DAGGER'S SLEEP

Dagger's Sleep

A Sleeping Beauty Retelling
Beyond the Tales Book One

Tricia Mingerink

Sword & Cross Publishing

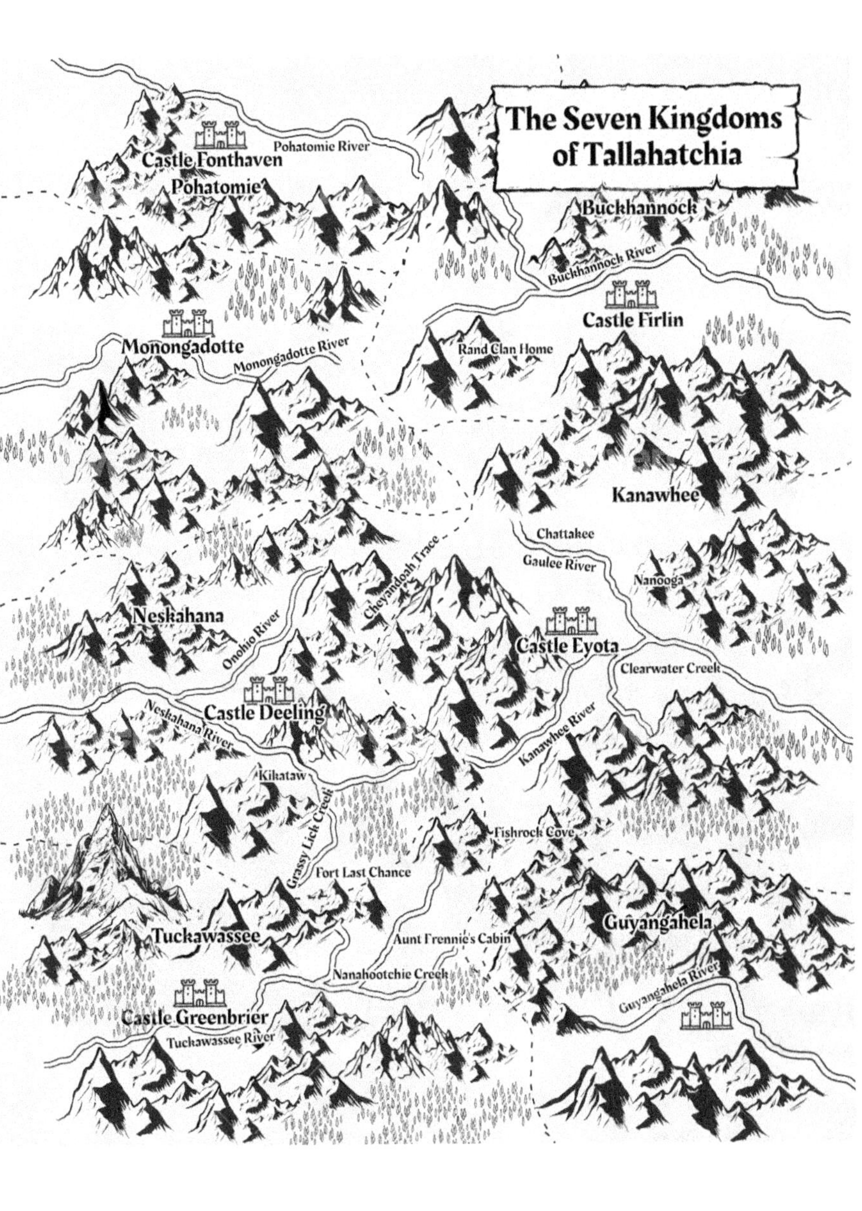

The Seven Kingdoms
of Tallahatchia
Castle Fonthaven
Pohatomie River
Pohatomie
Buckhannock
Buckhannock River
Monongadotte
Castle Firlin
Monongadotte River
Rand Clan Home
Kanawhee
Chattakee
Gaulee River
Nanooga
Neskahana
Cheyandoah Trace
Onohio River
Castle Eyota
Clearwater Creek
Castle Deeling
Neskahana River
Kanawhee River
Kikataw
Grassy Lick Creek
Fishrock Cove
Fort Last Chance
Guyangahela
Tuckawassee
Aunt Frennie's Cabin
Nanahootchie Creek
Guyangahela River
Castle Greenbrier
Tuckawassee River

Chapter 1

Rosanna

It was said that at the dawn of time, before the curse darkened the mountains, the kings of the seven great river valleys heard the trees singing.

The river roared beneath Princess Rosanna's birch bark canoe, the sound coursing deep inside her chest as if singing an ancient song. The Onohio River's steep sides blurred into all the greens of light and darkness. Ahead, boulders jutted from the raging river, shining slick and wet and deadly.

Rosanna dug her paddle into the water, turning her canoe deftly between the boulders. Her heart thumped into her throat. Not fear, exactly. Not on this river, whose moods and torrents purred through her blood. More like life itself thrilling with the reminder that death lingered at the edges, one ill-timed paddle stroke away.

Here on the river, she didn't have to be a princess. She

could dream about the far-off places in the Seven Kingdoms of Tallahatchia. The deep gorges with their unexplored rivers. The blue mountains stretching into the horizon.

Not that she was much of a princess. The Fallen Fae hadn't even considered her a princess enough to curse, nor had the Loyal Fae given her a gift, as if they both had forgotten a princess had been born in Neskahana twenty-one years ago.

In the prow of her canoe, Isi Degotaga—Rosanna's maid, bodyguard, and best friend since they were both ten —gripped her paddle, her knuckles even whiter than the face of the birch bark showing on the canoe's interior. Still, she dug her paddle in when their canoe needed the extra power.

Two canoes with two guards each hurtled down the river ahead of Rosanna's canoe, another two canoes and three guards following behind. At this point in the falls of the Onohio, the river ran too swiftly for anyone on the bank to pose a danger, and all her guards could do was wait to fish her from the river if she missed a stroke or timed the river wrong, a danger with the river swollen with the spring rains and mountains' snowmelt.

The Onohio dipped and swooped around a boulder. Rosanna braced herself and dug her paddle in deeper, focusing on the river ahead. If she hit this next rapid wrong, her canoe could be damaged or even broken in half.

The best part of the entire Onohio River, certainly. This raging, terrible section of it.

A swoop. A twist around a boulder, riding the roiling current. A course correction to keep her centered in the river.

Then the river dropped away before her in a two-foot-high waterfall gushing in a foaming wave.

Her canoe hurtled out into the air before crashing down flat-bottomed into the calm pool beneath. Spray shot up and over the bow, drenching Isi and splashing Rosanna's face.

Rosanna let out a whoop and dug in her paddle to steer their canoe out of the way of her guards following. "That was even better than last spring."

"If by better, you mean more terrifying, then yes." Isi swiped water out of her eyes. The morning sun glistened on her light brown skin smattered with freckles across her high cheeks and straight nose, much like her father's. Her curling black-brown hair, like her late mother's, frizzed from the braid and beads she'd used to attempt to tame it. "Ugh, I hate getting wet."

As they drifted clear of the small waterfall, a smaller canoe burst over and splashed down, water splashing over the bow and spraying across the canoe's lone paddler, Captain Degotaga, Isi's father and the captain of Rosanna's personal guards. His long black hair flowed across the top of his shoulders, a braid along one side beaded. Above his sharp nose and sharper chin, his eyes swept the surrounding landscape, searching for danger that might have been missed by the two guards holding their canoe steady at the edge of the waterfall's pool farther downstream.

Captain Degotaga edged his canoe between theirs and the nearest bank. "You shot that last set of rapids rather close, Princess."

Rosanna grinned, using her paddle to keep the canoe steady. She'd take that as a compliment, even if it was probably meant as a reprimand for putting her life in danger. "It wasn't that close. We cleared the rock by a good six inches."

A second canoe flew from the rapids and splashed down in the pool with Ahanu and Otho, two of Rosanna's guards, guiding it. They each gave her grins, swiping water from their faces and hair.

Captain Degotaga steered his canoe toward the waiting guards at the far side of the pool, and Rosanna maneuvered her and Isi's canoe to follow.

When they reached her guards, Chogan, the guard in the stern of the canoe, held up a hand. "Nikan and Garmund haven't checked in yet."

Rosanna flexed her fingers on her paddle as she kept her canoe steady. What was taking her guards so long to scout the river ahead? Usually this stretch took only a minute or two, and the guards returned before Rosanna finished her run down the rapids. "Should we send back up?"

Captain Degotaga swept his gaze around the Onohio's banks. "Not yet. Chogan, Ilma, if they aren't back in five minutes, go after them. Stay alert."

Ilma, a slender woman with dark brown hair, nodded while her husband Chogan mumbled, "Yes, sir."

Rosanna eyed the river ahead. To their left, the southern bank rose in a steep cliff, the rocks preventing trouble from that side and keeping the river narrow and fast even past the rapids. On the other side, the mountains sloped wooded and boulder-strewn to the river's edge. Treacherous to navigate, but not impassible.

In the front of the canoe, Isi tensed as she searched both banks as intently as the other guards. If trouble came, it would be Isi's job to get Rosanna out of there while the guards held their attackers back.

Would it come to that? Rosanna rubbed her thumb across the worn wood of her paddle. In the years of fighting along the border between her kingdom of Neskahana and its southern neighbor Tuckawassee, the Tuckawassee raiding parties rarely came this far north. When they did, they usually stayed along the Neskahana River to the south —a broader and more populated river—than the wild and rugged Onohio.

The dark shape of a canoe's prow swung around the far bend of the river, cut across the stream's current, and darted into the opposite curve where the river flowed back against itself and aided their journey upriver.

Captain Degotaga tensed and reached for the long knife strapped to his waist. The other guards did the same, though none of them drew the wide-bladed knives. Not yet.

Rosanna held her breath and poised her paddle to make a dash for the shore if necessary.

The morning sun splashed across the two figures in the far canoe, highlighting the beads tied in the strands of their brown and black hair and falling to the dark blue stripe painted along the upper edge of their canoe.

Her guards. Rosanna blew out a breath but didn't relax. Instead of giving a wave to signal the river ahead was safe, the guards thrust the canoe forward as if in a race, their muscles straining against their buckskin shirts and trousers.

Within minutes, they drew alongside, panting. Nikan, in the prow of the canoe, raised a hand and tapped his fist to his forehead in salute. "Captain, two bends down the river, we came across a lone man fighting what looks to be a raiding party of Tuckawassee. Taking care to stay hidden, we scouted the bank and confirmed it is a smaller raiding party, maybe nine or ten strong. While the man they are attacking is holding them off, it's doubtful he will do so indefinitely."

Captain Degotaga paused, glancing from Rosanna to the river ahead. "If we take to the shore, can we safely portage around them?"

"Perhaps, though we could not be sure there aren't more raiding parties deeper into the mountains."

Rosanna backed the paddle, gauging the power of the river dumping into the pool behind them. They couldn't go back, not without portaging around the rapids at their back. Nor would turning around gain them anything when the safety of Castle Deeling lay a mere half a mile in front of them, not behind.

If they avoided the Tuckawassee raiding party, an unknown stranger would most likely pay for Rosanna's safety with his life.

Rosanna straightened her shoulders. Captain Degotaga wouldn't like her suggestion. "Captain, I know my safety is your first priority, but any enemy of the Tuckawassee will most likely be our ally and thus shouldn't be allowed to die without us attempting to aid him."

After a moment's pause, Captain Degotaga gave a sharp nod. "Very well. We'll put in around the bend from the attack and strike from the mountain above."

They would be outnumbered, but only by three. Not horrible, but perhaps Rosanna could make it better. "Isi and I will dump in the river and push our canoe beside the cliffs."

"You'll still be in arrow range." Captain Degotaga shook his head.

Isi glanced over her shoulder, met Rosanna's gaze, and gave a nod. She faced her father. "We'll keep our heads down behind our canoe so they won't have a target. We'll be the distraction. If we get past, we'll make for Castle Deeling and send back reinforcements."

Captain Degotaga stared up at the sky for a moment, as if calculating the scenarios and costs.

Rosanna could make those same calculations, and Captain Degotaga didn't have a choice. It would be just as dangerous for her to remain behind. Any Tuckawassee either retreating or coming to reinforce the smaller raiding party could stumble across them, catching them without additional aid and cut off from the castle. Better if they pushed past the raiding party under the distraction of the fight to reach Castle Deeling as quickly as possible.

"Very well." Captain Degotaga straightened in his canoe. "Let's go."

With a firm stroke, Rosanna pushed her canoe forward. Her guards surrounded her canoe, their grins replaced with tight mouths.

The forested bank on one side and the cliffs on the other flashed by as they swept around the first bend and neared the second. Above the constant shushing, gurgling river, a crack of wood and shouts split the still air in the gorge.

As Captain Degotaga and the other six guards made for the north bank to disembark, Isi and Rosanna halted their canoe in the center of the stream.

Isi grimaced, swiveled as much as she could in the prow of the canoe, and slid her paddle into the wooden brackets along the canoe's inside. "Ugh. Time to get wet."

"This is partially your idea." Rosanna stowed her paddle along the side of the canoe and eased sideways in her seat. "Ready?"

With one last scowl, Isi gave a nod. Together, she and

Rosanna rolled backwards into the river. The icy water closed around her body, stealing her breath and tingling against her skin. This early in the spring, the river ran high and cold with the mountains' snow melt. She lifted her feet clear of the canoe, fought the current's pull, and gripped the canoe's upper cedar ribbing, tipping the canoe on its beam.

The few things Rosanna had with her in the canoe—just a pouch of dried meat for her breakfast and a canteen—tipped in the same direction but stayed inside thanks to the straps tying them to the canoe's ribbing.

"Do you think if we keep it tipped like this they'll think it's abandoned?" Rosanna kicked to steer them toward the cliffs.

"Possibly." Isi gripped one of the cedar thwarts near the front of the canoe.

Rosanna matched Isi's pace as they pushed the canoe forward toward the bend. As the sounds of the fight ahead grew louder, Isi stilled except for an occasional course correction.

Ahead of them, the river widened, the current slowing. Rosanna kept her body below the surface as she let herself and the canoe drift around the bend.

Boulders had tumbled into the river in some long-forgotten rockslide. Behind one, balanced on a rock barely above water, a young man whipped a quarterstaff up and drove it into the face of a man trying to inch around the boulder.

The young man's hair was of medium length, the strands brushing his jaw, a style of hair from the northern kingdoms. Blood trickled across his tan forehead. He had a dagger in a style that had gone out of use decades ago strapped to his waist.

His attackers gathered on the other side of the boulder and along the bank. Sunlight glinted on the strands of gold or silver woven through their black hair or at the neckline of their buckskin shirts, a Tuckawassee custom.

On the bank, the attackers' leader shouted orders, one hand pointing to the lone man behind the boulder and the other resting on her long knife belted to her waist. Her curly black hair was mostly tamed into a puffy braid interlaced with a silver thread and various gemstones.

Rosanna let herself sink lower into the water, hiding all but the young man with the staff from sight.

The man spun, his footing firm despite the slippery rock beneath his moccasins. The hardwood stave in his hands whipped through the air and cracked against an arm, a leg, a chin. A warrior, that's what he was.

"On the river! Archers!" A woman's voice rang against the water. Her words were longer, the vowels drawled, the consonants stretched in the manner of the southern kingdoms.

"Keep drifting. She can't see us, just our canoe." Isi kept her voice low, her mouth barely above the water.

An arrow crunched through the birch bark and struck the wood ribbing a few inches from Rosanna's hand. She gritted her teeth. She must not splash or give the archers a target.

Yelling and war cries poured from the mountainside.

Rosanna swiveled to peer around the stern of the canoe, keeping her head mostly submerged and hidden. On the bank, the Tuckawassee leader whirled and raised her long knife in time to block Captain Degotaga's thrust.

Something flashed bright out of the corner of her eye. The young man with the quarterstaff stumbled, staring at his hand as if he'd been injured. The two attackers on the other side of the rock leapt forward, one with a knife and the other with a war ax.

Still off balance, the young man tried to raise his staff in time to ward off the blows.

He wasn't going to make it. Either the knife would take him in the chest or the ax would split his skull.

The Tuckawassee weren't going to kill someone on her river. Not here.

Rosanna yanked her canteen free of its lashing and let go of the canoe. She gave a hard kick to thrust herself partway out of the water and threw the canteen.

The canteen struck the Tuckawassee closest to her in the shoulder. Not her best throw, but it had been difficult while in the river. Still, the Tuckawassee stumbled into the warrior next to him, both of their weapons going wide.

The young man whipped the staff around, cracking it across one man's back before jabbing it into a second man's stomach. Both attackers fell into the river. As soon as they surfaced, they stroked toward the shore.

"Pa has them on the run." Isi faced Rosanna and treaded water. "I don't think we have to worry about hurrying to the castle for reinforcements. Good thing, considering you were just asking to get skewered."

"Sorry." Rosanna reached for the canoe.

The Tuckawassee scrambled up the mountainside, quickly out of sight in the depth of the forest.

Before disappearing behind a dense section of trees, the Tuckawassee's commander glanced over her shoulder. Her eyes fixed on the young man before swiveling in Rosanna's direction.

Was that a frown? Rosanna couldn't tell at that distance, and a moment later, the commander followed her war party out of sight.

With the danger past and treading water, the ice-cold water shivered across Rosanna's skin. She clamped her teeth to stop her shaking.

"See." The word hissed through Isi's chattering teeth. "This is why I don't like getting wet. It's cold and miserable and we're going to be cold and wet all the way home."

On shore, Captain Degotaga kept Rosanna's guards behind trees and boulders, probably in case the Tuckawassee archers stayed in range or doubled back. Still, he waved Rosanna and Isi to come to the bank, held up his hand, then waved again. The signal to come in cautiously.

Perhaps they could go straight to the bank, but they would be exposed on the open stretch of river. Or she could push the canoe to the boulder only a few yards away where the young man leaned on his staff, glancing between the bank, Isi, and Rosanna. Captain Degotaga probably wouldn't agree it was the safer option, but it was time Rosanna met the man the Tuckawassee had ventured this far into Neskahana to attack.

Rosanna stroked forward, pushing the canoe. "Head for the rock."

Isi raised her eyebrows but joined her in pushing the canoe. Since she was at the prow, Isi reached the rock first.

After setting aside his quarterstaff, the young man knelt and reached a hand to Isi. He lifted her from the water and helped her climb onto the rock. Isi crouched and gripped the prow of the canoe. Out of the water, Isi shook, her mouth tinged gray with the cold.

Considering Rosanna couldn't feel how cold the water was anymore, nor the brush of her buckskin clothes against her skin, she needed to get warm just as much as Isi.

She swam to the rock and pressed a hand against its slick, algae-covered side.

The young man's dark brown hair fell along a sharp jaw dusted with dark stubble. He looked to be somewhere in his early twenties, maybe twenty-five at the most. She looked up into deep brown eyes the rich color of riverbank mud. He held out his hand.

As she took it and tugged to leverage herself from the water, the sunlight caught on the clear stone set in a silver ring, much like her father's signet ring. A fancy ring for a man dressed in buckskin that, this close, had worn spots on the knees and scuffs on the moccasins.

His eyes widened, and he stumbled, losing his balance and pitching forward.

Rosanna ducked, expecting him to fall on top of her. Instead, he shoved off the rock and plunged headfirst into the river behind Rosanna. Icy water splashed her back and neck.

When he surfaced, he shook water from his hair and swiped his face.

This wasn't her best first impression, accidentally throwing a man off-balance and pulling him into ice water. She exaggerated a wince. "Sorry."

"No, my own fault." He stroked forward and joined her against the rock. "After you."

Isi stretched out a hand. "I should leave you there since you like getting wet so much."

"Very funny." With Isi's help, Rosanna heaved herself onto the boulder. Water streamed from her clothes. She swiveled and held out her hand to the young man still in the water. "I'm glad we came along when we did to chase the Tuckawassee away. Why were they after you? Who are you?"

He grasped her hand to let her pull him free of the water. "I'm Daemyn Rand."

Daemyn Rand. As in the son of the renowned Arlen Rand, a friend of her father's back in the day. Her grip on him slipped as her own balance wobbled. If not for Isi's quick reflexes in grabbing Daemyn Rand's arm, he would've tumbled back into the river.

"Sorry." Rosanna sat back on her heels as he clambered, dripping onto the boulder. With the three of them perched on it, the space grew crowded. Over Daemyn's shoulder, Captain Degotaga motioned, his face hard. Of course, he wouldn't like his daughter and princess so far from him with an armed stranger.

Isi shook her head, her wet curls shining black. "We'd best get to shore before my pa sends the guards down on us."

Daemyn picked up his staff and led the way around the upright boulder and across other half-submerged boulders to shore. Rosanna followed while Isi towed the canoe.

Onshore, Rosanna ignored Captain Degotaga's crossed arms and gestured at Daemyn. "This is Daemyn Rand."

Captain Degotaga swept his gaze over him. "You do have the look of your father. What made a Tuckawassee raiding party chase you this far into Neskahana?"

"I was doing some scouting in Tuckawassee, caught their attention, and haven't been able to lose them. But as for the reason I'm in Neskahana . . ." Daemyn faced Rosanna. His eyes held something she couldn't quite name, but it sent a shiver down her spine anyway. "I came looking for you."

Chapter 2

Rosanna

*Though given the whole earth, the seven kings, instead of
being content, turned to pride and warred among themselves
as to which one should rule over the others. Their war cursed
themselves, their descendants, and the whole land so that the
trees lost their song and the Highest King no longer walked
among them.*

Rosanna blinked, shook her head, and shivered.
"Why were you looking for me?"

"I'll explain, but not here." Daemyn glanced
up at the mountainside where the Tuckawassee had disappeared. "We shouldn't linger."

Captain Degotaga gave a sharp nod. "Chogan, Ilma,
Otho, fetch the canoes."

Rosanna rubbed her arms. The buckskin of her sleeves
squished beneath her fingers and stuck to her skin. It was
going to be one long half mile to the castle.

When her guards returned towing the canoes, they all climbed in, Daemyn Rand sharing a canoe with Captain Degotaga.

After three more long sweeping bends and one small set of rapids, the towers of Castle Deeling appeared above the trees.

Rosanna drew in a deep breath, warmth settling in her chest. As much as she longed for adventure, there was something about the sight of Castle Deeling's gray stones and square, squat towers perched on a cliff overlooking the convergence between the Neskahana and Onohio Rivers that sang her heart's song as if the stones had soaked up her childhood memories and radiated their warmth.

Farther to the west, the town of Deeling stretched along the cliffs and flowed down the slope as the cliffs flattened into a broad valley. Only a few of the rooftops poked above the town's stockade wall of large, pointed logs. At the point where the town met the shoreline, a cluster of docks extended into the river. A large trading canoe and its fleet of smaller guard canoes was in the process of pulling alongside a dock, bringing a load of glass and pottery into Deeling from the smaller towns downriver.

Rosanna's guards led the way to Castle Deeling's small dock where they disembarked and carried the canoes to racks in a stone shed. From there, they marched up the long, winding stairs carved into the cliff's side. As they climbed higher, Rosanna glanced down at the Neskahana River rippling brown far below and the mountains rising and falling, green near the castle and deepening to blue in the distance.

A few stairs below her, Daemyn Rand also stared off into the horizon. But something about the set of his chin and the depth to his gaze told her he saw what lay beyond those distant mountains.

The sunlight fell across a scar running along the underside of his jaw on his neck, as if someone had tried to slit his throat at one point. They must have been close to succeeding since the scar appeared to run across the large vein. For Daemyn to have survived, the actual wound must not have been as deep as the scar seemed to indicate.

As if sensing her gaze, he looked up. His dark brown eyes locked with hers, filled with some emotion she couldn't name. Resignation, perhaps? Sadness?

A shiver shook her as a breeze cut through her wet clothes. She focused on the steps in front of her and kept climbing.

Finally, they arrived at the postern gate. The guards on the wall top hailed Captain Degotaga and swung the gate open.

Her father met them inside the entry hall, his hands smudged with dirt as if he'd come from overseeing their guards' morning training. His black hair flowed loose around his shoulders without his crown to hold it in place, though some of it stuck to the patches of sweat on his forehead. Although he stood several inches shorter than Daemyn or Captain Degotaga, he carried his shoulders back with the authority of the king he was. "Ro, you're soaked. What happened?"

"We ran across a Tuckawassee raiding party and chased them off. They were attacking him." Rosanna shivered, her teeth chattering, and waved over her shoulder at Daemyn.

Daemyn stepped up next to her, his hair and clothes also still damp.

Father's eyes widened. "Daemyn, isn't it? You're the spitting image of your father. If I didn't know better . . ."

"I've been told I resemble him greatly." Daemyn bowed low. "He spoke very highly of you, King Faron."

"I was very saddened to hear of his passing last year." Father gestured for Daemyn to straighten. "He was a good man. I learned a lot from him when he spent time here years ago."

Rosanna had heard some of the stories. Something about Arlen Rand, Daemyn's father, helping her father when he became king after Grandfather was killed by the Tuckawassee. From the news they'd received last year, Arlen Rand too had eventually fallen to the Tuckawassee.

Daemyn nodded, but his tone was distant as he spun the clear-stoned ring around his finger. "Your Majesty, I was actually on my way to speak with you, and that matter has become even more urgent in light of recent events."

"Of course. I'll have refreshments sent to the hall. Do you wish to freshen up first?" Father eyed Daemyn's damp and dirty clothing.

Rosanna edged away. She needed to change out of her own buckskins, which were growing increasingly itchy and stiff as they dried. Behind her back, she motioned for Isi to leave to change and find dry clothes for Rosanna.

"If you'll provide me with the room and dry clothes, I'll take a few minutes to change." Daemyn gestured to Rosanna. "I would like to request that Princess Rosanna be present for this meeting. This concerns her."

Why would this concern her? Besides her accidentally saving him, she couldn't think of anything.

Father motioned for one of the maids and asked her to show Daemyn to a guest room. Rosanna headed for the stairs, but her father caught her arm. "Could you wake Berend? I'll fetch Willem and your mother. If there's a

Rand involved in this, it's going to be concerning to all of us."

Rosanna grimaced. Her younger brother Berend was a bear to wake in the morning. Partially because he was an eighteen-year-old who enjoyed his sleep, but mostly because he spent his nights as a large black bear, thanks to his Fae curse. Not that he acted like he considered it a curse. "I'll get him, even if I have to toss him into the river to wake him up."

She hurried up the stairs, leaving a trail of damp footprints, and halted before Berend's room. If only she could change out of her stiff, damp clothes first, but Berend would need all the time he could get to be fully awake in time for the meeting.

With a deep breath, she pushed open the door to Berend's room without bothering to knock.

In the dim light filtering between the closed shutters, Berend was a tangle of blankets and limbs. There was his arm flung around a pillow. There his bare foot stuck out from the blankets. A soft, growling snore came from the mound of blankets near the foot of the bed. Apparently, he'd curled up backwards on the bed again, his head at the foot and his feet propped against the headboard.

She made it most of the way across the room before she had to let out the breath she'd been holding. Even though she tried to take shallow breaths, the stench of wet, musty animal and dirty woolen socks still burned her nose and into her mouth. Even worse than last time she'd ventured in here. If her brother didn't clean this room soon—since none of the maids dared enter the bear prince's lair even if it was perfectly safe—she and Isi might have to tackle the room themselves.

Reaching the bed, Rosanna tossed back the blankets.

Her brother wore the same rumpled buckskins he'd worn yesterday, now even dirtier. His black hair, cropped even shorter than Daemyn's, frizzed around his head and had leaves and twigs tangled in it.

She shook his shoulder so hard his head wobbled back and forth on his pillow. "Berend. Wake up."

His snores continued with barely a hitch in their rhythm.

"Berend, it's time to stop hibernating and get out of bed." She dragged all the blankets off him. When the cold didn't make him stir, she grabbed an arm and pulled him off the bed, letting him thump onto the floor.

He muttered, rolled over, and curled into a ball as if he was about to go into winter hibernation.

"Sorry to do this, but you leave me no choice." Rosanna rolled him onto his back and turned his face up. His mouth fell open into a long snort. Locating a wet section along the hem of her buckskin shirt, she wrung out the cold river water. It splashed onto his face and dribbled onto his neck.

With a growl, he bolted upright, flailing with his arms.

Rosanna ducked under one swing and jumped back to avoid another. "Wake up, Bere-Bear."

He blinked deep brown eyes first at the windows, then at her. "What'd you wake me for? I've only been asleep for a couple of hours. Let me go back to bed."

He reached for the bed as if intending to crawl back into it. Not if she could help it. Rosanna flicked water from her fingers at his face. "Not a chance. There's a meeting in ten minutes in the hall."

Berend swiped the drops from his eyes. "You didn't have to splash me, Ro-Row. I'm up. Just give me a minute."

She crossed her arms. Of course, she splashed him. He wouldn't wake up otherwise. "I was attacked by Tuckawassee this morning."

He straightened as if she'd dunked him in the icy river water. "Tuckawassee? This far north? Are you all right?"

"I'm fine." She blew out a breath and sat cross-legged on the floor. For the first time that morning, something quaked inside her, as if the true depths of fear she should've felt on the river facing the Tuckawassee finally hit her now. "I wasn't in that much danger."

Berend huffed much like he did when he was a bear. "Guess I'll have to chase them off tonight."

"Don't." Rosanna shook her head. Even as a bear, Berend wasn't invincible. "The Tuckawassee aren't going to follow Father's law forbidding hunting bears at night. Besides, they weren't after me. They were attacking Daemyn Rand, and I saved him, sort of, then dragged him into the river, then I nearly dropped him into the river again, and he came back to the castle to talk to Father about something important and Father wants us there."

Shaking his head, Berend pounded on the side of his head with the flat of his hand as if trying to shake something loose from his ear. "I know I'm still sort of sleepy, but did you say you pulled the Daemyn Rand—the bane of the Tuckawassee and scourge of river pirates—into the river?"

"Yes. Headfirst. I caught him off balance." Rosanna shrugged. He had been distracted by something, as if he'd noticed the ring on his hand for the first time. But that didn't make sense. Why would he be surprised by his own ring?

"I wonder what he's doing in Neskahana? Trouble seems to follow Daemyn Rand wherever he goes, and by trouble, I mean more than a paltry raiding party of

Tuckawassee. I don't have to be a scholar like Willem to know that." Berend pushed to his feet. "Let's find out what he wants."

Rosanna scrambled to her feet and managed to catch Berend's sleeve before he trotted from the room. "After you clean up and change. You smell like a wet bear."

"And you smell like pond scum." Berend grinned and reached for what hopefully was a clean buckskin shirt from a pile on his floor. He shook his hair, raining bits of leaves and twigs onto the floor.

She shook her head and left. When she entered her room two doors down the hallway, Isi had already changed into a blue cotton dress and laid out one of the only two dresses Rosanna had, a deep forest green one with Isi's intricate beadwork around the neckline. Fabric was too scarce to waste on an excess of gowns, even for a princess. Not that Rosanna minded.

Isi looked up from the chair where she sat beading a pattern around the neckline of a buckskin shirt. "I was beginning to worry I'd have to go back and rescue you from some dastardly villain who'd struck when my back was turned."

"Nothing that terrible." Rosanna propped her foot on a chair and worked at the stiff, damp laces of her knee-high moccasins. At this point, she just about agreed with Isi. Getting wet wasn't enjoyable at all. "I had to wake Berend."

"That explains it. In that case, I'm amazed you got here so quickly." Isi set down her beadwork and knelt to help Rosanna unknot the moccasin laces. "Now let's get you changed and presentable before Prince Berend manages to beat you to the meeting."

When Rosanna arrived in the castle's great hall a few minutes later with Isi at her heels, her father, Captain Degotaga, Daemyn, and Colonel Hassun, the commander of father's guards, were already there, sitting at the large table on the raised dais at the far end of the large expanse. Behind them, the red and white Neskahana banner waved in a draft.

A few of father's guards stood at each of the exits, making sure the hall remained empty, while her father's bodyguard loitered along the wall by the dais.

Rosanna nodded at the guards by this door and stepped inside.

Before she could shut the door, her older brother Willem caught it with an ink-stained hand and stepped in behind her. Taller than her or Berend, Willem's wiry build and darker skin reflected more of their mother than their father.

He nodded. "Good to see you're in one piece."

"I'm fine, really." As Isi leaned against the wall where she could keep an eye on the room, Rosanna took a seat along the table.

When she glanced up, she met Daemyn's dark brown eyes. He wore a plain blue shirt, his hair still damp, but he'd shaved off the scruff he'd had earlier. His hardwood staff leaned against the wall behind him. Why had she picked the seat directly across from him?

She focused on the tray of cheese and bread placed on the table barely out of her arm's reach. Her stomach gurgled.

Willem claimed the seat next to her and eyed Daemyn as if he was a puzzling plot hole in one of the legends the traveling bards told. Rosanna nudged him, but Willem didn't seem to notice her or her favorite cheese within his reach. Instead, he faced Captain Degotaga across from him and started up a conversation.

No one seemed to be paying any attention to the food. Should she interrupt Willem to ask for him to pass the tray? Or lunge over him to reach for it?

Her stomach growled again. It had been hours since her pre-dawn breakfast. If she didn't do something about silencing her stomach, it would growl loud enough for everyone to hear.

Daemyn reached over, grabbed the tray, and held it out to her the way a servant would, silent, his eyes down.

"Thank you." She claimed two pieces of cheese and a slice of bread.

Daemyn shifted the tray to hold it out to Willem, who took a slice of bread without breaking stride in his conversation.

Why was Daemyn serving them when he was the guest? Rosanna chewed on a piece of cheese seasoned with a hint of rosemary. He did it so naturally no one else had seemed to notice.

No sooner had Rosanna taken another large bite of cheese than her mother glided into the room. Her long skirt swished over the floor, cut in the latest fashion with a tapered waist and rounded neckline so that few would guess that same dress had been reworked many times over the years. The deep yellow of the fabric set well against her dark skin, curly hair left loose, and perfectly pink lips. The beauty was the result of Mother's Fae gift, but the poise was all Mother.

Daemyn stood and bowed. "Queen Erina."

Mother inclined her head. "Daemyn Rand. My condolences on your loss a year ago. Your father is still very missed."

"Thank you, Your Majesty. It has been an adjustment since he's been gone." As Mother sat, Daemyn returned to his seat.

The door flung open, and Berend strolled inside, dressed in what appeared to be clean buckskins. While still mussed, his hair no longer sported twigs or leaves. He plopped into the chair next to Rosanna and snatched the food tray. "If I'm going to be up, I might as well eat. I'm hungry as a bear."

Rosanna rolled her eyes. "I'm so glad you think you're funny."

"I think what you mean is I'm *bear*ly funny."

Willem halted his conversation and leaned forward, his mouth straight. "Your humor is un*bear*able."

She groaned and dropped her head in her hands. Brothers. They would go on and on if they got started. "Please, not the puns."

Berend grinned and shook his head. "I believe our dear sister would like to beg our for*bear*ance."

"I see. But I don't see why her preference should have any *bear*ing on our conversation." Willem kept his grin in check, though his eyes crinkled, giving him away.

"That would be rather over*bear*ing of her." Berend linked his hands behind his head.

Rosanna bit the inside of her cheeks, but she couldn't help it. "Your puns are getting a little thread*bare*."

Berend tossed back his head and howled a laugh. Willem slapped the table, grinning at last. "I knew it would be more than you could *bear*."

At the end of the table, Father coughed. "If we could get this meeting started?"

Willem straightened in his chair, his grin dropping

from his face. Berend clamped his mouth shut but couldn't hide his smirk.

Father motioned to Daemyn. "If you would care to proceed, would you like to explain what a raiding party of Tuckawassee was doing this far north?"

Daemyn stood, his hands clasped behind his back, as if standing was his natural posture for reporting to kings. "Several weeks ago, I slipped into Castle Greenbrier."

Rosanna stared. How had Daemyn managed to sneak into a castle belonging to the Tuckawassee king? Perhaps he was as skilled as the stories about him said.

"You got into Castle Greenbrier?" Colonel Hassun leaned forward. Gray streaked through his black hair. "We've been trying for years to get someone inside. How far did you get?"

"Close enough to search the king's desk and meet most of his daughters. My family has become familiar with the castle over the years." Daemyn's voice remained flat. Almost bored. As if it wasn't anything difficult to sneak into the Tuckawassee stronghold. "As you can imagine, they didn't take it kindly when they discovered my intrusion."

Beside Rosanna, Berend snorted and muttered. "No wonder they weren't happy."

Rosanna nudged Berend under the table to quiet him. Her father would go to similar lengths if any of them were in danger.

"Thus they sent a raiding party to track you all the way here." Captain Degotaga crossed his arms.

"Yes, led by Major Beshko. She and I have clashed before." Daemyn paced to the wall and picked up his staff, rubbing his thumb over the smooth wood. "While I was there, I saw Tuckawassee plans to invade Neskahana."

Father stiffened. Berend growled low in his throat. Mother and Willem both wore frowns, though Willem's pinched lines around his mouth.

Not again. Rosanna tried to keep her breathing steady. In the last major fighting between Tuckawassee and Neskahana twenty-years ago, her grandfather had been killed before she ever truly got a chance to know him, since she was only a year old at the time.

Would the other four kingdoms be drawn into the conflict this time? Twenty years ago, both Monongadotte to the north and Guyangahela to the southeast hadn't come to Grandfather's call for aid, though they hadn't reinforced the Tuckawassee either. Buckhannock in the northeast would've sent aid, but its armies had been too busy holding off incursions from the Pohatomie, the other kingdom to side with Tuckawassee in this ongoing war.

A war that had lasted nearly a hundred years over the seventh kingdom, Kanawhee, and the legendary high prince of the Seven Kingdoms of Tallahatchia, asleep behind his hedge of thorns.

Colonel Hassun shook his head, his expression unchanged. "While the information will be valuable, it isn't unexpected. The Tuckawassee have raided every ten to twenty years or so, every time it appears possible the time might be right for the high prince's promised cursebreaker to be found. We've fought them off before, and we'll do it again."

It was said, at least in Neskahana and the other kingdoms loyal to the high prince, that when he woke, he would restore peace and prosperity to Tallahatchia. The Highest King himself had promised a princess would wake him from his curse, something Tuckawassee and Pohatomie fought to prevent.

As a little girl sitting by the fire in the great hall on winter nights, Rosanna would lean forward and beg for details. The bards would oblige with tales of romance and peril and true love's kiss waking the sleeping prince. But that was before she realized the story was more than just a story. That legend had gotten her grandfather killed, and now it brought the Tuckawassee onto her river.

Daemyn's shoulders hunched as if he carried Tallahatchia's mountains on his back. "It won't be that simple this time. This time, the promised cursebreaker has been found."

Father straightened in his chair. "How can you be certain? Many have claimed to be able to tell the time and the means. All hoaxes and frauds, in the end."

Daemyn leaned against his wooden staff, the clear stone in his ring glinting in the lamplight. "It has been given to me by the Highest King to know the princess who will wake the high prince from his cursed sleep, as evidenced by my family's faithful service to the high prince these past hundred years."

If anyone's word could be trusted on this matter, it would be Daemyn Rand's. There was good reason the Tuckawassee had been trying to kill him and his ancestors ever since the high prince fell into his curse.

Daemyn wasn't looking at her, yet Rosanna found herself holding her breath, something growing cold deep in her stomach. Somehow, she knew his next words, their beats drumming their truth into her chest, even before he said them.

"Princess Rosanna is the one destined to wake High Prince Alexander and restore the high king to his throne."

CHAPTER 3

ROSANNA

As a sign of the greater curse unleashed upon all, it was decreed a curse would fall to the descendants of the kings given rule over others. Yet the Highest King also promised hope in the form of a gift and a sign of a cursebreaker that they might know that no curse remained out of his power to break.

Rosanna struggled to draw in a deep breath as Daemyn Rand's announcement echoed in the great hall. Her? The one destined to wake the sleeping prince? Surely not. She was so invisible she hadn't even been given a gift or a curse. Why would the Highest King choose her?

Father stiffened, his eyes resting on her as if Daemyn's words had been a death threat. Mother's face whitened, and she gripped Father's arm, as if begging for strength. Willem rested a hand on the long knife on his belt, his body tensing. Captain Degotaga drew in a sharp breath and stared up at the ceiling while Colonel Hassun remained stoic.

Rosanna's chest tightened, a chill slicing from her stomach down to her toes. Her family wasn't the type given to loud outbursts. No, they absorbed shock with silence and outward calm. And right now, the silence could've cracked stone.

"Are you serious? Our Ro-Row?" The front legs of Berend's chair slammed to the stone floor. Of course Berend would be the first to speak. He gave a laugh, only to trail off. "You're not fooling. You really think she's the princess promised in the legends?"

Daemyn's gaze focused on the wall as if seeing something beyond the stone and tapestries. "There are legends, then there are *the* legends. The ones so breathed with truth their tellers take care never to change a word. Some of the tales about the sleeping prince are just tales embellished for campfires. But others . . . those are true. The Highest King promised a cursebreaker, and Princess Rosanna is that cursebreaker."

She was the cursebreaker for the curse that had torn Tallahatchia apart.

If the Tuckawassee and Pohatomie learned what she was, they would do all in their power to stop her from reaching Castle Eyota and waking the high prince. They couldn't let the high prince return, not after a hundred years of fighting those still loyal to the united kingdoms Tallahatchia had once been. Next time, the Tuckawassee raiding party wouldn't be after Daemyn. They would be looking to kill her.

She swung her gaze to the pairs of guards at each of the

doors to the great hall and from there to Isi. Isi's eyes were wide.

The guards were loyal, but the Tuckawassee and Pohatomie would discover she was the cursebreaker. This was the sort of secret no one could keep. Nowhere would be safe. Not her beloved Onohio River. Not even Castle Deeling.

The only way to end this—to end the war—was for her to wake High Prince Alexander. Didn't the legends say his waking would bring peace to Tallahatchia? Wasn't it his destiny to reunite them?

Her grandfather had died fighting for Neskahana and his loyalty to the high prince. Generations of warriors in Neskahana had fought and died along the border with Tuckawassee. Who was she to shirk duty?

Besides, this was her chance to see those distant blue mountains she stared at each time she had to turn her canoe around to head back home. Was it this destiny that had called to her from beyond the horizon?

She raised her chin. "I'll go."

Silence settled on the great hall. She braced herself. What would her family's reaction be? What could they say?

Father's shoulders rose and fell. When he raised his head, his face was set in tight lines. "It's an honor to do the Highest King's will, and our family is blessed to have been given the privilege of this duty. We'll do all in our power to aid Rosanna."

An honor. A privilege. Rosanna straightened her shoulders. There was no question of heeding this call. If she was the one called to wake High Prince Alexander, she would have to do it.

She met Daemyn's gaze. "When do we leave?"

"It'll take a few days to notify the barons and gather the

army, but we march to Castle Eyota as soon as the men are prepared." Father's eyes became distant, as if he already saw a list of all the preparations that had to be accomplished before they could leave.

Rosanna struggled to swallow. An army. That wasn't the sort of adventure she had in mind. Not one so surrounded by her father's warriors that she wouldn't have a chance to paddle her own canoe or get dirt underneath her fingernails.

Daemyn shook his head. "I'd prefer to travel with the princess and a handful of guards. When your army moves, it'll draw the attention of the Tuckawassee and Pohatomie. Their armies will do their best to counter yours, and Princess Rosanna would find herself in the middle of a battle. If the Tuckawassee don't set off after your army, they'll attack Neskahana while it's vulnerable."

"No good options either way." Father shook his head. He rested a hand over Mother's where she still clutched his arm. "I don't like leaving Rosanna lightly defended."

"My guards and I will continue to protect her with our lives, as we have always done when she's on the river." Captain Degotaga crossed his arms, his gaze flicking briefly to where Isi stood along the wall. "We're familiar with the princess's skill with a canoe, and she's comfortable and safe with us. I do not say this lightly. As the princess's body-guard, my own daughter will be at risk as well."

"A risk I would rather neither of our daughters faced." Father sighed. "But if there's no choice, there's no one I trust more."

No choice. Rosanna shivered. There wasn't much of a choice, was there? She could try to hide from her destiny, but that would leave her country at war and wouldn't stop the attack Tuckawassee was planning anyway.

If she traveled with Father's army, she would be the center of the war. But with only Captain Degotaga, Isi, and her other six guards, she was vulnerable if a larger Tuckawassee force discovered them.

"I don't think it's a coincidence that the cursebreaker was revealed only five weeks before the high prince's birthday marking the hundredth year since he fell asleep. I believe, though I'm not certain, that's the day the princess has to wake the prince." Daemyn twisted the signet ring on his finger. "I'm not sure what would happen if we were delayed and missed the day."

"Another point in favor of a smaller, nimbler raiding party guarding the princess." Captain Degotaga rested his crossed arms on the table.

Odd that he would be for a smaller group, considering Isi would be put at more risk. But perhaps he thought being in the center of an army would be just as bad. Rosanna glanced at Isi again. Isi's hand rested on her long knife, her mouth pressed tight. When their gazes met, Isi gave a slow nod as if to say she believed they could handle it.

"I have friends and family across Tallahatchia who will give aid." Daemyn's mouth almost twitched into a smile. "I'll send a message tonight."

Father still scowled as if unconvinced. Not that Rosanna could blame him. She wasn't sure which option she hoped for. A possibly safer, slower journey with Father and the war party he'd raise or more adventure.

Colonel Hassun leaned forward, a section of his silver-black hair falling across his shoulder. "If we can't keep this a secret—and we can't, not something like this—then we should make as big a show of it as possible. Announce that we have the promised cursebreaker. Rally the other kingdoms. March on Kanawhee with as much fanfare as we can muster. Draw the attention of the Tuckawassee and Pohatomie to us and away from the princess as she sneaks into Kanawhee quietly."

Rosanna glanced around the room, trying to gauge her family's reactions. Except for Berend's wide-eyed look, the others kept their faces too blank to read.

Finally, Willem nodded, his fists curling in his lap as if he didn't like his own answer. But that was Willem. He wouldn't like the thought of sending his little sister into danger. "The Tuckawassee will expect Ro to be with the army. After all, the Tuckawassee king has twelve daughters he reportedly dotes on. Sending his daughters with an army is what he would do, and thus what he will expect us to do."

"That might work." Father fingered the beaded strand in his hair, as if already contemplating adding the black beads signaling war.

"It would work better if I went along." Mother's spine might as well have been made of a long knife's blade. "The Tuckawassee will have spies. They'll soon see the army lacks a princess. I know I'm about thirty years too old, but from a distance, I believe I can still pass as Rosanna."

Her Fae-enhanced beauty would help. Rosanna studied Mother's line-free face, black hair trailing gracefully around her face. How many of the Tuckawassee knew what Rosanna looked like, besides the small raiding party she'd met that morning? Had they ever paid attention to her?

Probably not. Without a gift or a curse, there wasn't much to her. Not until this, anyway.

Father's eyes crinkled, as if he wanted to say something romantic but didn't in front of all of them. His expression sobered back into tight lines seconds later. "I don't like the thought of you going into danger."

"A hundred years ago, our ancestors pledged that they, their children, and descendants would remain loyal to the high king. That vow applies just as much to me as it does to Rosanna and you. Besides," Mother squeezed Father's arm, "with the army marching on Castle Eyota, this castle might not be much safer than traveling with the army."

Father rested his other hand over Mother's. "Very well. You'll travel with me and the army."

Willem stared at the tabletop, hand flexing, perhaps thinking about the pen he would soon wield. "I'll stay here and look after the castle. Tonight, I'll work on missives we can send to the other kingdoms."

At the wistful sound in his voice, Rosanna tried to meet his gaze, but he wouldn't look at her. Was he too thinking about lack of choices? Thanks to his curse that he couldn't leave Neskahana's borders, Willem had no choice but to stay behind, even if, as crown prince, it was the wisest decision anyway.

Perhaps that was why he'd been given the gift of charismatic writing. With a pen, he could convince just about anyone over to his way of thinking if he had a mind to.

"I can go with Rosanna." Berend leaned his chair back onto two legs once again. "With me around, she'll be *beary* protected."

"With all due respect, Your Highness," Captain Degotaga shook his head, his mouth twitching as if he was trying not to smile, "while I would appreciate the gift you would bring, I don't think your sleep schedule is compatible with the sort of traveling hours we will need to keep. We might travel during the night occasionally, but not the whole way due to the unpredictable terrain and unfamiliar rivers."

"Oh." Berend frowned, but the frown only lasted a second. "Then can I go with the army? You'll be moving a lot slower and will have supply boats and wagons I can curl up in if I need to during the day. I can help scout ahead during the night and stuff like that."

Father heaved a sigh but nodded. "You'll have to obey Colonel Hassun's orders. No going off by yourself."

Colonel Hassun cleared his throat, stood, and pulled one of the rolled maps from the trunk along the wall behind the dais. "We should discuss the routes we'll take, so we can see to properly outfitting both the army and Captain Degotaga's men for the journey."

He unrolled the map on the table, and Captain Degotaga set river pebbles at the four corners to hold it flat.

Daemyn stepped closer and pointed. "I think you should take the army on the northerly route up the Onohio River to the Cheyandoah Trace and from there down the Gaulee River to Castle Eyota. It's the route the Tuckawassee would expect you to take, and it's the best suited for moving large numbers of men. You should have the support of Buckhannock, and possibly Monongadotte as well."

Rosanna leaned forward in her seat to see the map, trying to picture Tallahatchia spread out in waves of green-covered mountains. How much of it would she be able to see on this journey?

"Yes." Father stood as well. "And it'll force the Tuckawassee to travel long distances to attack us. But where will you lead Rosanna? You'll have to stay far away from my army if you want the distraction to work."

Daemyn paused, glanced at Father, then back down at

the map. "I'd like to travel by river, taking mostly the small streams. We'll take the Neskahana River to Grassy Lick Creek, portage across the mountains, and from there work our way on a southern loop until we reach Castle Eyota from the south."

Father stiffened. "That will take you through Tuckawassee."

"Exactly. They wouldn't expect the promised princess to walk right through their kingdom. And most of their men will be fighting you to the north." Daemyn tapped the map. "No route is safe. No matter what way we go, Major Beshko is here. She'll do her best to track us on whatever route we take. If we can lose her by going south, it'll be worth the risk."

Rosanna rubbed the callouses on her palms, gained from years of paddling her canoe on both the Neskahana and Onohio Rivers. She'd wanted an adventure, but was she ready for an adventure like this? Cutting right through the heart of Tuckawassee?

If she was the princess promised a hundred years ago, what choice did she have? Maybe this was the reason she wasn't given a curse. She had been cursed, or perhaps honored, long before she'd been born.

Yet why hadn't she been given a Fae gift to help her on this journey?

She would have to handle this just as she was now. She was strong. She could paddle her own canoe. That had to count for something. "How soon do we leave?"

"Tomorrow morning, if His Majesty believes that will be enough time to gather the supplies we'll need?" Daemyn gave a half bow to Father. "I will also need access to the highest tower and a torch to send my message signal tonight."

The lines on Father's face deepened. "Of course. I'll begin preparations for the army at once to cover the packing for your journey."

Tomorrow morning. Rosanna sucked in a breath. So little time to get used to the idea of leaving her family. Of this quest and danger.

And adventure.

Father stood. "This meeting is adjourned. We have a lot to do before tomorrow morning."

As the others stood, Willem grabbed Rosanna's arm. "Wait up a moment."

Rosanna crossed her arms and waited. Berend grinned and sauntered from the room. Father, Mother, Colonel Hassun, and Captain Degotaga strode past deep in conversation. Daemyn slipped out after them. As he shut the door, he glanced at her before the oak closed between them.

When Rosanna faced Willem, he remained frowning at the door where Daemyn had disappeared. "You had something to say?"

Willem sighed, his shoulders hunched. "Just . . . be careful, all right?"

"I know. I'm going to have all of Tuckawassee, Pohatomie, and anyone else who doesn't want to see the high king return after me." Rosanna rubbed her arms. Even saying it out loud didn't make it real. How could she be such a threat?

He shook his head. "No. Well, yes. But be careful of Daemyn Rand too."

"Why? He's loyal to the high king, isn't he?" Rosanna glanced at the door to the great hall, but it remained closed. The only ones in the room were the guards by each of the door and, along the far wall, Isi talking with Willem's bodyguard.

"Yes. That's not a question. His family has been instrumental in stopping or warning about every Tuckawassee raid and attack for the past hundred years." Willem met Rosanna's gaze. "You wouldn't remember. You were too young. And Father and Mother won't talk about it. But I was seven when Grandfather died. Grandfather and his men were led into a trap. Arlen Rand learned it was a trap and went after them, but he was too late. When Father and the reinforcements arrived, Arlen Rand was the only survivor."

"What does that have to do with Daemyn Rand?" Rosanna crossed her arms tighter. Dribbles of the stories about the Rand family trickled through her mind. Something about the Rands knowing more than they should, and the Tuckawassee hunting them because of it.

"Nothing, maybe. I don't know." Willem shook his head again. "But it isn't the first time a Rand was the only survivor. Daemyn is the only survivor of the attack that killed his father, according to the story. What I'm trying to say is, I don't want you to be another casualty."

"I won't be." Rosanna clenched her fists against her biceps, feeling the strength she'd built up over years of canoeing on the rivers. "Captain Degotaga, Isi, and my guards will make sure that doesn't happen."

Did she believe that? It was hard enough to believe the danger was real, much less know how she would respond. Was this really happening? Danger? Adventure? Hopefully by tomorrow when she climbed into her canoe, it would feel like more than a legend.

CHAPTER 4

ALEXANDER

ONE HUNDRED YEARS AGO

The seventh king, realizing what they had done and what it would cost, fell on his knees and begged forgiveness before the Highest King. For this reason, this seventh king was made high king over the others.

Alexander, high prince of Tallahatchia, strode into his bedchamber and tugged off his boots, muddy from the hours spent outdoors training with his dagger. His shirt, soaked with sweat, landed on the floor a moment later. "Jadon! Baron Galilahi is here. I need a clean shirt—the black one should do—and my crown. You have it polished, right? And my black boots. You polished those too, I trust."

"Yes, sir." Jadon Rand, Alexander's manservant, set the pitcher of water he carried on the washstand next to the basin. "I also fetched warm water."

Good. That was one thing he appreciated about Jadon.

Sometimes he managed to anticipate an order before Alex gave it.

Alex used the towel to wash the sweat and dirt from his chest, arms, and neck. Not necessarily for Baron Galilahi's benefit. The baron, whose estate of Fishrock Cove rested in the mountains at the border of Kanawhee and Tuckawassee, was a good ally and deserved the respect of decent clothing, but he was also a warrior who understood the sweat and grime that came with training with the spear, dagger, and war ax.

No, the change of clothes and washing up had more to do with Mirabelle, Baron Galilahi's daughter.

Mirabelle. With snapping eyes and curving mouth. Alex smiled as he pulled on the black shirt with gold embroidery, gold circlet, and signet ring with its sapphire stone that Jadon handed him. Hopefully Alex would be able to get her alone for a kiss or two or six before Baron Galilahi had to leave.

"Do you require anything else, sir?" Jadon stood back, head bowed, and shoulders hunched, as if to disguise the fact that he stood a few inches taller than Alex. Rather annoying, that, having his manservant taller than him. But, it couldn't be helped. He should've guessed, when he picked a mountain boy as his manservant ten years ago, that Jadon would outgrow him.

"No, I believe that's all. Please have my ax, spear, and dagger polished before I return." Alex didn't wait for Jadon to answer. His order would be done. Jadon was efficient like that.

Alex strolled from his chambers, down several hallways, and up a curved staircase inside one of the towers until he reached his father's study.

When he stepped inside, his father, High King Atohi,

already leaned against his desk. His crown held back his black hair, several eagle feathers dangling from the section of hair along the right side of his face. "Alexander. Good. You're just in time."

Alex joined Father, Baron Galilahi, and Colonel Micco, the commander of the castle guards, and peered at the map laid out on the desk.

Lord Galilahi pointed at the border between Kanawhee and Tuckawassee. "My scouts spotted King Hakan drilling warriors through these mountains here. If I didn't know better, I'd think he's working on the best strategy to move large numbers of men from Tuckawassee to Kanawhee as quickly as possible."

Alexander gritted his teeth. Seven kingdoms ruled by seven kings. They would dissolve into chaos if not for the high king uniting them into one country. For Tallahatchia to survive, the high king had to be strong.

Father was strong. But his enemies knew the exact day when he would become his weakest. Alexander's twenty-first birthday. The day when, according to the curse placed upon him by a Fallen Fae, he would prick his finger with his own dagger and fall into a sleep like unto death, never to wake, along with everyone within Castle Eyota's outer walls.

Apparently Tuckawassee was already planning to pounce, claiming the power of the high king. The other kingdoms would follow, along with all their barons. Tallahatchia would erupt into war as each of the kings fought to be the new high king.

Colonel Micco studied the map from the short side of the desk, a frown crossing his weathered face. At one time, Colonel Micco had been Father's manservant, much as Jadon was Alex's, but Father had released him to join the castle guards many years ago. "We should order the barons to call up the militias in Kanawhee. They should, at the very least, be prepared in case they are needed."

Father's shoulders were straight, but the muscles strained as if it took all his willpower to keep from slumping. "If Kanawhee calls up its militias, the other kingdoms will follow. War will be only one wrong word away."

"War is already one word away, if Tuckawassee's actions can be confirmed. Better we are ready than taken unawares."

Baron Galilahi crossed his arms. "You doubt my report?"

"I'm sure Colonel Micco didn't mean anything by it." Father shook his head. "We don't doubt your report, but it's good to question the interpretation to make sure we do nothing in haste."

Alex closed his eyes and drew in a deep breath. What did they know? Tuckawassee appeared to be arming, preparing for a strike once Kanawhee was vulnerable. Did that mean they wanted war? Or perhaps they merely prepared in case one of the other nations intended to attack?

How many of the other kingdoms were already planning the same? Might they all be planning, in some way, to step in and seize the power of high king once Alex fell into his cursed sleep?

There would be a power void. The Seven Kingdoms would lose their high king, one of the few things that bound them together as a nation. And Kanawhee, one of the seven, would be kingless.

Baron Galilahi cleared his throat. "I know you don't wish it, but please, Your Majesty, at least consider staying outside the castle on the high prince's birthday so that if the worst happens, Tallahatchia won't be without her high king."

"No." Father's face hardened until the angles in his face cast shadows across his cheeks. "If Mirabelle was the one with this curse, would you leave her side? Would you let her sleep, never to wake, on her own? No. Whatever Alexander's end, High Queen Verena and I will share it."

Alex shifted. He didn't like to contemplate what the curse would mean. Sleep without end. Never to live or move or wake until death or time ended, he didn't know which. For that was the curse the Fallen Fae had spoken over him eight days after he was born.

Baron Galilahi drew in another breath, but Alex spoke first. "Besides, whether my parents fall asleep now or die years later, it doesn't make a difference in the larger scheme of things. I am their only heir. If the curse happens, the line of the high kings dies with me no matter what happens to my parents."

Baron Galilahi's shoulders slumped, and he nodded. Of course, he did. Alex was the intelligent one. He could see all the obvious answers everyone else wasn't gifted enough to notice.

Alex didn't voice the other solution he could pursue— perhaps should've pursued a year ago. He should've gotten married, even if it meant marrying young, and had a child by now to leave behind an heir when he fell asleep.

Yet what good would that have done, to leave a young wife and child behind? If the Tuckawassee king or any of the other kings of Tallahatchia were desperate enough for power, they could take it just as easily from a young queen and her babe as they could with no heir at all.

"You haven't found another who you can name as heir?" Colonel Micco waved a hand toward the stacks of genealogy records filling one of the corners behind Father's desk.

"None close enough to be considered an heir in the direct line. Almost all the other six kingdoms have some ancestor related to the high kings, giving all of them a nearly equal claim to the high king's crown, should they pursue it." Father rubbed at his face, as if he was weary enough to need never-ending sleep after all the late nights he'd spent lately.

Who could sleep well with Alex's curse hanging over them, inevitably drawing closer with each day?

Alex traced a hand over the jewel-studded end of the high king's scepter where it lay across its stand at the corner of Father's desk. It was an ugly scepter, a misshapen log some long ago king had deemed important enough to dress up with a few jewels.

Who would wear the crown and carry this scepter if Alex couldn't?

He curled his fingers. That crown and scepter were his birthright. He was the high prince. By right of his birth, he deserved to one day wield all the power signified in those objects. What a high king he would be, with his superior intelligence. He would create a Tallahatchia like no one had seen before.

Why did all of that have to be snatched away by some Fallen Fae's petty curse?

Alex stepped away from the desk and paced. Did he have to fall to the curse? That was a question he'd asked himself ever since his seventh birthday when he'd learned about the curse.

On that day, he'd come up with a plan. He'd convinced Father to allow daggers back into the castle, on the condition they would be banished again on Alex's twenty-first birthday since the curse wouldn't strike until then. He himself had trained with a dagger so pricking himself wouldn't happen due to clumsiness or unfamiliarity with the weapon. He would give his dagger away the night before his birthday, since the wording of the curse specifically said he would prick his finger on his *own* dagger.

What else could he do to avoid it? Surely he hadn't been gifted with intelligence without a purpose. There had to be a way for him to think his way out of this in the three months before his birthday.

Perhaps he didn't have to avoid it. Or end it. No, he had to get it removed. Take away any possibility the curse could happen at all.

A Fae had cursed him. Only a Fae could undo it.

The plan unrolled until Alex couldn't say which part of it fell into place first.

He halted and turned toward Father, Baron Galilahi, and Colonel Micco. "Queen Kimi of Buckhannock is due to birth their first child in about two months or so. One of the Loyal Fae will be there to bestow a gift. I'll ask this Fae to have the curse removed. Surely the Lord of the Fae doesn't intend for the balance of power placed in Tallahatchia to fall."

Colonel Micco didn't react, as if he didn't believe the Fae would remove the curse. Baron Galilahi stared while Father paused, then nodded slowly. "Yes, we must do something drastic. We can't let this curse happen."

"I will leave immediately for Buckhannock."

Father straightened. "I'll send a division of guards to escort you."

"No." Alex shook his head. He'd already thought of all the possibilities and settled on the best one before Father could even begin to process a plan. "We can't let any of the other kingdoms know we might have a solution. Right now, they think they know the exact day when we'll be vulnerable. Let them continue to think so. We can better counter their moves when they're predictable. No, it would be best if I traveled alone, dressed as a lowborn traveler."

Father scowled. "I don't like it. You're too vulnerable alone."

"I'm intelligent and good with my dagger. I'll take Jadon with me, of course, so he can keep watch while I rest." Alex crossed his arms. "I'll be able to move much faster and be inconspicuous with just Jadon to aid me."

It took a few more minutes of arguing, but Father and Colonel Micco eventually agreed. Of course, they did. Alex was the one gifted with intelligence, after all. Most people eventually saw the logic of his words.

With the meeting adjourned, Alex slipped from the tower and strode through the entry hall filled with antiques from the various kingdoms, including a whitetail deer formed of iron from Buckhannock, a tapestry of geometric designs in vibrant purples and greens from Guyangahela, and a bowl of delicate, blown-glass fruit from Neskahana.

After exiting the main doors, he found Mirabelle waiting for him in their usual spot in the garden near the postern gate, under the climbing roses filling the arbor and sheltering them from prying eyes. At this time in the early spring, most of the plants barely poked through the brown dirt only recently revealed under melted snow.

Mirabelle had her back to him, stroking one of the rose stems. As she stroked, leaves burst along the stem, followed by a bud. A few moments later, the rose bloomed, a burst of brilliant red against the green leaves. She leaned over and sniffed.

Alex wrapped his arms around her waist. "Your Fae gift

suits you. What else would someone as beautiful as you be able to grow except roses?"

Mirabelle leaned against him. Her dark brown hair flowed over her shoulders and the back of her deep red dress. "Are you sure your gift wasn't flattery instead of intelligence?"

"It means I'm smart enough to know a beauty when I see her." Alex loosened his hold, and Mirabelle turned in his arms.

She wrapped her arms around his neck, her mouth curving in that coy way that sent his head spinning. She drew him closer and pressed her lips to his. He returned the kiss, long and deep, again and again. He pulled back just enough to whisper, "Marry me. Now. Before the curse." He bent to claim yet another kiss.

She shoved away from him. "Not a chance."

Alex drew in several deep breaths and pulled her closer once again. "Why not?"

Mirabelle yanked out of his grip. "I'm not going to tie myself to your curse. There are plenty of princes out there. I'm sorry, but I'm not about to spend all of time sleeping. Or living alone essentially a widow, yet unable to move on because my husband is still alive in a cursed sleep. I have too much life to live yet."

Something was shattering inside him. Not that he loved Mirabelle. Not the way Father loved Mother, anyway. But he'd still imagined that someday, if he could avoid the curse, maybe he and Mirabelle . . . well, they had plenty of passion between them. That certainly counted for something.

He reached for her again. "What if I found a way to end the curse? To keep it from happening?"

Mirabelle slapped his hands away. "If you find a way to

prevent the curse from happening, then I'll consider resuming what we have. But until then, don't expect any more kisses from me. With my beauty, I have plenty of other men clamoring for my attention. All I have to do is crook my finger and they'll grovel at my feet. I don't need you."

She ripped the rose from the arbor, whirled, and swished away, her hips swaying as if to remind him of all he had to lose.

He had to end this curse. No matter what it took.

CHAPTER 5

ALEXANDER

ONE HUNDRED YEARS AGO

*But the true hope rests in the Cursebreaker for only he holds
the power to break the curse that destroys the world and fully
corrupts the hearts of men.*

The sun barely peeked over the far horizon, an awful hour to be awake. Alex stifled a yawn and tried to appear alert as his father went through yet another lecture on being safe and smart as they stood before Castle Eyota's postern gate, a small iron-banded door set in the back wall of the castle facing the Kanawhee River far below. Frost still covered the ground and much of the castle's garden nearby.

Jadon stood off to the side, head bowed respectfully, their pack on the ground at his feet. At the gate, Colonel Micco removed the locking bar, having sent the guards away.

Finally, Father paused for a breath, and Alex jumped in

before he could start off on another lecture. "I under-stand." Alex nodded, and the motion felt strange with his hair trimmed short and missing the eagle feather he normally wore next to his right ear.

He had decided it would be smarter to travel as a castle servant from Buckhannock like Jadon. Thus, he wore plain, unadorned buckskin traveling clothes with his hair cropped short. Thanks to his mother—who had been a princess of Pohatomie before she married Father—his skin was lighter than most in Kanawhee, more like those in Buckhannock. Even his name sounded more Pohatomie than Kanawhee.

The buckskin rubbed against his skin, stiff compared to the fine shirts and breeches in his wardrobe.

Alex adjusted his sapphire-stoned signet ring where it hung from a leather string around his neck. Besides his dagger, his signet ring was the only piece of his status he was taking with him. One thing to remind him of home and all he had to lose if he failed on this quest. "I'm going to get this curse removed."

Father patted Alex's shoulder. "I know you will."

Mother stepped forward, her dark purple dress swishing around her feet. She hugged him tightly, her long blond hair tickling his chin. "Stay safe."

"Of course." Alex extricated himself from Mother's hug. "I'll be fine. Don't worry."

With a final nod, Alex spun on his heel and motioned to Jadon. Jadon hefted their pack on his back and fell into step behind Alex. Colonel Micco swung the gate open, and Alex strode through.

As soon as Jadon stepped through behind him, Colonel Micco swung the postern gate closed. No turning back now. There were only the steep cliffs down to the river, the thin path leading to the main trail to the town, and the removal of his curse before him.

Alex led the way down the winding path along the cliffs and around the base of Castle Eyota. No other castle in Tallahatchia held the majesty of Castle Eyota with the spindles of its many towers rising into the sky, the sun splashing against the red-gold of its stone walls. Tiers of rooms and sprawling courtyards, gardens and strong encircling battlements. Surely a castle fit for the high kings.

Perched as it was on a high bluff over Kanawhee River, it dominated the landscape and its section of river. Even the town of Eyota downriver appeared small from the castle's lofty heights, as if to remind everyone who saw the castle that his family ruled Tallahatchia.

A rule some would dare to question if his curse wasn't removed.

Alex gritted his teeth and forced himself to pull a hood over his head and duck as he and Jadon neared the bustling trail heading into Eyota. Farmers hauled carts loaded with their produce, furs, and meat to trade in the town for cloth from Guyangahela or glass from Neskahana or metal goods from Buckhannock.

Ahead, a man led a small wood buffalo—one raised and trained to be a pack animal—by its leather halter. The mound of packs strapped to its thick-furred, humped back swayed with the animal's lumbering gait. Probably one of the traders having come over the mountains from Guyangahela.

The bustle thickened the closer they came to Eyota. Here, unlike any other town in Tallahatchia, the Seven Kingdoms mixed into one. In the crush of people along the main street, a group of men from Guyangahela, the rich cloth of their shirts and leggings dyed in deep blues and greens that stood out against their dark skin, haggled with a Kanawhee merchant selling dried corn from Pohatomie.

A man from Monongadotte—distinguishable by the elk's head and antlers he wore like a hat and the fur draped over him for a cloak—laughed and stroked his red-brown beard as he conversed with a man wearing gold chains and jewels around his neck in the style of the Tuckawassee.

This was what the high kings made possible. Trade between the kingdoms. Kanawhee—and the town of Eyota in particular—was the center of that trade.

Alex drew in a deep breath of the town's smell—a combination of animal manure, tanned fur, baking corn-bread, and the general odor of too many human bodies for a small space. This was home. The legacy of the high kings he would maintain, if he wasn't forced to sleep on his twenty-first birthday.

Jadon pushed past him. "Best let me lead, sir. We'll have to shove our way to the passenger docks."

Alex grimaced and nodded. Normally when he visited Eyota, he was accompanied by a contingent of guards who saw to it the road cleared before him. It wasn't fitting for a high prince to rub shoulders with the lowly people he ruled. But he wasn't going to have a choice today.

Jadon weaved through the traffic on the street, dodging around people walking in every direction.

Alex hurried to keep up while avoiding eye contact with those around him. What would happen if someone in the crowd recognized him, he didn't know. But he'd rather not lose any time on this quest to a crowd fawning over their high prince.

Alex caught glimpses of the river in breaks between the buildings. Docks crowded along the bank, and rivermen poled their boats into docks or unloaded the goods a merchant would soon display in their shops or on their tables along the road.

The river itself teemed with nearly as much traffic as the town with everything from small two-man birch bark canoes to the larger twenty-foot cargo or passenger canoes, to the riverboats poled by lines of men walking along narrow decks on either side of the boat.

Finally, they reached the far end of the town near where the Gaulee River converged with the Kanawhee. The docks for the passenger canoes and riverboats were crammed with people waiting to catch a boat up or down the Kanawhee or Gaulee.

Alex followed as Jadon shoved his way through the crowd to the dock master. Jadon pointed at the riverboats. "We need a boat headed up the Gaulee. Are any of them going all the way to Chattakee?"

The dock master chewed on the end of his corncob pipe and eyed the boats in the docks in front of him as if consulting a list in his head. Finally, he took the corncob pipe from his mouth and used it to point at a riverboat weathered to a light gray with the name *Mae Belle* barely visible on the side.

It was average size for a passenger riverboat with two narrow decks running alongside the raised center section where cargo was stowed. Rows of benches lined the roof of the cargo area while a rudder stuck out from the stern. "That one there is going as far as Nanooga. You might be able to catch a boat from there to Chattakee."

That one? Alex had to fight his scowl. That riverboat looked like it could barely float, much less make it to Nanooga.

"Thank you." Jadon hitched the pack higher on his back and headed for the riverboat.

Alex trailed behind. If a riverboat wasn't the fastest way up the Gaulee to Buckhannock, he would turn around now and walk all the way.

A small group of people already waited by the boat, some sitting on wooden benches, others standing and talking quietly with piles of baggage around their feet. Off to one side, a man dressed in a purple silk shirt perched on a bench next to a woman in the finest green silk from Guyangahela. The baron and baroness of Nanooga returning home.

Alex ducked and tugged the hood of his cloak lower over his face. He couldn't let them recognize him. With the baroness's gossip skills, all Kanawhee and half of Buckhannock would know he had left Castle Eyota by nightfall.

Jadon approached the white-haired man leaning against the hull of the *Mae Belle*. "Do you have room for two more passengers to Nanooga?"

The riverboat's skipper rubbed a hand over the sparse hair on his tanned scalp. "Got room for one more riding passenger, but plenty of space if you want to work your way upriver."

"That will be satisfactory." Jadon pulled a handful of etched wooden tokens out of his pocket and handed them to the skipper.

The tokens were meaningless in themselves, but they were redeemable in Eyota for a set number of goods as marked on the tokens' face. The merchants and market in Eyota determined how much all the tradable goods were worth, and Alex's father looked over the accounts to make sure everything remained fair and none of the merchants attempted to cheat each other or the traders from the other six kingdoms.

After an hour wait, the skipper finally called for passengers to board. The baron and baroness climbed aboard first, navigating onto the raised platform above the cargo area and claiming the bench at the front. That would've been Alex's seat, if he'd been traveling as himself.

Once all the other riding passengers clambered on, Alex strolled past Jadon, the other working passengers, and the ten men who formed the regular crew and stepped onto the riverboat. The wooden deck rocked under his weight. Most unpleasant.

He squeezed onto the end of the last bench next to a family returning to Monongadotte, judging from the various animal skins they wore. The bench had so little room he actually had to sit shoulder to shoulder with one of the teenage boys in the family and had to duck the whitetail deer antlers set into the boy's wood and fur hat every time he swung his head to gawk at his surroundings.

This was going to be a long, uncomfortable two days to Nanooga.

While the crew took down their poles and shuffled into position, Jadon shoved their pack on top of the stack in the hold and claimed one of the long poles from hooks set along the side of the cargo area. It looked to be an unwieldy thing, nearly as long as the boat, and probably weighed several pounds.

It was a good thing there had been one seat left in the passenger area. Alex would've given himself away if he'd had to pole the boat alongside Jadon.

The skipper hopped on board and gripped the tiller. "Listen up. Passengers up top stay seated at all times and keep your hands and feet inside the passenger area. We don't need you tripping up the men poling this tub. You on the poles, listen to your front and rear men. Stab the poles in and lean into them when you walk and give them a good yank when it's time to walk forward. Right then, shove off."

The crew and the two working passengers on the starboard side who appeared to have done this before thrust their poles into the water until they struck bottom and shoved. The riverboat eased away from the dock. Alex gripped the edge of his bench and tried to stay in his seat as best he could as the boat lurched into the river's current.

Along the foot-wide walkway, Jadon had joined the other men poling. It looked like exhausting work. They stabbed the pole into the river bottom, leaned against it while walking to the stern to shove the boat forward. Once there, they yanked the pole free and marched to the bow of the boat to start the process over.

Terribly monotonous. Almost as monotonous as the endless trees and mountains rising on either side of the river. They probably wouldn't even be attacked by river pirates, as much as that would break up the tedium. But river pirate attacks were rare, thanks to his father's soldiers patrolling the river.

Alex craned his neck. Behind them, the spires of Castle Eyota rose against the distant western sky like the mountain's golden crown. He couldn't lose the glory of that castle to his curse. He wouldn't allow it to happen.

CHAPTER 6

ROSANNA

The legends told, though not truly, that a princess would wake the high prince from his cursed sleep with true love's kiss.

Rosanna secured her pack in the center of the canoe she would share with Daemyn. Except for a few essentials, most of the camping gear was already tied down in two of the other canoes, each with two of her guards.

The morning sun still lay below the shadowed crests of the far mountains, the sky pink and blue in a rare clear day this early in the spring.

Captain Degotaga helped Isi into their canoe. She wore a fringed buckskin skirt that fell to her knees with a pair of leggings beneath and fringed shirt. Her moccasins laced up to her knees.

Rosanna wore similar traveling clothes, but without

the red and white beadwork that Isi's shirt had. Isi shot her a grin as if she didn't care that, with the extra beadwork, she was supposed to be mistaken for Rosanna if they were spotted.

Before Rosanna could brace herself, Berend hugged her, squeezed her tighter and tighter, grinning when she wheezed and wiggled.

"I'm going to need my ribs in one piece." She swatted him on the shoulder.

"Just had to give you one last bear hug." He released her, tugging the sleeve of his shirt down over his left hand.

Trying to hide the flash of white bandage tinted red in the center. Rosanna crossed her arms. "You got hurt chasing after that Tuckawassee major, didn't you? Come on. Fess up."

Berend glanced over his shoulder, winced, and lowered his voice. "Don't tell Father and Mother, all right? It's just a little spear poke in my paw. Nothing big."

Perhaps. But there was something in his stance. He leaned to the right, his back stiff. And he hadn't pulled her off her feet with his bear hug like he usually did. "Don't lie to me, Bere-Bear. Where else?"

He shifted, the tips of his ears going darker beneath his bronzed skin. "That Major Beshko apparently isn't the screaming type. She's more the strike out with a spear and attack type. I, well, had to beat a hasty retreat and, uh, my . . . rear end is a bit of a bigger target as a bear."

Rosanna wasn't sure whether to laugh or shake her head. "Don't you think everyone is going to notice when you don't sit down for a week?"

"Willem is going to cover for me. Maybe. At least, I don't think he's confessed about yanking the arrow out of me yet." Berend grimaced and shrugged. "What are big brothers for?"

Rosanna glanced past Berend to Willem, who was strolling toward them. Willem tipped his head toward where Father stood off to the side, frowning, arms crossed.

That explained things. Rosanna gave Willem a nod in return. Willem trusted their father was too smart not to see through Berend within minutes.

Knowing Willem, he had probably accompanied his arrow-yanking with a lecture for Berend to be more careful and tell Father and Mother himself.

Willem reached them, and Rosanna stepped into his hug. A firm hug, but less rib-crunching than Berend's. Someday—if Willem ever found the right girl within Neskahana's borders—his wife was going to feel protected and loved with his hug. "I'm going to miss you."

Willem released her and stepped back. "Stay safe, all right? You're the only sister we have."

Rosanna forced herself to grin, and she had to swallow several times to clear the lump in her throat before she could talk. "I'll be fine. If all the stories are true, Daemyn Rand knows what he's doing. The Tuckawassee will never catch him."

"Just as long as they don't catch you." Willem squeezed her shoulder before he stepped back, bumping into Berend's left side as he did. Berend winced and scowled.

Mother took Willem's place, hugging Rosanna. "Stay safe."

"You too." Rosanna swallowed. She hadn't expected her voice to get rough and scratchy like that. But Mother had volunteered to be bait and would be braving weeks of rough travel with an army.

But what else could they do? She couldn't run from

this duty, but she wasn't sure how determined she was to go forward. She was going more because she wanted the adventure than any driving conviction to wake the high prince.

What would she be expected to do, if she succeeded? The stories said the princess who woke him would be his true love. Would she have to marry him? She'd never met the man, only heard a few stories passed down from her great-grandfather to Grandfather to Father to her.

Father rested his hands on Rosanna's shoulders. "I'm proud of you. No matter how this turns out—even if you fail to wake the high prince in the end—I will still be proud of you."

Rosanna hugged him. "I'm going to miss you so much."

Dreaming about adventure was one thing. Actually leaving was something entirely different.

He patted her back as he stepped out of her hug. "We'll see each other at Castle Eyota."

Most likely after she'd woken the high prince, if the Tuckawassee army delayed Father and Mother like Daemyn Rand predicted. But at least that gave her something to look forward to. Wake High Prince Alexander, then she could be reunited with her family as they basked in the high king's gratitude.

Rosanna forced herself to spin on her heels and climb into the front of the canoe. Daemyn shoved them from shore and gained his seat in the canoe as fluidly as the water now gurgling against the birch bark hull.

Chogan and Ilma, the husband and wife pair among her guards, set out in the lead with Nikan and Garmund following.

The crisp morning air turned into a breeze as Rosanna

and Daemyn dug their paddles in and propelled the canoe forward. Mist hung over the far stretches of the river and dripped from the trees along the gorge's sides, turning the leaves blue and purple in the distance. The mountain peaks gleamed in dark greens and deep blues along the horizon, as restless and wild as the rivers they contained.

Rosanna thrust her paddle into the river, pulled backwards with her whole body, especially her torso and shoulders, and feathered her paddle from the water Although she didn't turn around, she could feel by the steady glide of the canoe that Daemyn matched his rhythm to hers with the ease of someone who had traveled with her for years. Or, perhaps, someone used to adjusting to new travel companions as needed.

She forced herself not to turn around. She wouldn't watch as Castle Deeling and the walled town it protected slid out of sight behind the mountains. Would she see her home again?

Not just the castle, but this stretch of river, the trees she'd watched grow from saplings into towering trunks, and these mountains—these ever-changing mountains with their moods and river-carved faces that had seen the days when the Highest King himself walked the earth to talk with the seven kings and listen to the singing trees— would she ever see these mountains again?

Maybe. Maybe not. But she would see more mountains, the deep blue ones she'd stared at on the horizon all her life. Perhaps they, too, would sing home in her veins.

The miles blurred beneath the canoe, blending into a soothing rhythm of paddle strokes and the gurgle and pock of the river against the canoe's sides. Sometimes Captain Degotaga and Isi glided next to them, sometimes behind them, as the river's currents demanded.

Going upriver as they were, they snaked back and forth across the current rather than fight it, using the natural eddies around the river's bends. Otho and Ahanu formed the rear guard in the final canoe.

As the sun rose, it glinted off the water ahead of them until Rosanna had to squint to read the river's swells and currents.

Daemyn's rhythm halted behind her. After a few seconds, something tapped her arm. When she swiveled, Daemyn held out a small tin filled with a thick, dark gray-colored paste. If it was anything like the similar clay pot she had in her pack lashed in the center of the canoe, it consisted of charcoal and bear grease. Daemyn had already smeared a layer underneath both of his eyes. "This will help."

She grimaced, balanced her paddle across her knees, and took the tin from him. "I know. But it's so difficult to scrub off after I'm done on the river I usually avoid it." Partly the reason she woke so early in the morning and headed up the Onohio before the sun rose, then downriver with the early morning sun at her back.

He resumed his steady strokes. "Not something you'll have to worry about on this trip, Your Highness. Put it on thick. You might be wearing it for a few days before you'll have a chance to wash it off."

All a part of the adventure. Rosanna dug her fingers in and smeared the black paste underneath her eyes. As she did, she noticed Captain Degotaga and Isi drawing alongside them. Isi applied some of the grease below each of her eyes in neat, swooping lines.

Rosanna washed her fingers off in the river as best she could and closed the tin. The black grease cut the glare from the sunlight enough that she no longer had to squeeze her eyes into slits. Twisting in her seat, she shoved the tin into one of his packs where the covering oil skin had been pulled back. After tucking the oilskin back into place, she lashed it tightly once again.

When she looked up, Daemyn's gaze flicked between the river ahead and studying her. Was he annoyed she'd touched his pack without permission? "Sorry, your pack was open, and I figured . . ." She shook herself. Why was she apologizing? It would've been more of a hassle if she'd handed back the tin expecting him to put it away.

"No, it's fine." Daemyn shook his head, his gaze going to the pack she'd lashed back into place. "It wasn't what I was expecting. But I'm glad you know your way around a canoe and a proper knot."

Something in his mild tone struck her, like he would've been just as patient had she refused to paddle her own canoe and fumbled with the basics of travel. She faced forward and gripped her paddle again. "What had you been expecting? A condescending princess ordering you around?"

"Actually, yes, before I met you." The rhythm of Daemyn's strokes remained steady behind her. "I couldn't be sure what the promised cursebreaker would be like."

"What would you have done if I had been annoying and bossy?"

"I would've seen to it you arrived at Castle Eyota on the right day in one piece with as few discomforts as possible."

If Berend had said those words, they would've been sarcastic. But Daemyn's tone remained sincere, as if he meant them. "Isn't that exactly what you're doing now? It makes no difference to you if I'm arrogant or helpful?"

"Don't get me wrong. I'm thankful you're going to make this a whole heap easier." Daemyn's voice remained low, just as she'd kept hers, to make sure their conversation wouldn't carry too far over the water. "But my duty remains the same."

"The duty to guide me to Castle Eyota?" Rosanna gazed at the riverbanks. Were Major Beshko and her raiding party out there somewhere, hiding behind the familiar landmarks? Had Father's scouts tracked them down by now? "You seem to know Tallahatchia rather well."

He couldn't be that much older than Rosanna's twenty-one years. Possibly around twenty-five. How young would he have started wandering Tallahatchia to know it so well already?

Daemyn dug his paddle into the river and drew it back, the late afternoon sun glinting off the clear stone in his ring. As his shoulders sagged, something in his eyes appeared old. Far too old for his unlined face. "I may appear young, but I've known my duty for a long time."

Daemyn Rand and his father and grandfather before him dedicated their lives to fighting the Tuckawassee and Pohatomie to restore the high king to his rightful throne. Did Daemyn fear he would give his life for this cause the way his father had done only a year ago?

Rosanna struggled to keep her breathing even. What would she be called to sacrifice?

Her family risked their lives—as well as the lives of their people—to see that High Prince Alexander woke. That was the depth of the loyalty Father still carried to the high king even though Tallahatchia hadn't had a high king in Father's or Grandfather's life times.

"Why?" Rosanna wasn't even sure she'd asked the question out loud until Daemyn's paddle stroke hesitated for half a beat. She swallowed and glanced over her shoulder. "Why are you doing all this? What has High Prince

Alexander ever done for you? He's been asleep for nearly a hundred years. You've never met him. Your father and grandfather never even met him."

Daemyn's gaze drifted to the river, as if he stared into the far mists of the past. "It's what the Highest King has called me to do. I can do no less."

She straightened in her seat to hide her shiver. No, she didn't have half the conviction of the man sitting in the canoe behind her. If she was the princess destined to wake High Prince Alexander, then, a hundred years ago, this moment in her life had already been planned out. Generations in Tallahatchia depended on her to succeed.

Yet here she was, going along more for a lark than actual commitment to the duty asked of her. If they ran into danger, how determined was she to carry out this calling?

To their right, a stockade came into view halfway up the hillside. Its thick log walls probably protected a cluster of homes. The faint sound of barking dogs and shouting men carried down to them on the river, and within moments, faces lined the wall of the stockade's parapet, axes and spears gleaming in the sunlight.

Something ached deep in Rosanna's chest. Even here in Neskahana where her father did his best to protect their people, no one—not the large towns or the small settlements deep in the mountains—dared live outside fortified walls. How much worse must it be in other places in Tallahatchia? Especially Kanawhee whose king slept behind his wall of thorns?

Could she stop the war by waking the high prince? If she was the promised princess, why did she still feel so small? Invisible? Shouldn't she have gained some sort of strength or gift or something?

"I'm sorry, Your Highness. We'll be camping out in the forest on this trip." Daemyn's voice remained too low to carry to the settlement fading into their wake.

Focus on the adventure. She had always wanted to camp out in the forest. "I'll be fine. And this is going to be a long trip. You don't have to call me 'Your Highness' the entire time."

"If that is what you wish, Princess."

Try as she might, she couldn't detect the flippancy she might've expected. If Berend had said something like that, it would've had an eye roll and a smirk to go with it. She glanced over her shoulder. "You aren't being sarcastic, are you?"

He gave her such a wide-eyed innocent look with those deep brown eyes of his that she nearly apologized for making such a wrong assumption. Then the corner of his mouth twitched, softening the line of his jaw beneath the shadow of stubble. "Best set yourself right and get paddling, Princess. We have a heap of miles to make before dark."

Perhaps it was the trace of the mountain speech in his voice, but she found herself smiling as she dug her paddle deep, facing the river before them once again.

Captain Degotaga and Isi's canoe pulled alongside, and Captain Degotaga scowled at Daemyn as if he blamed him for the delay. Isi flashed Rosanna a grin, a twinkle in her eyes as if she thought she knew something. Rosanna didn't know what Isi thought she knew, but she grinned back anyway.

Her grin faded as her gaze strayed to the mountains rising steeply on either side of the broad expanse of the Neskahana River. Were Major Beshko and her Tuckawassee raiding party out there watching even now?

She drew her paddle through the water, feeling the power of the river beneath the thin birch bark skin of their canoe. They had hundreds of miles to travel across three kingdoms.

It would be an adventure. That much was certain.

CHAPTER 7

ROSANNA

Every waterfall is an echo of the final WaterVeil that separates this world from the one beyond, the Highest King's own realm where he rules as the Lord of all Fae and Men. Their thunder is a whisper of his voice.

When Rosanna woke after a third night of camping outdoors, her hip bone and her shoulder ached from the night curled in her blankets with only a thin padding between her and the hard ground. When she pushed herself upright, she had to bite her lip to stop a groan at the pain shooting down her arms and back. She'd never paddled so many hours against the current before.

But she couldn't complain. This was the adventure she'd always wanted. Paddling her canoe into the far-off horizons, exploring the depths of those blue mountains.

Isi still slept on her bedroll on the other side of the tent, her breaths rising and falling in a slow rhythm. Might as well let Isi sleep. At least someone found some rest on the hard ground, especially after they'd gone late into the night for the past three days to put as much distance as possible between them and Major Beshko.

Rosanna crawled from the tent, shook out her long, black hair, and straightened her buckskin shirt and trousers.

Captain Degotaga was already up, nudging a few twigs into a flame to get a fire started. Morning mist hung heavy over the river and its bank, obscuring any smoke the fire might make from prying eyes. Garmund and Nikan walked the perimeter while Otho laid out ingredients for breakfast on the bench of one of the canoes.

A lone figure perched on a rock overlooking the hushed river, his staff held across his lap. Rosanna walked toward him, purposely crunching last year's leaves under-foot. She didn't want to startle him.

He stiffened for a moment before relaxing, but he didn't turn her way or acknowledge her presence as she eased onto a seat on one of the rocks a few feet away. She did her best to get comfortable against the rock and a tree growing from the rocky slope.

The silence was too still, too deep for her to try to break. Mist curled between the treetops and danced over the river as if a ghost of the memories these mountains had seen. Only the river dared add a whisper to the quiet. The breeze, the trees, even the mountains held their breath as a line of pink broke through the deep blue on the horizon, a trumpeting herald to the sun's ascent into the heavens.

Across the river and upstream, a large shape moved from the mist, solidifying into a shaggy, bull buffalo. His low grunt echoed down the river gorge, answered by his herd following close behind. He dipped his head and drank. As he moved off, the rest of the herd slurped at the water before they too disappeared back into the mist and mountains.

And Daemyn Rand remained as still as if he was as a part of these mountains as the trees and the river. Perhaps in the pulse of the river he heard his own heartbeat. Much as she did.

Maybe that was what had drawn her here. The feeling like he might be one of the few people who could under-stand her. Who heard the mountains the way she did.

Someone who could be a friend.

She had been blessed with Isi's friendship, even if Isi didn't share her drive for adventure any more than she shared Isi's love for fine beadwork.

The weight of her questions ached in her chest, but she couldn't put words to one that would be worthy of breaking this silence.

Finally, she forced a single question into the morning, one she should've thought to ask the night before. "What is it like, having traveled and seen all of Tallahatchia?"

He didn't turn to her, just leaned against the staff resting between his knees. "There is always another horizon in the distance, no matter how many horizons have already been crossed. And even a familiar one looks different with each new dawn. A gift from the Lord of the Fae."

"Makes me wonder what it all used to sound like when the kings of old could hear the mountain's music." Rosanna closed her eyes and let the silence wash over her once again. After several minutes, she glanced at Daemyn. "Where are you from?"

"Buckhannock. Deep in the mountains." Daemyn

flexed his fingers on his hardwood staff as if he needed its support.

"Do you have any siblings?"

"Yes. Several brothers and sisters. All younger." Daemyn stared up at the sky, something weighing his shoulders and features. "It's been a long while since I've seen them."

"It must have been different, growing up with that many siblings." Rosanna glanced over her shoulder but didn't see Isi moving about the camp yet. She must still be in their tent. "I had my brothers and Isi. We're as close as sisters."

"My childhood wasn't quite what you imagine." Daemyn shook his head.

"Well, I'm sure there was the added pressure of your family's duty. Growing up being told that you would someday have the duty to find the princess meant to wake the high prince and lead her to Castle Eyota must have been daunting."

"Yes. At times."

"I'm glad I didn't know about all this growing up." Rosanna waved at the rippling expanse of the river before them. "It was hard enough growing up without a gift or a curse."

"It isn't such a bad thing, to have neither." The clear stone in the ring on Daemyn's finger flashed in a flare of dawn's light piercing through the trees. "Sometimes gifts can be just as much of a burden as the curses."

Was it the gift of being the one to find the high prince's cursebreaker that so burdened him? Or something else?

Whatever it was, she wasn't comfortable enough with him yet to ask. Nor was he likely to answer her. She smiled.

"Hopefully this will be over soon, and you'll be able to see your family again."

A half-sad, half-hopeful smile creased his face. "Yes, I believe I will."

His voice had that odd tone, like his words held more meaning than what seemed on the surface.

He pushed to his feet. "Breakfast is ready."

After claiming a bowl of oatmeal, Rosanna found a seat on a nearby log. Daemyn didn't join her even though she'd left plenty of room. With a nod in her direction, he headed for Captain Degotaga.

Isi perched on the log next to Rosanna, stirring maple syrup into her oatmeal. "Do you know we're going to have to ration our supply of maple syrup? We might be able to get more at the army outpost by the border, but that's it. How am I ever going to survive endless breakfasts of oatmeal without maple syrup to make it edible?"

"I'm not sure." Rosanna fought her smile.

Isi grinned, though her grin faded as she sighed. "You didn't brush your hair this morning, did you?"

Rosanna pulled a section of her hair over her shoulder. It might be a bit frizzy. "No, I didn't. Didn't seem important."

Isi shook her head, making her perfectly slicked and polished braid swing across her back. "Guess that's probably true. From a distance, no one's going to think you're the princess and I'm the bodyguard if your hair is as wild as the river. Now finish your oatmeal, and I'll braid your hair."

Once everyone had eaten and Isi had braided Rosanna's hair, the tents were taken down and their gear stowed in the canoes. Each canoe was carried down the bank and set in the water. When everyone slid into their seats and claimed their paddles, they set off upriver once again.

Rosanna slipped back into the steady rhythm of paddling, her stiff muscles easing into a warm burn with the exertion. The hours and miles rippled past in with a comfortable familiarity of motion and strain that claimed every muscle so fully she didn't try to think or feel. Just breathe in the scents of deep forest and river.

As evening neared, Rosanna sat straighter and tilted her head as a sound echoed across the water. She glanced over her shoulder. "Is that a waterfall?"

A hint of a smile cross Daemyn's face. "Yes."

She didn't have to ask which one. It had to be the Kikataw Falls, the largest falls on the Neskahana River. "I've always wanted to see . . ."

For some reason, she didn't try to finish that sentence.

"You'll see them now." Daemyn dug his paddle in again as the canoes behind them neared to within a few feet.

With each paddle stroke, the rumble built into a roar, then into a thunder. They curved around a bend in the river, then there it was. The Kikataw Falls rose in the distance, framed by jagged cliffs and tumbled boulders. The waterfall plummeted down in a brown wall, landing in a swirl of foam at the bottom. The new green of the spring foliage crowded along the rocks and contrasted with the solid blue of the sky above.

Rosanna missed a paddle stroke as she stared at the falls rising above them. An urge built in her chest to paddle their canoe right to the brink of that pounding foam and feel the power of the water surge through her blood. "Can we go closer?"

"Only if your guards allow it." Daemyn steered their canoe closer to Captain Degotaga and Isi.

Captain Degotaga was giving instructions to the two lead canoes for the guards to scout their landing site.

Daemyn jabbed the end of his paddle toward the falls. "We're going to go closer while we wait for the scouts."

Captain Degotaga glanced from Rosanna to the falls. "All right. But we'll come along. Otho, Ahanu, stay fifty feet out and keep watch."

Rosanna dug her paddle into the water and felt the canoe glide forward. The waterfall's rumble grew until it vibrated into her bones. Daemyn took their canoe all the way into the churned water at the edge of the foaming chaos.

After resting her paddle across her knees, Rosanna tipped her head up and held her hands out as the spray sprinkled across her face in the river's cool kiss. She drew in a deep breath of the water-filled, crystal air. "It's even more magnificent than I imagined."

A breeze touched Rosanna's face, reminding her of whispers and thunder, songs and ancient stories passed down in all their careful wording from fathers and mothers to sons and daughters because they meant something beyond mere stories, especially the stories of the Cursebreaker.

The Cursebreaker, of whom a cursebreaker like her was a sign.

Rosanna swayed with the tug of the river, the stir of the breeze. Why had that burden been placed on her? Why did she have to be High Prince Alexander's cursebreaker?

And why, if she was in the line of kings given to rule, had she been given neither curse nor gift? Especially the gift meant to symbolize hope, if she was supposed to bring hope?

Would she banish this vague restlessness stirring inside

her? A restlessness that whispered this wasn't her calling, even though Daemyn Rand, the one given to know High Prince Alexander's cursebreaker, had said otherwise.

When she tore her gaze away from the waterfall, Daemyn was studying the riverbanks as if he could see beyond the trees to the danger that might lurk there.

"Do you think Major Beshko is following us?" Rosanna had to raise her voice to speak over the waterfall's roar. It had to be unlikely they were followed, wasn't it? Major Beshko couldn't possibly have found out Rosanna was the promised princess before she left, and Father's men surely had driven her and her men deep into the mountains where they wouldn't be able to observe Rosanna and her guards leaving.

"I don't know, but it never hurts to remain wary even while we are still in Neskahana." Daemyn lifted his paddle. "Your guards have signaled it's safe. We'll camp within sight of the falls tonight."

If she could, she would stay in this place of mist and thunder for hours. But the sun was already sinking, turning the world orange, then gray. At least she would fall asleep to the waterfall's music tonight. She picked up her paddle and stroked toward shore.

CHAPTER 8

ALEXANDER

ONE HUNDRED YEARS AGO

After five days traveling by riverboat, Alex kept his pace steady as he hiked along a branch of the Cheyandoah Trace, leaving the small outpost of Chattakee behind. He refused to slow, even to catch his breath. The sooner he got to Buckhannock, the better.

Behind him, Jadon huffed and panted even worse than Alex. Perhaps due to the pace Alex was setting or because Jadon carried the pack, as was only right, since Jadon was the manservant.

He should slow down to give Jadon a rest. He couldn't have the man collapse on him before they'd even left Kanawhee, especially not after Jadon had poled the two days from Eyota to Nanooga and had to pole two of the three days from there to Chattakee.

The path leveled out, winding next to a jagged line of fifteen-foot cliffs on one side and a steep slope down to Wolf Creek hundreds of feet below on the other. Alex squinted to the west. Was that a line of clouds moving in? Rain. Just what they needed.

The burn in his calves changed to his thighs as the path sloped downward once again. Through the trees, he caught a glimpse of the swaying rope bridge spanning the small creek winding its way through the mountains. They'd already crossed several such bridges as they followed the path headed toward the Trace.

Alex remained silent as he hiked down the last stretch of path down to the bridge. The river gurgled over boulders. Somewhere in the new, spring leaves of the trees, a lone bird twittered. The branches clattered against each other.

But this was still silent compared to the hustle of Castle Eyota. There, Alex was always in some sort of meeting with his father or talking with the young nobles or bantering with the captains on the training ground.

But now he'd just spent five days in near silence. It wasn't like he made small talk with the peasants he'd been forced to share a bench with on the trip from Eyota.

Now there was just Jadon. His manservant. Alex didn't exactly converse with Jadon at Castle Eyota. He gave Jadon orders, Jadon quietly and efficiently followed them, and that was that.

But they had a long way to hike. It would be unbearable to go the whole distance with nothing but the birds' chatter to listen to.

Alex set out across the wooden bridge. The ropes stretched under his weight while the bridge swayed in time with his footsteps. To the right with his right foot, to the left with his left foot. He strolled forward, rolling his body in time with the sway.

Alex waited until both he and Jadon were on firm ground. How did a prince go about starting a conversation with his manservant? He normally didn't have to worry about starting conversations. Usually the men and women of the court just found him, asked him a question or two, and let him talk.

"Do you have any family?" That was a safe topic, wasn't it? Jadon's family was somewhere deep in the mountains. Alex couldn't remember what kingdom.

Jadon halted. "Sir?"

Alex sighed and halted as well. The least Jadon could've done was keep walking and not delay them. "I'm trying to make conversation. It's what people do when they are on a long hike. Now answer the question."

Jadon adjusted the strap of the large pack resting against his back. His shoulders hunched forward, as if the pack weighed him down. "Yes. My parents, three brothers, and two sisters. They live in Buckhannock. I haven't seen them in years."

"I see." Alex gave a sharp nod. Of course, Jadon hadn't visited his family in years. It wasn't like manservants could just skive off whenever they wanted, and Jadon's parents were probably of the poor, rural variety who couldn't afford to step away from their farm long enough to see their son at the castle.

Spinning on his heel, Alex set out on the trail again, forcing down a twinge of something. Not guilt. He had nothing to feel guilty for. It was a great honor for Jadon to have been chosen out of all the other boys born the same day as Alex to serve him at the castle.

Besides, Jadon's life now was much better than it would have been had he been left to grow up as a peasant's son.

"If we pass close to your parents on our way to Castle Firlin, maybe we can take a few minutes to stop." Alex didn't look over his shoulder. He shouldn't have made the offer, really. They didn't have a lot of time. But perhaps that vague something in his chest would rest somewhat appeased.

"Thank you, sir." Jadon's low tone didn't hold the excitement it should've for Alex's gracious consideration. It sounded more like Jadon didn't believe Alex would carry through with the suggestion.

Alex kept marching forward along the dirt path meandering up the side of the next mountain. Jadon should've been grateful Alex would deign to make such an offer. Or even converse with him.

Perhaps it was better to hike in silence.

Around them, the mountains rose in green-covered peaks, the trees broken only by the occasional rock outcropping and the slice of the creeks and rivers running through the bottoms of the valleys. The stone gray sky overhead hung low, threatening to turn into yet another round of drizzle that rarely let up this time of year.

The forest grumbled a low hum formed of creaking trees, the distant rush of the river, the faintest breeze stirring the leaves at the tops of the mountain peaks.

A path split off to their right. Peering down it, Alex spotted three log cabins in a small clearing. Turkeys pecked at the dirt yard while bear, elk, and buffalo hides stretched across drying frames. A terrace cut into the side of the mountain behind the cabins held a vegetable patch. Somewhere in the distance, children squealed, and a dog barked.

Alex shook his head and kept walking. These mountains were littered with squat little cabins like those. Besides the few villages scattered in the valleys, most of the population of Tallahatchia lived in small clusters of cabins.

Jadon's family probably lived in a cabin like that somewhere in Buckhannock.

It was Alex's duty to protect the small, simple people in these mountains from the difficulties and squabbles of the bigger world. As the high prince, he must keep all seven of the kingdoms in line. A war between Tuckawassee and Kanawhee would ruin everyone from him and his father down to the lowliest peasant of mountain stock.

Alex had to end this curse. That was all there was to it.

They hiked the rest of the day in near silence. Jadon occasionally pulled out their chart to make sure they were headed in the right direction when trails forked from the Trace, but Alex didn't need to check the map. He had it memorized. That was the benefit of superior intelligence.

As night fell, they came across a section where the trail split off into another cluster of log cabins and rudimentary farms.

Alex eyed the log cabins. If he were traveling as himself with an entourage, he would've been able to march up to those cabins and demand they give him a place to stay for the night. They would trip over themselves at the honor of hosting their high prince.

But he had to keep his presence here a secret. If they stayed with one of those peasants, he would have to pretend he was nothing more than another peasant farmer.

Jadon adjusted the straps of the pack. "Perhaps we should stay in the forest tonight. It would be easier for you to remain unnoticed."

Alex grimaced and glanced at the sky. "It looks like it is going to drizzle again. I would prefer a roof over my head. I believe it would be best to ask for the hospitality I've heard these peasants are known for."

Jadon cleared his throat. "If you wish, sir. But it might

be best if I did the talking. Begging your pardon, but your accent sounds like the castle, or at the very least, a valley dweller. You don't sound mountain."

Alex opened his mouth to refute Jadon's insult, but his intelligence caught up with him before he said anything. Jadon wouldn't dare say something like that unless he had a valid point. Alex had grown up at Castle Eyota. The only time he'd traveled the Trace and the river system before, he'd been with soldiers who were the younger sons of the nobles who also spoke with the same accent as him.

But Jadon had spent his first ten years with his mountain family until he'd come to the castle. It had taken several years before Jadon's dialect had smoothed out, and even then, Jadon had the unfortunate tendency to drop back into it on occasion.

"Very well. I will follow your lead in this one." Alex spun and stepped onto the small path leading to the log cabins.

"Um, sir." Jadon didn't move. "It would appear odd if only one of us is carrying a pack."

Alex suppressed a sigh. Jadon had a point. If they were traveling as two peasants, they would both have packs. "Fine. What can you shift over to me?"

Jadon slid the pack from his shoulders, and it thumped on the ground louder than Alex would've expected. After a few minutes of pulling stuff out and undoing knots, Jadon produced a second pack, filled it with a few items, and handed it over.

Alex grabbed it, nearly dropping it at the weight. What had Jadon put in here? A few rocks?

If his feet and calves weren't so sore from a day of hiking up and down the mountain sides, Alex would've taken the time to put Jadon back in his place. But now wasn't the time, not if he wanted a hot meal and a soft bed for tonight.

Jadon swung what remained of his pack onto his back and trudged past Alex. He didn't say it out loud, but his stiff posture and purposeful stride was as good as an order to follow him.

Alex gritted his teeth. He had to put up with Jadon giving him orders tonight. Just for tonight.

As they neared the cabins, several dogs barked and bounded forward. They bared their teeth as they growled, the ruffs around their necks and the fur down their back standing on end.

Jadon halted and cupped his hands around his mouth. "Hullo, the cabins."

Alex froze where he was. Those dogs didn't look like the friendliest of creatures.

A door opened, and a man and boy stepped out. The boy held a lantern and a pitchfork while the man had a bow with an arrow already drawn. "State your business, strangers."

His mountain dialect was so thick Alex could barely understand him.

Jadon held up his empty hands. When he spoke, the mountain dialect was back in his voice, though not as thick as the man's. "We ain't looking for trouble, friend. Just passing through to Buckhannock. Would appreciate a spot to set for the night."

The man's gaze gave them a thorough once-over before he nodded as if satisfied. He relaxed his stance and slid the arrow back into his quiver. Then he snapped his fingers, and both dogs ceased growling and sat. He waved to the shed behind the log cabin. "You can stay in the barn. Come inside and the missus'll scrape a lick of stew for you."

The man leaned down and said something to the boy, sending him scurrying off to the shack these peasants so grandly labeled a barn.

Alex trailed behind them as the man led them past the dogs and opened the door to the cabin. Jadon stepped inside without hesitation, and Alex forced himself to follow.

The log cabin smelled faintly of smoke and tanned hides. The tiny main room barely had enough room for the table and the hearth. As they entered, a woman exited one of the two doors at the back of the cabin and froze when she spotted them.

The man stepped inside and shut the door. "Can you scare up some stew for these strangers? They're passing through."

"There ain't much left." The woman grabbed a stew pot and hung it over the coals.

"We'll be fine. Thank you, ma'am." Jadon set his pack by the door and sank onto one of the benches by the table.

Alex followed his example. Not that there was anything else he could do. There was barely standing room in there.

The door at the far side of the room cracked open and a face peered through the crack, followed by three more a moment later.

Counting the boy still outside, that made five children. In this tiny place? Alex did his best not to stare. He'd never stepped foot in a peasants' cabin before. It was dark and far too warm. The one window was covered with a heavy shutter on the outside and a thin wax paper on the inside instead of the glass panes of Castle Eyota.

The man laid his now unstrung bow across pegs above the door while the quiver hung next to it. He took a seat on the bench across from them. "So you're headed to Buckhannock? From 'round there?"

"I am. Been trading by Eyota for the past few years." Jadon rested his elbows on the table as if completely relaxed.

Alex kept his back straight, his hands at his sides. If he said so much as a word, these people would know he was high born.

"Reckon they're a mite in a tizzy down there with the prince's curse coming up and the Tuckawassee getting riled."

Alex tried to keep his expression neutral. He wasn't sure he wanted to hear this peasant's opinion of politics at Castle Eyota.

Jadon shot him a glance before turning back to the peasant. "I reckon High King Atohi will have it handled."

The man snorted. "The prince can't avoid it, and the high king and queen ain't gonna let him sleep for a hundred years alone."

Alex bit his tongue and fought the weight in his stomach. This ignorant man didn't know anything. Just because he said the curse couldn't be avoided didn't mean anything. Alex was the one with the gift of superior intelligence.

The peasant man rested his elbows on the table. "Don't matter to me what the high king and queen do. Us mountain folk survive. Let the kings fight it out themselves, I say."

Jadon glanced at Alex again but kept his mouth shut.

Alex clenched his fists below the table. Why didn't Jadon come up with some reply?

The peasant woman approached the table and set wooden bowls in front of Jadon and Alex.

Alex frowned down at the stew. It looked thick and

rich, that wasn't the problem. But it only filled an inch or so at the bottom of the bowl. Barely enough of get him started, much less satisfy his hunger.

Jadon elbowed him and picked up the spoon the woman set on the table. After dipping his spoon into his stew, he blew on it and took a bite. "Powerful good stew, ma'am."

She gave them a tight smile. "Sorry there ain't more."

"You had your family to feed first." Jadon's smile was soft, disarming. Different than the stiff expression he wore around the castle.

Alex blew on his spoon of stew and took a bite. It was tolerable. The meat a little tough, the broth watered down. But now wasn't the time to voice his opinion, and at least the stew was warm.

It only took a few bites to scrape the last of the stew from his bowl. His stomach wasn't near full, but they could always dig into their packs for the dried meat once they were in the barn.

As the woman collected their bowls, the bar across the door lifted with a pull string and the boy stepped inside. "Barn's set, Pa."

"Good." The man motioned to Jadon and Alex. "You can sleep in the loft."

He showed them into the barn and left them a lamp once Jadon assured him he would make sure it was properly blown out before they slept.

Alex tried to make himself comfortable on the pile of itchy, poky straw covered with blankets that smelled faintly musty. A far cry from his down-filled mattress at the castle.

He closed his eyes and tried to get comfortable between the poking hay and aching muscles. He probably wasn't going to sleep, but he might as well try.

A HAND SHOOK HIS SHOULDER. Alex groaned and forced his eyes open. He had to blink several times to make Jadon out in the gloom. "What time is it? It can't be morning."

"It's early. Time to get going." Jadon swung the pack onto his back. "We've imposed on these good people long enough. If we stay long enough for breakfast, we'll be taking food out of the children's mouths."

He eyed Alex as if expecting him to protest. Alex groaned and tugged on his boots. How could he protest when Jadon put it that way? Even if the thought of eggs and sausage sizzling over the fire in that cabin set Alex's mouth to watering.

"Fine. Let's get moving." Alex forced himself to his feet and headed for the ladder out of the loft. They had a lot of miles to walk today. Might as well get to it.

Chapter 9

Rosanna

The roar of the Kikataw Falls rang in her ears as Rosanna bolted through her breakfast the next morning and set to work packing their camp. Instead of lashing their gear into the canoes, they divided it into packs for the portage up and around the falls.

Rosanna crouched and reached for the sides of the canoe. "I can carry the canoe."

Daemyn glanced from her to the canoe. "It weighs nearly fifty pounds."

"Our supplies probably weigh as much or more, and it would be better if you were less encumbered. I carried my own canoe during the portages back home." Rosanna tightened her hold on the canoe.

"All right, but we can switch if we have to." Daemyn set aside the packs and reached for one end of the canoe.

With his help, Rosanna turned the canoe upside down and settled the carrying yoke with its layer of rabbit fur padding onto her shoulders.

Gathering her legs beneath her, she drew a deep breath

and forced her legs upright, her muscles straining with the effort. Once she was upright, she settled the canoe's weight more comfortably on her shoulders. The rear of the canoe leaned behind her while the front tipped into the air. She would have to be careful she didn't snag it on any low-hanging branches, but she could see where she was going.

After a brief word with Captain Degotaga too low for Rosanna to hear, Daemyn disappeared along the faint trail winding its way up the riverbank.

Captain Degotaga called orders and arranged the guards. Each of the guards carrying a pack fell into line in front of their canoe bearer to hold low hanging branches out of the way as well as give protection at each place in line. Rosanna was arranged near the middle behind Captain Degotaga and Isi, who would have to hold the branches aside for both her father and Rosanna since Daemyn was ahead scouting.

As they set off, Rosanna leaned into the hike up the side of the mountain. Her calves burned while her shoulders already ached with the weight of the canoe sitting across the muscles there. She steadied the canoe with one hand, then the other to distribute the pain back and forth between her arms.

The trail wound upward along the ridge facing the river, just a sliver of worn dirt among the leaves, rocks, and underbrush. The roar of the waterfall followed them as they climbed first alongside, then above the roaring torrent.

After about twenty minutes of walking, Captain Degotaga signaled a halt. The pack carriers set the packs on the ground, carefully spacing them out so that the canoe bearers could set the canoes down bottom side up resting on the packs.

After Isi helped her set her canoe on the packs,

Rosanna took out her canteen and drank several large gulps, the muscles in her shoulders cramping.

Once most of her thirst was satisfied, she dribbled some of the water over her canoe to keep the birch bark moist. It wasn't too warm this time in the spring, but the day was sunny and the new spring leaves didn't completely block the sunlight. Rosanna wouldn't risk the bark drying out and cracking. Better to sacrifice a little water.

She sat cross-legged on the ground and opened a pouch filled with crumbles of dried meat, berries, and nuts. Her stomach rumbled, and she dug into the food. She had to keep up her strength to carry the canoe for the next leg of the portage.

As she stuffed another pinch into her mouth, Daemyn hurried from the underbrush hiding the bend of the path ahead. He strode into the center of their resting men and canoes, gripping his staff. "A band of ten Tuckawassee are heading this way. We have to get off the path quickly."

Captain Degotaga pointed at a tumble of rocks down the slope from them. "Behind there. Now."

Rosanna jumped to her feet, closed the pouch of food, and stuffed it into her pack. By the time she crouched to lift the canoe to her shoulders, Daemyn was there to help heft it to her shoulders. She straightened, and Daemyn gathered one of the packs that had held up her canoe. Garmund grabbed the other.

Gripping the canoe with both hands, Rosanna picked her way down the slope. The loam slipped beneath her moccasins, and she had to turn sideways, both to better slide downward and keep the end of the canoe from hitting the ground.

Daemyn and Isi got to the rocks ahead of her, tossed

down the packs, and took the canoe from her before she'd even fully rounded the first boulder.

Heart pounding, Rosanna turned to Otho arriving with a canoe and helped him set it down across more packs and a tree branch.

Daemyn raced up the hill and followed the stragglers, brushing at the furrows left by their sliding feet down the slope, straightening brush, kicking loam back into place, to disguise the all-too-clear marks of their passing.

Even with his efforts, Rosanna could still see the faint hints of the darker ground beneath peeking through and the way some of the undergrowth refused to stand fully upright again. Hopefully the Tuckawassee would be moving too fast to pay attention to the signs of disturbed ground or would mistake it for deer making their way down to the river.

"Everyone down. Don't move." Daemyn flattened himself to the ground a few feet away from Rosanna near the base of one of the boulders. Rosanna lay on her stomach as everyone else did the same.

From where she lay, she could just glimpse a section of the path above between two of the boulders and the trees. She stilled, breathing as lightly as possible.

The minutes stretched until Rosanna couldn't tell how much time had passed. Feet tramped against the trail above. Beside Rosanna, Daemyn was so still he might as well have been a tree or a stone, a part of the mountain itself.

Rosanna peered at the trail above. The tramping grew louder. Movement flickered, and a man marched past, carrying a laden pack. Two men followed carrying more packs. Spears, bows and arrows, knives, and axes flashed.

Another Tuckawassee raiding party, marching deeper into Neskahana, not back to Tuckawassee. Were they on the way to reinforce Major Beshko and her men? Or merely under orders to cause more chaos, destruction, and pain?

Rosanna lost count of the number of men and canoes that marched by overhead. Under their trampling feet, any traces of her group's passing were worn away everywhere except for their descent to their hiding place.

On the path above, one of the men carrying a pack hesitated and stared down the slope in their direction.

Had one of them moved? Had he spotted their canoes or the flash of their black hair against the shadows by the boulders? Or perhaps he'd noticed the hints of their flight down the slope that Daemyn hadn't been able to hide.

The man slapped the arm of another and pointed down the slope.

Rosanna bit her lip to stop herself from making a sound. They had to stay still. There were too many Tuckawassee for them to fight, and they couldn't outrun them forever, even if they left their canoes.

The other Tuckawassee shrugged, and the two of them kept walking.

Rosanna didn't take in a deep breath until the last Tuckawassee passed and the crunch of footsteps disappeared into the distance.

After a full fifteen minutes had passed, Daemyn eased to his feet. "Let's get moving. Quick as we can."

Rosanna stood and brushed herself off. The sooner they could put distance between them and the Tuckawassee, the better.

Within a few minutes, she had the canoe balanced on her shoulders once again. She climbed the ridge behind Daemyn and Captain Degotaga. Her calves and back burned with the strain, but she forced herself to continue trudging up the slope, then along the trail.

As they crested the ridge, Daemyn stiffened and knelt by something lying across the path.

Captain Degotaga spun and put a hand on her arm. "You should stay back, Princess."

If he thought to protect her from the sight before them, he was already too late.

A man lay in the dirt, an arrow sticking from his back. His shirt and the ground around him were covered in a dark, red substance already beginning to dry brown and flaky at the edges. He was so unnaturally still that something cold swept through Rosanna's chest.

She'd never seen a dead body before, but she didn't have to be told the man was dead. There was something so empty about that body lying in the dirt and blood, as if her soul could sense that his had long crossed the WaterVeil into beyond.

Beyond the man lay another body. A woman, looking barely older than Rosanna. Also still. Also dead.

Behind the body, smoke poured from the doorway of a cabin, its door askew, windows shattered.

Down the slope far below a stockade surrounded a cluster of buildings, some gushing smoke much as the cabin before her. Some of the figures moved and shouted, but others remained still.

Dead.

Rosanna eased the canoe from her shoulders and set it on a patch of pine needles. She pushed past Captain Degotaga to stand next to the bodies laid out in the dirt. A man and his wife, killed because they couldn't reach the stockade or their home fast enough when the raiding Tuckawassee came.

"Princess?"

She wasn't sure who had spoken, if it was Captain

Degotaga or Daemyn. She shook her head as she knelt by the bodies.

Something moved below the shelter of the dead woman's arms. Rosanna eased a warm bundle free. The baby blinked up at her, wide-eyed, as if too confused and terrified to cry.

This quest was real. It wasn't a lark. It wasn't a grand adventure.

It was life and death in a way she hadn't understood before. She couldn't have understood it until the look of death carved into a man's face.

If the Tuckawassee had their way, that would be her. Dead before she could reach Kanawhee and wake the high prince.

But if she didn't succeed and stop this war? How many others would die? Not just here, but also in Tuckawassee if her father or one of his barons sent a raiding party in retaliation? Or Buckhannock and Monongadotte, under attack by Pohatomie? Or Pohatomie with the retaliation raids by Monongadotte?

That was the tragedy of the war. They were all Tallahatchia. There was no pain like that of a nation at war with itself. Even if she woke the high prince, it wouldn't erase this pain.

But at least it would prevent more.

CHAPTER 10

ALEXANDER

ONE HUNDRED YEARS AGO

The past week of travel had been the most miserable of Alex's life. He'd even had to sleep on the ground in a primitive camp several times. Like a commoner. Who would have guessed the Cheyandoah Trace was so backwoods and uncivilized?

Rain dripped down his hair. He was soaked. His spare clothes were soaked. His feet squished inside his moccasins. If this rain didn't let up, he might be tempted to wear one of those raccoon hats like the peasant folk to keep his head dry.

Alex set out across yet another bridge across a decent-sized stream. Jadon followed with the packs. Silent, as they had been for most of the past week. They had run out of things to talk about in that short conversation the first day of hiking. What else was there to talk about? The weather? It was raining. Nothing to talk about there. And it wasn't like he was going to discuss complicated political matters with his manservant.

Only another week of hiking until they reached Castle

Firlin. Just nine more days and the little inconvenience of his curse could be disposed of. He would be able to move on with his life like a normal prince without a care to trouble him besides the minor annoyance of lesser kings who wanted more than their due.

The bridge gave a strange lurch under his feet, off-rhythm from the normal sway. A groan shuddered from the ropes.

Alex froze. The bridge stilled as Jadon halted as well. The ropes must have a worn spot that had frayed nearly to the breaking point. Alex gritted his teeth. He would have to have the inspectors for this section of bridges fired and replaced if they had missed a stress point so blatant.

"In front of us or behind?" Alex half-turned to glance over his shoulder at Jadon.

Jadon hunched as he gripped the rope handrails. "In front, I think. We'll have to go back."

They had to get off this bridge. The creek below them wasn't deep, its bed filled with rocks and boulders. They were about thirty-five feet up. Too far for them to survive the fall. If they did, it would only be to spend their last few hours of life in pain-filled, broken bodies. And right now, they had about forty feet of bridge between them and the safety of the mountainsides. If the bridge snapped, they would smack into the rocks below before they ran out of rope.

"Only one of us should move at a time. We don't want to put any more stress on the bridge than we have to." Alex slowly pivoted on the bridge. He had to get back to the side beyond Jadon.

Jadon swallowed, his grip white-knuckled on the ropes. "You go. I'll stay here."

It was only right, Jadon staying behind while Alex went first. Alex was the important one. He was the prince.

Logically, Jadon should move first. He was closer to the safe side of the bridge. Carrying the packs as he was, he weighed more than Alex and put more stress on the ropes.

But Alex wasn't going to argue. Jadon was about ten feet behind him. He stood a better chance of surviving if the bridge snapped.

Alex inched forward. The ropes gave a small groan, but nothing like the shriek before. He eased forward a few more feet.

He reached Jadon. He should pass and keep going. Jadon was just a manservant. Disposable.

Why was he hesitating?

"Go. Don't worry about me, Your Highness. Go." When he met Alex's gaze, Jadon's eyes were strangely dull. As if he already stared at the WaterVeil.

Alex flexed his grip on the handrail ropes. He shouldn't care.

But Jadon had been Alex's manservant since they both were ten. Those years of service deserved some sort of consideration.

Jadon leaned against one of the handrails to give enough room for Alex to pass. Alex shuffled next to him.

The ropes twanged and the boards below their feet dropped.

Alex fell. His own weight ripped his hands free from the rope made slick from the rain. His chest seized so tightly he couldn't cry out. He couldn't breathe. Not with his hands and feet flailing but finding nothing but air.

Something snagged the back of his shirt.

Jadon groaned and heaved Alex upward. "Grab the rope."

Alex latched onto the remaining footbridge rope and clung to it.

Jadon let go and adjusted his own grip on one of the handrail ropes. He had braced his feet on the footbridge rope. But with the continued drizzle making the ropes slick and the weight of the packs, Jadon didn't seem to be in much better shape than Alex.

The dangling boards dug into Alex's underarms as he tried to pull his lower body over the rope. He gritted his teeth and tried to twist his body up and around, but he didn't have the upper body strength.

He couldn't stay like this. He wouldn't be able to pull himself along the rope or upright like Jadon.

Jadon reached down, gripped the back of Alex's shirt, and tried to pull him up higher. Alex curled his body, trying to get a leg over the rope. But he couldn't. Already his arms shook with the weight of his body. He didn't have the strength.

The rope Alex gripped made a snapping sound. It sagged a few more inches but didn't break. Yet.

What could he do? He was supposed to be the intelligent one. He should be able to think of a way out of this predicament. Surely there had to be something.

He needed time to think. Something he couldn't do while he clung to the rope with a sickening drop beneath him and his heart pounding in his ears.

He couldn't think. But he had to.

Jadon let go of Alex's shirt. Was he going to leave Alex here and scramble to safety on his own?

Gripping the handrail with one arm, Jadon loosened the straps holding the pack to his back and let it drop into the gorge below. It thudded on the rocks, some of the packs bursting open and spilling onto the rain-drenched stone, a reminder of what would happen if either of them fell.

Jadon bent down again, and when he yanked on the back of Alex's shirt, Alex was able to hook a toe into the footbridge rope. He waited only a moment to catch his breath before he began pulling himself along as best he could, maneuvering around the dangling boards. "We have to keep moving."

They had to reach the bank before the second footbridge rope gave, or at the very least, they had to get close enough so that the impact into the tree and dirt covered side of the gorge wouldn't kill them.

Alex tried to pull himself on top of the ropes and boards, but they twisted. Best not to keep trying that and putting more stress on the weakened rope. He hung underneath. The footboards smacked him in the face and chest as he moved.

Jadon shuffled behind him, feet on the footbridge rope and both hands on one of the handrail ropes. The ropes kept trying to swing in opposite directions, but Jadon somehow maintained his balance.

The end of the bridge crept closer. Alex hardly dared to breathe as if the added weight of air in his lungs could be the feather that broke the last strand of the footbridge rope that carried the bulk of his and Jadon's weights.

Five yards to go. Four. Three.

The ropes gave another moan.

It was too much stress on the ropes. They weren't going to hold.

Another shuffle. A snapping sound, and Alex fell again, his hands and feet still gripping the ropes now no longer attached at the far side of the bridge.

But this time, Jadon fell with him. In the split second as

they dropped, Jadon must've let go of the handrail and latched on to what was left of the footbridge with Alex.

This time, Alex did cry out. He was pretty sure Jadon did too, but he couldn't be sure over his own shout and the rushing wind as they swung toward the side of the gorge.

At the last moment, Jadon twisted. Alex smashed into him as Jadon took the brunt of the impact against the gorge with his back. His mouth flew open, and Alex felt him sliding as his grip loosened on the ropes. Alex wedged an arm around Jadon until he managed to reclaim his grip on the ropes.

Jadon closed his eyes and sucked in a large gulp of air. "Are you all right, Your Highness?"

"I'm fine." Alex glanced upward, then down below them. The ends of the two snapped footbridge ropes trailed in the creek and sprawled across the tumbled boulders surrounding the banks. If they climbed down, they would be able to retrieve their pack before they crossed the creek and attempted to climb out the other side. "We're climbing down."

Now that the fallen bridge rested against the side of the gorge, the boards tied between the two ropes formed something of a ladder.

Alex picked his way down one hand or foot at a time. He had to wiggle his toes between boards to make enough of a gap for his feet to fit.

Jadon followed, giving him enough room to make sure the boards wouldn't slide down and pinch Alex's fingers.

Alex hopped off the makeshift ladder and stepped from one boulder to the next, placing his feet carefully to avoid slipping and falling on the wet rocks. He knelt next to their scattered packs. Their pots and camping supplies had spilled, but their food seemed to be still all right. It wouldn't be too difficult for Jadon to repack.

A small, stifled groan came from Jadon's direction. Alex turned as Jadon eased to the ground and hobbled toward the creek, a hand pressed against his ribs.

Had Jadon been hurt? He had taken the worst of the impact against the side of the gorge.

Jadon shuffled another few steps closer, grimacing.

Alex sighed and returned to Jadon's side. "How bad are you hurt?"

"I don't think anything's broken, but I have a few bad bruises." Jadon straightened and shoved past Alex. "I'll fetch the pack."

His mouth tightened as he knelt and gathered their camping supplies.

Jadon was hurting, even Alex could see it. As much as he wanted to, he couldn't expect Jadon to carry the pack, cross the river, and still be in some sort of shape to make it up the other side. As distasteful as it was, Alex would have to carry at least some of their supplies.

Alex knelt next to Jadon. "What can you split into a second pack? I'll carry some of it."

"Are you sure, Highness?" Jadon didn't look up as he wedged a pot back into the pack.

No, Alex wasn't. But Jadon had taken the brunt of that fall. Had he done it on purpose to spare Alex? He'd let Alex pass. He'd stayed clinging to the ropes when he could have left Alex behind. Alex owed Jadon something for all that trouble.

"Yes, I'm sure. You're hurt. It's only logical I take some of the load." Alex straightened. "While you divide the packs, I'll see what I can salvage from the bridge. We might be able to use some of it to help us get up the far side of the gorge."

Alex pulled the end of the bridge out of the creek. The boards and rope dripped with both rain and creek water. When he found the ends, he frowned. While half of the fibers were frayed as if they had snapped, the other half were neatly sliced through.

Why would someone cut this bridge? No one knew Alex was here. Even if they did, they couldn't know Alex would be the next person to cross this bridge or that it would snap when he was on it.

No, this seemed to be more of a random act of sabotage.

But even random sabotage was an act against Alex in a roundabout way. This was one of the bridges along the Trace, the official route of the high king's message runners. To destroy this bridge on purpose was to strike against the rule of the high king.

He had to break this curse before it happened. There was no telling what sort of chaos would be unleashed on Tallahatchia if he didn't.

CHAPTER 11

ROSANNA

It was said that only those who faced death knew the true horror of the curse.

As they placed their canoes in the water the next morning and shoved off, Rosanna glanced over her shoulder at the small crowd of the survivors of the settlement of Kikataw. In the front, an older woman hugged the orphaned baby to her chest.

Off to one side, the rotted stumps of what had once been docks jutted from the water. A hundred years ago, Kikataw had been a major stopping point along the river where goods had to be portaged around the waterfall.

She blinked and forced herself to face forward. "Do you ever get used to it? Seeing pain and death like this?"

"No. Perhaps a person becomes harder. Less sensitive of the sights and smells of death. But not immune to them. If anything, the more I see, the more I recognize the horror of it all." The sunlight glinted on the scar along his neck, a reminder that he had watched his father die.

It had been easy to say she had been sensitive to the plight of those hurt by the Tuckawassee. She'd claimed to be horrified at the reports of those killed. But it was another thing to witness it for herself.

Rosanna dug her paddle into the river. The surge of her muscles, the rush of the water beneath the canoe, helped calm the churn in her stomach. "Do you think waking the high prince will solve the problems we're having with the Tuckawassee? What can he do that we can't?"

The king of Tuckawassee and his warriors terrorized five of the other kingdoms of Tallahatchia, but Tuckawassee and Pohatomie were still part of the seven. To war against them was to war against themselves.

But this couldn't continue. The Tuckawassee and Pohatomie kings had to be stopped.

Daemyn pulled back on his paddle, the muscles taut along his forearms. "Until we have a high king again, the kingdoms can't unite under one leader."

The silence lengthened, broken only by the swishing of their canoe through the river and the splash of their paddles.

What must this river have been like a hundred years ago when trade between the kingdoms flowed uninterrupted? The river would have teemed with canoes and riverboats carrying metal objects from Buckhannock, gems from Tuckawassee, fabric from Guyangahela, corn from Pohatomie, and taking the glass and baskets and clay dishes from Neskahana to all the other kingdoms.

Was that Tallahatchia gone forever? Or could it be restored by the high prince?

Daemyn's voice broke into her musing. "Pirates plague

the stretch of river up ahead. We'll have to try to slip past them in the night. The gorge is too narrow to try to sneak through the forest, especially not while carrying our canoes."

River pirates? Rosanna drew in a deep breath as the daydreams about the Tallahatchia that once was faded.

This was her reality. Rotted docks. Abandoned outposts. Rivers overrun with pirates her father couldn't control without pulling warriors away from their stations on the border with Tuckawassee.

Yet another thing the high prince would have to solve when he woke.

Hopefully he was the prince Tallahatchia needed him to be.

The sky remained a dark, heavy blue glittering with stars in some places, flat and lifeless in others where clouds drifted. A slice of moon rose above the far distant mountains.

Rosanna dug in her paddle, feeling the momentum as Daemyn timed his stroke with hers. The banks rose black on either side of them, the outermost leaves catching hints of moonlight. Only the flash of silver on the crests of ripples distinguished the river from mountain and sky. Ahead, her four guards in their two canoes were nothing but black shapes.

How long did they have until they passed the river pirates' hideout? She didn't dare talk. Voices carried too far over the water, especially at night.

She drew in a shuddering breath, and only then realized her pulse pounded in her throat and buzzed in her head. The paddle shook in her hands, and water splashed. Too loud. Much too loud.

She gulped in several deep breaths. She mustn't panic.

Wiggling her toes, she felt for the palm-sized rocks she'd piled in the bottom of the canoe within easy reach. If they went into battle, she would at least have something on hand to throw.

Their canoe rounded a bend in the river. Ahead, cliffs rose black against the dark sky to one side of the river.

She eyed the cliffs. Was that where the river pirates holed up? Why wasn't Daemyn steering their canoe to hug the far bank? Perhaps the river pirates stowed canoes on that bank too, ready to shove off and claim the prize once the paddlers were shot and killed with the arrows from the cliffs.

Nikan and Garmund dropped back so that their canoe fell into place on her left while Isi and Captain Degotaga took station on her right. Chogan and Ilma held point only ten feet in front while Otho and Ahanu remained in rearguard only a few yards behind. If they were attacked, they needed to be in a tight formation, not strung out.

Breathing as lightly as possible, Rosanna eased her paddle into the water. She couldn't bobble her paddle now. Or bump the sides. They couldn't do anything to alert the river pirates.

The river's speed changed as the river narrowed between the cliffs and the far bank. Rosanna struggled to keep her paddle strokes silent while fighting the strong current running against them. She searched what she could see of the water ahead. If there were rocks ahead, none of them would see them before it was too late.

Daemyn kept them in the center of the river.

Hopefully that meant he knew this stretch of river as well as he claimed and wouldn't steer them into any boulders.

The dark cliffs drifted by, hulking and silent. Were they going to make it without alerting the river pirates? Her heart throbbed in her throat.

Something bumped and scraped against the underside of Chogan and Ilma's canoe. Rocks rattled and fell somewhere at the base of the cliffs.

Daemyn muttered something under his breath and dug his paddle in harder. As Rosanna drew on her paddle, it snagged on something in the river. Something snaked across the river in both directions, black against the deep gray water.

A rope. That's what it had to be. Strung across the river to alert the pirates if anyone tried to cross in the night. It scraped along the bottom of their canoe, sending shudders into her toes and knees.

Light flared along both banks, first in small pinpricks, then large bonfires flaring bright enough to cast light and shadows all the way across the river.

She threw her shoulders and body into the strokes. Even and fast. She could see the dark water below and the color of her buckskin leggings in the light of the bonfires on both shores.

Something zipped through the air and splashed into the water near her. She caught the fuzz of goose feather fletching before the current carried the arrow away.

More arrows splashed into the water around them. Something thudded into their canoe.

"Into the water." No sooner had Daemyn given the order before he tipped their canoe over.

Rosanna grabbed a breath as she smacked shoulder first into the water, icy with the spring runoff from the mountains. She pulled her legs free from the canoe to avoid damaging it and did her best to stow her paddle in the tilted canoe while treading water.

An arrow cut through the birch bark above her head.

She drew in a breath, gripped the side of the canoe, and ducked as low as she could in the water. She shoved with her legs and swam with her free arm. At the stern, Daemyn kicked hard as well.

She risked a glance over her shoulder. All their canoes were tipped sideways. Isi paddled gamely in the water, her mouth pinched in a tight line as if angry at the river pirates for causing her to get wet. The guardsmen hunkered in the water as they shoved their canoes forward.

They would all tire quickly in the frigid water swimming against the current.

The river pirates shoved canoes into the water. Rosanna kicked harder. Would they be able to outswim the river pirates? They wouldn't be able to fight them off, not while being in the water while the pirates had the advantage of canoes.

"Can you tow the canoe by yourself?"

"Yes." The word came so automatically she didn't think about the consequences until his steady pressure vanished. She grunted as the full weight of the canoe with their supplies still strapped inside tugged at her arm. No, she couldn't tow it by herself, not and still make headway against the current.

The river pirates gained on them swiftly. They had long, sleek war canoes with eight to ten men packed into each one. She counted four canoes rushing toward them, two from the rear, one from the front and one directly at them from the bank. Arrows still rained from the cliffs above, smacking into the water and their canoes. If they survived this mess, they'd have to take the time to repair the damaged canoes before they could continue.

The first of the war canoes reached Ahanu and Otho. Her guards struck upward but couldn't do much against the river pirates stabbing down with spears and long knives. Someone cried out. One of her guards? Which one? In the darkness, she couldn't tell how badly he was injured. If not killed.

Rosanna fought to pull the canoe farther forward. Her arms shook—with cold, with the exertion, she couldn't be sure. Her legs burned as she kicked.

River pirates attacked Chogan and Ilma only a few feet away. Rosanna halted, treading water. She was trapped in the circle of her guards and the surrounding river pirates.

Isi appeared at her side, a knife in her hand. Captain Degotaga's canoe drifted with the current back the way they'd come.

With a whoosh, Captain Degotaga burst from the water, gripped the side of one of the war canoes filled with river pirates, and yanked it downward, sending all eight of the pirates splashing into the river. The water roiled with fighting bodies and flashing long knives.

She glanced behind her. Nikan, Otho, Ahanu, and Garmund struggled to hold off two war canoes. Several of the river pirates stood in their canoes, spears raised to better deliver killing blows.

A dark shape exploded from the water next to the war canoe like a monster rising from the depths of the river, gripped its side, and submerged swiftly. Their canoe pitched over, flinging the pirates into the river with barely a time for a shout.

Ahead, a river pirate raised a spear to bring it down

onto Ilma as she tried to get close enough to unbalance the canoe.

Rosanna grasped one of the rocks in her canoe, struggled against the current, and threw. The rock struck the river pirate in the leg, causing him to cry out and nearly drop his spear. His unintended motion wobbled the canoe, nearly tipping it over.

Out of the corner of her eye, she saw the eight river pirates in the water close on Captain Degotaga. She tapped Isi's shoulder. "I have plenty of rocks left. I'll be fine. Go help your father."

Even as Isi nodded and dove back underwater, Rosanna grasped another rock and threw it hard at another pirate attacking Chogan and Ilma. Not a good throw. Her fingers were too wet and throwing while half-submerged too awkward.

As the stone plunked harmlessly into the water, she picked up a third and this time her thrown rock caught the pirate in the shoulder.

Still, it wouldn't be enough. They were outnumbered thirty to ten, and she hardly counted as her thrown rocks were more annoyances than lethal.

She hurled two more stones, smashing a pirate's head and another's elbow. Only four more stones rested in her canoe. Not nearly enough.

Shouts echoed off the cliffs from behind her. Rosanna glanced over her shoulder. She couldn't be sure what they were yelling, but the pirates in the upright canoe were pointing at Daemyn standing in the other canoe, a paddle held in his hands like a quarterstaff.

The arrows from above stopped. The river pirates reversed their canoes and raced toward the bank. Those in the water swam as if a many-toothed monster snapped at their toes.

Isi reappeared at Rosanna's side. "They're leaving. Why would they do that when they were about to wallop us?"

"They're scared." Rosanna couldn't make those words come out in anything above a whisper. Who was Daemyn, really? Why would thirty river pirates turn tail and run the moment they got a good look at him?

Captain Degotaga caught up to them, towing his canoe. "Get going, Your Highness. We must not dally in case they change their mind."

Rosanna forced her legs and arms back into motion once again. When they stopped to right their canoes and attempt to dry out their clothes, she was going to have a few questions for Daemyn Rand.

CHAPTER 12

ALEXANDER

ONE HUNDRED YEARS AGO

Alex held his breath as Jadon picked his way across yet another rope bridge. In the past three days as they had crossed from Kanawhee into Buckhannock, they hadn't had any more bridges collapse under them, though they had come across two bridges already fallen and another with ropes that had been nearly sliced through.

Jadon reached the far side, and his shoulders relaxed. He knelt and inspected the ropes for the handrails and footboards before standing. "All clear."

Finally. A bridge that hadn't been tampered with. Alex had begun to wonder if the bridge saboteurs had completely wrecked the infrastructure of the entire seven kingdoms.

He hefted his portion of their packs onto his aching shoulders and strode onto the bridge. After three days of carrying half of their packs, his back and shoulders should've gotten used to the exertion. Instead, those muscles cramped so much he couldn't lift his arms above his head.

But he wasn't going to complain. At least, not too often. He was the high prince. Surely he could push through some pain, couldn't he?

If he gave up, he wasn't sure he'd like what that said about him. And that was a rather uncomfortable feeling, thinking there might be something about himself he didn't like.

The bridge swayed with comfortable firmness beneath his feet. He stepped onto the far side and let himself smile. That bridge cutting must just be a local, disgruntled peasant who wouldn't be too troublesome to deal with. At the next large town, he could send a message back to his father to have it handled by the time he and Jadon returned this way after getting the little matter of his curse taken care of.

Footsteps pounded on the path ahead of them. Alex put a hand on his dagger but didn't draw it.

Moments later, a runner sprinted down the path, wearing nothing but leggings and moccasins, his chest glistening with sweat. A wood medallion with an emblem of the high king's scepter dangled from a length of rawhide around his neck, designating him as one of the official runners that connected the seven kingdoms to the high king via the Trace and its branching paths.

Alex and Jadon stepped off the path to give the runner room. With their system of relays along the Trace, the runners could carry a message from the farthest north of Tallahatchia to the south in a matter of days.

The runner skidded to a halt next to them, jogging in place, and cocked his head at the bridge.

"It's safe. We just inspected both ends and crossed."

Jadon pointed at the bridge. "But the bridges over the Bearwallow, Mud Shoal, Shallow, and Blackwater Creeks are out or unsafe."

The runner halted then, putting his hands on his knees. "Then it isn't just Buckhannock's problem."

Something tightened in Alex's stomach. "They're having problems with bridge cutting too?"

The runner nodded. "King Othniel of Buckhannock is sending a message to High King Atohi asking for help. But if this problem is spreading, it's going to take a while for the high king to get the message, much less respond with help. He will have his own troubles."

Yes, he would. Between the curse looming, the rumors of unrest in Tuckawassee, and now this, Father would be struggling.

What was happening to the seven kingdoms? They had lived peaceably for generations. What had changed?

Or perhaps this had always been there, waiting for a weakness in the high king's family. Ever since the beginning of time itself there had been this underlying tension between the six kings and the seventh high king. Each generation, each gift, each curse reminded them of what had caused all this.

Jadon held out his canteen to the runner. "Would you like some water?"

The runner shook his head and jogged in place once again. "I have to keep moving, especially now that climbing up and down those gorges will add to my time. You'd best get moving too. The next few bridges are all out."

"Thanks." Jadon lifted a hand as the runner jumped into a sprint, not even slowing his stride across the swaying bridge.

Alex probably should've offered some sort of parting

wave as well, but he couldn't seem to move. How dire were things in Tallahatchia?

As the afternoon lengthened two days later, Jadon slowed near a turn off from the Cheyandoah Trace.

Alex halted and pointed down the trail. "What's down that way?"

Jadon hesitated but didn't turn toward him. "My family."

Alex couldn't force himself to move, his chest tight. He had promised they would take the time to visit Jadon's family. He couldn't go back on a promise like that. It wasn't what an honorable prince like himself would do.

But did they have the time? Something was going on in this region, and they should hurry to Castle Firlin as quickly as possible. Alex needed to consult with King Othniel of Buckhannock.

The expected prince or princess of Buckhannock wasn't due to be born for another month yet. Jadon and Alex had made good time, despite the rough going with the sabotaged bridges. They could spend a few days with Jadon's family and still get to Castle Firlin well before the child was born. Even if the baby was born, they would have to wait around for eight days until the Fae showed up to bestow the gift.

Besides, Jadon's family was common folk. They might know more about what was going on than Buckhannock's king, and they would talk openly to Jadon, since he was family.

Jadon turned away from the path, his jaw tight. "But I understand, Your Highness. We need to keep moving."

"No, we have time." Alex cleared his throat. He could afford to be magnanimous to his manservant after the trek they'd done. "Your family might have insight into the trouble that's been happening. I assume they'll speak freely to you?"

Jadon coughed and glanced up at the clouds overhead as if they were a riveting diversion. "They'll speak freely, all right. If there's one thing my family is good at, it's speaking their mind."

"Very well. Lead the way." Alex adjusted the straps of his pack. It would be good to take a few days' rest.

Jadon turned down the path and set out. He halted a few times when trails branched off, as if unsure of the correct direction.

When was the last time Jadon had visited his parents? Alex tried to remember when he'd given Jadon enough time off to walk all the way to Buckhannock and back. Had he ever given Jadon time to visit his family? Surely he had. He just couldn't recall it at the moment.

After an hour, Jadon took the right hand fork up the slope of a mountain. His steps quickened, and Alex had to trot to keep pace.

A dirt lane opened before them, small shops lining each side of the little street. At this time of evening, candles shone in the windows of the second floors as families sat down for their evening meals.

Jadon turned another right before they reached the town and jogged up a nearly invisible path into the undergrowth.

Just when Alex was about ready to call a halt to catch his breath, the path opened onto a small cabin in a grove of trees. Alex couldn't make out many details of their surroundings in the descending darkness, but the cabin itself glowed with candlelight.

Jadon stepped onto the porch but froze with his fist poised above the door's timbers. His shoulders rose and fell before he straightened and knocked.

Alex counted his own heartbeats as he waited on the step below the porch. For some reason, even his chest was tight.

Something thumped from inside the cabin. Then the door opened, framing a hunched man with steel gray hair leaning on a cane. His right leg crooked at an odd angle, as if a break had healed badly at one time. "What you want, stranger?"

Jadon swallowed, holding out his hands as if begging the man to recognize him. "It's me, Pa. Jadon."

The cane fell from the man's hand as he took one hobbling step forward. He gripped Jadon and pulled him into a hug, mumbling something too low and broken for Alex to make out even standing a few feet away.

Shrieks and the sounds of pounding feet came from the cabin before a thin, gray-haired woman pushed through the doorway, tears streaming down her face. She pushed between Jadon and his father and kissed Jadon's cheeks, his forehead, and his cheeks again.

Alex rocked back on his heels and stared up at the porch roof. He got the odd sense that he shouldn't be here, and that wasn't a feeling he'd gotten before. A prince never intruded. Everyone else simply intruded on him.

But this . . . he was intruding here.

And even odder, he had nowhere else to go.

More footsteps, and three more boys and two girls crowded through the doorway. The oldest of the boys, looking only a year or two younger than Jadon, smacked

Jadon on the back. "Glad to see that tyrant prince finally let you out of his sight."

Tyrant prince? Alex sucked in a breath and clenched his fists. Was Jadon's family a bunch of traitors?

Jadon stiffened, his jaw tight, and shot a glance at Alex. "Luke, he's not a tyrant. He's our high prince, and we owe him respect."

Was Jadon saying that because Alex was standing there? What would Jadon have said if he hadn't known Alex was listening? Did he harbor traitorous thoughts like his brother?

After ten years of loyal service, it was hard to imagine. Jadon never acted like he planned to do anything but serve Alex with the respect owed him. But one couldn't always tell.

Alex would have to find out. He couldn't have a man with anything less than loyal thoughts serving him. Especially not with the current tensions.

"Your brother is right. The Lord of the Fae placed the high king and high prince over us. We must give them respect despite their weaknesses." Jadon's father had his head bowed, as if such respect was hard to give.

Alex felt the lump of his signet ring tucked under his shirt. He wasn't hard to respect, was he? Surely not. He'd always treated Jadon plenty generously. Hadn't he?

Luke crossed his arms. "Ten years, Pa. Ten years and Jadon ain't been allowed one visit. And what about the raids? What have the kings done about them? Nothing, that's what. They're too busy living in their fancy castles to care what happens to us mountain folk."

Jadon cleared his throat and gestured to Alex. "I brought . . . a friend. From the castle. He's . . ."

Alex stepped forward, barely finding space on the

crowded porch. How should he introduce himself? After the anti-prince sentiment expressed, he wasn't about to say he was the very prince they had lambasted. Though it would serve them right to know their traitorous words had been noted.

Speaking freely, indeed.

Why hadn't Jadon defended him? Or even Jadon's father? But they all stood in silence, accepting the change of topic as if they couldn't refute Luke's outburst. They could only ignore it.

Alex forced himself to smile and extend a hand. He had to prove them wrong, at least part of it. "I'm . . . Alex. I work with Jadon. At the castle."

One of Jadon's sisters giggled. "That there castle speech is right fancy."

"And Jadon's got that fancy speaking." His other sister grinned. "Could you learn us some of that proper talk too? Maybe I'll catch a castle boy with it."

One of the brothers tugged his sister's hair. "You ain't gonna want one of those sissy castle boys. They ain't got the stomach gutting a deer or eating good varmint stew."

The sister smirked and turned her dark brown eyes on Alex. "Well, castle boy. You want to come in and share our stew? Possum and coon, maybe some squirrel. Can't recollect all we put in it."

Alex swallowed. Were they fooling him or serious? He couldn't be sure and didn't dare ask. "If you're inviting me in for supper, I would be happy to accept. We haven't eaten in hours."

"Of course, come in. Set back down, young'uns. Nancy, fetch bowls for Jadon and Alex. Luke, Silas, slide over and make room on your bench."

In a matter of minutes, Alex found himself wedged

between Jadon and his loud-mouthed brother Luke, so close he had to keep his elbows pinned to his sides and his shoulders turned sideways.

Nancy, the sister who had invited him in, set a bowl of a thick stew in front of him. Bits of corn, carrots, potato, and meat floated in the dark brown gravy.

He dipped in his spoon, blew on it, and eyed the mystery meat. Was it raccoon? Possum? Squirrel? Some other small rodent or animal?

The back of his neck prickled, and he glanced up. Everyone around the table eyed him. Jadon's siblings had various versions of a smirk on their faces while Jadon's parents had lines across their foreheads as if they were worried about offending their son's uppity friend from the castle.

Jadon's mouth pressed tight. Out of his entire family, he was the only one not staring at Alex. His knuckles were white on his own spoon, his breaths so shallow his shoulder didn't bump into Alex's like Luke's did.

Was Jadon fighting . . . anger? It was almost as if he was worried about Alex throwing a spoiled princely fit and offending his mother and her cooking right there in his family's cabin.

Well, he might be a castle boy, but he'd been raised with proper manners. With a deep breath, Alex popped the bite into his mouth and chewed.

The meat had a tang to it, but it didn't seem all that different from the venison or bison meat they got at the castle. Best if he didn't think about what he was eating and just savor it. It was the best meal he'd had since they'd left Castle Eyota.

Focusing on the warmth of the stew, he smiled and

lifted a second spoonful in a salute. "This is excellent stew, ma'am."

Jadon's mother smiled back, and Jadon's family returned to their meal. The dull thunk of pewter spoons on wooden bowls filled the small kitchen.

Next to Alex, Jadon's shoulders relaxed, and he finally dipped his spoon into his stew.

Had he really thought Alex was so self-centered and arrogant that he would insult Jadon's family to their faces?

Alex dug in. If he didn't think about the fact that he might be eating rodent, the stew was rather tasteful. The meat gave it a certain depth of flavor, the gravy rich and thick enough to just about need chewing. Actually, if rodent tasted this good, Alex might not mind so much after all.

It took a few minutes, but the conversation finally picked up. No politics. Jadon's family filled him in on the local happenings. Lots of marriages and births and deaths of people Alex didn't know and didn't care to ever know.

Once they finished eating and the dishes cleared away, Jadon's mother pointed toward the loft above the back half of the cabin. "Jadon, Alex, I think there's enough room to squish you upstairs with the boys. There's still a tick up there for you, Jadon."

Ten years, and Jadon's family had left a bed open for him in case he had a chance to go home.

A chance Alex had never given him.

Why did he have such a sick churning in his stomach over that? It was Alex's right to demand loyalty and hard work out of his servants. He was the high prince. He deserved such respect.

But was it right?

Alex swallowed. Had he ever asked that question before?

Jadon nodded and strolled around the table. "I'll show you upstairs, Y—Alex."

Alex grabbed his half of the pack, swung it onto his back, and followed Jadon to the ladder nailed to the wall next to a doorway into one of the two tiny bedrooms that took up the back of the cabin. The door to one bedroom leaned open, giving Alex a glimpse of a bunk bed and a trunk taking up most of the floor space. The entire room was about the same size as his large bed back at the castle.

Jadon climbed the ladder, a wince creasing his forehead. His ribs were probably protesting the movement.

Alex followed, barely managing to get himself and the pack through the opening in the floor into what passed as the cabin's second story. He peered into the dark interior, trying to make out details in the dim light spilling through the opening around the ladder.

The sloped roof of the cabin went all the way to the floor on either side. Even the center was so low Alex wasn't sure he'd be able to stand straight even there. Straw ticks lined up all in the row down the center of the space, three on one side of the ladder and two on the other. Trunks sat at the foot of each of the ticks, probably holding all each boy's clothes and possessions.

People really lived like this? With next to nothing?

Jadon pointed to the two ticks to the right of the ladder. "My brothers will all squish onto the other side. Get some rest, if you'd like."

Alex nodded and set the pack at the foot of the tick at the far end. He probably should stay here and let Jadon have some chance to reunite with his family on his own. It was the polite thing to do, after all.

As Jadon turned back toward the ladder, Alex caught his arm. "Was that really possum? In the stew tonight?"

"I'm not sure you want to know, Your Highness." Jadon's head and shoulders hunched as he returned to the servant's posture he'd always had at Castle Eyota.

"Yes, I think I do. I wasn't lying when I said the stew was tasty, regardless of its content."

"Honestly, I don't know what was in that stew. We eat possum, coon, squirrel, and rabbit out here. They're easier to shoot or snare. It's much harder to take down an elk or bison, especially not with one arrow. And when the family does get big game, the choice cuts are sold down the mountain to feed the town folk and the rest smoked for winter." Jadon shrugged. "Meat is meat. Don't matter if it comes from a possum or a deer if it's cooked right."

"No, I guess not." Alex flopped down onto the straw tick, and his back jolted when the mattress didn't give as much as he'd expected. There wasn't much to this straw tick, but at least it would be better than sleeping on the ground. "I'm turning in. I will appreciate a few extra hours of sleep on a decent bed for once."

Jadon nodded and disappeared down the ladder.

Alex spread his bedroll on the bed, took off his boots, and sprawled out, yawning. He hadn't been lying. A few extra hours of sleep would be appreciated. He might even be able to sleep in without windows for the sun to peer through and wake him up at such an annoyingly early hour as it did when they camped in the open.

Voices drifted from the kitchen below. A steady hum, low and almost soothing.

Too bad every inch of the wooden floor pressed painfully against his back through the woefully inadequate straw stuffing. He rolled, squirmed, scrunched, and stretched, but nothing made the mattress more comfortable.

After sleeping on the hard ground for nearly two weeks, a straw mattress should be a luxury. But the ground was expected to be hard. A mattress should be soft and comfortable, not scratchy and lumpy.

Feet and hands scuffed on the ladder, and Alex lay still and peered through slitted eyes.

Jadon's youngest two brothers glanced at him before they headed for the straw ticks on the far side of the attic room and settled in for the night. In the rooms below, the doors for the bedrooms opened and shut. Goodnights were exchanged.

Alex waited, but neither Jadon nor his brother Luke climbed the ladder and headed for their beds. A low hum of voices remained from down below, even if the fire's glow dimmed to a dull orange.

At the far side of the attic, one of Jadon's brothers snuffled a snore. The other's breathing lengthened and steadied. How were they both asleep already?

Alex stifled a sigh and propped his hands behind his head. So much for extra sleep.

His name spoken in the hushed voices below caught his attention. He eased upright, cocking his ear toward the hole in the floor. Had he just imagined it? Or were Jadon and Luke talking about him now that they assumed he was asleep?

Whatever they were talking about, Alex had to find out. What if it was talk of treason? Something about the bridges?

Easing forward, Alex crawled over the straw ticks and lay on his stomach in the shadows near the ladder. The snoring and loud breathing from Jadon's youngest brothers remained steady.

Jadon's voice was low. "We were sent to the king of Buckhannock for a special mission for the prince. I can't say more than that. Since we were so close, we took the time to stop. I'm not sure how long I'll be able to stay."

"So this ain't a proper visit. After ten years, that arrogant prince can't see more than his own nose. You had to sneak off to see us. It ain't right." Luke's tone cut sharp enough to slice the floorboards even if they were barely above a whisper.

Alex gritted his teeth. It wasn't like Jadon had ever asked for time off to see his family. Surely Alex would've granted him leave if he had.

Wouldn't he? Or had Jadon been too afraid of Alex's answer to even dare ask?

No, that couldn't be it.

Jadon sighed. "He does the best he knows how. It's not his fault he wasn't raised to have much in the way of compassion. I'm sorry, but this is the way things have to be."

"Do they? Really? Half the time SueAnne forgets she even has another brother. She was all of two when you left. The only memories she's got of you is your letters. What sort of brother can you be to her like that? It ain't right."

"I know." Jadon's voice cracked. "But there ain't nothing I can do."

"Ain't there? You could quit. You don't have to serve him like a hound dog." Luke snorted. "But you're the everperfect brother. You even talk all fancy like them castle folk. Got all friendly with them too. Soon you'll up and marry one of those castle girls and you ain't never coming back here."

"Don't you think I'd like nothing better than to settle

down with a girl and raise a family? But it ain't gonna happen. I'm too castle for the folk around here and too mountain for the folk back there. I don't belong nowhere no more." Feet scuffed on the wooden floorboards, as if Jadon was standing, trying to hold himself back from shoving his brother.

"That ain't true. You belong here."

Silence filled the room below. Alex shouldn't be listening. This argument wasn't even about him anymore, though he was connected to it. But he didn't move. He'd never heard Jadon so . . . angry.

"I know. My home will always be here." Wood squeaked against the floor, as if Jadon had returned to his seat. His voice had returned to his mild tone. "But I believe my place is at Castle Eyota right now. Ma and Pa need the money I send home."

"Reckon they did back when you left. But not no more. We're grown now. We can take care of ourselves, and Ma and Pa."

"You're going to be marrying your MaryKate in a few months. You'll have a family of your own to worry about."

"We'll make do. But Pa ain't helpless. He's been making the handles and fitting the ax heads for one of the smiths from the village. It brings in enough."

"Maybe. But if I can keep you, Silas, and Hasil from the mines, then it's worth it. I ain't going to ask Ma to watch her sons walk into a mine after what happened to Pa."

Had Jadon's father been hurt in a mining accident? Alex couldn't remember if this part of Buckhannock was known for mining iron or the coal used to smelt the iron into proper steel for weapons.

"Don't sneer down your castle-refined nose at working

in the mines. It's good, honest labor and don't you say it ain't."

"I didn't say that."

"You don't have to. Well I got news for you. We don't need your charity for your poor, unintelligent mountain family and your crippled pa. We're doing just fine. Pa and Ma ain't said a word against me and Silas taking a few shifts at the mine. I'm proud to be a miner's son and grandson, and if that's the kind of life I give my family, I'll be right proud of that too."

"I'm not . . . it's . . ." Jadon blew out a breath. "It ain't charity. I'm doing my part to provide for this family and honor the Highest King just like you. Now I've had enough."

Boots stomped across the room. Alex scrambled over the straw ticks and slid into his bedrolls as hands and feet scuffed on the ladder. He rolled onto his side and tried to still his breathing to pretend to be asleep.

Jadon thumped into the attic, his footsteps pausing as if he were watching to see if Alex was asleep. Apparently satisfied, he headed for the straw tick in the eaves of the attic next to Alex, the mattress his family had kept waiting for him for ten years.

Alex gripped the blankets tighter around his chin and tried to relax.

But it would be a long time—well after Luke settled on his mattress and his and Jadon's breathing deepened into sleep—before Alex managed to relax enough to sleep.

CHAPTER 13

ROSANNA

As dawn broke between the mountains, Rosanna squished from the water and collapsed to her knees, shivering. She rubbed her hands together, trying to return feeling to their tips.

After evading the river pirates, they had stopped briefly to climb back into the canoes that weren't too damaged, assess the wounds that Ahanu and Nikan had received, and towed the damaged canoes until Daemyn finally called a halt when they turned off down a side creek.

Isi stumbled from the creek and stuck her hands under her armpits. "I hope we're allowed to make fires. I might hop into one to get warm."

"I won't be far behind you." Rosanna clenched her teeth and forced herself to her feet. She had to help Daemyn carry their canoe from the water, even if her buckskins remained damp and the chill ached into her joints.

Wading into the river, she reached their tilted canoe— one of the damaged ones—as Daemyn untied the straps holding their packs inside. Water splashed through the two holes near the waterline, currently tipped upward.

As Rosanna pulled the packs free, water dripped off them. Hopefully the oiled skins protected the clothes. More than anything, dry clothes would be appreciated.

She tossed the packs onto the bank and lifted the canoe from the river. Water flowed from the holes.

Together, they carried it from the creek and set it down on a stretch of grass. Daemyn returned to the water to help Otho carry Ahanu from a canoe to the bank. Blood soaked the bandaged tied around Ahanu's leg above his right knee. Behind them, Garmund steadied Nikan as he waded from the creek. Blood saturated Nikan's sleeve from the wound on his shoulder.

Captain Degotaga swept a glance over them. "I suppose we'll have to risk a fire. But we'd best hurry and patch the canoes as best we can. We don't want to linger in case the river pirates come after us."

Daemyn helped Otho lay Ahanu on a dry patch of dead leaves and straightened. "The river pirates won't come after us. We can take some time to rest here before we continue."

How could Daemyn be so sure? What hold did he have over the river pirates?

Captain Degotaga studied Daemyn for a few seconds, as if assessing the confidence Daemyn placed in his own words. "Very well. We'll tend the wounded, patch the canoes, and catch a few hours of rest."

While Chogan tended to the wounded and Ilma built a fire, Isi and Rosanna dug out clothes from their packs and retreated behind a boulder to change. The new clothes were damp, but at least they were drier than the buckskins they'd worn all night.

They hung their wet clothes from branches and stood next to the fire. Rosanna extended her hands. The heat tickled her palms. Warmth seeped into her face and clothes.

"Pardon me, Princess." Otho pushed past her and Isi with a jar of animal fat in one hand and a pot in the other.

Rosanna stepped aside and suppressed a sigh. As much as she wanted to stay there all day, they had canoes to repair and a few hours of sleep to catch. "I guess we'd better start harvesting the birch bark."

Isi held up a small knife. "Ready when you are."

Rosanna and Isi set out with Chogan into the surrounding woodlands to search for birch trees. Once they found a stand only a few hundred yards into the brush, Rosanna selected a section of the bark and made a slit down the middle of the tree, careful to only cut through the top, pliable layer of bark and not touch the hard layers underneath.

After slitting the top and bottom of the piece she'd selected, she and Isi eased the bark from the tree, doing their best not to tear it. It didn't come easily. Peeling birch bark was best done in the hottest months of summer, not mid-spring.

Rosanna and Isi peeled bark from several more trees until they had a heap of birch bark at their feet. Chogan helped them carry the birch bark back to their camp alongside the river. By the time they returned, Otho had spruce pitch boiling in his pot. Taking it off the heat, he added charcoal and a dollop of the animal fat.

Nearby, Garmund soaked spruce roots in the river while Ilma pulled out one that had already been soaked and set to work stripping off the outer bark on the root to make it pliable.

Daemyn knelt next to their canoe, inspecting the three

holes. Rosanna set a stack of birch bark next to him and knelt on the other side.

Ilma delivered a pile of peeled spruce roots, now white and slippery.

"I'll cut the patches, if you want to get a start sewing them in." Rosanna picked up a piece of birch bark, measured it against the largest hole in the canoe, and began cut it into shape. She kept her eyes on her work as she dared to ask the question that had niggled at her all night. "What did those river pirates shout last night? Right before they ran?"

When Daemyn remained silent, she looked up and held out the birch bark.

He took the bark from her, placed it with the white side toward the inside of the canoe, and started poking tiny holes along the edge with the tip of his dagger. "They call me the Cursed One."

"Cursed One?" She snatched peeks at him as she measured and cut the other two pieces of birch bark. "You aren't cursed, are you?"

"No, I'm not. Though some might call it a curse." Daemyn's voice was low, as if he might be one of those who did. He threaded a strand of spruce root through the holes to sew the bark into place.

What did he mean by that? What curse-that-wasn't-a-curse did he have on him? Was it because of his duty to find and escort her to wake the high prince? But why would that duty strike such fear into the river pirates?

"That doesn't explain why they ran off like that." Holding her patch over the smallest hole in the canoe, she punctured small holes all around the edges of the bark with her knife.

"I've run into that particular band of river pirates

before. They have vivid memories of that last battle." Daemyn finished securing the largest patch in place and started on the second.

"What happened?" Rosanna worked the spruce root back and forth through the small holes.

"I . . ." Daemyn raised his head, sweeping his gaze over the camp as if searching for a reason to avoid answering her. "Looks like the resin is ready."

Rosanna glanced up as Otho approached and held out a small ceramic pot filled with cooling spruce gum.

She grimaced. Gumming the seams in the canoe was the messiest part of the job. With the animal fat and charcoal added, the gum wasn't as sticky as the raw resin, but it still was a pain to get off fingers.

Daemyn gave her a cock of an eyebrow and a twitch of his mouth that was the equivalent of a grin for him. He held up a length of the spruce root. "I'm still sewing."

"Fine." Rosanna dipped two fingers into the gum and spread it over one of the finished patches. She made sure all the holes around the root stitches were filled with gum before she smoothed a layer of gum over the whole section of birch bark. The birch bark glowed with a hint of yellow when she finished.

He had sidestepped the topic of the river pirates. Why? What had happened that last time he'd faced the river pirates to make them so fear him?

She finished that patch and moved on to the next one. As she reached for another glob of resin, her hand bumped into Daemyn's as he too reached for the resin, having finished sewing the second patch in place. "I'm sorry."

He waved at the jar and gave her a nod. "You first, Princess."

Together, they finished spreading the gum over the

final patch. Daemyn stood and held out his resin covered hand to her. She took it with her own equally sticky hand and let him haul her to her feet.

Captain Degotaga strode toward them. "It appears that all the canoes will be able to be patched, though I'm not sure one will hold for long."

"They only have to take us another day and a half up the Grassy Lick Creek before we'll have to leave them to hike over the mountains." Daemyn scraped his fingers together as if trying to get the resin off.

If his attempts were going anything like hers, they weren't doing any good. Rosanna peeled her fingers apart. The stickiness tugged at her skin. "How are Nikan and Ahanu?"

"Both will recover, though neither will be able to wield a paddle or hike over the mountains." Captain Degotaga rubbed at the back of a hand where a red slash marred his skin. A scratch he must have received in the battle the night before.

"The captain at Fort Last Chance at the headwaters of the Grassy Lick is a friend of mine. He will be willing to tend to them." Daemyn frowned down at his hands.

Fort Last Chance. The last outpost in this section of the mountains before Tuckawassee. Rosanna clenched her fingers over her sticky palms. Only three more days until they entered Tuckawassee and the real danger began.

CHAPTER 14

ALEXANDER

ONE HUNDRED YEARS AGO

A hand shook Alex's shoulder. Back at the castle, he wouldn't have even stirred that early in the morning. But now he only allowed himself one groan before he sat up.

Jadon withdrew his hand and nodded toward the ladder. "Breakfast will be in a few minutes."

Alex glanced around the attic. He and Jadon were the last ones left. Apparently Jadon had let him sleep later than the others.

Voices rose from the kitchen below. Lots of them. With laughter and the raised voices of a family comfortable with each other.

When was the last time Alex's family had laughed and talked with such abandon? As if they could ignore propriety and just laugh?

He couldn't remember ever doing it. Even when it was just the three of them, they were always the high king, queen, and prince. Even with each other.

And Mirabelle. She had her tinkling laugh, but how

much was that as forced and restrained as his laugh when he was with her? Did either of them even know how to be themselves?

Probably not. Because Alex was nothing if he wasn't the high prince. It was his identity. He couldn't set it aside even to relax for a moment.

Jadon turned, but before he could reach the ladder to descend into the kitchen, Alex stopped him. Jadon glanced back. "Sir?"

Alex released his arm, trying to put some of his thoughts into words. The ones that came to mind sounded too much like an apology. And high princes didn't apologize. "We have time. We can stay a few days before we set out for Castle Firlin."

"Are you sure, Your Highness?" Jadon's face went blank, as if he didn't trust Alex's word.

Was he sure? He didn't relish staying with this family for long, not with the anti-prince sentiments expressed.

But he could afford to be gracious to Jadon, just this once. Give him a little time with his family.

Besides, Alex could observe them more to see how deep the discontent with him ran. Was Jadon's brother Luke behind the bridge cuttings? There seemed to be too many for one man, but perhaps he had joined some secret organization that even now plotted against Alex and his father.

It would be worth putting up with this rustic mountain family for a few days if Alex could find a few answers about the downed bridges.

"Yes, I'm sure." Alex pushed past Jadon and climbed down the ladder.

The youngest girl—SueAnne—was setting the pewter plates on the table, while the youngest brother—Hasil if Alex had it figured right— set tin cups next to each plate.

Nancy stepped inside carrying a bucket of milk, probably freshly milked from the few goats out in the barn.

Jadon's mother smiled as she stirred a bunch of eggs, meat, and various vegetables around in a pan. "How'd you sleep?"

"Nice and cozy, Ma." Jadon jumped from the ladder, strode past Alex, and kissed his mother on the cheek. "Pa tending the animals?"

"Yep." Jadon's mother stirred the eggs once again. "The vittles are about done."

Jadon's father lurched inside, leaning on his cane, followed by the rest of Jadon's siblings. Alex hung back, but he didn't have to worry about finding a seat. Jadon and Luke left plenty of space between them on the bench.

Jadon's mother set the pan on the center of the table and the siblings dug into the eggs, dishing them into their plates. Alex barely managed to claim some.

"Were you going to be leaving today, Jadon?" His mother's mouth was tight.

Jadon shook his head, his eyes flicking toward Alex before focusing on his mother. "No, actually we can stay a few days, if you don't mind putting us up for that long. Our message for the king isn't urgent."

A smile softened her features. Jadon's sisters squealed, and one jumped up to hug Jadon.

Luke leaned around Alex to slap Jadon on the back. A brotherly gesture, if with an edge even Alex could hear. "In that case, you can go hunting with us today. I bet it's been years since you've been on a good buffalo hunt."

"Not since I left here." Jadon grimaced and glanced down at his plate.

"And your castle friend for sure ain't never been on a hunt." Luke smirked.

No, of course Alex hadn't. But he wasn't going to back down at all. Surely he could handle something as plebian as a hunting expedition.

Silas—a lad of fifteen or sixteen—speared a bite of eggs. "Maybe we'll teach him how to gut a carcass. That'll make him think twice about what he's eating."

Alex was already thinking twice or more, but he wasn't going to say anything. He swallowed. "Sounds . . . entertaining."

Luke grinned. "It will be."

ALEX JUGGLED the stack of long spears he'd been given. Somehow, he'd been nominated to be their weapons carrier. Luke had a sense that he didn't dare refuse and had no problem taking advantage of that.

Jadon's brothers Luke and Silas each carried a bow and a quiver filled with long, metal tipped arrows as did Jadon and his sister Nancy. Hasil carried a bundle of hardwood stakes, their ends carved to points.

The only sibling not tagging along was SueAnne, and Alex got the impression she stayed behind because she was the youngest, not because she was a girl. Shocking, really, seeing a girl like Nancy lugging around a bow. Perhaps the rumors of these backwards people were true. They really did teach their girls to shoot and fight as well as their men.

It was just as odd to see Jadon dressed in buckskin carrying weapons like a warrior instead of wielding cleaning brushes and polishing rags.

How did they plan to take down a buffalo? They were big animals to kill with a few small spears and arrows. But what did Alex know? He'd never questioned how his meat was caught. A lot of meat came from buffalo raised in farms for meat. But others were caught in the wild.

After two hours of hiking through rough country deeper into the mountains away from well-traveled paths, Luke pointed at the ground near a small creek. Even Alex could spot the churned up ground and a few large hoofprints.

Luke led the way in the direction the herd had traveled. Alex tried to keep his breathing steady as they hiked up the side of a mountain and around a steep cliff.

A small meadow opened below them, dotted with the moving and lowing forms of the wood buffalo.

Luke dropped to his stomach. Alex set down the bundle of spears and sank to the ground a few feet away.

Luke pointed at a buffalo at the edge of the herd nearest them. "That one."

"That's what I reckon too." Silas nodded toward a cluster of low boulders to their right. "Let's set up there."

Alex did his best to stay out of the way as Jadon, Luke, and Silas pounded the stakes into the ground, their sharpened ends pointed down the slope toward the herd. Nancy and Hasil dragged downed brush into lines on either side of the boulders, creating a funnel toward the stakes at the end.

Luke smirked and pointed at the pile of spears by Alex's feet. "Ready to cut out?"

Alex took the spear. Cut out? As in drive the buffalo away from the rest of the herd? Were they insane?

Hasil and Nancy grabbed spears, wielding them with ease.

Jadon claimed a spear as well, holding it as if remembering an old skill. "You don't have to. We can cut out with three."

Maybe so, but if Nancy was doing it, he wasn't about to refuse. A surge pulsed through his veins. Something shaky, yes, but also thrilling. More thrilling than anything he'd done before, except perhaps for kissing Mirabelle. "I can handle it."

Jadon eyed him like he wasn't convinced. "All right. Follow my lead. If you run into trouble, plant your spear like this and brace it toward the buffalo." Jadon demonstrated a maneuver where he jabbed the blunt end of the spear into the ground, kept it in place with one foot, crouched, and braced it at an angle with his arms.

"Will that stop a charging buffalo?" One little stick with a small iron head to stop a massive, charging beast?

Luke slapped Alex on the back again, hard enough to send Alex stumbling forward. "Possibly. If the spear don't shatter or your grip don't falter, and if the buffalo dies before its charge carries it all the way to you."

Alex tightened his grip on the spear's hardwood shaft. This was not an intelligent idea. Not at all. What were these crazy mountain folk thinking?

Nancy and Hasil jogged down the slope, sure-footed as squirrels even while lugging spears taller than they. With a motion for Alex to follow, Jadon slunk down the mountain and crept toward the herd.

At the edge of the meadow, Jadon crouched behind a tree. "I'll make sure the rest of the herd doesn't spook and head in this direction if you think you can get the buffalo started toward the trap. Hasil and Nancy will back you up."

Hasil could be no more than thirteen. Nancy only a year older. He was in trouble. Alex gripped the spear tighter and crept into the meadow after Jadon.

A few of the wood buffalo eyed them, but most of

them kept grazing. Apparently, buffalo were docile animals until roused.

Jadon halted facing the herd, his back toward Alex and the chosen buffalo. He sank into a crouch, his spear in his hand as if this came all naturally to him even after ten years of living as Alex's manservant at Castle Eyota.

Alex tiptoed over to the buffalo they intended to trap and kill. It rolled its eyes at him, but continued grazing. He hit it across the neck.

The buffalo turned to him and pawed its front hoof.

Alex hit it again, this time across the nose.

The buffalo made some sort of low, bellowing sound and charged forward.

That wasn't good. Alex spun and ran as fast as he could for the trees only five feet away. He might have let out some sort of shout, but he couldn't be sure.

Behind him, hooves drummed. If it was just the one buffalo or the whole herd, he couldn't tell past his own pounding feet and heart.

He reached the trees and sprinted up the slope as quickly as possible.

Hooves thundered closer. Closer.

He couldn't outrun the creature. He spun on his heels, stabbed the end of the spear into the ground, and crouched to brace the spear.

The buffalo bellowed again and lowered its head, looming so close Alex could just about reach out to pet the thick, dark brown fur curling around its face and neck.

He squeezed his eyes shut, bracing himself for the impact and pain of slicing horns and crushing hooves.

Someone yelled something bloodcurdling and raw, though not with pain. Alex peeled his eyes open in time to see Nancy dodge out of the way of the buffalo's swinging head, her spear dancing in her hands as she poked the buffalo's side.

It skidded and whirled to charge after her. She dashed up the slope, the buffalo closing hard on her heels.

Before it could trample her, Hasil burst from behind a tree with a similar, eerie yell and jabbed at the buffalo.

Alex couldn't force himself to uncurl from his crouch on the ground. He'd heard about how wolves took down large prey, working as a pack to wear the animal out before they went in for the kill. That's exactly how Jadon's family hunted this buffalo.

Jadon sprinted upward with his spear in his hand. The rest of the herd was running, spooked by the commotion, but they stampeded down the length of the creek's valley, not up the slope. Jadon motioned. "Come on."

Alex would, if he could get his legs to stop shaking long enough to take a step.

Hasil and Nancy had herded the buffalo to within ten feet of the trap. Jadon joined them, stabbing, jumping back, stabbing again, until they had the beast inside the jaws of the enclosure. At the far end, Luke and Silas raised their bows and loosed a pair of arrows.

The buffalo let out a bellow filled with more pain than rage, one arrow in a shoulder, the other buried in a rear leg.

With Hasil and Jadon in front of her, Nancy dropped her spear and took up her bow, joining Luke and Silas in releasing another volley of arrows.

As the buffalo fought a few steps deeper into the trap, Jadon too dropped his spear, unslung the bow from his back, and took aim with an arrow, sending it plunging into the animal's rear leg.

The buffalo staggered, its rear legs buckling. It fell to

the ground, still bellowing and pawing with its front hooves.

Hasil leapt forward and plunged his spear into the buffalo's chest, leaning with his whole body to drive it deep.

The buffalo gasped, blood streaming down its sides. With a groan, it rolled onto its side. Its legs twitched, a breath snorted from its nose, and it lay still.

Alex dropped his spear. His hands trembled. His teeth rattled. That had been close. Far too close. These mountain folk were good at what they did, but crazy wasn't a strong enough word for it.

Luke drew a rather large knife from a sheath at his waist. "Might as well get to it."

While Jadon, Hasil, and Silas also drew knives, Luke leaned over and sliced open the buffalo's stomach.

Alex caught one glimpse and one whiff, and his stomach churned up into his throat. He clambered to his feet, stumbled a few feet away, and stared up at the sky. As much as he wanted to prove he was tough, he wasn't going to watch. He was already dangerously close to losing his breakfast, and actually vomiting would be far more embarrassing.

After pacing until his stomach calmed down, Alex found a seat on a fallen log. Except for the siblings talking as they gutted the dead buffalo, the only sounds were the faint rustling in the tree tops, a twittering bird, and the rumble of the herd running into the distance.

Somewhere up the slope, something crunched against the layer of fallen leaves coating the mountainside.

Alex stiffened, his heart racing in his throat once again. Had the buffalo herd circled around? Or was that a pack of wolves attracted by the scent of blood? Or a bear?

He gripped the wooden staff he'd used on the buffalo and stood as the crunching sound rushed down the mountain's slope toward him.

The woods were empty.

No, not empty. A squirrel careened down the slope and launched itself into a tree. After a moment, it scrambled down and raced off in a different direction, each jump raising enough noise to sound like a full-grown man barreled through the forest.

Who knew such a small critter could much so much noise? Alex released a breath and relaxed onto the fallen log.

"Alex. We're done."

Alex turned at Jadon's shout and strode down the hill.

Not much remained of the carcass, and Alex did his best not to look too closely. The buffalo's fur with the meat presumably tied inside had been lashed two sturdy saplings.

Luke smirked and pointed at one end of the poles. "So, castle boy. You have a weak stomach. Do you have a weak back too?"

Alex gritted his teeth. He shouldn't have to prove anything to these peasants. He was the high prince. His worth was measured in his intelligence, not his brawn.

But that didn't stop a part of Alex from wanting to prove his brawn as well. He couldn't refuse Luke's challenge, not if he wanted the goading to stop.

Alex marched to one end of the carrying poles and lifted. He staggered under the weight, his arms shaking as he tried to heave the poles upward.

Jadon's siblings chuckled, with Luke snorting the loudest of all. Of course he did.

But Jadon crossed his arms. "Luke, it's fine if he

doesn't want to help. He isn't used to hard labor at the castle."

"I reckon his job must be a mite easier than yours. Maybe you should apply to get his job instead of slaving for that arrogant prince."

Alex ground his teeth together so hard the corners of his jaws ached. Now he couldn't refuse this. In Luke's eyes, he was just as worthless in his pretend role of a servant as he was in his real one as prince.

And he was far from worthless.

He set the poles down and stepped back, catching his breath. Jadon's siblings snorted louder—even Nancy—and shouted something at him, but he ignored them. He needed to apply some intelligence to this problem instead of tackling it only with strength, which he admittedly lacked.

Leverage. That was the key. Leverage and using his strongest muscles instead of his weakest.

He crouched and strained to lift the poles to his shoulders, bracing his elbows into his thighs to give himself better purchase.

The ends of the poles settled onto his shoulders. The weight dug into the muscle there, but he steadied himself and glanced over at Jadon and his brothers.

They had stopped laughing. Luke still sported a smirk, but Hasil had his eyebrows raised in what could have been grudging respect.

Alex raised his eyebrows. "Well? Is anyone going to help me carry this, or will I have to do all the work myself?"

Jadon stepped forward, but Luke beat him to it. He crouched much like Alex and lifted the poles to his shoulders with much less effort.

Once Luke had the poles balanced on his shoulders, he

eased to his feet, and Alex matched his movements, though a tad slower as his leg muscles strained to get him upright.

The others gathered the spears, bows, and quivers, and Hasil led the way up the slope back the way they'd come.

Within a few steps, Alex realized his first mistake. He'd claimed the back end of the carrying poles. The bundle of fur and meat blocked his view of anything but a few feet in front of him, making it hard to watch his step as they hiked up and over the mountain's ridge and down toward the small stream on the other side. Every time he panted in a breath, he gagged on the stench of raw meat and the buffalo's pungent, greasy fur.

But he couldn't complain. Nor give up. He had gained some measure of respect in their eyes, and he wasn't going to lose it now.

Why was that respect so important to him? It wasn't like he'd ever see Jadon's siblings again after he and Jadon left for Castle Firlin. They were just lowly peasant stock who didn't matter in the larger scheme of Tallahatchian politics. Alex was the high prince. He didn't need their respect. Just their unswerving allegiance.

But it did matter, somehow. Respect had always been something Alex had due to his title. It had never been something he'd personally earned.

He was earning it now with every staggering step and shaking muscle. And this earned respect tasted sweeter, weighed heavier, than the automatic respect given due to his rank.

How far had they gone? Alex didn't dare raise his head from staring at the patch of ground in front of his feet.

A large root crossed the path. He raised his foot, but not high enough. His toe caught, and he staggered, nearly falling to his knees.

"I reckon it's time to switch carriers." Jadon stepped to his side and lifted the poles from Alex's shoulders.

Alex didn't argue. He rolled out of the way and pushed to his feet. He hadn't been the one to ask for a rest, and that was the main thing.

Nancy relieved Luke of his end of the poles.

Alex leaned his hands on his knees, trying to catch his breath and still the muscles that cramped and shook even worse now that they'd been relieved of their burden.

Nancy and Jadon set out after Hasil and Silas once again. Alex straightened to follow, but the blunt end of a spear jabbed into his chest.

Alex faced Luke as Jadon and his other siblings disappeared over the crest of a ridge.

Luke planted the staff in the ground. "I know who you are, Your Highness."

CHAPTER 15

ALEXANDER

ONE HUNDRED YEARS AGO

Alex stiffened and tried to get his cramping muscles to cooperate. He wasn't in much of a position to defend himself if Luke turned out to a traitor in deeds as well as words. "How did you know?"

Luke snorted. "Just because you're gifted with intelligence don't mean no else got a fair measure of sense. It were obvious as a skunk on the porch you ain't no servant."

Alex sighed. Apparently, he lacked sufficient acting skills to fool a peasant. "What do you plan to do now? You've been talking like a traitor. Are you going to act like one too?"

Luke crossed his arms. "No. But I aim to look out for my brother."

Alex would've crossed his arms as well, but his shoulders and arms ached too much for him to move them.

Luke glared. "We missed him all these years. A few letters ain't enough. Our sisters barely know him. That ain't right. And Jadon ain't the brother I recollect leaving here. He don't smile or laugh the way he ought."

Alex tried to meet Luke's gaze but couldn't hold it. That guilty feeling was back in his chest. Incredibly uncomfortable, that feeling.

Worse, he was right. Jadon should've had a chance to visit his family over the years. Alex hadn't taken the time to realize what his demands were costing his servant.

How many other servants at Castle Eyota had gone years without seeing their families because of his family's orders?

But Alex wasn't going to admit any of that to Luke. "I see. I will take that into consideration."

Luke jabbed Alex in the chest with the spear again. "You'll do more than that. You treat him right, or else."

Alex raised his eyebrows. Was this peasant threatening him? "Or else what? What could you hope to do to me?"

"I'll march to the castle and personally beat you with this spear. That's a promise." Luke held Alex's gaze. "Do you doubt me?"

Staring into his dark brown eyes—hard as the cliffs below Castle Eyota—Alex couldn't doubt him. This peasant would march all the way to Kanawhee to personally administer a beating, even knowing he'd earn himself a beating or an execution in return. "No, I don't. But it won't be necessary."

"See that it ain't." Luke backed off a step, but his posture didn't relax. "And what about your curse? What do you reckon to do then? Will you hold him to his duties and make him suffer the curse too?"

Alex stilled. In all the years of trying to find a way to avoid the curse, he hadn't given too much thought to what would happen if he couldn't avoid it. Would he and his father require the servants to stay and sleep until the end of time with them?

No, Alex couldn't ask that. Perhaps he'd ask for volunteers and make sure whole families stayed together whatever their decision. But no one should be forced to endure his curse. That was the double curse he already knew all too well.

This time, Alex could meet Luke's eyes and not flinch. "I promise that if I should fall prey to the curse, Jadon won't suffer it with me. He'll be released from his duties and may return here."

Some of the tension eased from Luke's shoulders. "Good. That's all I ask. I reckon we ought to catch up to the others."

Alex only nodded and followed when Luke set off down the trail once again.

That night, squished on the bench between Jadon and Luke, Alex dug into the buffalo roast. Instead of curbing his appetite, his part in hunting down this buffalo added a relish to the meal.

Never mind that he could barely lift his arm to bring his fork to his mouth. He'd taken several turns carrying one end of the poles on the hike back.

When had he ever had this sense of satisfaction back home? He couldn't recall any, except perhaps for the day when he'd convinced his father to allow daggers, axes, and knives back into the castle. He had taken pride in being intelligent enough to dissect the wording of his curse to find ways to avoid it.

But this was a different sort of pride. The kind of hard, physical work and aching muscles.

Perhaps, for all their rustic ways, these mountain folk did have something going for them. The ease they had with each other. The quiet confidence of knowing what they could accomplish with their own two hands. The laughter and smiles that filled this table.

When they left, Alex would take a piece of this moment with him. Somehow in the time he had left before his curse, he had to find a way for his family's table to be like this. Warm. Relaxed.

Happy.

ALEX HIKED along the trail spur leading down the mountain where it would eventually connect with the main trail to Castle Firlin. The pack on his back tugged on his shoulders with the extra supply of smoked buffalo meat, cutting into his shoulders.

He adjusted the straps, trying to make them sit more comfortably against his muscles.

"Would you like me to carry the pack, Your Highness?" Jadon's voice had gone back to a quiet, subservient tone.

After the last five days with Jadon's family, the tone grated. Alex tightened his grip on the straps and kept marching forward. "No, I'll carry it."

"My bruised ribs are fine now, Your Highness."

"I know." A week ago, Alex would've gladly handed over the pack, thinking it was only right that Jadon carry the full load. But now he could still feel Luke's staff jabbing him in the chest and his warnings in his ears.

Luke may have been partially right. Alex had been a mite arrogant at times. But he had just spent five days living in a backwoods cabin, sleeping on a straw tick on the floor, and eating who only knew what meat without complaint. And participated in a buffalo hunt and a few quaint farm chores while he was at it. He was vastly improved now, and he would show it by carrying this pack all the way to Castle Firlin.

Though, once the castle was in sight, he might have to transfer the full load back to Jadon. It wouldn't do to have the high prince show up at the doorstep of Buckhannock's king toting his own pack.

He could afford to be generous right now. It no longer sat right to stroll ahead like this, not after spending nearly five days treating Jadon as nearly an equal.

Alex halted and turned to Jadon.

Jadon stopped as well, his head bowed as it had been before they visited his family, his posture stiff. "Is there something you require, Your Highness?"

What did he require? Alex stared at the overcast sky, trying to put something of the knot in his chest into words. Was it guilt? Missing the closeness that Jadon shared with his brothers? The lack of family?

"You don't have to . . . just don't act like that. Not here. We're in the middle of the forest. It's ridiculous for you to keep acting like a manservant." Alex huffed out a breath. "You're more like a traveling companion. A bodyguard, maybe, if you can use a hardwood staff half as well on a person as you can on a buffalo."

"Are you sure?" Jadon raised his head, though his expression remained far too carefully blank. Such a practiced, servant's expression.

And it wasn't right. Not anymore.

"Look. I'm sick and tired of silence. Walk up here where I can talk to you without craning my neck all the time. It's uncomfortable." Alex pointed to the patch of ground next to him. "Do I have to make that an order?"

"No, sir." Jadon stepped forward to claim the spot on the path next to Alex.

Alex set off down the trail once again. This time Jadon kept pace with him. Seeing his easy stride and remembering the way Jadon's siblings had covered ground in a hurry on the buffalo hunt, Alex got the uncomfortable feeling that Jadon could have hiked the distance in far less time if he had been setting the pace instead of Alex.

Alex did his best to lengthen his stride. Wouldn't Mirabelle be impressed when he returned? He'd shed a few pounds around his middle. Stood a little leaner than he had before. And he'd helped hunt down a buffalo and lived to tell about it.

If he closed his eyes, he could picture the curve of her mouth as she smiled that coy little smile at him. That smile would grow and turn into a kiss or two once he was able to announce to her the curse had been lifted before it had a chance to occur.

Only a few more weeks. The queen's child would be born, and eight days later the Fae would come to give a gift. Once Alex gained an audience with the Fae, surely the Fae would lift the curse as soon as Alex explained the consequences of what would happen if the curse remained.

Alex cleared his throat. "When we get to Castle Firlin, I will probably have to wait for several weeks until the babe and then the Fae arrive. I'm sure King Othniel will be more than happy to provide me with any servants I might require. No need to have you stay. Once we arrive, you may return to your family for a few weeks. Just make sure you return to Castle Firlin in time to accompany me back to Castle Eyota."

Alex looked over at Jadon, only to realize Jadon had halted.

"Do you mean that?" Jadon swallowed and looked away.

Did Jadon doubt him that much? "Yes. We swung by your family just like I promised, didn't we? Now keep up. The sooner we get to Castle Firlin, the sooner you can return to your family."

Jadon trotted a few steps to join him once again. "Thank you, sir."

"Don't thank me. Use the time to convince your brother I'm not quite the arrogant prince he thinks I am." Alex shrugged, making the straps of his pack dig deeper into his shoulder muscles.

"I'll do that, sir."

Perhaps Alex would be able to sleep a little easier now, knowing Luke wasn't about to come after him on some dark night with a buffalo spear.

Still, to make sure that didn't happen, Alex had one more promise to make. "I've also decided that on my birthday, none of the servants will be required to remain in the castle unless they wish to do so and knowingly risk being cursed to sleep. I'll make sure my father signs a proclamation releasing all of you from your duties should the worst occur."

Alex had to swallow back a tightness in his throat. If he couldn't get the Fae to end this curse or if he couldn't figure out of a way to avoid it on his own, he wouldn't see his family again. They and he would sleep until the end of time—or perhaps until death. The wording "sleep like unto death for all time" was too vague to know for sure.

Either way, Alex would never marry Mirabelle. Never hold children or grow old. Never rule Tallahatchia. Never do anything for history to remember him except sleep.

Luke, for all his pushy ways, had been right about this. Even a high prince could not order—could not even ask—his servants to share that end with him. They all should be free to live and smile and laugh, from the lowliest scullery maids to the soldiers guarding his father's throne. None of them should be forced into this curse with him.

Surely the Fae would remove Alex's curse. The Lord of the Fae wouldn't allow a curse like this to ever happen. It was too horrible. Too unfair. Alex didn't deserve to have his life cut short like this.

Somewhere during Alex's thinking, he and Jadon had reached the main trail and turned toward Castle Firlin. They passed a few small settlements and even one that could almost count as a village.

A few miles from the village, the pounding of running feet came from farther up the trail.

Alex and Jadon stepped to the side as a king's runner dashed down the trail. Alex waved him down, and the runner halted, pacing to keep limber. Alex pointed the way the runner had come. "News from Castle Firlin?"

The runner nodded. "The queen's babe came early."

A lump settled in Alex's chest. "When? How long ago?"

"Four—no, five days ago. The way I was told it, the king waited to send the runners until he knew the babe would live. A girl. The queen's still doing poorly. Might not make it, they say."

The runner said something more about passing the message on to the outposts and the other kings and the high king, but Alex couldn't concentrate on the words.

Five days ago. The same day he and Jadon had turned off the main trail to visit Jadon's family.

That meant there were only three days until the Fae visited the child to bless her with a gift.

At the pace they had been traveling, it would've taken

them nearly four days to reach Castle Firlin. Too late. Alex struggled to breathe past the squeezing in his chest.

They couldn't be late. Too much hung on ending this curse.

With a final nod in their direction, the runner took off once again.

Jadon straightened his shoulders, his face a blank mask once again. "We had better get moving, Your Highness. Would you like me to set the pace?"

Alex could only nod.

CHAPTER 16

ROSANNA

As long as the bridges remain, Tallahatchia will never fall.

The mountains closed in tighter around the Grassy Lick Creek than they had around the broad Neskahana River. Shade from the overhanging trees covered the creek. Without the rush of so much water, the creek felt stiller, calmer than the broad stream even if it flowed faster.

As she climbed up the side of the gorge, Rosanna glanced over her shoulder at the twenty-foot waterfall pounding downward in waves of shining, frothing water to their left. The roar of tumbling water echoed around them, masking the sounds of their footfalls.

They'd left their canoes hidden behind the waterfall where the damp would keep them from drying out. Daemyn said he had a friend in Tuckawassee who would provide them with canoes once they reached there, a mere mountain ridge away.

Behind her, Nikan hiked under his own power, his left arm cradled to his stomach. Garmund and Otho carried Ahanu between them on a stretcher. He was conscious, but blood soaked the bandage wrapped around his leg above his knee.

Rosanna's calves and thighs burned as they climbed the steep, switchback trail up and out of the gorge. As they reached the top, the mountains fell away around them, peaks and valleys stretching on into the deep blue distance.

Isi blew out a breath. "It doesn't look like it will ever end. Like the entire world is mountains."

"There is other land out there. Deserts and plains and bodies of water so vast they are called oceans." Rosanna shook her head at the horizon ringed with forested peaks.

"I can't imagine it. How can an ocean be bigger than our mountains? I don't think I want to ever see that. It must be terrifying." Isi's breath came out harder. "Sometimes it seems like we will never reach Castle Eyota. We aren't even out of Neskahana yet."

"We'll reach it. Eventually." Rosanna tried to keep her own travel-weariness out of her voice. She'd longed for adventure. For the far distance mountains. But the reality of travel was harder than she'd expected. Not all of it. The thrill of the next bend, the awe of a new waterfall, that remained.

Still, it would've been nice to have been able to pause and breathe for a day. To have time to take in the new sights around her instead of skimming by them too fast to appreciate them.

She wasn't here to satisfy a longing for adventure. She had a duty. A destiny.

Daemyn reappeared on the trail in front of them, strolling toward them at a brisk, but unhurried pace. "No one ahead of us for a few miles. I didn't see any signs of recent travel, either. The Tuckawassee must be sticking to the larger trails."

Captain Degotaga nodded. "Very good."

Daemyn reclaimed a pack from one of the guards. Instead of strolling next to Captain Degotaga, he matched his stride to Rosanna's.

She wasn't sure why walking in stride with him felt so natural, as natural as matching her paddle stroke to his. "How much farther to Tuckawassee?"

"We'll be there tomorrow morning. The Cheyandoah Trace is just ahead, and we'll stay at Fort Last Chance tonight." Daemyn held a branch out of her way. "It's a small outpost. This isn't a high priority trail to protect. Too rough for a whole army to easily move through. The Cumber Gap to the south is your father's primary concern."

The Cumber Gap. The place her grandfather was killed fending off the Tuckawassee the last time the tensions flared into a fighting war.

The trail before them opened and leveled out, joining a broader trail than the one they had been on.

Daemyn reached a hand and pulled her up a large step formed by a gnarled root. "Welcome to the Cheyandoah Trace. Part of it, anyway."

Rosanna stepped onto the worn track, wiggling her toes in her moccasins as if she could feel the history soaked into that dirt. The Trace was flattened and hardpacked from hundreds of years of human and animal feet alike.

This trail had once been the jewel of Tallahatchia. The trail, the bridges, and the runners that traversed them, connected the seven kingdoms together. The rivers made them kingdoms, but this trail united them.

Within a few miles of hiking, the trail ended at the lip of a small gorge about thirty feet wide and as many feet deep. At its bottom, a creek bubbled over rocks in miniature waterfalls a few inches to a few feet high.

The stubs of two rotting posts were barely visible on this side of the gorge. The rope bridge that had once strung between them and the long-gone posts on the other side had rotted away decades ago. Even the boards were gone.

A thin trail, newer than the Trace, switchbacked down into the gorge, across the creek, and up the other side.

How much easier would it have been in those long past days when the bridges still stood? Travelers like her could've crossed that gorge in a few strides on a sturdy bridge instead of trekking down and back up while carrying their gear.

"The bridges must have been a sight to behold back then. We still have a few that my father and ancestors maintained in Neskahana, but it must have been amazing to cross all of Tallahatchia without ever descending below the tops of the mountains." Rosanna halted to close her eyes and try to imagine it.

"It was." Daemyn's voice was low, almost as if he was looking back into the past with her. When she glanced at him, he shrugged. "Or so I gather from the stories. It was the bridges the Pohatomie and Tuckawassee destroyed first, even before High Prince Alexander fell under his curse."

Would the high prince rebuild the bridges and Tallahatchia's unity when he was restored to his rightful throne? Or were the Seven Kingdoms too fractured, too broken for a high king to unite them any longer?

Daemyn glanced past her shoulder. "Go on after

Captain Degotaga, Princess." He strode around her and reached to steady Nikan. Nikan's face had paled. With only one hand and the blood loss, he'd struggle to navigate steep descent.

Isi grabbed Rosanna's arm and tugged her forward, following Captain Degotaga and Chogan. The rest of her guards trailed behind her.

When they were halfway down the gorge, Isi leaned closer. "Daemyn seemed to be awfully interested in talking today."

"He's our guide." Rosanna shook her head and glanced over her shoulder. Daemyn remained out of earshot, half-carrying Nikan. "Besides, I'm supposed to wake up High Prince Alexander. Doesn't that mean I'm his match or something like that? Waking him up with true love's kiss?"

"Don't see how you can do that if you've never met the man. Unless he looks terribly adorable in his sleep." Isi gave an exaggerated flutter of her eyes. "If that's the case, I might kiss him first."

"Go ahead." Rosanna slid the last few feet to the bottom. She balanced on the wet stones as she crossed the small creek. "Let's hope we survive long enough to have to worry about how to wake the high prince. Things are only going to get harder from here."

The grin dropped from Isi's face. "I know. But I'll get you through it."

What would history say about her quest years from now? Would she be a hero who saved her country? Or was she on a hopeless, last-ditch effort for a doomed nation before unending war consumed them all?

The fort's stockade silhouetted sharp against the orange sky as the sun set to the west. The figures of men with bows and arrows appeared between the sharpened points of the stockade's logs.

But beyond the stockade, a ridge stood against the sky. On the other side lay Tuckawassee.

As Captain Degotaga halted them in front of the gates, a voice boomed out. "State your business."

Daemyn stepped next to Captain Degotaga. "Daemyn Rand, requesting entrance for the night."

The men on the stockade stirred, and an order rang into the night. One of the two wooden gates swung open.

Captain Degotaga led the way inside. Rosanna stared up at the solid walls and the ranks of solemn men along the parapet. Fort Last Chance. The last outpost in Neskahana. Their final chance to stop an invasion if it came from here.

A stocky man with gray hair down to his shoulders clapped Daemyn on the shoulder. "Ar . . . Daemyn! Glad to see you made it here in one piece." The man peered past Daemyn and pointed at Isi. "That her? The promised princess?"

Wait, how did this man know about her? Mostly about her, anyway.

Daemyn's mouth twitched in his version of a smile. He steered the gray-haired man past Captain Degotaga, who had a hand on his long knife, and halted in front of Isi and Rosanna. Daemyn gestured to Rosanna. "Princess Rosanna, this is Captain Hezekiah Boda. Hezekiah, this is Princess Rosanna and her bodyguard Isi Degotaga."

Captain Boda bowed. "It's an honor."

"Pleased to meet you." Rosanna glanced from Captain Boda to Daemyn and raised her eyebrows.

"Captain Boda is a relative. He received the message I

sent from Castle Deeling." Daemyn leaned against his hardwood staff. "And when we leave tomorrow, he'll keep an eye on our back trail."

Something in her relaxed. After two weeks not knowing if Major Beshko followed them, they would have someone watching their backs. If all was well, Captain Boda would have nothing to report.

ROSANNA EYED the crest of the ridge in front of her, the border of Tuckawassee. Captain Degotaga and Daemyn strode in front of her without pausing, as if the thought of entering Tuckawassee didn't daunt them as it did her.

She had only four guards around her now, along with Isi, Captain Degotaga, and Daemyn. They'd left Nikan and Ahanu behind at Fort Last Chance.

Isi linked her arm through Rosanna's. "Together?"

Rosanna gave a firm nod. "Together."

They strode forward two steps, then three more, and crossed the mountain's crest. The mountains fell into the distance below them, the sharper peaks rising all around them with their tree-covered tips stretched toward the sky.

They were in Tuckawassee.

Shivers traced along Rosanna's spine and fingertips.

They hiked silently, faces tight, as if all smiles and laughter had been left behind at the border. Daemyn scouted the path ahead, moving with the wariness of a deer sensing the hunter's presence.

That night, they camped in a cluster of boulders near the headwaters of a small mountain creek that Daemyn said would lead them to the mighty Tuckawassee River as it carved its way down the mountains' sides.

As Rosanna gnawed on her supper of dried venison and even drier hard biscuits, a flash of light in the distance caught her eye. She stood, moving to where Daemyn leaned against a boulder at the edge of the circle. The light came again, from near the ridge they had crossed that morning. "What was that?"

"Hezekiah. Sending a message." Daemyn didn't take his eyes from the blinking light as he answered her. His mouth tightened as the light's random pattern continued. "He and his men spotted a band of eighteen Tuckawassee following our trail, led by a woman. He tried to delay them, but they got away."

"Major Beshko." Rosanna wrapped her arms around her stomach. She'd thought it would be better to know for sure, but was it? Or was it worse feeling the danger creeping closer behind them even as they strode deeper into the danger before them. "How far back?"

The flashing light ended in the darkness. Daemyn turned to her. "Not even a day. They're catching up."

Chapter 17

Alexander

One Hundred Years Ago

Alex gasped for breath as he and Jadon jogged as fast as they still could after their third day of rough travel. Castle Firlin perched next to a broad bend in the Buckhannock River. The castle was nothing more than a ten-foot-tall wall ringing a broad stretch of land filled mostly with wooden buildings and a single, tall stone tower.

At this time of night, a few hours past midnight the morning of the new princess's eighth day, the massive wooden gates were locked tight, though due to the day, the guards were alert and pacing as if they could stop the Fallen Fae's curse on their princess through their watchfulness.

Alex could've told them it would do no good. His parents had stationed guards in the room with them from midnight on. Still he'd been cursed.

As he and Jadon skidded to a halt in the torchlight in front of the gate, the guards pointed their spears and bows and arrows down at him. The guard in the center brandished his spear. "Leave. This castle is closed tight for the night."

For the first time since they'd left Castle Eyota, Alex withdrew his signet ring from the underneath his shirt, untied it from the leather cord, and slipped it onto his finger. The sapphire in its center shone even in the low light of the torches. His mission was at an end. Now was not the time to hide his identity.

Alex raised his hand for them to see the ring. "I am High Prince Alexander of Kanawhee, son of High King Atohi of the Seven Kingdoms of Tallahatchia. I demand that you give me entrance."

The guard peered down at him. "How do I know you're the high prince? Just because you're flashing a fancy ring at me doesn't mean anything."

"It will to your seneschal. It's his job to recognize my signet ring and seal." Alex huffed out a breath. The guards probably should be complimented on their diligence, but he didn't have the time or the patience to deal with them at the moment. "I order you to fetch him at once and to give us entrance while we wait. At best, you will have given the hospitality due your high prince. At worst, you will have a rabble-rouser you can throw into the dungeons. Do you wish to risk my wrath if I am who I say I am just on the small chance I might not be?"

It was so obvious. Even with the guard's lesser intelligence compared to Alex's own, the man really should've seen it long before this.

The guard scowled. "All right. You may enter while I send men for the seneschal."

When the gate was cracked open, Alex strode inside, his head high. He didn't bother checking to see if Jadon followed. Of course he did, once again carrying all their packs.

They were shown a bench where they could sit and wait. Alex sat, but he couldn't help tapping his foot. Yes, it was the middle of the night, but surely the seneschal would jump to respond when he heard who was at the gates.

Finally, the guard returned, leading a small, wiry man with thinning hair. Though small, the man carried himself and his weapons with an easy confidence.

Alex stood and held the hand with his signet ring up for the seneschal to inspect. "I am High Prince Alexander."

"Hmm . . . yes. I suppose you are. The ring is right." The seneschal eyed him. "You realize it's the middle of the night. And not a good time for our king. His wife died yesterday, and the new princess will be cursed before today is out."

Alex hadn't come all this way to be lectured by a lowly seneschal. "I know. But this is of utmost importance. I don't even have to speak with your king. I came to speak with the Fae who will gift a blessing to your princess. It can't wait. I don't know when I will have another chance to find a Fae."

"No, I suppose not. They don't exactly come and go at the beck and call of us mortals, even for kings." The seneschal cocked his head. "I'll lead you to our princess. But I warn you. We're all very loyal to her and to our king. If you do anything that threatens them, I won't hesitate to respond in kind, high prince or no."

What was in the rivers up here in Buckhannock that so many citizens from the mountain peasants to the castle seneschal were willing to threaten the high prince to his face? It really was astounding. If Alex hadn't been in such a hurry, he would've pursued the matter further. Perhaps he still might, once he returned to Castle Eyota free of his curse and with an abundance of time to deal with insubordination.

But right now, the minutes were ticking by. For all he knew, the Fae had already come, given a gift, and left.

"I understand." Alex strode forward to force the seneschal to start walking.

The seneschal made some sort of humming, huffing sound and took his place in the lead with a few quick steps. He led the way, turning toward a row of the cottages along the outer wall instead of the tower. Probably another precaution as the king tried to prevent his newborn daughter from receiving a curse.

A burst of something—a deeper darkness—came from one of the cottages. Shouts. A flare of torchlight that did little to pierce blackness.

The seneschal raced forward, drawing his dagger as he ran.

Alex ran after him, though he didn't bother with his dagger. If it was the Fallen Fae delivering the expected curse, weapons wouldn't do any good. Somewhere behind him, he could hear Jadon's footsteps, but he didn't look. All that mattered was getting to that cottage in time for the Fae's gift.

He burst inside at the seneschal's heels. They were just in time to see a blur of darkness swirl and vanish. A stocky man with a crown perched on his black, curly hair rocked a baby in his arms, crying as if he didn't care who saw their king openly sobbing.

Alex probably should go to the king, ask about the curse, or something like that. But, not yet. Instead, he scanned the room. He didn't see the Fae here. Maybe he wasn't too late.

Then, the Fae was there in a luminescent glow that seemed to emanate from the Fae's clothes and skin. The Fae's form was enough like a woman for Alex to think of her as she, though the Fae was so much beyond human that she wasn't female the way a human woman was.

Her skin was gold as the sun, her eyes like the warm coals glowing on a winter's day. But most stunning were the crystal wings spreading behind her, many pairs of them. They were shaped like a butterfly's wings, translucent like a dragonfly's, but etched with patterns more intricate and delicate than the most pristine snowflake.

He stepped forward, but the seneschal halted him with his spear. "Wait until after the princess has been given her gift."

Alex swallowed back his impatience. The sobbing king probably could use some hope after the week he'd had, but Alex had been living with his curse for nearly twenty-one years. He needed it gone, and he needed it gone now.

The Fae's voice was a golden whisper, too soft for Alex to hear what the gift was, though the king stopped weeping.

The Fae turned away from the king and the babe in his arms.

"Wait." Alex shoved the seneschal's spear out of the way and dashed forward. "I must speak with you."

The Fae halted in a corner. With everyone rushing forward to surround the king and princess, the corner was as private as it could get in this tiny cottage.

Alex couldn't look the glowing Fae in the face, so he stared at the log corner post instead. "I need you to remove my curse."

Warmth bathed his face from the Fae's light. "To remove your curse is beyond my power. I am but a messenger. I speak only what I am given." Her voice was a whisper with all the power of a waterfall.

"Please. You have to try. I can't fall asleep forever just because of some evil Fae's whim." Alex nearly grabbed the Fae's arm but stopped himself. Something told him he wasn't allowed to touch, even a sleeve.

"A whim of one of the Fallen ones, yes, but still the Highest King's plan."

Alex didn't understand. If this was some plan, then why must he sleep? It wasn't fair. "Why? Why didn't that Fae just curse me with death and be done with it?"

"That is not a power they possess, for they do not have the authority to decide when life ends here and begins beyond." Only the warmth in the Fae's tone kept Alex's anger from boiling out of his chest and into words. When he finally glanced up at the Fae, the fiery eyes were somehow sad. "They are the Restless ones. True rest is denied them, so they turn even sleep into a curse."

If this Fae couldn't end his curse, then was he doomed to sleep until the world ended?

No, he wouldn't allow that to happen. There had to be a way he could end it before it even began. "Are you sure you can't even try?" Surely if the Fallen Fae had the power to unleash a curse, a Loyal Fae could undo it.

"Only the Lord of the Fae has the power to give and to take. I am but a messenger. I speak only what I am given, even now."

Alex drew himself straighter. If this Fae wouldn't help him, then he would go to the Lord of the Fae himself and demand that he remove Alex's curse. "Then I will go to the Fae land. How do I get there?"

A soft smile illuminated the Fae's golden face. "You will find the entrance to Beyond in the heart of the water's veil.

The breeze—the breath that created all breezes—will guide you."

What did that mean? Alex glanced over his shoulder at Jadon. Could this Fae get any more cryptic?

When Alex turned back to ask for more answers, the Fae was gone. No warning. No flash. Just gone.

Alex blew out a breath. That was a waste of time.

If only he could storm out of that cottage and be done with the place. But as the high prince, it was his duty to at least attempt to offer some comfort to King Othniel.

Alex strode to King Othniel, glaring the king's guards and seneschal out of his way.

King Othniel glanced up from the baby in his arms, but he stared at Alex with such a blank expression in his eyes Alex wasn't sure the king understood whom he was seeing.

Alex tipped his head in a respectful gesture. "I am sorry for your loss."

King Othniel blinked. "Who are you?"

Alex straightened and held out his hand. The sapphire in his signet ring flashed in the candlelight. "I am High Prince Alexander." When the king's expression didn't change beyond the blank stare, Alex added, "I came here seeking a removal of my curse by the Loyal Fae."

King Othniel sprang to his feet and gripped Alex's sleeve with one hand, his other arm still cradling his daughter. "Please tell me there's hope. Tell me."

Alex glanced around the room, but none of King Othniel's men moved to dislodge their desperate king's fingers from Alex's sleeve. How dare the king lay a hand on him. He was the high prince. He should order the man to unhand him and yank his arm free.

But something in King Othniel's eyes stopped him.

This king had lost his wife. He'd had his daughter cursed moments ago, and the curse must be a terrible one. If there was one thing Alex knew, it was the weight of a curse.

Alex rested a hand on King Othniel's shoulder and steered him back into his chair. "What is the princess's curse?"

King Othniel released Alex's arm and stroked a finger across his daughter's cheek. "The moment her teeth bite into an apple, she will fall into a sleep like unto death."

What was it with the Fallen Fae and sleep? "Was that the whole curse?"

King Othniel nodded.

A curse much like his own, though perhaps even worse. No specific day mentioned. No hope of her father sleeping with her. Her curse could strike at any moment, snatching her away.

And apples were common, grown in abundance to the northwest in Pohatomie and traded throughout all Tallahatchia.

When King Othniel met Alex's gaze, tears pooled in his eyes. "My daughter is my heart. She's all I have left. Please. Tell me there's a way I don't have to lose her."

Alex opened his mouth, but words wouldn't come. Did he have any hope to offer King Othniel? He'd been so sure the Fae would remove his curse, but that hope had been dashed. Now there was only the Fae's cryptic instructions and his own determination.

"I don't know." Those weren't words he'd said often. Not with his superior intelligence. "But I'm not giving up hope. I'm going to keep seeking to remove my curse. You'll know if I succeeded on my birthday." Alex straightened, spun on his heels, and marched from the cottage.

He halted in the castle's lawn to wait for Jadon. Far

above, the stars twinkled and glittered, as if reminding him that they would continue to coldly, heartlessly shine regardless of whether he slept or lived.

Jadon stopped next to him. "Where to now?"

"I don't know." Annoying words to have to utter twice in as many minutes. Alex stared at the black shapes of the mountains rising around the castle. "I think the water's veil means a waterfall, but there are thousands of waterfalls in Tallahatchia. I don't have time to check each one for an entrance to the Fae's land. And how do I follow the wind? It makes no sense."

"Perhaps we have to trust the words and follow them before they make sense." Jadon held his hand out, fingers splayed, as if he felt a breeze, even on this utterly still night.

"You aren't making sense either. Give me a minute, and I'll figure something out." Alex squeezed his eyes shut. With enough time, he could think his way out of any problem.

Something stirred the dust in front of his boots. At first, he didn't feel anything. Then the whisper's touch of a breeze grazed his face.

The breeze built around him, whirling, swirling, cutting through him until it shoved with such force he couldn't resist taking a step forward. To the west.

Which made no sense. The prevailing winds, the strong winds like this one, came out of the west heading east. But this breeze was coming from the east headed west.

Alex hiked his pack higher on his back. Follow the breeze.

Apparently, they were headed west.

Chapter 18

Rosanna

Rosanna scanned the trees around them as she trotted to keep up with Captain Degotaga's pace. As they pressed deeper into Tuckawassee, the landscape had changed to lower mountains, swampier forests. More sycamore with their scaly bark dotted the forest with only scattered maple and beech. The oaks were broader and scragglier instead of tall and straight.

But the forest remained no less dense or old, still filled with shadows.

The hair on the back of Rosanna's neck prickled, as if she could sense Major Beshko behind her. Her back muscles tensed as if expecting an arrow at any moment.

Daemyn was somewhere behind them, scouting their back trail. How far behind was Major Beshko? Would they be able to outrun the Tuckawassee hunting them?

The muscles in Rosanna's legs burned. She couldn't think about the danger. She had to concentrate on the next step. The next gasp of air into her lungs.

Captain Degotaga lifted a hand, signaling them to a halt. "Ten minute rest. Grab something to eat and drink."

Rosanna leaned her hands on her knees. The straps of her pack dug into her shoulders, the muscles there cramping, but she didn't dare take the pack off. She wasn't sure she'd put it back on when their rest was over.

Isi stopped next to her, a hand on her waist. "I'm in good shape, but not this good."

"Me either." Rosanna sank onto a log, drank water from her canteen, and pulled out her pouch of dried meat and fruit. After she popped a handful in her mouth, she held the pouch out to Isi.

Isi pinched some for herself. "I'm really getting sick of this stuff. What I wouldn't give for fresh meat. A nice venison steak. And freshly baked biscuits."

Rosanna gnawed on her own bite of the dried meat. It had been a novelty, living off what they could carry in their canoes or backs, a few weeks ago. But now? Yes, she'd love a fresh, juicy side of meat. Warm bread. Fresh preserves. "It might be a while. I don't think Castle Eyota has much in the way of fresh food considering all of the people inside have been asleep for nearly a hundred years."

Isi heaved a sigh. "Don't dash my hopes. I need something to look forward to. You have your handsome, sleeping prince. I need a nice steak."

Rosanna shook her head. Something in her eased, even if she couldn't smile. "He isn't *my* prince. I'm just supposed to wake him up. That's it."

She found her gaze straying toward the stand of forest where Daemyn had gone. Why did Isi's teasing make her look for him? She wasn't thinking about him that way. She couldn't. Now wasn't the time to start developing feelings for anyone. Daemyn, High Prince Alexander. No one. She had a duty to perform, and she had to concentrate on doing it.

Footfalls crunched in the forest. Captain Degotaga and the other guards whirled.

Daemyn jogged toward them and skidded to a halt. Something in his stance had Rosanna jumping to her feet, her stomach sinking.

Daemyn leaned on his staff. "They're gaining on us."

They weren't going to outrun them. The Tuckawassee were a raiding party. They trained to jog for miles over rough country. Her guards weren't trained to fight like that, nor were she and Isi.

Captain Degotaga's expression didn't change from hard lines and harder eyes. "Ditch the tents, the camping supplies. Take only the basics. Food and water only. Let's get moving."

Rosanna dumped her pack, groaning at the relief on her aching back and shoulders. She pulled out her canteen and the pouch of dried meat. Nothing else mattered.

Daemyn led the way into the forest. This time, they weren't following a portage trail but set off into the trackless trees.

Rosanna tried not the trip over the raised, gnarled roots and the uneven clods of dirt. Branches scratched her face and tugged at her hair. Sweat trickled between her shoulder blades and under her hairline.

The slope steepened. Rosanna panted for breath. She was in good shape, but not good enough to run miles and miles without rest, even freed from the weight of her pack.

They weren't going to make it.

Shouting broke out in the forest behind them. Distant crashing, growing closer.

"We have to split up." Daemyn slowed to a fast walk as he glanced over his shoulder at Captain Degotaga.

Captain Degotaga shot a look behind them, his mouth pressing into a thin line, and nodded.

"Scatter and try to lose them. Head for the convergence of the Nanahootchie Creek and the Tuckawassee River. A relative of mine will be there." Daemyn gripped his hardwood staff. "I'll take Princess Rosanna."

"But the princess . . ." Captain Degotaga stepped closer to Isi and glanced from her to Rosanna, something pained in his eyes. His warring responsibilities must be tearing through him.

Rosanna couldn't ask Captain Degotaga to put her safety before Isi's. Not in this. Right now, his first concern should be his daughter, not his duty. "I'll be safe with Daemyn."

With his skill in the forest, she was probably safest with him.

Captain Degotaga put his arm around Isi's shoulders. "All right."

Isi patted her father's hand, her face tighter and harder than Rosanna had ever seen it. "We'll buy you time. If the Tuckawassee see me, they'll think I'm the princess. We can lead them away from you."

"Isi, no. You can't do that. Not for me." Rosanna shook her head.

"I'm your servant and your bodyguard. This is what I've trained to do." Isi's eyes had a sheen to them, as if she believed this might cost her life.

Rosanna halted and pulled Isi in for a hug. "No. You're not my servant. You're my friend. You hear me? My *friend*. And you're not allowed to die, understand?"

Isi squeezed her back. "Don't you die either."

The shouting and crashing brush was growing louder. Louder. They were wasting too much time, hugging and saying goodbyes, when they should run.

But if Isi died, Rosanna would regret not taking this time. If she couldn't she certain she would ever see her friend again, she had to be certain there was nothing left to be said between them.

Isi stepped back and gripped her father's hand. She met Rosanna's gaze and nodded once. A solemn farewell.

Chogan and Ilma held hands as they prepared to scatter. Otho and Garmund gripped their long knives, as if they intended to turn and attack the Tuckawassee regardless of being outnumbered eighteen to two.

With one last salute to Captain Degotaga and a bow to Rosanna, the guards she had grown up with as they paddled their canoes beside hers for so many years dashed into the forest. Toward the Tuckawassee.

With one last glance, Captain Degotaga and Isi spun on their heels and ran. Also toward the Tuckawassee.

Rosanna's throat squeezed so tightly she could barely breathe. She turned to Daemyn, and he held out a hand.

This was the moment she wasn't supposed to waste her friends' and guards' sacrifices. She should gain as much distance as possible to make their sacrifice worth it.

It wouldn't be worth it. Her life wasn't worth such loss.

But she placed her hand in Daemyn's, and together, they sprinted deeper into the mountains.

CHAPTER 19

ALEXANDER

ONE HUNDRED YEARS AGO

lex jogged along a mountain trail, the breeze stirring the pine needles at his feet and an ever steady pressure on his back.

It was a strange breeze that led them, though somehow familiar. He'd felt it on the day he'd decided to leave to end his curse and every day on the trail. This breeze never left, even when the leaves on the trees around them remained still and the air didn't stir.

How many days they'd been running, he didn't know. They halted at night and slept, but beyond that, they ran. They ran farther and longer, beyond what he would've thought his own endurance.

They saw no one else, the path they ran unknown, though their feet knew every stone, every root, even if their eyes didn't.

On and on they ran. They'd left Buckhannock, of that much Alex was certain. But whether they were in Monongadotte or in some wild land beyond, he didn't know or care.

He should care. He wasn't sure how they'd find their way home. But while the breeze stirred his hair and guided his feet, his home at Castle Eyota remained too far away to matter, as though his home lay in front of him instead of behind.

The torrent of wind they'd followed for days ceased.

Alex stumbled at the change in pressure at his back. He blinked and drew in a breath, as if he'd woken from a deep sleep filled with untold, golden dreams, and now had to remember what reality looked like.

Jadon blinked and turned in a slow circle. "Is this it?"

A creek lay in front of them, about ten feet across. Alex couldn't tell how deep it was for, instead of the clear waters of most streams in Tallahatchia, this creek's water flowed a strange, bright turquoise the same color as a robin's egg.

The back of his neck prickled. Water wasn't supposed to be that color. What was this place?

The trees and undergrowth along the banks waved leaves in an unnaturally bright green. Pink and purple flowers winked among all the green, though it was surely too early in the spring for such flowers.

But Alex didn't see a waterfall.

The breeze stirred for a moment, waving the thick grass around their moccasins toward downstream.

Alex turned and strode along the creek, his gaze fixed on the luminous water. The bank down to the creek steepened the farther they went, and he and Jadon stuck to the ridge of earth above. The greenery grew so thick Alex sometimes lost sight of the creek for a few strides.

A noise murmured ahead. Not the roar of a large waterfall, but the rush of a smaller falls. The greenery parted enough to reveal a foot-high tumble of the turquoise water, frothing white.

But the breeze didn't stop, stirring the foliage farther downstream.

The farther Alex walked, with Jadon trotting at his heels, the more vibrant the water became, as if the source of the odd coloring came from downstream, an impossibility for a flowing creek such as this.

Again, the rush of a waterfall came from in front of them, louder, more insistent this time.

Was this the right waterfall? Alex's heart thumped into his throat. Today might be the day he stood before the Lord of the Fae and demanded an end to his curse.

It had seemed so simple in that cottage in Buckhannock. But seeing this unnatural water and having run with the power of the wind, he wasn't as sure.

Through the brush, the waterfall became visible. Water tumbled four feet over a line of stones now more orange than the tan they'd been at the first waterfall.

But this time too, the breeze didn't stop.

Alex kept going. Surely this creek had to be the right one. He'd come too far and done too much to admit defeat now. He would follow this creek to its end if he had to.

As they rounded a bend, he heard a third waterfall. Not muted this time, but a roar.

He hurried forward and halted at the edge of a small gorge. A thirty-foot-tall waterfall plunged white and frothing down into a pool of brightest turquoise.

And the breeze, finally, had gone still.

"This has to be it." Alex found a narrow ledge of dirt and inched along it down the gorge. The trail widened after the first few yards as it zigzagged down the face of the gorge between rocks and trees.

The trail ended at the bottom behind a large boulder that blocked most of the waterfall from view. Alex scrambled around the boulder and found himself on a flat, muddy bank on one side of the pool. Bright orange rocks and boulders lined the pool and tumbled along the sides of the waterfall, a sharp contrast against the green undergrowth and vivid water.

Despite the tightness in his chest driving him forward, this place demanded he stop and stare for a minute to take it in. The forest, the mountains, the rivers always had a living stillness about them, but nothing like the life flowing here.

Jadon set his pack on the ground, knelt on one of the orange boulders, and dipped his fingers in the water as if transfixed by the stillness of this place, a quiet solemnity even with the waterfall's roar.

Alex half-expected Jadon's fingers to turn to diamond or gold. Water like that couldn't be of this earth. But nothing happened.

"I think this is it." Alex whispered the words, though a whisper wasn't necessary. They were alone, except for the *presence* of this place.

He let his pack fall to the riverbank next to Jadon's. Where was the entrance to the Fae land? Was it behind the waterfall?

The rocks along the shore pressed too tightly around the falls for him to circle behind it on land. Alex touched the water. Cold. Frigid, even. It wouldn't be a pleasant swim.

He waded into the pool. His moccasins protected his feet from the sharp edges of the orange rocks filling the pool's bottom, but the buckskin quickly squished and filled with icy water. When the water reached his knees, a shiver raced through his body.

Bracing himself, he dove forward, getting all but his

head wet as he launched himself into a swimming stroke. The cold tore through his buckskin shirt, wrapping around his skin.

He crossed the pool in three long strokes and pulled himself onto a jumble of boulders next to the falls. One boulder lay completely submerged at the base of the falls, and he could stand on it with only his feet wet to the ankles. Leaning forward, he stuck his hand into the torrent of water gushing down from above.

Nothing happened. No tingles shooting up his arm besides shivers. No door opening in the water.

He climbed around to the back of the falls and felt the cliff's stone face. Just rock. He examined the boulders, but nothing appeared to be an entrance to anything bigger than a snake or a rodent den.

With a shiver, he returned to the boulders at the base of the waterfall. This didn't make sense. Why had the Fae sent him here if there wasn't an entrance after all? Had it been a trick?

Jadon had waded knee-deep into the pool. Alex waved him over. "Help me look."

Jadon grimaced and plunged into the water. He paddled over, and Alex helped him onto the boulder. Together, they searched behind the waterfall once again. The stones were cool and slick with water and algae beneath Alex's fingers.

No secret latches clicked. Nothing moved. No bright flashes of light.

Alex sat on a boulder next to the waterfall, held out his hand, and let the foaming water run through his fingers. His wet shirt and trousers clung to his skin and dripped onto the stone. The breeze had left, thankfully, or he'd be shivering worse than he already was.

He had to think. Where would the Fae hide the entrance to their land? He must be able to find it. Alex flicked the water from his hand. "It has to be here."

"Where do you think the heart of the waterfall is?" Jadon sat with his feet dangling in the water.

This was what Alex did best. Think. Answer riddles. He squeezed his eyes shut and let out a long breath. What would be the heart of a waterfall? Was it the place where it tumbled over the edge? Or the water as it tumbled through the air? Or . . .

He leaned forward and studied the white foam where the water from the falls stabbed into to the pool with a wild confluence. That was the heart, where the water plunged and roiled and thundered with all its power.

But entering there would be dangerous. At that point, the waterfall created a powerful undertow. A large waterfall could pin a man to the bottom with a force too strong for him to fight, drowning him.

"I think we have to go down there." Alex swallowed and stood on the boulder at the base of the falls, his toes curling at the frigid water.

Jadon glanced from him, to the waterfall, and back. He straightened his shoulders, his face blank. "I see. I'll go first, sir, to scout. No need for you to risk yourself."

A few months ago, Alex might have ordered Jadon into such a danger without a second thought. But now, there was Luke's poking staff and the miles of travel stopping Alex from giving such an order lightly any longer.

Perhaps it would've been wiser to send Jadon first. He was the servant. But if there was an entrance to the Fae land, then Alex didn't want to wait. "No, I'll go. You follow and get ready to pull me out if you have to."

Jadon nodded and braced himself against the boulder

as if preparing to yank Alex from the waterfall's grasp if need be.

Alex eyed the waterfall's plummeting deluge until its thunder resonated in his bones. With a deep breath, he jumped.

The water swallowed him in a chaos of foam and confused currents. It pounded against his chest, driving him downward so quickly he couldn't tell how deep the pool went.

This hadn't been a good idea. The roar, the strength, the pummeling all gripped him too tightly. He could die down here, searching in vain for an entrance that didn't exist.

His feet, then his back struck the bottom and shot pain up his spine. Water, with power the likes of which he'd never known before, pressed him to the pebbles beneath as if it never intended to let him go.

Was he going to die down here? His lungs hurt with the pounding water and the need for breath. He peeled his eyes open, but the water stung. All whirled in explosions of bubbles and silt.

The entrance. He had to find it. Struggling against the force pinning him to the bottom, he felt about him, searching for something besides water and rock. Wiggling a few feet, he stretched to search more. His lungs ached for breath.

As he shifted a few more feet, the water caught him again, whipping him upward on the outflow. His shoulder bashed into a boulder, then he popped out at the surface, pressed against the boulder where Jadon stood.

Jadon helped him out of the water. "Are you all right?"

Alex coughed and gasped in a breath. "I think so." He groaned. His shoulder, his back, his head all hurt. "That was even worse than I thought it might be. And I didn't find it. I'm not sure it's down there."

Jadon glanced at the waterfall and sighed. "I'll try."

Alex shook his head. "No. The current is too strong. I only made it out by accident."

"There has to be a way. The Fae said we'd find entrance here." Jadon tensed, as if prepared to cast himself into the waterfall despite Alex's order.

"I am the only way to enter there."

Alex jerked at the sound of a stranger's voice. He glanced up to see a man sitting on the boulder next to the falls. The stranger looked like a man, but there was something about him. Something *more*. "Are you the gatekeeper or something?"

"I have been called the gatekeeper, but I am also the gate."

This stranger was probably Fae, then, based on how cryptic he was being. Some Fae guardian of this pool or something like that. It would've been helpful if he'd shown up before Alex had nearly drowned himself trying to get to the gate. "Well, then, if you could open the entrance?"

The stranger waded into the frothing water near the falls. "You can only enter by me."

Jadon held the stranger's gaze for a moment. Then he stepped forward as if he was willing to follow this stranger to his death at the bottom of this waterfall without question. The stranger gripped Jadon's arm.

Alex eyed the pool. Did he dare follow this stranger into that turbulent water? What if he decided to drown them? They didn't know anything about him.

The stranger held out his hand. "Come." There was something of a command in that word, for all the mildness of his tone.

The breeze, so still a moment ago, swirled up from the pool behind Alex and cut through his wet clothes into his chest.

What did Alex have to lose, really? He had come all this way to end his curse. If he failed and returned with his curse still hovering over him, he might fall into a death-like sleep. Or he could die here and now.

Or, maybe, this stranger was telling the truth, and he would open the way into the Fae's land.

Aided by the breeze at his back, Alex stepped forward.

The stranger grasped his arm.

Before Alex even had time for a decent breath, the stranger dragged him and Jadon into the waterfall's heart. The water surged around Alex even more powerfully than before, shoving and slamming as the gatekeeper dragged them down.

Alex waited for them to strike the bottom. He counted two heartbeats, then two more. Surely he had struck bottom before now last time.

He peeled his eyes open and squinted past the sting of the water. All he could see was turquoise water going down into depths. The surging bubbles and crossing currents tore away all sense of direction until they almost seemed to be going upward when he knew for a fact they were still being dragged deeper.

His lungs ached. His chest squeezed. How much farther? Where was the bottom of this pool?

The pressure built. His lungs spasmed, and he had to fight to keep from gagging in a mouthful of water.

He was going to drown. This was no gatekeeper. He was going to kill them both.

Alex flailed, trying to break free of the stranger's iron grip on his arm. Next to him, Jadon remained still, as if trusting this stranger was the gatekeeper and not the bearer of death.

Alex couldn't break free. The water and the stranger held him too tightly. His chest heaved with his lungs' need to draw in breath. His head buzzed and swirled until he couldn't think. He couldn't think, and they were both going to die in the seemingly bottomless deep of this waterfall.

His arms and legs were too heavy. He couldn't find the strength to fight, to move. Unable to resist any longer, he gave in and opened his mouth for a lungful of water.

But instead of darkness, light crowded in at the edge of his vision, growing brighter and brighter until it swallowed him.

CHAPTER 20

ROSANNA

She choked on each breath. Her heart thundered in her ears. Too close. The Tuckawassee were too close. Her legs weren't strong enough. Her gasping lungs wouldn't hold out.

Her hand in Daemyn's grew hot, sweaty, but she didn't let go. He didn't either, as if by his grip on her he could save them both.

He couldn't. She slowed him down.

They were running downhill now. Ahead lay a small waterfall and creek set in a hollow too peaceful for the danger stalking their heels.

Daemyn jerked her to the right. "Over here." He led her to a section of boulders just below the hollow's rim. Moving aside a fallen log, Daemyn exposed a small nook created by a crack in a boulder. It would be barely big enough for Rosanna, if she curled up small. "Get in."

She didn't question him. The dirt and leaves in the nook pressed damp against her hands and knees. She couldn't think about the spiders or rodents or snakes that might inhabit a place like this. Sitting with her back to the stone and her knees tucked against her chest, she fit.

Daemyn crouched and met her gaze. "Whatever happens, don't move. Don't make a sound. Stay here. I'll be back for you. It might take a while, but I will come back."

How could he be so sure? "What if they kill you?"

His mouth quirked at one corner. "I'm rather hard to kill, as they'll soon learn. Don't worry. I'll come back for you. Please promise you'll stay here."

She nodded. "I promise."

He pulled the straight-bladed, old-fashioned dagger from his belt. After taking the clear-stoned ring from his finger, he held both the ring and the dagger out to her. "Take care of these for me, all right?"

She took them. Why was he giving these to her? He had seemed so sure he wouldn't be killed, yet giving her the ring and dagger seemed like he thought he would be. It didn't make sense.

But Daemyn didn't have time to waste explaining to her. "Be careful."

With a nod, he moved the log back into place and scattered dead leaves and fallen twigs across it until only a few shafts of sunlight pierced through. From the outside, he must be making it appear as if that log had been undisturbed for years.

The rustle of leaves and scuffing of his feet moved off slowly. Rosanna leaned forward to peer through one of the remaining gaps.

Daemyn smoothed the leaves and twigs where they'd left the trail, then he barreled down the rest of the trail to the creek in a rush, leaving enough disturbed leaves and skid marks in the dirt to look like at least two people had come through.

When he reached a broad, flat stone beside the creek, he turned and planted his staff as if forming a wall the Tuckawassee wouldn't be able to knock down.

What was Daemyn doing? Shouldn't he be trying to outrun the Tuckawassee? Use the creek to hide his tracks and get away? Instead, he looked like he intended to fight the Tuckawassee armed with nothing but a stick.

Thumping feet crashed over the rim of the hollow. "There he is!"

Something zipped through the air.

Daemyn doubled over, an arrow protruding from his stomach.

Rosanna pressed both hands over her mouth and leaned back from the peephole. But only for a moment. She couldn't stop herself from peeking out again, even knowing she was about to watch Daemyn die to protect her.

Daemyn was straightening. With a grimace, he yanked the arrow out as if in complete disregard of the internal damage he might inflict to himself and tossed it aside. Blood flowed down his buckskin shirt and dripped onto the stone below him, but he stayed standing, his staff gripped in both hands now.

"I want him alive." The woman's voice rang with authority. A voice Rosanna had heard once before on the banks of the Neskahana. Major Beshko. "We need him to tell us where the princess has gone."

The crashing footsteps came toward her hiding place from above. Rosanna pressed herself against the stone away from the gaps and the peepholes in case one of them should glance in this direction. She couldn't give away her position. Not when Daemyn was out there now, bleeding and probably dying to keep her hidden.

When the crashing disappeared past her, Rosanna eased forward again to peer out. The Tuckawassee circled Daemyn. There were nine of them. Four had bows with arrows nocked while another four held their long knives ready.

The last one, Major Beshko, strode down the slope, one hand resting on the knife on her belt. The gold strands in her curly, black braid winked in the afternoon sunlight. Her buckskin shirt and leggings were neat, even after the long trek from Neskahana.

They wouldn't get away this time. That sank deep into Rosanna's chest. Major Beshko had tracked them too far to let them slip through her grasp now.

"You won't get her. I won't let you past me." Daemyn held his staff steady, his body tensed for battle.

"She went down the river past you, did she? Hoping to hide her tracks." Major Beshko shook her head, her thick black hair puffing around her head. "How far do you really think she'll get on her own?"

Even now, Daemyn led the Tuckawassee off course. Even if he died right where he was, the Tuckawassee would search for her downstream while she hid here. Something in her chest warmed, even as her fingers grew chilled.

"Far enough. If I buy her enough time." Daemyn glared at Major Beshko as if he intended to not just fight all eight men but defeat them.

"You won't." Major Beshko paced back and forth. It wasn't the worried sort of pacing. More the sort of pacing done subconsciously while talking. "Do you know how long I've been hunting you, Daemyn Rand? I hunted your father before you, though his demise wasn't of my doing, more's the pity."

"If I remember right, both my father and I defeated you several times before." For someone whose blood pooled on the stone beneath his feet, Daemyn's voice and stance remained rock-steady. "You won't succeed this time, either."

Major Beshko's posture didn't change, as if bored. "We'll see."

She gave one flick of her hand.

Daemyn stepped forward before the Tuckawassee archers could lift their bows. He parried a knife with one end of the staff and whipped the other into a Tuckawassee's face. Blood gushed from the man's nose, and he stumbled backwards even as Daemyn punched the hardwood into another Tuckawassee's stomach.

Spinning on his heel, Daemyn cracked the staff down on a Tuckawassee's arm as the man prepared to stab him, then whipped it around with a whir of air against wood. It connected with a sharp crack against the Tuckawassee's shin. The man howled and dropped his knife as he collapsed.

Before that man fell, Daemyn's staff took a fifth man, one of the archers, under his chin, laying him out with the others.

Rosanna drew in a breath, her thumping heart loud in the confined space. Was it possible Daemyn could survive this?

Major Beshko tilted her head and waved in Daemyn's direction. Her face remained smooth, unchanging.

One of the archers raised his bow, aimed, and released. One moment Daemyn was standing tall and strong. The next, the arrow punched into his stomach only inches from the first wound. At that short of range, the force of the second arrow drove Daemyn back a step.

Daemyn sank to his knees, the staff falling from his grasp.

Rosanna pressed both hands tight over her mouth. Hot, wet drops slithered down her face and splashed against her fingers, even though she'd known it would end like this, deep down.

The Tuckawassee that could still move pounced. For a minute, Rosanna couldn't see Daemyn past the bodies crowding around him.

When the Tuckawassee stepped back, they had Daemyn's hands tied behind his back. He knelt, choking on ragged breaths, as blood soaked his shirt, his trousers, and the stone around him all the way to the creek.

How was Daemyn still breathing? Surely after that much blood loss and pain, he should've been crumpled on the ground, gasping out his last breath.

But he raised his head to glare at Major Beshko with something raw and unnerving in his eyes, the look of a fox that had chewed off its own foot to escape a trap and still had the will to fight.

Major Beshko circled once around Daemyn before she paused. "In all my years tracking you and your father, I noticed something odd. No matter how hard we looked, there was only ever one of you. We couldn't find your mother. We couldn't find any siblings. We couldn't even find you while you father was still here."

What did Major Beshko mean? Daemyn had told Rosanna he had siblings. He wouldn't have lied about that, would he? Surely not to her. He trusted her more than that.

Daemyn swayed, though his eyes never wavered from Major Beshko. "The mountains hide . . . their own."

"Perhaps. But not this well." Major Beshko leaned forward. "Who are you really, Daemyn Rand? What are you? Are you some Fae masquerading in human form?"

"I'm as . . . human as . . . you." Daemyn's words were coming hard, but somehow, he remained upright.

"And yet, you never die when you're supposed to." Major Beshko gripped Daemyn's chin and yanked his face to the side, exposing the long scar along Daemyn's neck. "Didn't Arlen Rand have his throat cut? Yet you have the scar."

"I barely survived." Daemyn jerked his face free of her grasp.

Major Beshko rested a hand on her hip near her long knife. "Strange. All the official reports in my kingdom say your father was alone that day. Yet the stories say you were there as well. Odd, isn't it?"

What was Major Beshko talking about? Why didn't she leave Daemyn alone? Couldn't she just abandon him to die and chase down the river where she thought Rosanna had run?

"Why won't you die?" The question was all logical and calculation. Major Beshko grasped the end of the arrow shaft sticking out of Daemyn's stomach. She shoved it in farther. Daemyn cried out and doubled over.

Rosanna curled her hands so hard over her mouth her teeth cut into her cheeks. If only she could do something to stop this.

She could step out of her hiding spot. That would stop this torture, but only long enough for Major Beshko to see who she was. The major would promptly kill Daemyn, and probably Rosanna as well.

No matter what happened, she had to obey Daemyn's final order and remain here. It would do no good to toss away Daemyn's sacrifice and get herself caught.

Major Beshko thrust the arrow deeper still. Her expression remained blank, her eyes calculating, as if this was a mere problem she was studying. With a quick twist, she yanked the arrow from Daemyn's body.

Daemyn cried out and collapsed, going silent.

A sob caught in Rosanna's throat, but she bit her lip. She couldn't make a sound.

One of the Tuckawassee gripped Daemyn's arm and dragged him onto his knees once again. Daemyn's head lolled. Then, he raised his head, his chest rising and falling with breaths so ragged and pained Rosanna felt each one even from her hiding place.

Climbing to her feet, Major Beshko wiped her bloody hand on Daemyn's shoulder. "It's rumored the river pirates call you the Cursed One. They say you cannot die."

"Death . . . comes for . . . us all." Daemyn seemed barely able to speak, yet he craned his head to keep glaring Major Beshko in the face.

"Does it? Even for you?" Major Beshko stepped back. "Let's test that, shall we? Make it a lethal shot this time, please."

One of the Tuckawassee stepped to within three feet, raised his bow, and drew back the arrow. Daemyn kept his head high, glaring.

Rosanna wrapped her arms around her knees and buried her face in the crook of her elbow. She couldn't watch. It was already too much to hear the meaty sound of the arrow striking true, the boneless thump of a body striking stone, and one of the Tuckawassee men saying, "He's dead."

Major Beshko snorted with such contempt Rosanna could imagine her kicking Daemyn's lifeless body. "It appears the rumors were incorrect. As usual."

Somewhere in the distance, three blasts of what sounded like a signal horn blared.

Major Beshko's voice never wavered from her even tone, as if she hadn't just ordered a man killed. "They've caught the princess. Now, gentlemen, let's join the others and get this business completed."

Isi.

Rosanna curled tighter, pressing her face into the crooks of her arms. Not Isi. Would the Tuckawassee hurt her? Kill her? Rosanna could picture Isi with her nose in the air ordering the Tuckawassee to unhand her, making them think she was the princess.

Not more sacrifice. How many of Rosanna's friends would die to save her? Almost she would give herself up to spare them, except that it would be a useless gesture in the end.

Rosanna huddled in her hidden nook, not even daring to peek out, as rustling and tramping marked the Tuckawassee's progress away downstream.

She didn't dare breathe. If she did, the tears inside her might escape. Her whole body shook with the force of the soundless sobs trapped in her chest. She must not cry. She must not make noise. She must not move.

The minutes ticked by. The forest returned to its normal, quiet rustling and sighing. Somewhere a bird called. Another answered.

Still Daemyn didn't come.

Of course, he didn't. He was dead.

She had to know for sure. What if he wasn't dead, but

lying there dying without someone to help? He'd told her to stay here, but she couldn't. Not any longer.

She would venture out long enough to check on him. The Tuckawassee were long gone down the river, confident they already had the princess they had tracked across the mountains in their grasp.

Peering through a gap in the leaves and twigs, she searched as far as she could see. Nothing.

She shifted the bottom of the log, pushed the leaves aside, and froze, listening. Nothing moved in the forest beyond the faint breeze stirring the treetops.

Should she risk it? She'd promised Daemyn she'd stay here.

But he wouldn't be coming to get her, and she had to see him for herself. She couldn't do this on her own. She couldn't.

After crawling from the nook, she tiptoed down the slope, scanning the woods for any Tuckawassee lingering there. The hollow remained quiet.

Near the bottom of the slope, she drew in a deep breath, braced herself, and turned to Daemyn.

He lay with the same unnatural stillness she'd seen only once before outside of Kikataw, his eyes open, unblinking, and far too empty. His body sprawled at an odd angle with his hands bound behind him. An arrow was buried nearly to the fletching in his chest.

Prickles tingled along her arms. She didn't have to go closer to know he was dead. He *felt* dead, even from where she stood.

But she couldn't turn away now. As much as her stomach heaved at the blood and the thought of touching a dead body—even a body that had once belonged to a friend—she had to be sure.

The pool of blood around Daemyn's body spread so wide she couldn't get to him without stepping or kneeling in it. She crept closer and knelt. Dampness soaked into her knees, the blood already cold from the stone beneath.

With a shaking hand, she pressed her fingers to Daemyn's neck. No pulse. She checked his wrist. Nothing. She didn't try to find a heartbeat, not past the arrow sticking up from the left side of his chest.

The Tuckawassee had been right.

Daemyn Rand was dead.

CHAPTER 21

ALEXANDER

ONE HUNDRED YEARS AGO

Alex opened his eyes. It wasn't like waking after a long sleep where his eyes were gritty and his mind groggy. No, this was like blinking. One moment his eyes were shut, then he was looking around, fully alert and awake.

He and Jadon sat beside a pool of aqua water, the roar of a waterfall somewhere in the distance. Oddly, Jadon now wore a white shirt and trousers.

When Alex glanced down at himself, his clothes too—though they resembled the shirt and trousers he had been wearing in cut and shape—were white, but a strange sort of white that went beyond the mere absence of color. They were white like light, every color of the farthest reaches of the rainbow mixing together into a white that glittered like diamonds.

The grass beneath Alex's hand bent with the softness of velvet, though it sparkled the same color as a finely cut emerald.

Trees surrounded them, as if they were in a deep forest.

At least, *tree* was the only word Alex had to describe the lofty trunks and leafy branches spreading over him, though the word seemed too small. Their trunks stood straighter and grander than the proudest oak, the bark glinting like a brown version of quartz. The leaves, if they could be called that, spread in shapes Alex had never seen and ranged in color from amethyst to diamond, deepest garnet to emerald.

"What is this place?" Alex stood on shaking legs.

"You sit at the threshold of Beyond."

Alex turned at the voice of that gatekeeper-stranger who had dragged them here.

The gatekeeper stood a few feet away, now dressed in a white shirt and trousers like Jadon and Alex. A thin gold circlet sat on his brow, somehow powerful in how under-stated it was.

Alex got the feeling this stranger was more than just a gatekeeper for this place. "Who are you, really?"

Jadon pushed to his feet, his eyes locked on the stranger. After a few hesitant steps, Jadon knelt. "You're the Prince above All Princes. The son of the Lord of the Fae."

Alex should've seen it. The circlet. The power and authority to bring them here. Of course, it could be none else. He knelt beside Jadon. "We seek an audience with the Lord of the Fae."

"Rise. Come."

By the force of the word, Alex stood. And followed.

The Prince led them between the tall, broad trunks of the trees. The grass made no noise beneath their white moccasins. Nothing stirred except an occasional tinkle of leaves as if that guiding breeze remained with them even now.

The farther they went, the louder the waterfall's roar became until it thundered more than the largest waterfall in Tallahatchia. Still, Alex sensed he would have been able to talk and hear comfortably over it without shouting, though none of them spoke.

The Prince led them around one especially large tree, and a small glade opened before them, a massive wall rising from its far side.

No, not a wall. A waterfall. Plunging down from heights too far above for Alex to see the top and disappearing into the ground in a plume of mist. To his left, the waterfall stretched into the distance. To his right, it cut through the middle of a gateway, leaving only one of what he assumed were two doors visible on their side.

As they strode closer, swirling spots, and flashes became visible in the rushing water. All the storms of the earth—from the largest hurricane to the mightiest storm cloud—were no bigger than a pinprick of light and a teaspoonful of clouds in the torrential wall of water before them.

And beyond the waterfall lay something hazy. More land. People. He couldn't tell. It was all too indistinct.

But there was singing. It rose and fell over the mighty roar of the waterfall in a language unknown. A chorus of voices, in harmony, in unity.

The singing had Alex transfixed where he stood. Something rose inside him, a longing for the place beyond that waterfall. For the beauty of which those voices sang. For the knowledge of the full meaning of the words of their song.

Jadon took two steps forward, his hand stretched toward the waterfall in front of them as if he intended to open a door and step through.

The Prince stepped between them and the waterfall. "We stand on the threshold where the living may enter. Only the dead may step through the WaterVeil into Beyond. But someday, this Veil too will be torn down."

So they were still among the living. Alex hadn't been sure.

Jadon glanced from the Prince to the mighty WaterVeil, his face twisting with a longing so deep only the language of the land beyond could've described it, though that language knew no such pain.

The Prince's eyes held compassion. "It is not your time to enter. I have much work yet for you to do."

Jadon blinked and nodded.

The Prince led them to the gate divided by the WaterVeil. A giant, arching tree formed the gateway imbedded in a golden wall that stretched into the distance on the side of the WaterVeil they could see.

There was an impression of rising turrets and spires of a grand palace rising behind this door, but Alex wasn't sure if he could see the palace or just sense that it was there beyond what his eyes could take in.

The door shimmered with the same opalescence of the inside of the oyster shells traders brought inland from the sea. The Prince raised a hand. "These may enter for they are mine."

The gate swung open as if pulled aside by a footman for the master's entrance. Jadon followed first, then Alex.

They entered a long corridor all in crystal and gold, though here too the WaterVeil sliced down the center so they could only see and walk in the right side. Along the one wall, living paintings swirled and moved in brightest colors.

In one of them, Alex caught a glimpse of himself and

Jadon crossing one of the bridges in Tallahatchia. In another, a girl in travel-stained buckskins cried next to an arrow-shot body, her sobbing shoulders and hair obscuring the body's face. Yet, even this scene of death and blood was a plan carried out. It was good when seen here.

"What is this place?" Alex halted, scanning the paintings. Something told him that if he searched long enough, he could see his end written here.

"This is the Hall of Things That Are and Have Been and Will Be." The Prince didn't pause as he led them onward.

Jadon reached out and touched the frame of the painting with the crying girl. His eyes narrowed, a wrinkle forming between his eyebrows. What did he see in the painting that Alex couldn't?

Alex bumped his shoulder. "What is it?"

Jadon shook himself. "Nothing. We're falling behind."

They hurried to catch up with the Prince's long strides. The farther they walked, the brighter the corridor grew until Alex squinted to see Jadon's silhouette a few feet in front of him.

The Prince reached another door at the far end of the corridor. This door too opened soundlessly.

Light beyond all else streamed through. Alex covered his eyes, trembling under the power of it. He sensed, more than saw, Jadon collapse to his knees.

This was the throne room of the Lord of all Fae and Men. Even with his eyes shut, the light poured into Alex until he still saw the crystal floor spreading out, the WaterVeil curving to stand between the throne and the door where Jadon and Alex trembled.

But the golden throne . . . with light and power spreading out, the scepter and crown glittering with gemstones beyond those found in the earth . . . and the Highest King that reigned there . . .

Even as he sensed and saw, he knew he wasn't sensing the truth. Not the full truth, anyway. Only a small revelation of truth in a form Alex's brain and eyes could process.

Alex couldn't take a step closer, not to enter that throne room. Every inch of his skin burned with the light's heat. His legs shook, and only the fact that his knees had locked in place kept him standing.

The Prince halted in the center of the room before the WaterVeil, standing between them and the throne. He turned and held out an arm to them. "Come."

More than an invitation, it was a command that couldn't be resisted, even if Alex's muscles didn't have the strength to move.

The breeze wrapped around Alex, flowing into him until he could stagger a step, then two.

Jadon reached the Prince first and fell to his knees, his face to the crystal floor. Alex sank to his knees a moment later at Jadon's side. Even with the breeze's strength in him, he shook. In this throne room, no one but the Prince himself could stand tall and steady.

"Ask."

The word boomed off the crystal walls and the lightning-streaked WaterVeil. With his face pressed to the quartz-like floor, Alex didn't know if it was the Prince or the Lord of the Fae who had spoken.

He wet his lips. "I have been cursed to sleep like death for all time. I need to have the curse removed."

"I gave you no curse."

"I know you didn't. It was one of the Fallen Fae." Alex clenched his fists, his shaking growing worse.

"All things are from me." The voice spoke again, and it

was as if three voices spoke in all the octaves of harmony, yet it was one voice. It boomed from beyond the Veil, from the Prince, and from the breeze building with each word spoken.

"Please. I need it taken away." Alex couldn't believe he was begging, yet he was. His voice choked in his throat. "Please. It's important. I can't live with it."

"What you call a curse will not be removed."

Alex swallowed, but it wasn't despair that tightened his throat now. A heat built in him. He'd gone all this way, come so far, only to be told *no*? It wasn't fair. He shouldn't have to suffer this. He deserved to have this curse taken away after all he'd done. Surely the Lord of the Fae could remove it if he wanted to. But he refused for no reason Alex could see.

"Why not? The whole of Tallahatchia will be in peril if I sleep!" Alex clenched his fists, and this time, he didn't shake. He was too angry for the light of this place to tremble through him. "This curse has to be removed. There isn't any other way."

"I have promised a cursebreaker. When time is complete and complete again, a princess will come, and you will wake. So I have spoken, and thus it will be done."

What sort of promise was that? When would Alex wake? How long? What princess? Would it be Mirabelle waking him after a short time? No, it couldn't be her. She wasn't a princess, not in the strictest sense of the word. Would Alex sleep for hundreds of years until some princess stumbled her way to Castle Eyota to wake him?

"Please." For the first time since they'd entered the throne room, Jadon spoke. He lifted his head to the Prince. "Please, if it is possible, may I be the one to lead the princess to Castle Eyota?"

The Prince looked at Jadon with something like compassion in the depths of his eyes. "You do not understand what you ask. The time will not be short as earth measures time. You will lose much if granted this request."

The time wouldn't be short? Alex swallowed down the burning in his chest. Why not? Why did he have to sleep for such a long time? Why did this have to happen to him?

Jadon shook, but his gaze didn't waver. "I understand."

"So it shall be. You will lead the promised cursebreaker, and you shall be granted the life and strength to see this duty to its end."

"How will I know her when I find her?"

The Prince waved toward Alex. "As a sign, the stone in the high prince's signet ring will turn clear when in the presence of the promised cursebreaker."

Alex glanced down at the sapphire glinting a brilliant blue in the signet ring he had forgotten to remove after seeing King Othniel. How could a sapphire turn clear? It didn't make sense.

And why was Jadon's request granted so easily? One request, that's all it took for Jadon. Yet Alex had begged and pleaded, and his was refused.

The Prince turned to Alex. Behind him, the light streaming from the throne grew brighter and brighter until Alex could barely see the Prince's form in the light scorching his senses. "Which is the curse, and which is the gift? Someday I shall ask an answer from you, High Prince Alexander. And, someday, you shall know it."

The light—painfully white—brightened still further, overwhelming, until Alex drowned in it as surely as he had the turquoise pool.

CHAPTER 22

ROSANNA

osanna swiped at her tears, swallowing back the tightness in her chest as best she could. She couldn't stay here, sobbing.

But she couldn't leave either. Where could she go? Her guards were gone. Isi, her best friend, was captured, possibly hurt or even killed. And there was nothing Rosanna could do. Not alone as she was now.

Nor could she leave Daemyn like this. Seeing that he had a proper burial was the one thing she could do.

She reached for the arrow shaft sticking from Daemyn's chest. Even knowing he was dead, she couldn't just rip the arrow free. She peered over him. The arrow had gone all the way through him, its tip protruding, bloody, from his back.

Gripping the shaft with two hands, she strained to snap it. The sturdy shaft refused to break, not with the lack of leverage she could put on it with most of the shaft inside Daemyn's chest. Gritting her teeth, she put a last burst of strength into her fingers.

The shaft snapped. She pulled the fletched end out first, then eased the broadhead out of his back.

With the dagger he pressed into her hands before confronting the Tuckawassee, she sawed through the ropes binding his hands behind him. When the rope fell away, his arms flopped limply apart.

She sucked in a breath, her stomach churning. A second wound marred Daemyn's lower back. Major Beshko had shoved the arrow all the way through before tearing it from him.

Her breathing hitched, choking, gasping. She stumbled to her feet, staggered a few steps, and braced herself against a tree. She couldn't do this. The blood. His torn body. She couldn't see him like this.

Did she have a choice? She couldn't help anyone. Could she walk away from the one thing she was capable of doing to honor her friends?

With a deep breath, she returned to Daemyn's body and touched his eyelid, dragging it closed over his staring eye. She hurriedly closed his other eye too.

With the arrow gone and his eyes closed, he looked like he was sleeping instead of dead. Yet, his chest remained still, and that empty sense about him still shivered across her skin.

She couldn't leave him here in the pool of his blood. Scavengers would pick his body to nothing. He deserved better than that.

Grasping under his arms, Rosanna leaned all her weight backwards to move him up the steep slope of the creek's bank. Her hands, her feet, were slick with his blood. Her back and shoulders ached with his weight. Sweat dampened her shirt and hair as she dragged him inch by inch.

Finally, she managed to lay him in a hollow at the base of a boulder about fifteen feet above the creek where she would be able to pile rocks on him to bury him.

She sank to her knees, unable to make herself fetch that first stone. Once she placed it on him, he would truly be gone. She would be alone on this journey that still didn't feel hers.

She'd gone this far for Daemyn, not for some legendary prince asleep in his castle. She'd gone for the man who had never questioned her ability to paddle a canoe or navigate a rough section of rapids. A man who struggled under a weight she didn't always understand.

She couldn't do this. Not alone. Yet she couldn't go back.

Tears pricked her eyes even as she fought to hold the pain inside. "I can't do this without you, Daemyn. You seemed to think I had a gift or talent or something special, but I don't. I'm useless."

"Rosanna."

The voice was quiet, but resonant. Rosanna glanced at Daemyn's body, still lifeless before her.

But there, a few feet higher on the slope in front of her sat a stranger. Yet something about him felt like he was someone she should know or already knew. He dressed in simple clothes, and his voice didn't have the accent of the Tuckawassee. In a way, it held all accents and dialects, as if all languages were known by him.

She swiped at her face, trying to erase some of the tears. "Who are you?"

"You know who I am. Before the mountains were, I am. Before the rivers, I am. I am he who chose you for this purpose before you were born."

A breeze drifted through the gorge and ran soothing fingers over the tear stains on Rosanna's face.

And Rosanna knew this stranger. He was the Highest Prince, the son of the Lord of Fae and Men. Now that she looked closer, she could see the golden circlet on his head. A wonder she hadn't noticed it before with the way the gold glinted far brighter than with a mere reflection of the afternoon sun.

"I'm sorry. I can't do this." Rosanna shook her head and scraped at the dried blood on her hands. "I'm useless. I don't know why you chose me. I wasn't even given a gift when I was born."

"Just because a Fae wasn't sent to declare your gift doesn't mean I never gave you one." The Prince's voice didn't waver from its quiet, compassionate tone. "I give many gifts, and it is often the gifts that can't be seen that are the greatest of all."

"I don't understand." Rosanna shivered, but the breeze wrapped her with warm tendrils. "Will you please tell me my gift?"

"You have been given many gifts, but first among them is the gift to hear." The Prince's smile warmed her to the depths of her soul. "Now, listen."

It was a command, but the sort of command it was a privilege to obey.

Rosanna closed her eyes and listened.

At first, nothing in the breeze's gentle breaths, the trees' constant rustling sounded any different than the hundreds of times she'd stepped into Tallahatchia's mountains.

Then, a pure note soared, not with the suddenness of a song beginning, but with the continued flow of a song already long begun.

More notes joined the first, swooping, soaring, ringing in a purity not found in any flute or mouth pipe. The chorus swelled with many voices in notes unknown to human ears.

The trees. The trees were singing.

The stalwart oaks boomed in low, bass tones with all the grandeur of their mighty branches. The maples rang with husky voices as weathered as their gnarled trunks. The willows and birches swished and swooped in whispery breaths. The sycamores belted out a harmony as old as their heartwood. And above them all, the glistening, crystal notes of the beech trees—those elegant, silver queens of the wood—filled the mountains with a song so pure, so enduring, it shattered the sky above to pour into the realm beyond.

More voices bubbled with laughing joy—the rivers adding their part to the song.

A deep hum as old as time itself thrummed through the earth beneath Rosanna's fingers. The mountains themselves singing their ancient song.

The words the trees and mountains sang was the language of things beyond, a tongue few knew to utter. Still, the truth of the words, a taste of their meaning, beat in Rosanna's chest. *Worthy. Holy. Majesty.*

This was the song she'd longed to hear all her life, as if a piece of it had lodged in her chest from before she was born.

But this was more beautiful than she could've dreamed, for the trees, the rivers, the mountains, they didn't sing for her. Or themselves. They sang for the Highest Prince sitting near her, for the Highest King on his throne, for the Breath of all breezes that gave life in the beginning.

"It's . . ." Rosanna couldn't think of a word to describe

the wonder. Beautiful fell short. Magnificent wasn't grand enough.

"Listen." The Prince commanded again.

Rosanna strained her ears harder, trying to sink deeper into the song.

The voices of the trees rose in pitch until they were a painful wail. The beeches keened in purest agony. The mountain's rumble broke, weeping as one forsaken. The rivers themselves were the tears of the mountains flowing down their faces in a torrent of unending sorrow.

Pain. Corruption. Death.

The keening pierced Rosanna's chest. She pressed her hands over her ears, but she couldn't block out the screaming, wailing trees.

This was the curse her ancestor had unleashed upon the innocent mountains, the guileless trees. The weight of that guilt burdened her still, that worst of all crimes still unpunished.

Even now, she couldn't undo what had been done. She could do nothing but carry that guilt as the mountains wept for the beauty that had once been, the trees cried for justice for the wrong done to them, and the rivers ran with the torment they suffered because of mankind's original folly.

And the curse was dark and cold within her. She didn't need another curse to be placed on her as a sign to hear the darkness resonating from her own heart.

Rosanna covered her face and wept along with the mountains. "I'm sorry. I'm sorry this can't be undone."

When she glanced up, the Prince's eyes also shone with tears, as if the agony of the song wailing around them pained him even more deeply than it did her.

"Listen." He commanded for a third time.

She didn't want to strain her ears to hear more of this pain. But she squeezed her eyes shut and listened anyway.

A single, quavering voice rose above the keening. Still pained. Still tormented. But rising with a new strength that couldn't be snuffed out by all the darkness of the jangled song around it.

Rosanna didn't have to understand the speech of trees and earth to know the word of which this voice sang, for an answering song beat inside her own chest.

Hope.

Hope for the Promised Cursebreaker who would end the curse and restore all beauty.

This was the hope she was meant to be in her own humble and stumbling way to point to the greater Hope still coming.

So far, she'd journeyed for herself or for Daemyn. But from now on, she would journey for the Cursebreaker.

Weeks ago, she'd asked Daemyn why he undertook such a task for a prince he'd never met. Back then, she hadn't understood when Daemyn had said he didn't do it for the high prince. Of course, he didn't. He labored for the Highest Prince of above all princes.

As must she. For it was truly the only reason to do anything.

She looked to the Prince. "What would you have me do?"

"If I asked, would you go on alone?"

Rosanna glanced down at Daemyn's body. If the Prince told her to go, she'd have to leave. Immediately. Without giving Daemyn the burial he deserved. Or trying to help Isi. No looking back.

How could she hesitate when the Prince for whom the trees sang asked her to go?

The breeze touched strands of her hair, and Rosanna drew in a deep breath of it. This was her gift, small as it was. She'd been given the gift to hear.

She would hear, and she would obey. "Yes. Whatever you ask, whenever you ask, however you ask, I will go."

"Then so be it."

Rosanna braced herself. He would tell her to go now. She must not look back.

"Take up your canteen and fill it in the creek yonder."

An odd request, but Rosanna fetched her canteen from where she'd left it in the nook where she'd hidden, strode to the creek, and dipped the canteen in, holding it under until it was full.

She returned, knelt, and held out the canteen.

The Prince gestured to Daemyn's body. "Do not fear. He but sleeps, and it is time for him to wake. I have more work yet for him to do."

He slept? Rosanna pressed her hand against Daemyn's wrist. His skin was already too cold for there to be life, his pulse gone. No, Daemyn was dead. "I don't understand."

She looked up, but the Prince was gone. She glanced around, but she was alone with Daemyn's lifeless body. Even the trees had stopped their singing—or rather, she had stopped listening—and the loss of the song sunk deep into her chest.

What was she supposed to do now?

She had a canteen of water in her hand and a man in the deep sleep of death who had to wake. There was only one thing to do, something she'd done many times to wake Berend. She upended the canteen and dumped the water on Daemyn's face.

He didn't bolt upright like Berend did when splashed with cold water. Not even a flinch or wince. The water ran down his face as if he were nothing more than a dead rock shedding water after a rain.

Surely, he would wake. The Prince had spoken it.

She rested her hand on his chest a few inches away from the gaping wound where the arrow had transfixed his heart.

The breeze stirred the dead leaves around them and brushed across the back of Rosanna's fingers.

Beneath her hand, Daemyn's chest rose and fell with a breath.

ROSANNA

Rosanna pressed a hand to Daemyn's neck. Though light and fluttery, a pulse now pounded there.

A pulse. Life. Hope.

With his heart once again pumping, blood started seeping from his wounds, though not as much as Rosanna might have expected considering one wound had torn open his heart.

While he probably hadn't been given life again to bleed out moments later, losing more blood wouldn't help things either. Rosanna scrambled to find something to staunch the bleeding. Since they'd abandoned all their spare clothes and medical supplies with their packs, all they had were the clothes on their backs.

After hacking a section of the buckskin off the bottom of his shirt, she pressed it against the wounds in his stomach and chest. Not that the buckskin would do much for soaking up blood, but the pressure would help, wouldn't it?

Daemyn groaned, his head moving back and forth as if he was trying to shake himself awake.

She pressed one hand to his forehead. "Lie still. I think you were dead for a few minutes there."

"Wouldn't . . . be the first time." Daemyn's mouth barely moved.

Now wasn't the time to ask for details, though she could guess some of it. He had earned the name Cursed One from the river pirates for a reason, and she didn't think it was because the river pirates had missed with their arrows.

Rosanna refilled the canteen and pressed it to his mouth. "Can you manage a few sips?"

He did but turned his face away after a few swallows, coughing. He cracked his eyes open. "You didn't stay hidden."

"No, but I waited until the Tuckawassee were well gone." She gripped the canteen tighter. "They captured Isi, thinking they have the princess."

Daemyn arms moved and his head lifted as if he was trying to sit up. He sucked in a sharp breath and flopped back to the ground with a moan, a hand pressed to the wound in his chest.

Rosanna rested a hand on his shoulder. "Unable to die or not, you won't be going anywhere for a while."

"Can't . . . stay. The Tuckawassee might be back." Daemyn's breathing grew more ragged, as if the pain of his wounds had returned after the numbness of death wore off. "Can you . . . get to the convergence . . . by yourself?"

It was the second time she had been asked to go on alone. It wasn't something she could refuse. She swallowed. "I think so. But I don't want to leave you here. You need help."

Daemyn had his eyes squeezed shut. "Get help. Come back for me."

All right, she could do that. "I'll go."

Daemyn gripped her arm. "It's southeast of here. There'll be a friend."

"All right." She set the canteen within his reach and propped his head up with a few handfuls of leaves. The convergence of the Nanahootchie and Tuckawassee was only a couple of hours away. Daemyn would need water more than she would. She also took the time to track down his hardwood staff where it had fallen on the creek's bank.

With a single backward glance, she set off alone into the woods, keeping the sun behind her right shoulder.

She could do this, right? Find her way by herself through the woods. As long as she never strayed too far from the Tuckawassee River, she wouldn't get lost.

The forest stretched into the vast mountains. She glanced about as she walked. What if she stumbled across a bear or a wolf? Or worse, one of the rare black panthers that wandered this far north from the swamps of the nations to the south.

She gripped Daemyn's dagger tightly, though it would do her little good if she came across a dangerous man or beast.

Something large crashed through the undergrowth ahead of her. She froze, clutching the dagger.

A white tail flashed in the woods before she lost sight of the deer over a rise.

Just a deer. Nothing to get all spooked over.

She kept walking, up and down mountain ridges, passing small waterfalls as she navigated over and through small creeks on their way to the Tuckawassee River.

A few times she spotted a log cabin or two at a distance.

She skirted around those. Here in Tuckawassee, they would be enemies rather than friends.

The sun sank lower behind her, casting long shadows between the trees around her. Sunset and darkness came fast in the deep woods.

Her stomach rumbled, and her mouth dried. Her feet and legs ached with the miles she'd walked and run that day.

But Daemyn lay badly wounded back in that hollow. What if the Tuckawassee returned to find him and kill him again? Or a pack of wolves came to the scent of so much bloodshed?

And what about Captain Degotaga, Isi, and the others? Had they been captured—or worse, killed—by the Tuckawassee? She couldn't let herself imagine Isi lying there, shirt bloodied, eyes empty, as Daemyn had been.

The forest appeared bathed in gray now. She veered to the right, going down the crest of the gorge, until the Tuckawassee River came in sight. The Nanahootchie couldn't be that much farther ahead. It was too big to cross accidentally.

A piercing yip rose into the sky in the distance, joined by a chorus of other barking howls. Coyotes. A long way off yet, but the sound still chilled her skin and had her casting about looking for eyes in the gloom around her.

Every fallen log and rotting stump appeared as black shapes in the indistinct forest. She jumped at every sound and imagined movement.

There, barely visible ahead in the fading light, a stream dumped into the Tuckawassee from the north. The water roiled where the two collided.

Rosanna hurried down the slope of the gorge as best

she could in the gray haze of almost night. Trees appeared in front of her as if suddenly planted there.

She glanced around. She couldn't see any one in the dim haze. Was she the only person here? What if the person supposed to help had left to set up camp elsewhere for the night?

Should she call out? What if some of the Tuckawassee were here and heard her?

She had to risk it. "Hello?" She kept her voice low. It could still carry on the quiet night, but not too far. "I need help. Daemyn Rand sent me."

Nothing stirred in the night except for the churning river waters ahead of her.

"I believe you're looking for me," a cheery voice spoke from behind her.

She whirled. A tall figure carrying a staff stood a few feet away. In the uncertain light, she couldn't make out much of his features besides his dark hair.

"I think so. If you're Daemyn Rand's friend." She gripped the dagger's hilt with one hand, though she wasn't sure what she'd do with it if she drew it from its sheath.

Something about his features told her he was smiling even though she couldn't see his expression in the darkness. "I'm more than that. I'm his nephew." The man strode closer. "My name's Ezekiel Rand, though friends, family, and friends of family call me Zeke."

"Has anyone else come here? I was traveling with six guards—four men and two women—when we were attacked by the Tuckawassee and had to split up."

"No, I'm sorry. You're the first all day."

She squeezed her eyes shut. Did that mean all of them were captured? Or dead? Perhaps they still fled, the Tuckawassee dogging their steps.

As much as she worried for them, she could do nothing to help them now. But she could help Daemyn.

"When we were attacked, Daemyn held off the Tuckawassee so I could hide and was . . . gravely wounded." She wasn't sure how to go about explaining to Zeke that his uncle had been dead for a while that afternoon.

"I see." Zeke set out in the direction she'd come, something in his tone suggested he understood exactly what she'd meant. "And he's probably not healed enough to move about on his own yet. How far away is he?"

Rosanna trotted to catch up, her muscles aching. "About two hours from here."

"By Falling Rock Creek?"

She nodded, though she hadn't known the creek's name and could only guess Zeke knew the right one. Did she have the strength to walk all the way back there, only to have to hike two more hours helping Daemyn? She barely stumbled forward now.

"And you look done in." Zeke headed down the bank toward the Tuckawassee River. "We'll have to chance my canoe. You won't make another five hours of hiking."

Downstream of the convergence, Zeke uncovered a fifteen-foot canoe with a few bundles of supplies in its center. It must have taken some tricky paddling to get it here by himself.

Zeke pointed at a rock. "Here. Sit. Let me get you food and water before we go on. Better to take a few minutes now to revive you than have you pass out trying to paddle."

She sank onto the rock. When he handed her a canteen, she drained a third of it in a few large gulps. The bread and cheese he handed her was gone in a few bites.

"Sorry that's all I have. When we reach the cabin

tonight, I have a pot of stew I can set to simmering for you."

Warm stew. She closed her eyes. What would it be like to have warm food to fill her stomach?

She sipped at the canteen again and studied Zeke. He couldn't be much younger than Daemyn. Maybe twenty to Daemyn's twenty-five, though she was guessing on both their ages. Zeke's features had some resemblance to Daemyn, but not enough that she would've picked them out as related. "There must be quite the age gap between your father and Daemyn for you and your uncle to be practically the same age."

A lopsided grin crossed Zeke's face. "Something like that. I'll have to let Uncle Daemyn explain if he has a mind to. Are you ready to get moving, or do you need a few more minutes?"

"I'm ready." She stood and handed back the canteen. All she wanted to do was curl up on a bed in that cabin Zeke mentioned. But she couldn't rest for the night until Daemyn was fetched and tended.

He had died to protect her from the Tuckawassee. The least she could do was make sure he was given warm food and a comfortable bed before she sought her own rest.

After she helped Zeke set the canoe in the water, he eyed her as he held the canoe steady. "Can you paddle?"

"Yes. I've spent years in my own canoe on the Onohio and Neskahana Rivers." She slid into the canoe, took up the paddle, and poised it to begin a stroke.

"Perfect. Now no more talking until we reach Daemyn. Sound carries on the water." Zeke climbed into the canoe and grabbed his paddle.

Rosanna nodded and dug her paddle into the water.

She didn't have to be reminded to stay quiet, but Zeke didn't know that.

Something in her chest eased at being in a canoe again, a paddle in her hand. The Prince had told her truly. Sometimes the small gifts could be the best ones, overlooked as they were.

She set a fast rhythm, which Zeke matched, though not with the ease Daemyn had. Daemyn seemed to sense her timing as if they shared the same rhythm with more than just their paddles.

She and Zeke were going with the current and here the Tuckawassee River clipped along. What had taken her two hours to hike took only twenty minutes by canoe.

Zeke turned the canoe into the mouth of a creek, and they paddled hard against the current for a few minutes until a tumble of boulders and a stepped waterfall blocked their way. They lifted the canoe onshore and hiked upward along the creek.

She struggled to keep up with Zeke and keep her footing in the dark. On the river there had been the faint glow of stars to guide them, but under the trees it was nearly black as a bear's fur. But they couldn't light a torch, not without alerting the Tuckawassee who, based on the flicker of a fire farther up the gorge, weren't far away.

After too many minutes of stumbling upward in the dark, the outline of the slope and the rumble of the waterfall rose from the darkness.

Rosanna hurried past Zeke and led the way to where she'd left Daemyn.

When she knelt by the boulder, she rested her hand on what she guessed was Daemyn's shoulder. "I'm back. And I found your nephew."

Zeke knelt next to her. "I hear you got a mite beat up,

Uncle Daemyn. You need to learn to take better care of yourself."

"I'd like to see you . . . do better." Daemyn's voice sounded stronger than it had when Rosanna left but still weak.

"How many of them was there this time?"

"Nine." In the dark, Rosanna couldn't tell if Daemyn's eyes were open or closed.

"Only nine? You're slipping in your old age." Zeke's chuckle held a mock scolding.

"Respect your elders." Daemyn sounded like he was smiling.

A chorus of long, eerie howls rose into the sky, closer than the coyotes had been, though not yet a danger. A pack of wolves preparing to hunt.

"Sounds like we best get you out of here before those wolves come in for blood."

Together, Rosanna and Zeke got Daemyn to his feet, and Zeke draped Daemyn across his back and shoulders. He grunted as he lifted Daemyn. "I think you're heavier than last time."

She didn't hear Daemyn's murmured reply. She found her canteen and Daemyn's staff before she caught up with Zeke.

After hiking down the slope, they reached the canoe. Rosanna lifted most of the canoe into the water while Zeke lifted with one hand, Daemyn still draped across his shoulders and back.

As she held the canoe, Zeke did his best to lower Daemyn into the center near Zeke's supplies without hurting either Daemyn or the birch bark.

Once Daemyn had been settled in a half-sitting, half-lying position, Rosanna and Zeke slid into the canoe and grabbed their paddles.

Fighting up the Tuckawassee River took twice as long as it had to paddle down with the current. Rosanna's arms struggled to remember their strength enough for each stroke. Her eyes hurt, and her joints and bones throbbed with a weariness deeper than she'd known before.

But she had to keep moving. She forced herself to go numb to the ache and exhaustion and just keep paddling as if her body had forgotten how to do anything else.

When they reached the convergence, Zeke turned them up the Nanahootchie.

The current fought against them on the narrow stream. It took all her remaining strength to pull the canoe forward against the stiff current with every stroke. From the grunts behind her, even Zeke struggled.

At last, he turned them into a small creek and from there up a dead-end seep that trickled off to nearly nothing. They left the canoe beached on the sand, and Zeke led the way into a hollow carrying Daemyn.

Rosanna followed with Daemyn's staff and as many of Zeke's supplies as she could carry.

Something glowed in the forest ahead, solidifying into a cabin with the faint light of embers lighting it within.

Rosanna hurried ahead and opened the door for Zeke. He carried Daemyn inside and laid him out on the wooden trestle table taking up most of the space in the room.

Zeke grasped a lamp and set to work lighting it. "Can you stoke the fire? The pot of stew is off to the side if you want to set that on."

Rosanna added smaller kindling, then a few larger logs over the glowing coals. It took some blowing to coax flames to catch. When the fire blazed, she hung the pot she'd found filled with a meaty stew on the hook over the flames.

By the time she finished, Zeke had eased Daemyn's shirt off. The three arrow wounds gaped red, still dribbling blood. White scars marked Daemyn's chest and stomach, stark against his bronze skin. How many times had Daemyn been hurt?

Zeke shook his head. "These aren't pretty. Going to lay you out for a day or two, even with how fast you heal."

"Can't be helped." Daemyn didn't open his eyes, his fists clenched at his sides.

Rosanna glanced from Daemyn to Zeke. He shouldn't be alive, much less only take a day or two to heal from these kinds of arrow wounds.

But now wasn't the time to ask. "What can I do to help?"

Zeke handed her a bundle of cloths. "Press these to two of the wounds. Don't matter which. Uncle Daemyn would heal just fine without help, but he heals faster if given a mite of aid."

Rosanna folded the rags over the two wounds in Daemyn's stomach and leaned on them.

Daemyn groaned. He cracked his eyes open and glanced at her. "Sorry to be a bother."

"It isn't a bother." Not after seeing Daemyn dead. Rosanna could put up with any amount of blood after that.

Zeke returned holding a ceramic jug. "Good news. I got a full jug of Aunt Frennie's best moonshine. Actually, there's a whole keg of it out back."

"That's good news?" Daemyn squinted at Zeke and scowled. "Hopefully you don't drink it. That stuff could rot out your guts and leave a hole through your center."

"True, true. But ever since the moonshine kept cousin Hez from getting an infection, we've used it on every wound." Zeke shrugged. "And it's good for starting fires in a pinch. A keg or two of the stuff could set a whole castle on fire."

"Not going to be pleasant, is it?" Daemyn clenched his fists. His chest heaved with a deep breath.

"Reckon not." Zeke grinned. "This ain't gonna go right on through you when I pour it on that wound, will it? Because that would be mighty disturbing."

Daemyn scowled. "I'm fairly sure I no longer have a hole all the way through my chest."

"Good." Zeke dumped the jug over the arrow wound.

Daemyn groaned, and his muscles tensed beneath her hands. The moonshine reeked so strongly it burned her nose even a minute later. It must've burned even worse in that wound.

Zeke pulled out a needle and thread and began to stitch the wound closed. The muscle at the corner of Daemyn's jaw tensed. When Zeke finished with that wound, he handed her a jar of something he said to spread over the gashes.

While Zeke poured more moonshine over the other two wounds, Rosanna dipped her fingers in the balm and spread it over the new stitches. Then she wrapped a bandage over the balm.

Rosanna helped Zeke spread more balm over the wounds in Daemyn's stomach and put the first layer of bandages across them.

Zeke helped Daemyn sit up. When he let him go, Daemyn swayed.

Rosanna put an arm around his shoulders. "Lean on me."

Daemyn fought for a moment before he sagged against her. He rested his forehead on her shoulder. "I'm sorry, Princess."

"Don't be." She had to curl her free hand to stop herself from running her fingers through his hair. To soothe him, of course. She couldn't be attracted to him. Not to a man with too many secrets. As soon as she woke the high prince, Daemyn would disappear back to wherever he'd come from, and she'd still be a princess.

In a few minutes, Zeke had the two wounds in Daemyn's back patched up.

Daemyn pushed from Rosanna and swung his legs over the edge of the table. When Zeke stepped forward, Daemyn waved him off. "I'm fine."

He pushed from the table. His legs buckled, and his knees slammed into the wooden floor.

Zeke heaved a sigh and hauled Daemyn to his feet. "Come on. Let's get you to bed."

Daemyn nodded, his eyes barely cracked open. He and Zeke staggered the few feet to one of the two doors across the room. When the door opened, Rosanna caught sight of a set of bunk beds against one wall.

Rosanna sank onto one of the benches and stared at her hands. They shook, Daemyn's blood dried under her fingernails and in the cracks of her skin. Her whole body shuddered.

The door clicked shut. Zeke strolled back into the room. He straddled the other end of the bench facing her. After collecting a clean cloth from the pile left on the table, he picked up the jug of moonshine. "Hold out your hands."

Rosanna couldn't stop her hands quaking as she held them out. She should be stronger than this.

Zeke poured some of the moonshine over her hands, then worked to wipe the blood from her skin. "It's all right. All of us get the shakes now and then. You're going to be all right, and so will he."

"You do this often?" Based on Daemyn's scars, far too often.

"More than I like." Zeke finished cleaning her hands and started on the table. "Uncle Daemyn will sleep for hours. Probably won't wake until noon tomorrow. He tends to need a lot of sleep when healing."

When Zeke set stew in front of her, she wrapped her hands around the bowl and let the warmth seep into her. She should pull herself together, but all of her ached, wrung out and scraped raw.

But she would have to be fine. Daemyn, Isi, the rest of her guards . . . they didn't have time to waste on her falling apart.

She would be fine. She would be strong, and she would face tomorrow without complaint.

But, for tonight, she let her hands shake.

Chapter 24

Rosanna

Yawning, Rosanna lay in bed working up the willpower to get up. Warmth curled around her for the first time since she left Castle Deeling.

This room didn't have a window, but something told her she'd slept long. Sighing, she tossed the blankets aside and swiveled her feet to the floor. After running her fingers through her hair, she tied it back, straightened her clothes, and headed for the door.

Zeke bustled around the main room of the cabin. He looked up and grinned. "Glad to see you're awake. There's grits for breakfast. Or an early lunch, depending on how you look at it."

Rosanna claimed a seat on the bench by the table. "How's Daemyn?"

"Still sleeping." Zeke set a bowl of grits in front of her. The dried corn had been rough ground, then warm milk and butter stirred in to form a thick, porridge-like meal.

Rosanna dug in her spoon. It warmed her stomach, sticking to her ribs like nothing else did.

Zeke took the seat across from her. "I checked the rivers this morning. No sign of your guards. I'd like to scout around to see if I can find them, leaving now, if you think you'll be all right?"

"I'll be fine. Please find them." Rosanna set aside her spoon. How could she sit here stuffing her stomach without a thought for what Isi might be going through?

Zeke got to his feet and slipped on a quiver of arrows, his bow fastened to the quiver. "When Uncle Daemyn wakes, he might be hungry. There's more grits or leftover stew. Help yourself to anything in the cabin. I probably won't be back until after dark."

"Don't worry about us." Rosanna stirred her grits.

He grabbed his hardwood staff. "I'll find your friends."

Once Zeke left, Rosanna managed to finish her grits, and she set to work cleaning the cabin's small main room. Washing dishes wasn't something she'd done before she'd left for this trip, but it wasn't hard to figure out once she tracked down soap, water, and a cloth.

About an hour past noon, rustling and creaking came from the second bedroom. She scooped some of the grits from the pot where she'd kept it warm over a low fire and knocked on the door.

"Come in." Daemyn's voice sounded stronger than it had last night, even muffled by the door.

She pushed the door open, leaving it ajar behind her.

Daemyn sat on one of the lower bunks, leaning against the wall at the head of the bed with only an inch of headroom to spare under the top bunk.

He hadn't regained a shirt yet, probably because his had been too bloody and torn to be salvageable, and he had the bandage off the wounds in his stomach as he reapplied a new layer of balm. Even from a few feet away, the wounds were far less red and open than she would've expected, as if a week's worth of healing had happened in a single night.

Daemyn remained intent on his task and jabbed an elbow toward the table taking up the wall between the two bunk beds. "Just set it there. Smells like Rita's grits recipe. Just as long as it ain't spiked with Frennie's moonshine."

Rosanna set the bowl down on the table. "I don't think it is. At least, I haven't gotten tipsy, and I had a whole bowl."

Daemyn's gaze shot up, and he straightened so fast he bumped his head on the top bunk. "Sorry, Princess. I thought Zeke . . . never mind. I . . ." He glanced around, as if searching for a shirt.

Rosanna plopped on the other lower bunk. Based on the rumbled blankets, it was probably where Zeke had slept last night. "Don't stop changing your bandages on my account. I saw worse last night."

"I'm sorry. I would've spared you that if I could've. I'm almost done." He glanced over his shoulder as if to try to see the bandages on his back before he capped the jar of balm as if intending to pack up the medical supplies.

"It's all right to ask for help." She tried to meet his gaze, but he looked away, his jaw tight. "You died to keep me safe. Now let me help you in this one, small thing."

With a sigh, Daemyn leaned forward and rested his elbows on his knees. "Do you think you could change the bandages on my back?"

Two bandages were plastered to his back, one above his heart, and the other on his lower back near his spine. A scar the width of a long knife's blade sliced into his skin near the bandage by his heart, as if he'd been stabbed in the back. Other scars dotted his back as if he'd been arrow shot many, many times.

Surely one man couldn't live through so many wounds?

Or had he?

She'd thought he'd been joking when he said it wasn't the first time he'd been dead, but what if he had been telling her the truth? How many times had Daemyn Rand died?

His back tensed, as if bracing himself for an onslaught of questions that would pierce him like a barrage of arrows.

She drew in a deep breath. She'd offered to help him, not pry for answers he wasn't yet ready to give. Better to gift him with her patience than force the answers from him.

She stepped closer and reached for the bandages. "I don't have experience with changing bandages. I pull these off, check for infection, and spread more salve on, right?"

His shoulders fell as he released a long breath. "Honestly, they don't need changing if you don't want to do this. There won't be any infection, and Zeke can change the bandages when he returns. I'm fine."

He'd been dead yesterday. He was far from fine. Rosanna shook her head, though he wouldn't be able to see with his head bowed. "I can handle it, all right? Just because I'm a princess doesn't mean I'm useless in everything."

That brought his head up. "You're not useless. I didn't mean it like that. I just . . ."

"Want to protect me. I know." Rosanna tugged on the bandage plastered over his heart. "Now hold still."

He didn't so much as flinch as she pulled off the bandage. Beneath, the wound was mostly closed, now more pink than red. He held the jar of balm out to her, and she scooped some with her fingers and worked it over the wound. Once she had the new bandage on, she made quick work of the second wound.

She cleaned her fingers on a scrap of cloth and gathered the medical supplies into a pile.

Daemyn swiveled his feet to the floor and grimaced, pressing a hand to his chest.

Rosanna stopped him with a hand to his shoulder. "No, don't get up. You need rest."

"I need a shirt."

"I'll fetch one for you."

He leaned against the wall once again, grimacing even with that small movement. "The trunk at the foot of the bed. Just pick one."

Rosanna knelt before the wooden trunk at the far end of the bunk bed. Inside lay a few fringed, buckskin shirts and pairs of leggings. She grabbed the first shirt from the pile, shut the trunk, and handed it to Daemyn.

As he shrugged into the shirt, she regained her seat on the mattress of the lower bunk across from him.

Daemyn tied the laces at the neck of his shirt, still not looking at her. "You haven't plied me with questions yet."

"I reckon you'll tell me eventually." She gripped the edge of the mattress. She'd given him trust by not asking until now. Would he trust her in return? "Were you given the Fae gift of indestructability or something like that?"

Daemyn's laugh didn't have the joy a laugh should. "Something like that." He leaned his head against the wall. "The story is a mite long."

Rosanna shrugged and waved at the open door. "We have time. Zeke left to scout and said he wouldn't be back until dark."

Daemyn stared at the door as if he saw something beyond the log walls. "Not many people remember that when the high prince's curse was given, he was cursed to sleep for all time. No hope of waking. No promised princess. Nothing but endless sleep for him and all within Castle Eyota's walls. High Prince Alexander realized the kingdoms would crumble without a high king to hold them together so he and his manservant Jadon Rand set out to find a Fae to remove the curse."

"Jadon Rand, your great-grandfather?" Rosanna shifted on the bunk bed so that she, too, could lean against the wall.

Daemyn continued, as if the story caught him too deeply to hear her. "High Prince Alexander and Jadon traveled far across Tallahatchia to the very throne of the Highest King himself to ask for the curse to be removed."

"Really?" Rosanna savored again the memory of the tree's song. What glories must the high prince and his servant have experienced stepping foot into the throne room of the Lord of All Things? "Did your great-grandfather ever tell stories of what it was like?"

"No. The things he saw there were beyond what can be expressed with mere words." Daemyn had his eyes closed, as if lost in that moment long, long ago. "While Jadon knelt there in the presence of the Highest King, a calling settled on his heart so strongly he couldn't refuse. He asked that he might be the one to bring the promised princess to wake the high prince, and the Lord of the Fae granted his request, giving him life and strength to complete his task."

If the Highest King gave Jadon Rand the task to bring her to the castle, then where was he? What was . . .

No, that couldn't be. It was too impossible. She shook her head, though the movement did little to disrupt the whirl in her mind.

Daemyn lifted his head and met her gaze. "I'm Jadon Rand."

"But that . . . your father was friends with my father. You can't . . ." How could this be possible? That would make Daemyn over a hundred years old.

"A few years after the high prince fell asleep, I realized I wasn't aging. Not at all. As the years passed, I managed to age myself by putting ashes in my hair, but that couldn't go on forever. So, I invented a son and when the time came, I became that son. I've done that several times since." Daemyn lowered his gaze from hers and rubbed at an old scar across his palm. "I can't die. Not and stay dead, anyway."

That's why the river pirates called him the Cursed One. How often had the Highest Prince appeared beside Daemyn's—or Jadon's—lifeless body and woken him again for yet more years of toiling for this mission? She swallowed at the lump building in her throat. "How many times?"

"Eight."

He'd died eight times. Her gaze caught on the scar on his neck under his jaw. Arlen Rand had died by having his throat slit. *Daemyn* had died from that wound. From a knife in his back. From other wounds a total of eight times.

Perhaps the river pirates were right to call him cursed. It seemed like an awful thing to have to die several times over, yet never able to stay dead, until this one task was finished. A task that depended on her, of all people, to complete it. "What happens to you if I wake High Prince Alexander?"

He sighed and stared at the ceiling. "I don't know. Maybe I'll just start aging again. Or maybe all the years I've lived will catch up with me, and I'll die. Somehow, I suspect it will be the latter."

Rosanna dug her fingers into the mattress. How could she wake the high prince knowing that doing so could kill Daemyn? "That's horrible."

"Not really." He shook his head. "I've lived a hundred and twenty years. It will be a hundred and twenty-one on High Prince Alexander's birthday. I watched my parents, my siblings, my nieces and nephews, even most of my great-nieces and nephews die before me. There are times I'm so . . . tired. I'm ready, if that's what comes. I've glimpsed into Beyond. It's no horror to finally enter there."

She blinked and looked away from him. How could she selfishly want him to stay longer when he had lived so long, suffered so much? "And you never married?"

As soon as she said it, she gave herself a mental kick. Why would she ask something like that? It sounded like she hinted at something more. Which she never could. Now more than ever.

"No. I couldn't marry, knowing I'd watch my wife die, my children die, maybe even my grandchildren die, all without ever aging myself. I couldn't do that to them or myself." Something almost like a smile crossed Daemyn's face for the first time since he'd started his story. "But I've never been as alone as I thought I would be the day I asked for this task. I told my parents and my siblings as much as I could, and they made a pact that they and their descendants would aid me, and, though I certainly didn't ask for such help, there hasn't been a day when I haven't been grateful for it."

"So Zeke is actually your great-great-grandnephew?" Rosanna plucked at the rumpled blankets she'd shoved aside on the bunk bed. "And he knows all of this?"

"Yes, and he insists on calling me Uncle Daemyn, even though I've told him just Daemyn is fine. At least it's easier to say than Great-Great-Great Uncle Daemyn." His expression warmed until his mouth was fully tipped up in a genuine smile. "And he's been one of my staunchest friends and allies these past few years, as you probably gathered."

"And Captain Boda? You said he was a relative?"

"Yes, a great-grandnephew." Daemyn shrugged. "I have relatives scattered across all seven kingdoms. Not all of them know the whole story, but many have chosen to continue the family legacy."

"I'm glad you've had them. It would've been awful to have no one." Rosanna let out a shaky breath and forced herself to smile. "So, what should I call you? Daemyn or Jadon?"

"Daemyn. As far as the Tuckawassee know, Jadon Rand died from a knife when he was thirty-nine years old. I reckon the person I was as Jadon died then too. A hundred years—living so many names—changes a person."

She wasn't sure what to say. He was over a hundred and twenty years old. He had traveled with High Prince Alexander, seen the very throne of the Highest King, fought for nearly a hundred years to preserve Tallahatchia and find *her*. All for some promise, some duty, he'd taken on when her great-grand-father had been ruling.

It was the reason he hadn't aged instead of being given a long life. This task was one for a young man. It demanded the strength of the young as well as the experience and wisdom granted to the old.

It was all too much to wrap her head around. It wouldn't settle into her mind and heart the way it should.

She'd started to think he was the sort of man she could

be attracted to. Adventurous, daring, skilled, patient. Trusting of her skills without trivializing them. The way he savored the old things and stories as much as she did.

But of course he did. Those old things—like the bridges and the tales of what Tallahatchia had once been—he'd seen them. Lived them.

The distance he'd kept between them most of the time made sense now. Yes, she was a princess, and he was of the mountain stock, though respected or feared by the kings and nobility of Tallahatchia. And, yes, the fact that she was High Prince Alexander's cursebreaker seemed to connect them somehow, a connection almost expected to be romantic even if she and the high prince had never even seen each other, much less talked. From what Daemyn had told her, that part of the story was an embellishment anyway.

But more than that, Daemyn kept her at arm's length because of the *time* between them. He had lived nearly a hundred and twenty-one years. He had seen things, done things, experienced life in a way she couldn't in her own twenty-one years.

Besides, Daemyn wasn't sure he'd live past the high prince's birthday. The moment she broke the curse might be the moment Daemyn died for real this time, and Daemyn was far too honorable to start any deeper relationship with that possibility hanging over his head.

She shook herself. All thoughts of romance—and Daemyn's possible death—could wait. Thinking about the one was fruitless right now, and thinking about the other . . . if she thought about it too long, she might refuse to see this mission through.

She wrapped her hands around her knees. "What was —is—High Prince Alexander like?"

Daemyn blew out a breath. "I'm not sure I should tell you the truth. Many in Tallahatchia have pinned their hopes on High Prince Alexander waking, and he's . . ."

"That bad?" Rosanna winced, something in her chest crumbling. She needed to believe High Prince Alexander was worth waking. Surely he was worth the cost, right?

But what about her two guardsmen who had been injured? All the people killed by the raiding parties of Tuckawassee and Pohatomie? Those who would yet suffer as Tallahatchia dissolved further into chaos?

Isi. Captain Degotaga. Her other four guards. Captured or dead, she still didn't know.

And Daemyn. It had cost him a hundred years of living and could yet cost him his life before he'd had a chance at living apart from this duty.

What if High Prince Alexander wasn't worth it?

If that was the case, she wasn't sure she could step outside this cabin and continue onward. What was the point if it wouldn't solve anything?

Daemyn shook his head. "The prince was raised to be a high prince. He holds that birthright very tightly. It's everything to him, for good or bad, often leading to arrogance. But, he was different that last month before his birthday. How much of that change will continue after he wakes, I don't know."

"Will he be a good high king? Restore the bridges and peace and everything like people say?"

Daemyn didn't meet her gaze. "Honestly, I don't know."

That hurt deep down. She'd trusted that waking High Prince Alexander would make the chaos in Tallahatchia better.

And now that trust ripped from her fingers. What was

the purpose of everything sacrificed if Daemyn—the man who had once been Jadon Rand, personal manservant to the high prince—didn't even know?

"Why?" She clenched her fists, balling them against the mattress as if prepared to punch someone. "Why bother waking him if it won't make a difference?"

"Because the Highest King has commanded it." Daemyn locked his gaze with hers again. There was something pained there, along with a depth of trust she wasn't sure she'd ever have. "The Lord of All decreed that High Prince Alexander will wake and has tasked me and you as the means to see it done. We must obey and trust the end that has already been written in the Highest King's halls. I don't know what the result will be. I don't know if Tallahatchia will be restored or fall into deeper chaos. In the end, that doesn't matter because High Prince Alexander was never to be our hope in the first place. Our hope is beyond him."

Looking into Daemyn's eyes, it was as if the trees sang again of their hope for the Coming Cursebreaker. The trees, the mountains, they didn't know or care about High Prince Alexander's curse. Their song saw beyond the politics and daily life that muddied truth. The trees sang for the final cursebreaking, the one true hope in all.

Daemyn's gaze remained on her. "In less than two weeks, we will wake High Prince Alexander and trust what comes after will be what the Highest King has decreed."

She drew in a shaky breath and nodded. Perhaps it took a hundred years to learn a trust like Daemyn's. Or maybe trust like that was the only way Daemyn had been able to survive a hundred years of toil and fighting and struggle.

Her skin prickled with the whisper of a draft. One of the chinks in the cabin walls must be missing.

She had been given the gift to hear. And that gift only meant something if she obeyed what she heard.

The Highest King had commanded, and she would obey. "All right."

The cabin door slammed open, out of Rosanna's line of sight. She flew to her feet, but Daemyn placed a hand on her arm. He shook his head and pressed a finger to his mouth.

"Uncle Daemyn? Princess Rosanna?" Zeke called out.

Daemyn released Rosanna's arm and slid to his feet. He shuffled forward, a hand to his chest. But he waved her off, refusing her help.

She followed Daemyn into the main room. Zeke gripped his hardwood staff, his leggings wet from the knees down. She peered around him, but he was alone. "You're here earlier than you expected. Did you find my guards? Are they all right? Where are they?"

Zeke scratched the back of his head. "The Tuckawassee have them."

CHAPTER 25

ALEXANDER

ONE HUNDRED YEARS AGO

Alex shook his head and blinked at the darkness around him. Specks of the light of beyond still burst across his vision. He squeezed his eyes shut and counted to ten before he opened them again.

The sky above seemed darker than it should, the entire world cast in shadows of black and gray, even though, based on the location of the sun, it was just past noon.

He lay at the edge of a pool, a small waterfall dumping into one end. But it wasn't the turquoise stream where he and Jadon had entered beyond. This creek was the normal clear water with muddy brown bank beneath. Nothing unusual or special about it.

Alex groaned and eased upright. A few feet away, Jadon already sat up, scrubbing at his eyes as if he couldn't figure out how to make them work properly in the normal light of day.

"I think . . . were we dead for a while there? Did I just dream it all?" Alex rubbed at his temples. Surely the things he'd seen were not meant for the eyes of the living.

Jadon glanced from him, to the pool next to them, and back. "I'm not really sure."

Alex pushed to his feet and swayed until his sense of balance remembered which way was up. How long were they there? It seemed like moments, yet something in him ached like he no longer walked in the same step of time as the world around him. "Where are we?"

Jadon stood and turned in a slow circle. "If I didn't know better, I'd say this was Clearwater Creek only a few miles from Castle Eyota."

Alex spun as well, taking in the creek, the hollow around them, the trees. From here, one of the rope bridges was visible cross the gorge above the waterfall. "I think you're right."

Somehow, they'd been returned to Tallahatchia hundreds of miles from where they had left it. Even their packs had been returned to them, though they had abandoned them at the banks of that other stream before entering the waterfall. Alex shouldn't have been surprised, not after the things he'd seen. But the result was disorienting.

Alex shook himself. "I guess we should return to the castle."

After all they had been through, it was almost too easy to hike back to the castle in a short few hours along easy, safe trails.

But he'd failed. He'd gone to Beyond and back, and yet he would return with his curse still hanging over him.

If he were stronger, he'd go off to some hidden tower to await his birthday on his own. But he wasn't that strong. He didn't want to face the curse alone. Nor, if the Lord of the Fae's promise of a cursebreaker held true, did he want to wake alone. His parents should be there, if they wished to share his curse with him.

Alex took several strides toward the path, then halted. He turned around to face Jadon.

Jadon carried the pack, his eyes downcast in his servant's posture once again. Something about that rubbed wrong. Jadon had loyally gone with Alex to the ends of Tallahatchia and Beyond.

Alex swallowed and tried to find words. What could he say? "Jadon. . . thank you."

Jadon met his gaze and gave one nod.

It was enough. No more words were needed.

After spinning on his heels, Alex hiked up the gorge to the spur of the Trace following the ridge above. This trail would lead them back to the castle.

Alex halted after they had only gone a few yards. A short tree with bunches of white blossoms stood a few feet from the trail. Farther along, a similar tree bloomed in pale pink. "The rhododendrons are blooming."

Jadon joined Alex. "A month must have passed while we were in Beyond."

Meaning his birthday was only weeks away, not the months Alex thought he'd have to prepare. The precious time he'd had left had been wasted on that failed quest.

Or mostly failed. He at least had a promise he would wake. Eventually. It wasn't nearly good enough. Alex shouldn't be forced to sleep at all. But it was all he had.

He set out again at a faster clip. He needed to return home and spend time with Mirabelle. Perhaps with a promise to wake, she would sleep too, and they could be together.

The trail and ridge curved to their right, and the gorge

opened before them. The Kanawhee River sparkled with sun-flecked rivulets while the distant mountains blurred green and gold as the spring leaves caught the sun.

On the sand-colored cliffs above the Kanawhee gleamed Castle Eyota, its spires spearing the sky unbowed before the might of the surrounding mountains.

Home.

Alex strode forward. Just a short walk along the ridge to the dock on this side of the river where they could catch a ferry across the river to Eyota and from there walk to the castle. They would be home well before dinner.

Except the bustling surrounding the town was subdued. Where were all the merchant canoes and river-boats plying the river? They all seemed to be docked or . . .

On the river below them, a large raft with two outrig-ging canoes caught Alex's attention. The raft had a black canopy stretched over it and the red standard of the high king flew at all four corners. A fleet of canoes and other barges filled the river surrounding it.

Alex froze, something in him reeling. He'd seen a barge like that twice before. Once for his grandfather when he was ten and again for his grandmother when he was fourteen.

A royal funeral barge.

"No." He tore down the trail the way they'd come, swerving to avoid Jadon. He didn't take the time to explain.

He raced down the trail, then turned onto a spur trail down the side of the gorge. He slipped and slid most of his descent, reaching the shore as the funeral barge beached onto the pebbles.

His mother leapt from the barge into the shallows and

dashed toward him heedless of the water and the swarms of onlookers.

"Alex!" She clung to him, her body thinner in his arms than he remembered. Black crow feathers were braided in her hair, a sign of mourning. Her shoulders shook as she held him, though he couldn't hear her sobs.

Maybe this barge was for him. His parents had probably thought him dead when he didn't return when expected from his journey.

How he wanted that to be the case. But the longer he held his mother without his father regally disembarking to greet him as well, he knew. "Father?"

"Water hemlock. He died four days ago." Something in Mother's face went rigid and cold at the words.

Water hemlock. Poison. Alex's father hadn't simply died. He'd been murdered.

It was no light thing to murder a high king.

This was a silent, deadly declaration of war.

Alex shook and hugged his mother as the other canoes arrived. Guards, courtiers, and castle servants disembarked and solemnly gathered.

He was too numb to cry. He couldn't process anything long enough to feel the ache he should at news of his father's death, as if he was a log tossed on a flooding river with no say in where he went.

Someone found him a few spare crow feathers that he bound into his hair so they dangled near his right ear. Jadon relieved him of his pack, the lack of its weight a reminder of things lost instead of a freeing relief.

His father lay still and white on a stretcher of finest doeskin, a black bear's hide covering him. His dagger rested under his folded hands and a circlet glinted on his brow.

When the four stretcher bearers grasped the poles and

lifted, Alex took his place at the head of the procession. He marched up the trail ascending the gorge, then still higher into the mountains. If his calves burned or his heart pounded, he couldn't feel them.

Just below the crest, row upon row of carved boulders marked the tombs of his ancestors. Near the stones for his grandparents, a hole gaped into the mountain's side, prepared over the past days while his father must have lain in state in the great hall.

If he'd been here when his father died, he would've had time to prepare for his duties in this moment. Would it have made a difference? Would the loss have been any less sudden or the goodbye any less painful?

Perhaps, perhaps not. He hadn't known when he'd said farewell all those months ago that it would be the last time he saw his father alive. There were so many things he should've said back then.

Yet if he had been here, would he have said them? Or were some things always left unsaid when death came?

He laid a hand on his father's cold forehead. If he'd had time, he might have given a speech in this moment. But now, all he could think was to say the final blessing as was his duty as his father's firstborn son. "To the depths of the earth and the heights of Beyond I commit you until the end of time."

He let his hand fall away and stepped back.

The bearers slid the stretcher and body into the hole cut in the side of the hill. With the grating of stone, four men rolled a boulder over the tomb's entrance, sealing it for all time.

His father was dead. Alex closed his eyes, even now hearing an echo of the song beyond the WaterVeil. Had his father's voice been among the singers even as Alex knelt in that throne room? He ached for the WaterVeil that now separated him from his father, a door the living were not permitted to enter.

But he had duties here. Now, if he slept on his twenty-first birthday, it would be as the high king of Tallahatchia.

CHAPTER 26

ROSANNA

Rosanna wrapped her arms around her stomach. "Where? All of them?"

"They're holding them not far downstream." Zeke paused. "They captured three of your guards, along with your guard captain and maid. The fourth was killed. I found his body and gave him a decent burial."

Which of her guards had been killed? It wasn't Ilma since Zeke had buried a man, but what about Otho, Chogan, or Garmund? Which one now lay dead? She squeezed her eyes shut, fighting the ache in her chest. How much longer would they keep them alive? "We have to rescue them."

"There are nearly twenty Tuckawassee holding them. I'm not sure we have a chance to get anywhere near them." Zeke shook his head and glanced at Daemyn. "Even with your near invincibility, it would be tough to get all of them away without someone besides you getting killed."

"Now that Major Beshko thinks she's killed me, it

would be best if I stayed dead, at least as far as she's concerned." Daemyn pressed a hand over the bandaged wounds in his stomach. The way he was hunched over, he probably shouldn't be standing. "While I'm healing quickly, I won't be at full strength for a couple of days."

"Please. We have to try. We can't just leave them there." Rosanna glanced from Zeke to Daemyn. "I know time is short to reach Castle Eyota before the high prince's birthday, and I know I shouldn't risk myself. But I can't leave Isi there. She's my friend. And her father and my guards have loyally guarded me for years. I can't turn my back on them."

Daemyn met her gaze and nodded. "We'll do what we can. Tonight would be best, I think."

"Meaning we all should eat, sleep, and eat some more." Zeke turned to Rosanna with something like a grin. "Uncle Daemyn thinks better on a full stomach."

Rosanna crouched in the forest a few yards downstream from the Tuckawassee camp. Daemyn and Zeke had disappeared into the forest somewhere to her left.

Several fires blazed in pits cleared of undergrowth and dead leaves. Chogan, Ilma, and Otho were bound to trees on one side of the camp. Isi was tied to another tree a few feet away with Captain Degotaga. Captain Degotaga angled his body in front of her, as if he could protect her, tied as he was.

No Garmund. Rosanna let out a shaky breath. She couldn't absorb his death now. She had to focus on rescuing her friends still living.

She curled her fingers around Daemyn's dagger,

keeping it hidden beneath her arm so it wouldn't flash. As much as she wanted to charge over there and rescue Isi now, she couldn't do it. Not yet. She had to wait for Daemyn's signal.

Shouting came from the far side of camp. Two of the Tuckawassee strode into the firelight, rolling a large keg. They set it upright near one of the fires so the it could be seen clearly.

Major Beshko strode over to them. "What's this?"

The men saluted. "It appears to be a keg of some sort of mountain moonshine. We found it in a canoe abandoned in the creek just outside our perimeter. We were doing a wide sweep when we found it."

Major Beshko inspected the keg. She frowned, the frown deepening when she opened the keg and tasted a sip. "Unless this rotgut is poisoned, it seems to be exactly what it appears. I wonder what the mountain folk are up to?"

"The canoe had a hole in it." One of the Tuckawassee soldiers shrugged. "Maybe both the keg and the canoe had to be left behind when the canoe was damaged?"

"And no one else found it on previous sweeps?" Major Beshko shook her head. "I don't like it."

Straightening, Major Beshko shouted orders for ten of her men to search the woods around where the canoe had been found.

Rosanna held his breath as the men moved off. If one of the Tuckawassee stumbled across Zeke or Daemyn, or even her if they got out this far . . .

She swallowed and ran Daemyn's instructions through her head again. If the Tuckawassee came in her direction, she was to stay absolutely still. Unless they stepped on her, they wouldn't see her in the dark if she remembered not to move.

Crashing and tromping came from the forest, though most of it remained on the far side of the Tuckawassee camp.

Her heart pounding in her ears, she inched forward. Slowly. That's what Daemyn had told her. Feel for sticks in front of her. Ease the branches over herself. Creep forward inch by patient inch.

The minutes ticked by. Her muscles tensed with the warring needs inside her. She had to get as close to the camp as she could before Zeke and Daemyn made their move, yet she couldn't hurry. To hurry would be to make noise. And making noise could get her caught.

The fires in the camp still blazed, hot and furious. The keg remained where Major Beshko had left it, close to one of the fires with the lid removed.

Isi dozed, her head resting on Captain Degotaga's shoulder. Captain Degotaga swept his gaze around the camp, wary, probably looking for a way to escape.

And Rosanna planned to give him one.

She circled through the forest, coming from behind where her friends and guards were tied to trees. She was only a few yards away from the edge of the firelight when a pinprick of light flared in the forest across the camp from her.

Major Beshko shouted and pointed. Before any of her men could do more than straighten and grip their weapons, an arrow flew from the darkness, its tip on fire.

The Tuckawassee ducked, but the arrow flashed past them and landed in the keg of moonshine.

With a whump, the heated alcohol vapor caught and exploded, tearing the barrel apart. The heated, burning moonshine splashed several of the guards standing closest to the fire. They batted at their clothes, trying put out the fire and shouting. Their weapons fell from their hands in their haste.

Otho pressed his leg to the dirt, kicking to put out the fire. It snuffed out, leaving little of the fabric singed.

She couldn't hesitate. That was her signal. She rose to a crouch, dashed forward, and crashed to her knees behind the tree where Captain Degotaga and Isi were tied.

Huddled behind the tree, she couldn't see what was happening in the Tuckawassee camp. But Major Beshko was ordering her remaining men into the forest after the man who'd shot the arrow. Hopefully none of them would look this way.

Rosanna touched Isi's hand. "Stay still. Don't move until I've cut all of you free."

Isi's hand twitched. Rosanna took that as a sign that Isi understood. Sliding the dagger beneath the rope, Rosanna sawed as hard as she could. Sharp as the dagger was, it took some effort for it to part each strand.

Finally, the rope holding Isi and Captain Degotaga to the tree parted. Neither of them moved, but they rubbed at their wrists.

Rosanna peeked around the tree. Few of the Tuckawassee remained in camp. Crashes came from the undergrowth on the far side. Some shouting. The cracks of either Daemyn's or Zeke's hardwood staffs against flesh and bone.

She dashed to the next tree and touched Ilma's arm. "It's me. Rosanna. Don't move until I give the word."

She sawed at the rope again. This rope seemed to take even longer to part. When it did, she peered around the tree. The shouting and crashing was even farther away now. Any minute now Major Beshko would realize all the attacking and fighting was just a distraction. They had to get out of here. She leaned closer. "Time to go."

Her guards jumped to their feet and spun around the tree. She pointed and waved deeper into the woods. As the guards hurried in that direction, Captain Degotaga and Isi clambered to their feet.

Rosanna grinned at Isi. If they had time, she would've given her a hug. But Isi just grinned back and tilted her head as if to say, *Shouldn't we get moving?*

Rosanna led the way deeper into the woods, circling toward the river once they were well away from camp, just as Daemyn had instructed.

When they were about a mile upstream of the Tuckawassee camp, Rosanna found the cluster of boulders Zeke had shown her and Daemyn earlier that evening. The fifteen-foot canoe lay hidden beneath the undergrowth.

"We need to get going." Rosanna lifted one end of the canoe. "Otho, how's your leg? I hope you didn't get burned too badly?"

Otho shook his head. "No, Princess. But thanks for your concern."

She nodded, glancing between the faces of her remaining guards. An ache filled a part of her chest at those missing—the injured Nikan and Ahanu and dead Garmund—but she couldn't acknowledge it now.

Isi gave a muffled squeal and hugged her. "You were so amazing! I couldn't believe it was you back there rescuing us."

Rosanna grinned. "I had help. Daemyn planned it all."

"He got you away from the Tuckawassee safely, I assume." Captain Degotaga lifted the other end of the canoe. As they had run through the woods, he'd favored his right leg, but Rosanna hadn't seen any bloodstains. He must've twisted it while trying to escape the Tuckawassee before.

Rosanna hesitated. How could she explain about Daemyn's death, and how he didn't stay dead, and the whole part about him being Jadon Rand and over a hundred years old?

It was too much for tonight. Perhaps she never would tell them everything, not even Isi.

Daemyn had been right. There were some things that were too precious to speak out loud and too real to put into words. Perhaps Rosanna would never tell a soul about the song she'd heard the trees and mountains sing, except Daemyn. He was one of the few who would understand.

"Yes, he did. And we found his nephew Zeke Rand who was waiting to assist us. Now let's get this canoe in the river. The Tuckawassee should be busy for a while following Daemyn and Zeke downriver, but I don't want to take chances." Rosanna hauled her end of the canoe into the water as Captain Degotaga did the same with his. She held it steady while the others climbed in.

Rosanna claimed the seat in the stern and picked up a paddle. The extra paddlers would make going upstream much easier than it had been the night before.

Before they could get more than two yards out into the river, a silhouette appeared on the rocks above them, puffy hair in a braid. Major Beshko's voice rang into the night. "That was clever back there, Princess."

Rosanna drew in a deep breath to keep herself calm, gripping her paddle. She glanced at Isi, Captain Degotaga, and her three remaining guards. She had to get them away safely. "Don't try to stop us."

Captain Degotaga lifted his paddle as if he intended to leap from the canoe and fight Major Beshko.

"Most of my men are chasing ghosts in the forest." Major Beshko held out her hands. Even in the low light, it was clear her weapons remained in her belt. "I'm not here to try to stop you. Not tonight. You're free to go. But before you do, stop and think. Do you really believe your kingdom or mine will be better if you wake the high prince?"

"Princess . . ." Captain Degotaga's voice was low.

She should put her paddle in the water and shove off. Major Beshko was letting them go, conceding this battle to fight another day.

But, she couldn't force her muscles to move. She wasn't sure Tallahatchia would be better. Even Daemyn wasn't sure.

Major Beshko planted her hands on her hips. "Don't you see? Our kingdoms are free of each other, without the tyranny of the high king."

She met Major Beshko's calculating gaze in the dark. Something like understanding shivered between them. They both had their duty. They both loved their kingdoms.

But that's where the connection ended. Major Beshko had tortured Daemyn in the name of her duty, and that was something Rosanna would never understand.

"We aren't free, not as long as this war continues. Nor do I think we're better apart when we're stronger together." Rosanna shook her head and reached for her paddle. Captain Degotaga was right. It was time to get out of here.

Major Beshko took a step back, lowering her hands to her sides. "Next time we meet, remember, I tried. You wouldn't listen."

Rosanna let out a long breath. Time to leave. Together, she and her friends propelled the canoe across the night-shrouded river.

CHAPTER 27

ROSANNA

By the time Isi woke the next morning in the bunk across from her, Rosanna had changed into a clean shirt and trousers Zeke had scrounged from somewhere, probably from a cousin or aunt considering the clothes were only a mite big. Or maybe Zeke kept a whole trunk of clothes in various sizes for emergencies.

Isi yawned, stretched, and glanced over at Rosanna. "I'd forgotten how much I missed sleeping in a real bed."

Rosanna tilted her head as she braided her hair. "I'm going to be sad to leave. Warm food and real beds. It's amazing the things you take for granted sometimes." She paused and cocked her head so that she could meet Isi's gaze while gripping her half-finished braid in her hands. "Like you. I'm glad we were able to rescue you. I don't want to lose my best friend."

"Did you really think you could lose me that easily?" Isi shook her head, moved across the room, and plopped down next to Rosanna. "You can't function a day without my help, can you? I mean, look at this braid."

"That bad?"

"Worse." Isi took the braid from Rosanna's hands and combed her fingers through Rosanna's hair to start over. "If the Tuckawassee hadn't made me leave my beadwork behind, I'd do something about that shirt. Pitifully plain, really."

Rosanna doubted glass beads and thread were something even Zeke could scrounge up on short notice. "I'm fine, really. It's not like it matters here if I'm looking my best."

Isi tugged on Rosanna's hair as she began braiding. "It always matters. A girl who looks her best holds her head high. And you could use a little confidence. Then you'd actually tell Daemyn Rand you like him."

"What? I don't—" Rosanna tried to shake her head but couldn't with Isi gripping her hair. She sighed. Why fight it? Isi knew her like a sister. "It doesn't matter. It wouldn't work between us."

"Why ever not? I know you're a princess and he's not nobility, but he's well-respected. And marrying a commoner isn't as frowned upon as it was years ago."

"It just wouldn't. There are things . . . it's complicated." Rosanna couldn't explain. Daemyn had trusted her with his secret. She couldn't go blabbing to Isi the whole he's-actually-a-hundred-and-twenty-years-old thing.

"One more question, then talking about boys will be done for the rest of today. Would it bother you if I flirted with Daemyn's nephew?"

Zeke and Isi. A good idea, or a bad one? Rosanna grinned. "No problem at all."

"Good." Isi's hands paused halfway through the braid, her mouth flat and serious once again. "What really happened yesterday after we split up?"

How much could Rosanna tell? "Some of the Tuckawassee caught us. Daemyn was wounded, but he distracted them from my hiding place and they thought they'd captured me when they captured you." Rosanna swallowed at the lump in her throat. How close had she come to losing Isi? Isi didn't seem too eager to tell her about it.

"And they just left him behind?"

"He was wounded pretty badly. They left him for dead." Actually, he was dead. But that was verging into territory Rosanna couldn't talk about, not even with Isi.

Isi frowned. "I thought he moved slower last night, but he didn't seem too badly wounded."

"He heals fast." That was true. Not the full truth, but enough. "It's hard to explain."

"I'm beginning to see that." Isi's fingers flew through braiding Rosanna's hair. "Now that we've left the canoes and all our supplies behind, how are we getting to Kanawhee? I really hope we don't have to walk the whole way."

"I don't know. Zeke seems to have an excess of spare canoes lying around. Maybe he'll have a few more spares for us. And some extra food."

Isi smiled as she tied off the braid. "Oh, he will. I have complete trust in him."

Once Isi had a chance to straighten up her own clothes, Rosanna led the way into the other room.

Daemyn, Captain Degotaga, Chogan, and Ilma gathered around the table finishing off a breakfast of flapjacks and sausage. Zeke didn't appear to be anywhere in the small cabin while Otho stood next to the window, keeping watch.

While Captain Degotaga made room for Isi on one side

of the table, Daemyn shifted over on the bench for Rosanna. She perched next to him and reached for a plate. "How are your wounds today?"

Across the table, Isi snatched the bottle of maple syrup like it was filled with gold and proceeded to douse her flapjacks with enough syrup that they just about floated on her plate.

"Healing. I'll be able to pull the stitches tonight." Daemyn speared a flapjack with a knife and transferred it to her plate. "We'll be moving out again tomorrow, if we can."

Something in his reserved tone and expression spoke of distance, as if the presence of Captain Degotaga and the other guards reminded Daemyn of his station and place.

The distance rubbed at Rosanna. After all they'd been through, he could at least be easy and smiling with her. They were friends, even if they could be nothing more.

Friends. That's how she'd treat him, then. He certainly could use a friend or two.

Before she could think of anything else to say, the door swung open, and Zeke stepped inside. "The Tuckawassee are scouring the mountains around here. Major Beshko is madder than a bear with a hangover."

"Will they find us before tomorrow?" Daemyn straightened, as if preparing to push to his feet.

"Don't reckon so. They're mostly sticking to the main river." Zeke set his staff next to the door. "Eventually they'll come across our tracks and dog our heels all the way into Kanawhee."

"And probably catch us again." Captain Degotaga shook his head. "Any options?"

"Not many. They know where we are headed, and we can't risk taking a longer route and have them get ahead of us." Daemyn shook his head and poked at the last few bites of flapjack on his plate. "We'll just have to push harder. We have friends on both sides of the border. They'll have to be enough."

"I was afraid of this."

Rosanna glanced over her shoulder at Isi as they marched up a trail deeper into the mountains separating Tuckawassee from Kanawhee. "Just be glad we get to make this hike without portaging canoes."

Zeke grinned so widely it could only be called beaming. And the full force of that beaming was directed at Isi. "My thoughts exactly. Uncle Daemyn tends to get too attached to canoes and takes them with him. I decided it was easier to have my Uncle Clive and Aunt Nettie and that pack of cousins build me several canoes than portage one over a mountain."

Captain Degotaga glared at the back of Zeke's head. "Pay attention to the front. You're supposed to be leading us."

Zeke grinned and strode farther in front of them.

Rosanna glanced over her shoulder again, past Isi, Captain Degotaga, and Otho. Daemyn scouted their back trail. Should he have gone off by himself? What if his wounds started bleeding again?

Her toe caught on a stone in the trail, and she stumbled forward a few steps. Isi gave a muffled snort, and Rosanna huffed and faced forward again. She'd end up flat on her face if she kept trying to walk like that.

They crested another small rise before the trail dipped down for a short stretch before winding upward again.

With a crackling of leaves, Daemyn strode past her and

caught up with Zeke. "No sign of them on our immediate back trail. I think we should be safe at Frennie's tonight."

"Good. I don't want to lead trouble right to Aunt Frennie's doorstep." Zeke shrugged. "Though if anyone can take care of herself, it would be Aunt Frennie."

Rosanna quickened her pace until she walked next to Daemyn. "Aunt Frennie? Is this the same one who makes the moonshine?"

Zeke's grin widened. "She's a hoot and a holler, she is. When Uncle Ted was killed by the Tuckawassee, she had to support her and the young'uns somehow and that's when she took up moonshining. Sells it mostly to Tuckawassee soldiers, and after a few swigs, they are more than willing to share vital information she passes along."

"She sounds like an interesting character." Rosanna shot a glance at Daemyn, then lowered her voice so that Isi and the guards couldn't hear. "Does this Aunt Frennie know about . . ."

Daemyn nodded, and his eyes flicked back toward the others. "Yes. But it might be best if the others assume we're cousins or something, as she would be if I was a normal age."

Rosanna rubbed at the callouses on her palms. What was it like for Daemyn, living so far out of his own time? He no longer had any sisters or brothers. Just great-great-grand nieces and nephews. Blood kin, yes. Barely.

His face was set in tight lines, his grip white-knuckled on his hardwood staff. She resisted the urge to lay a hand on his arm. "Are you all right?"

"I'm fine." Daemyn kept his focus straight ahead. "Only a week more on foot, a few days on the rivers, and we'll arrive at Castle Eyota. This is almost over."

"Are you really so eager for this to be finished?" She

focused ahead as well, matching his stride. Was he in a hurry to get rid of her? Of his responsibilities? To die?

Did she want to know the answer?

Daemyn sighed and finally glanced at her, but only for a moment. "Yes. And no."

She should've expected an answer like that out of him. Complicated. That seemed to be his life, and now hers.

After hiking the rest of the day, Daemyn led them up a side trail deep into a mountain glade. A cabin nestled in a stand of pine trees, but the sort of cabin with narrow windows and gables that appeared more like watch towers.

Zeke halted next to Isi. "Aunt Frennie's place. Just to warn you. They're a bit . . . boisterous."

"To put it mildly." Daemyn's mouth twisted, as if he wasn't sure whether to grimace or grin.

As they stepped into the glade, a woman flung the door open. She was rail thin, but with wide, muscular shoulders for her small frame. She looked to be in her late thirties, maybe early forties.

She opened her mouth and caterwauled in a pitch that carried across the meadow. "Uncle Daemyn! Zeke! Come and set a spell. Sam! Jonny! MacyMae! Come see the company!"

"That would be Aunt Frennie." Zeke set out across the hollow. "Such a refined, dignified lady."

Isi's forehead wrinkled as she studied the woman who had called Daemyn her uncle. If Rosanna hadn't known the truth about Daemyn, she would've been puzzled too.

Captain Degotaga frowned, but he and the other guards didn't ask any questions. Yet.

"Well, come on in and rest your feet up." Aunt Frennie waved wildly in their direction.

Rosanna took Isi's arm. "You heard her. You usually don't turn down an opportunity for some fun."

Isi grinned and hurried forward. "You're right. Let's go."

Rosanna was soon wedged on a bench between two girls ages ten and twelve. There were three boys and another girl as well, and she struggled to remember their names as they all introduced themselves over each other in one rowdy bunch.

Aunt Frennie, as she had insisted they all call her whether family or not, served up a mess of hog jowls, corn pone, and biscuits, warm and tasty. Rosanna dug in and ate a large helping. The only reason she didn't ask for a second helping was that there wasn't any left by the time she cleaned her plate. The boys polished off everything and licked out the pot for good measure.

Aunt Frennie jumped to her feet. "Time for some music. Can't end a fine meal like that without a spot of fiddling."

The children rushed from the benches and soon held a variety of instruments from a mouth pipe to a moonshine jug to a hand saw that an older boy tucked between his knees and bent, a fiddle bow in his free hand.

Aunt Frennie produced a fiddle and glanced at Zeke. "Start with Wanderer Over the Mountain?"

Zeke picked up one of the mouth pipes. "Sounds about right, I reckon. Seeing as we are passing through."

With barely a pause, Aunt Frennie launched into the first strains of the song, her bow whipping back and forth over the fiddle strings. The oldest boy coaxed haunting, quavering notes from the hand saw while the middle two boys blew bass notes across the tops of the empty jugs. Two girls piped a harmony on the mouth pipes.

It was a haunting song, a hint of the mourning song the trees had sung. Rosanna leaned forward, letting herself fall into the notes of the song.

The youngest girl set down her pipe and began to sing on the next verse. Something about mountains, traveling, and going home after the weary, long road.

As the song finished, the last note of the saw hung on the air, quavering.

Aunt Frennie sniffed, and for a moment, Rosanna glimpsed a hint of pain and loss. Then Aunt Frennie grinned and poised the bow over the fiddle again. "Something peppy now. Jenny Ferling Hey-Dilly-hey-o."

The family launched into another song. Within moments, Zeke clapped along, and Isi, Chogan, and Ilma joined in. Rosanna grinned and tapped her foot as well. She didn't know these mountain songs, but something in them drew a smile.

This was the sort of life she wanted. Not the finery and bustle of castle life, as much as she appreciated the fine things she'd had growing up. Not even because her family lacked warmth, for she loved her family and they loved her as much as this family did each other.

No, there was just something about the forest, the rivers, the mountains, that called to her the way the town life didn't. She'd take a rushing river, a paddle in her hand, and a sturdy canoe beneath her over a new dress any day.

Not that beautiful dresses or intricate beadwork were wrong. Those things were gifts too, in their own way. Isi's means of expression were her hair styles and beadwork. Rosanna's was a canoe on the river.

Rosanna glanced at Daemyn. He had relaxed enough to clap along as well, but he wasn't singing the way Zeke was.

Less than two weeks. Did the lack of time weigh on him as it did her? Was he looking around this room thinking this could be the last time he saw these family members?

How could she wake High Prince Alexander knowing what it would cost? Not just her. Not even Daemyn. But the entire Rand clan scattered across Tallahatchia. They seemed to care for him more than just a long-living ancestor whom they had pledged to serve. They saw him as part of the family, an integral part.

Daemyn leaned closer and whispered. "You're frowning. Don't think about the mission tonight."

She forced herself to smile. "I won't if you won't."

Something of a smile crossed his face as well. "Then I'd better teach you the chorus so you can sing along."

Tonight, she'd sing. She'd clap. She'd smile.

And she'd forget.

Chapter 28

Alexander

One Hundred Years Ago

The large, geared clock in the grand entry outside the great hall chimed. As Alex strode through the crowd gathered in the hall and climbed the stairs to the dais, he counted the strikes. Noon. Twelve hours until his birthday.

With a deep breath, he faced the room and swept his gaze over the six kings standing in the front row, their entourages of guards arrayed behind them. With the last notes of the clock reverberating in his chest, Alex forced himself to stand tall. "Thank you for assembling today. As you know, at midnight, the clock will strike on my twenty-first birthday, the day I am cursed to fall into a sleep like unto death."

The king of Pohatomie, his blond hair tinged with strands of silver at his temples, stood with his arms crossed. If Alex had support from his mother's distant cousin, he couldn't read it in the Pohatomie king's impassive face.

Though gaunt and pale, King Othniel of Buckhannock stood tall and gave Alex a slow nod. In the summons, Alex allowed for a representative if King Othniel hadn't been able to come in person. Yet, King Othniel was here, and that meant something. An understanding of recent grief none of the others shared.

Alex kept his back straight, his voice firm. "But do not despair. I have journeyed long these past months and have gained a promise that I will not sleep forever."

A low murmur swept through the crowd. The king of Monongadotte leaned over to whisper something to his guard captain, his red beard gleaming in the sunlight pouring through the windows. When he straightened, the massive antlers from the elk's head he wore nearly poked King Hakan of Tuckawassee in the eye.

King Hakan glared, first at the king of Monongadotte, then at Alex, with eyes as glittering as the gems in his crown and the strands of gold draped from his shirt's collar. Of all the men in the room, only the king of Guyangahela, with his purple-dyed shirt made of the finest silk and cape sewn with a multitude of colors swirling about his shoulders, a stark contrast against his dark skin, dressed in as much finery as King Hakan.

Alex held up a hand to silence the murmuring. "A princess will wake me from my cursed sleep. I do not know when she will come, but I have been told it will be when the time is complete and complete again."

And that the time wouldn't be short, but he wouldn't tell these kings that. Nor would he mention Jadon's part in finding that promised princess.

Jadon stood with a knot of guards in the far corner, but even at that distance, Alex caught the slow nod Jadon gave him. They must never know Jadon was the key to finding the promised princess and restoring Alex to his throne or some of them might decide to kill him.

Would any of them piece it together? Jadon would have to get close to them, and their daughters, to find the princess who would wake Alex. Would someone notice?

Hopefully it wouldn't be necessary. There was still a chance —a very good chance—Alex would avoid the curse. "Tomorrow, I plan to do everything in my power to avoid falling into the curse. But as a precaution, I am ordering that this castle be evacuated before midnight. As you have probably noticed, the servants have already begun leaving."

Even now, the bustle could be heard filtering through the doors as the men, women, and children that lived in the castle gathered their few possessions and left their home.

Alex hardened his face and voice. "If I should fail to stop this curse, I expect you to show your loyalty to the high kings by remaining united and preserving this nation until such a time as I can regain my throne."

The kings in front of him stirred, some going stoic, some crossing their arms, as if none dared either stand for their loyalty or proclaim their rebellious intentions.

The king of Neskahana stepped forward. The collar of his red, silk shirt was adorned with rows and rows of beads made from the glass Neskahana was known for. "Neskahana will stand with you, Your Majesty."

Alex inclined his head to acknowledge the courtesy the king had given in using the address for a king rather than a prince. "Thank you."

"As will Buckhannock." King Othniel's voice held only a trace of shakiness.

The king of Guyangahela folded his great height in a dignified bow. "Guyangahela is loyal to you, sire."

"As is Tuckawassee, Your Highness." King Hakan bowed, causing the fringe of gold strands around his shirt's collar to flap.

Had it been merely correct titles that caused King Hakan to still name him a prince? Yes, he wasn't yet the high king, not having been formally crowned, but it was understood that he would be crowned as soon as this mess with his curse was sorted out.

The king of Monongadotte didn't bow as deeply as the others, probably because his elk headdress would tumble off if he did. "You can depend on Monongadotte."

"And Pohatomie." The Pohatomie king's bow was as smooth and slick as the first ice of winter. But was it as deadly?

Someone had cut the bridges from Kanawhee to Buckhannock. Someone had poisoned his father.

And one of these kings most likely knew about it, even sanctioned and encouraged it.

All six of them had pledged their loyalty.

One or more of them lied.

FROM THE WINDOW of the study that had once belonged to his father, Alex watched the long line of people stream from the castle, bundles of belongings on their back or perhaps piled in handcarts.

People packed into the surrounding city and the outlying villages. Far too many for those villages to sustain for a long period of time. But many of the servants didn't want to go far in case they were able to return if Alex didn't prick his finger as cursed.

But if he did? What would happen to the hundreds of people who were now displaced from their job and home? Some, like Jadon, had families they could return to. For others, they had served the high kings at Castle Eyota for generations. They had no other home.

He sighed and turned away from the window. What else could he do? It would be worse to demand they stay and condemn them to sleep for an unknown number of years. A few months ago, he might have done so, but not now.

Now he understood the pain of a permanent separation from family. Everywhere he looked in the castle, something reminded him of his father.

He was supposed to have had more time. He was supposed to have been able to sleep and awaken as the high prince with all the burdens of the kingdoms firmly resting on his father's shoulders. He should have both parents with him.

But his father had been stolen from him.

A knock came on the open study door. "Your Highness?"

Alex turned. Colonel Micco, his father's seneschal stood there, a hand resting on his dagger's hilt. His gray hair hung loose about his ears, more lines etching around his eyes than there had been a few days ago.

"Colonel, please have a seat." Alex directed the colonel to a wood chair before he took the seat on the other side of the sparse wooden table that served as the high king's desk. Alex straightened a few of the stacks of paper before he met the colonel's eyes. "How is the evacuation going?"

"At this rate, all of the staff and the guards' families will be out by evening. I have assigned the guards to new positions outside the castle wall." Colonel Micco sat straight and stiff during his report, his eyes focused on a spot above Alex's head.

Alex rubbed the back of his neck. At least the evacuation was going smoothly. "You understand your orders in case I should fall under the cursed sleep tomorrow?"

Colonel Micco nodded. "I will set up a guard rotation on permanent station surrounding the castle."

"Be alert. Those who poisoned my father will surely try something once I'm asleep and vulnerable." Alex's skin crawled at the thought. It was one thing to anticipate a knife in his back, poison in his drink, when he at least had a chance to defend himself. But thinking about sleeping too deeply to wake, completely helpless to those who killed his father . . . it took all of Alex's self-control to keep from shaking.

This was surely the reason Alex's father had been killed. There had always been a chance Alex's parents would remain outside the castle and evade the curse for the good of continuing to rule the kingdom while Alex slept. But now, Alex was the high king, though unofficially.

Sleeping or dead, the result would be the same. There would be no more high kings in Tallahatchia. Alex was the last of his line.

"Of course, Your Highness." Colonel Micco gave a nod that seemed more a bow. "Do you have any more instructions for me?"

What else did Alex have to accomplish before tomorrow? In the past month, it had been all he'd focused on, preparing for the possibility of his curse. He'd signed proclamations, put contingency plans into place, ordered the evacuation, and announced to the whole castle the curse wouldn't be forever.

He shook his head. "No, that will be all. You know your orders."

Colonel Micco stood and strode toward the door. In the doorway, he halted and turned back to Alex. "For what it's worth, Your Highness. I don't believe your father could've handled this day any better than you have."

Alex released a long breath but couldn't speak. What he wouldn't give to have his father here to handle it for him.

Colonel Micco bowed his head, rubbing his dagger's hilt with a palm. "I served your father for nearly forty years, first as his manservant, then his personal bodyguard, and eventually as his guard commander and seneschal. I know more about his failures and triumphs as a man, father, and king than even you will ever know, yet I served him loyally until his last day. I will give you that same loyalty for the rest of my days, whether or not the curse claims you tomorrow."

Alex hadn't realized how important such faithfulness was until he had to depend on it so fully. If he slept tomorrow, his life would rest in the hands of this colonel and the guards under his command. "Thank you. Your loyalty is much appreciated. I wish I could reward you more for what you have and will do, but I'm afraid such rewards may be out of my power if my curse takes me."

Colonel Micco shook his head. "There's no need. A loyalty that exists only for the reward gained is no true loyalty but merely a well-bribed selfishness." He took one more step through the doorway. "May the blessing of the Lord of All rest upon you tomorrow."

With that parting, Colonel Micco left.

Alex paced back to the window. A group of courtiers, with their servants pulling handcarts, lined up in the courtyard to exit. Even from this distance, Alex spotted Mirabelle's flowing, black hair.

Something in his chest seized. He couldn't let her sneak away like this, not without speaking to him. She'd offered her condolences after his father died, but she hadn't sought him out. He couldn't let this silence stand, not when this might be his last chance to ever see her again.

He dashed from the study and down the stairs to the courtyard. The courtiers parted, bowing when they caught sight of him.

Mirabelle's father spoke to her. Her shoulders rose and fell, then she spun to face Alex. For the first time since he'd known her, her mouth didn't curve with her coy smile. Her eyes didn't sparkle. With all trace of flirtation gone, her face seemed like smooth ceramic, breakable beneath its beauty.

"One last walk in the garden? Please?" Alex motioned in that direction. He shouldn't have to beg, not with her. Hadn't they meant more to each other than that? He'd wanted to marry her. If his curse didn't hit tomorrow, he still did. Why did she have to push him away instead of clinging to hope?

Mirabelle glided past him with a brittle grace, setting a quick pace toward the garden tucked along the castle keep's far side. He managed to catch up and fall into step with her just before they entered through the garden's arched trestle.

Halting by the rose bushes, Mirabelle ran a finger over a leaf, not facing him. "Your curse wasn't removed."

"No, but I was promised it would end." Alex's arms ached to hold her. She was just so beautiful.

"By a princess." Mirabelle spat the words as if they tasted like poison.

"She doesn't matter. You do." Alex rested his hands on her shoulder. "I still want to be with you. Please. Stay with me here. We'll wake together."

Mirabelle spun, shoving his hands away. "Do you really think I want to risk taking on your curse? I have a curse enough of my own. But, no, this always has to be about you, doesn't it?"

He stumbled back. Had he ever thought to ask Mirabelle about her curse? She was the daughter of a baron, high enough nobility to have been cursed. But he'd always been so focused on his own curse to worry about hers. "I'm sorry. Tell me your curse, and we'll deal with it together."

She snorted, a thin, high sound. "If your curse doesn't have a way to avoid it, then mine doesn't either. And believe me, my curse is just as terrible. No, I won't sacrifice my own happiness for you. I have to put myself first."

He stared. After all their kisses, all the dreams they'd whispered about, this was how it ended? She had claws he hadn't seen hidden beneath her beauty. Had any of her flirtation been real? Or was it all some sort of game to her, played merely for her own enjoyment?

He jabbed his finger toward the castle gates, out of sight beyond the hedge. "Then leave. And don't come back. Not even if I escape the curse tomorrow."

She raised her chin, her face smooth as the finest Neskahana glass. "Very well. Fare well, High Prince Alexander."

She swept from the garden with the grace and dignity of a panther, all claws and vicious teeth beneath the surface.

Sinking onto a bench, Alex leaned his head in his hands. How was he going to get through tomorrow? The weight of it pressed hard against him.

Why couldn't the Lord of the Fae remove his curse? It would've made tomorrow so much easier. He'd already lost his father. Must he lose Mirabelle and everything else too?

Heat burst in his chest. It wasn't fair. Why was so much demanded from him?

It seemed that he was on his own in this. No one would help him.

That was just fine. He had his intelligence and logic. No one else could help him as much as he could help himself.

Alex stood a few yards inside the castle's gate while his mother hugged a few of the women she considered friends.

With a deep breath, Alex straightened his shoulders, faced Jadon, and pulled off his signet ring. "I suppose you'll need this."

Jadon nodded, took the ring, and slid it on his finger. "I'll keep it safe until I can return it to you."

Alex unbuckled his dagger from his belt and held it out on his palms. "And I give you this. It's yours."

Jadon picked it up and gripped it by its sheath. "I'll return this to you too."

Alex shook his head. "No. It's yours. That's the point. The curse says I will prick my finger on my dagger. I can't do that if I don't *own* a dagger."

"Then I'll take good care of it." Jadon buckled it to his belt. He glanced from Alex to the gateway. Colonel Micco stood next to the open gate, ready to close it once the last person left the castle.

"Go to your family, Jadon. Spend a few years with them." Alex waved toward the mountains rising past the castle walls. "You deserve that much."

Jadon met Alex's gaze. "I promise I'll bring the cursebreaker to wake you. You won't sleep forever." Spinning on his heels, he marched from the castle.

With one last glance at them, Colonel Micco swung the gate closed. The hinges groaned until the doors thunked shut.

Alex turned to his mother. They were the only two people left in the castle. No one else had decided to risk sleeping with them. And any friends that offered, they had encouraged to leave.

He wrapped his mother in an embrace, tucking his head against her shoulder as if he was still the little boy who had cried in her lap.

Somewhere deep inside the castle, the clock began to strike the hour. Alex counted in his head until the clock struck twelve.

Today he turned twenty-one years old.

He might never see another dawn.

CHAPTER 29

ROSANNA

Sitting on a log with only the stars to light their camp on the banks of the Kanawhee River, Rosanna gnawed on a dry biscuit and washed it down with a sip of water from her canteen. Her calves and feet ached from the trek up and over Fishrock Gap into Kanawhee, pushing hard to stay ahead of Major Beshko. Except for a night's stay with the baron and baroness of Fishrock Cove, they'd had little rest.

Isi sat on a log near Rosanna, her shoulders hunched as she stared at the spot where a campfire would have been, if they'd dared light a fire. Isi's biscuit and dried venison rested uneaten in her hands, as if she were too tired to eat, much less move enough to spread out her blanket to go to sleep. Having abandoned their tents back in Tuckawassee, all they had were a few blankets given by Zeke and Aunt Frennie and the open sky above them.

Somewhere in the darkness, Zeke and Otho kept watch while across from Rosanna, Chogan and Ilma leaned against each other on a log, dark circles smudging their faces under their eyes. Even Captain Degotaga had lost his crisp posture after their hurried march over the mountains.

At least the hardest part was over. A line of four canoes rested on the bank near them, ready to be placed in the water tomorrow morning. With the current at their sterns, Castle Eyota lay only a few short days down the Kanawhee.

Only a few short days until Daemyn might die.

Daemyn rested with his back against a tree at the edge of their small camp near the river. Of all of them, he appeared the least worn by their travel, perhaps thanks to the gift of health and strength provided him by the Highest King.

They'd barely spoken in the last few days. Daemyn had almost seemed to be avoiding her, as if he could prevent her from becoming too attached to him.

Too late. He was a friend. No amount of silence and cold shoulders could take that away or undo the churning in her stomach at having to choose between Daemyn's life and waking the high prince.

Could she do it? Was she strong enough to look Daemyn in the eye and condemn him to death, as much as he seemed to wish it?

Crunching leaves and running footsteps jerked her upright. She reached for Daemyn's dagger she still wore strapped to her waist as the others around the camp did the same.

Zeke burst from the undergrowth and skidded to a halt, followed by Otho. "There's a bear out there. Must've smelled our food."

Rosanna stood. There were thousands of black bears in these mountains. But what if . . .

A low huffing, growling, grunting sound came from

the bushes. A black shape barreled through the undergrowth, headed straight for them.

Zeke spun, lifted his bow, and nocked an arrow.

The huffing snarl came again. Familiar. If she listened closely, Rosanna could almost hear her name.

Zeke drew back the bowstring.

"Wait! That's my brother." Rosanna leapt forward and grabbed Zeke's arm. Behind Zeke, Captain Degotaga and her other guards relaxed and sheathed their weapons. Isi shook her head and rolled her eyes.

"What?" Zeke froze, his bow half-drawn back.

Daemyn lowered his hardwood staff, but his stance remained tense. "Are you sure, Princess? We're a long way from Neskahana."

"I'd know my brother's annoying growl anywhere." Rosanna stepped forward and planted her hands on her hips. The bear had halted behind a tree, as if realizing he'd had an arrow pointed at him. "Bere-bear, what did you think you were doing, running up to our camp like that? You nearly got yourself shot. Again. And I doubt this arrow would've found its mark in somewhere unessential."

Berend lumbered out from behind the tree, head hanging. In his bear form, he was a skinny, yearling sized bear shorter than her waist when he was on all fours. His fur was a thick black with patches of brown around his face and paws.

Once inside their camp, Berend plopped into a sitting position and spread his front paws as if looking for a hug.

Rosanna sighed and leaned forward to give her bear brother a hug. He wrapped his furry limbs around her, grunting and huffing as if trying to talk to her. Since bears' mouths and tongues weren't created for speech, the best he could manage was a semblance of words even Rosanna couldn't translate.

Something wet and cold slobbered over her ear.

Rosanna jerked backwards and swatted Berend's muzzle away. "How many times have I told you? No licking."

Berend gave her a grin that showed all his pointed teeth. He cocked his head and jabbed a paw at something behind Rosanna.

She glanced over her shoulder. Zeke had lowered his bow, though the arrow remained nocked.

"That's Zeke. He's Daemyn's nephew. Long story." Rosanna faced the others and patted the top of Berend's head, his fur coarse and prickly. "Zeke, this is my younger brother Berend. He's cursed to spend his nights as a bear."

Zeke glanced from Berend to Daemyn. "You didn't think to warn me about . . . this?"

"I thought Princess Rosanna's brother had remained with her father's army." Daemyn leaned on his quarterstaff.

Father's army. Had something happened to it? Was that why Berend had sought her out? "Is Father all right? Mother? What are you doing here?"

Berend rolled to his paws, waddled a few steps away to give himself space, and reared onto his hind legs. Standing like that, he stood a few inches over six feet tall. He might have looked intimidating, except for the lopsided expression twisting his bear's face.

He trundled a few steps, arms at his sides. He waved, gestured, grunted, flailed about, before finally facing Rosanna and looking at her like he expected her to understand.

"I have no idea what you're trying to tell me." Rosanna knelt and cleared a section of dead leaves and pine needles from the dirt. "I know it's slower but write what you need to tell us."

With a grunt, Berend plopped onto his haunches next to the cleared patch of dirt. He brandished his paw and wiggled his claws as he tried to get them to move in a way a bear's paw wasn't designed to move.

Zeke, Daemyn, and Captain Degotaga gathered around her and Berend, though Zeke still cast glances at Berend as if he expected to be attacked and eaten alive at any moment.

Berend managed to get his index finger—claw—by itself and wrote in the dirt. *I hate to be the bear of bad news.*

"That was funny back when you were ten." Rosanna shoved Berend's furry shoulder. "Cut to the reason you're here without any fiddle-faddle."

Berend cleared the dirt with his paw. As he wrote, his mouth moved as if he was trying to say the words out loud as he scratched them with his claw. *Father was concerned when you hadn't reached the castle yet and sent me to find you. As I was tracking you, I discovered that Tuckawassee major hard on your trail planning to ambush you tonight. She'll be here in less than an hour.*

Captain Degotaga frowned as he climbed to his feet. "That doesn't give us much time. We should evacuate to the canoes. On the river, we'll be able to outdistance them."

"We'd best get moving." Daemyn nodded. "Prince Berend, keep pace along the bank. Warn us if they start getting too close."

Rosanna forced her aching legs and sore muscles into action. No rest. If Major Beshko couldn't capture or kill them, she'd run them into the ground.

She dashed back to their camp and rolled the blanket

she'd spread across a soft section of pine needles. After grabbing her canteen and a small pack of food, she tossed them into the center of a canoe and lashed them down with a few quick knots.

Daemyn was beside her a moment later, adding his blanket and canteen before helping Rosanna carry the canoe into the water.

Next to them, Isi and Captain Degotaga hauled their canoe from the bank.

Prickles formed on Rosanna's skin that had nothing to do with the cold water swirling around her knees as she shoved the canoe farther into the water. The forest around them remained too silent. Somewhere out there, Major Beshko hunted them.

Rosanna barely had time to swing into the stern and grab a paddle before the current caught them and pushed them downstream. Digging in her paddle, Rosanna helped Daemyn straighten out the canoe before it had a chance to broach and potentially overturn.

Captain Degotaga and Isi swung their canoe into line on her right while Chogan and Ilma passed her to take up point ahead. Zeke and Otho fell into station as rearguard.

The river before them spread dark and flat against the still darker mountains thrusting their tree-covered slopes against an indigo sky so covered with clouds only a few stars poked through. A light drizzle began to fall, spattering the river's surface.

No rest. Not while Major Beshko remained so close. Perhaps they wouldn't be able to rest more than a few hours all the way to Castle Eyota.

AFTER TWO DAYS of travel downriver with only a few hours of rest snatched when they could, Daemyn directed them up Clearwater Creek. He halted them in a pool at the base of a small waterfall. "We'll spend the night here and cross to Castle Eyota at dawn. It's only a few miles downriver from here."

A few miles. Rosanna climbed from the canoe, her chest so tight she struggled to breathe deeply. Tomorrow she'd wake High Prince Alexander. And, possibly, watch Daemyn die yet again.

Berend rolled out of the center of Captain Degotaga and Isi's canoe where he'd spent most of the morning and early afternoon asleep. Now the sun had dipped so low they could no longer see it beyond the orange glow lighting the horizon through the trees.

As he stood, he stretched his arms above his head. Patches of scruff dotted his chin, probably because he hadn't taken the time to shave while on the trail. "I'll be changing back to a bear in a few minutes. I'll find Father and let him know you're safe and in position."

Rosanna hugged him. It didn't matter that his buckskins smelled like musty animal and body odor. At this point, she didn't smell much better. "Stay safe, Bere-bear. There are whole armies in the forest tonight who would like nothing better than bear for supper."

"Don't worry. I have no intention of being turned into bear steak." Berend thumped her back as he pulled away. "And you be careful too, Ro-Row. Those armies are out there because they want to stop you."

"I know." She swallowed and crossed her arms over her stomach. Almost she wanted them to succeed in stopping her. At least then it wouldn't be her decision whether or not to wake the high prince and possibly bring about Daemyn's death.

As the light began fading to gray, Berend changed into his bear form. One moment he was her human brother standing before her, the next blink he was a furry, grinning black bear. He stood on his hind legs, patted her shoulder with a large paw, and loped off into the forest.

Isi nudged her. "Don't worry. You'll see him tomorrow after you wake the high prince and are hailed a hero and all of this war mess is straightened out."

"Somehow, I don't think it'll be that simple." Rosanna sighed and turned back to their camp.

In the nook sheltered by the creek's gorge, Otho had risked building a fire and Zeke picked up his bow and headed off into the woods as if determined they would eat fresh meat on tonight of all nights. Not bear, of course. But fresh rabbit or venison would be appreciated. She'd even take a squirrel with a single bite of meat for each of them at this point.

"No, it won't. But we can hope, and hope is what got us this far after all." Isi shrugged, but her mouth didn't curve with a smile. "If life was easy, we wouldn't need the Highest King's hope or promises or gifts. Those are the things that make life good."

"Thanks, Isi." No sister could have been a better friend. Whatever happened tomorrow, it would be less scary with Isi guarding her back.

"Just doing my job." Isi finally grinned and nudged Rosanna again. "Now go on and spend some time with Daemyn. I don't know why the two of you have been side-eying each other for the past few days, but whatever it is, you probably should get it straightened out tonight."

"I'll explain when this is all over, all right?" By then, it wouldn't matter if she told Daemyn's secret.

Isi nodded. "Go."

Daemyn leaned on his staff near the waterfall, gazing at it as if remembering something long ago. As she reached his side, he pointed at a thin trail leading to the ridgetop. "The bridge crossing the creek is long gone, but the trail is still there. It's only a short hike to a place where we can see Castle Eyota."

Peering upward, Rosanna could make out the rotted posts that once supported the bridge. "I'd love to see the castle." Before she had to face it in earnest tomorrow.

Daemyn faced the camp. "Captain, I'm going to take the princess to an overlook to see the castle and the positions on the armies."

Captain Degotaga stood, as if he intended to go with them.

Daemyn shook his head. "She'll be safe with me."

"See that she is." Captain Degotaga settled back onto the log. "Don't take too long. It'll be full dark soon."

"We won't." With a glance at her, Daemyn set out on the trail leading to the ridge above.

At the ridgetop, Rosanna fell into step beside Daemyn, the trail just wide enough to walk side by side. What should she say to him? What could she say?

He paused. In the gray twilight, she couldn't make out the expression in his deep brown eyes. He looked away to the slope falling toward the Kanawhee River out of sight behind the dense trees and undergrowth. "You don't have to look so sad, Princess. It really is all right."

If this was his last night, he probably didn't want to be surrounded by tears and frowns. Even forcing a small smile on her face hurt deep inside. But what else could she do but gift him with these few precious minutes. It took effort, but her smile widened to something that almost felt genuine. "Then I'm not going to cry. At least not tonight. So where is this castle you were going to show me?"

"Not much farther." Daemyn turned from the trail headed deeper into the forest instead of toward the river. "But first I have a few people for you to meet."

Who would Daemyn want her to meet? Rosanna pushed through the underbrush after him.

They broke into a cleared section along the side of the mountain surrounding a small cabin. She would've studied it more, except that all around the edge of the clearing, rows upon rows of people had gathered, talking quietly. As she and Daemyn strode farther into the clearing, the talking hushed, leaving the forest silent except for a few nighttime frogs and insects chirruping in the trees.

Her footsteps slowed. The clearing blurred with skin colors from dark brown to pale, hair from curly black to straight blond, and manners of dress and adornment she'd only heard about in stories, from the richly garbed Guyangahelans in fabric that looked so fine she wanted to reach out and touch it to the animal hides and headdresses of the Monongadotte to a cluster of Tuckawassee with black gems woven into their dark hair.

There was even a group of men and women from Neskahana, their shirts beaded and fringed. A few gave her smiles and nods, as if recognizing their princess.

Never had she thought to see men and women from all seven kingdoms of Tallahatchia gathered together peacefully like this. This was something from legends, from a time when the town of Eyota was a center of trade, mixing of their cultures and binding them into one. A time no one but Daemyn Rand still lived to remember.

But the war still touched here too. Every man or woman standing there carried weapons, axes and spears, long knives and old-fashioned daggers, bows and arrows. The people from each kingdom clustered together, eying those from the other kingdoms as if here too war might break out.

Daemyn halted her in the center of the cleared section and waved at the people around them. "Princess, these are a portion of my many-time-great-nieces and nephews."

Only a portion of them? There had to be over a hundred people gathered in that clearing.

Her gaze snagged on the largest group, those from Buckhannock in their simple buckskins and abundance of weapons. One of the young men in the front wore an iron circlet. Was he the prince of Buckhannock?

"How many relatives do you have?"

"Over a thousand, I think." Daemyn shrugged. "A few had big families."

She'd known in her head that he was old beyond what he appeared to be, but seeing the results of a hundred years of his siblings' descendants rallying around him made it real in a way it hadn't been before. All the people standing before her, from the gray-haired man from Pohatomie to the young man with the crown from Buckhannock had known Daemyn from the day they were born. While they had changed, he had not, except for the occasional name change.

Zeke slipped into the crowd near those from Buckhannock, giving her a nod.

Daemyn faced the crowd. "For a hundred years, you have been my friends and family thanks to the promise your ancestors—my siblings—made to me. I thank you for all you have done to aid me. Tomorrow, your task will be complete for this" he paused and gestured to Rosanna, "is Princess Rosanna of Neskahana. She is High Prince Alexander's cursebreaker."

A few murmured to their neighbors or shifted, but most studied her as if trying to determine if she was worth the sacrifices their families had made for generations.

She couldn't meet their gaze. She wasn't strong enough to bear so many people's hopes resting on her. What if she failed tomorrow?

But what if she succeeded? She would take away the one man who united these people. They didn't fight and sacrifice for a high prince. They fought for a beloved friend and uncle.

"There will be fighting tomorrow, and it saddens me to think that some of you will be forced to fight each other. It's my hope that we'll be able to stop the fighting before too much blood is spilled for Tallahatchia to ever reunite into one nation, as it once was." Daemyn bowed his head, as if the weight of all Tallahatchia rested on his shoulders. "Now you'd better return to your kingdoms' armies before you're missed."

The crowd moved but not away into the forest. Instead, groups of two or three approached Daemyn, clapping him on the shoulder, shaking his hand, hugging him.

Saying goodbye.

Rosanna's smile ached as she forced it to stay in place. Some of Daemyn's relatives murmured to her, and it was all she could do to nod back. She couldn't take in their words beyond their collective meaning. *Do what you must do tomorrow. We'll be all right.*

By the time the last disappeared into the forest, the light had faded until it was nearly gone.

Somehow, after over a hundred farewells, Daemyn's

mouth twitched into something almost like a smile. "I still have to show you Castle Eyota."

As they regained the trail, the ground rose into a steep curve silhouetted against the purple, blue, and gray sky. Daemyn dropped into a crouch, then onto his stomach. Rosanna followed his lead and crawled on her stomach to the top where she lay flat.

The land spread before them, the tips of the mountains flaming with the sunset. Streaks of orange painted across the Kanawhee River as it wound between the mountains far below.

Nestled on a clifftop next to a bend in the Kanawhee River, Castle Eyota burned in a halo of light cast by the sun's last rays. A castle fit for a high king, all in the limestone found in these mountains. A tall tangle of some sort of plant grew around the castle, so tall she couldn't see much of the outer wall at this distance.

"I think that's your father's army over there." Daemyn pointed, keeping his hand low.

She looked in that direction. A few fires twinkled along the slope of a mountain north and east of them.

More campfires burned among the trees closer to the Kanawhee River. "Would that be the Tuckawassee army?"

"Yes."

As the night darkened, more campfires flared. Patches to the north of her father's army were probably Monongadotte and Pohatomie. An encampment to the northwest was Buckhannock. To her right on the southern side of the Kanawhee, another patch of lights could only be the army from Guyangahela.

At the base of the hill where Castle Eyota stood, more fires burned. The remnant of Kanawhee protecting their sleeping high king.

There would be a war here tomorrow. That's what those campfires declared in each flicker, each puff of dark smoke. Every king stated his army's presence and intention to do battle in the morning.

Tomorrow there would be war.

CHAPTER 30

ALEXANDER

ONE HUNDRED YEARS AGO

Alex paced across the throne room as the first rays of dawn spread across the ceiling from the great hall's high windows. After staying up all night, he should feel be exhausted.

Instead he paced with an energy that twisted inside him until it might tear him apart. The clock ticked away the seconds in the entry hall. Would this day never end?

Mother slumped in her throne next to the larger one where his father used to sit. Alex had yet to claim that throne. It hadn't seemed right trying to fill his father's place with the curse still hanging over him.

With only him and Mother in the entire castle, the stones were dead in a way they'd never been before. Each creak of wooden beams, each pop of shifting stone, echoed through the keep. The clock's ticking might as well have been a drum beat.

Was that footsteps? Alex froze, cocking his head to listen. Surely not. He had to be imagining things, this wretched silence eating into him.

There it was again. The sound of feet scuffing on stairs. Alex whirled toward the door, his hand closing on the empty space where his dagger usually hung.

But he didn't have a dagger. He was unarmed.

How had someone gotten past the guards? Had Colonel Micco and his men been killed during the night?

No, if that was the case, then there would be more than one intruder. Someone must have hidden in the castle while everyone left yesterday.

Besides, how the person causing those footsteps got in didn't matter at this point. He or she was most likely an enemy, and Alex didn't have a weapon.

Whoever had killed Alex's father apparently didn't plan to wait until his curse made him vulnerable. He was vulnerable already. Alone except for his mother. Unarmed. All the guards far away beyond the castle's outer walls.

Alex spun and dashed toward the dais, taking the stairs two at a time.

Mother straightened, her eyes widening. "What is it? What's wrong? The curse?"

He shook his head. "I heard someone. Get back behind the thrones."

Mother scrambled to her feet and crouched in the shadows behind the bulk of the three thrones on the dais.

A weapon. Alex needed a weapon. After a glance around, he picked up the scepter from its stand next to his father's throne.

The scepter was a two-foot-long length of carved hard-wood, its rounded end embossed with gold and iron and studded with jewels and glass. Swung hard enough, it could make a decent dent in someone's skull, if needed.

One of the double doors at the far end of the room swung open. King Hakan of Tuckawassee strode inside, the gold fringe along his silk shirt swaying with each purposeful step. In his hand he carried a gleaming dagger.

Alex tensed, raising the scepter in a defensive position. He should've known it would be the Tuckawassee behind all this trouble. They had been murmuring and complaining for years about his father's rule. Alex's father hadn't given it much thought. All the kingdoms grumbled a time or two.

But this time the Tuckawassee had changed grumbling into action and that action into treason.

"Come to kill me like you did my father?" Alex held to his position on the dais. The added height would give him some advantage should King Hakan lunge at him with the dagger.

"I considered it. It would save time and my sacrifice, but no. There's a good chance you would kill me first or get away long enough to call your guards." King Hakan strode across the throne room as if he owned the place. "Besides, one high king dying under mysterious circumstances already has the other kingdoms wary. I can't have them turn their wrath onto Tuckawassee all at once, which they would if the last of the high kings died by my hand. But if you succumb to your curse, no one will blame Tuckawassee for something that has been decreed since your birth."

"I have been promised I will wake." Alex remained tense. Just because King Hakan said he wasn't there to kill Alex didn't mean he wasn't lying.

"My son and his descendants will see to it that you never do." King Hakan halted a few feet in front of the dais.

"You'll sleep too. For all time if I never wake." Alex

caught the note of desperation in his own voice, but he couldn't help the thread of panic. Why hadn't King Hakan sent a servant for this? Why risk the cursed sleep himself?

"A sacrifice I'm prepared to make." King Hakan shrugged, his eyes gleaming with the light of a fire consuming itself. "My wife has been dead these past five years, and my son has been itching to rule. Better I end my reign this way, a hero to Tuckawassee, than die by his hand when he can no longer stand me hanging on to the throne that should be his. Instead of hating me for standing in his way to gain power, he and all his sons and their sons into the far distant generations will revere me for giving them power beyond what I ever had. I will buy them freedom from the rule of the high kings."

He was mad in some way. Power hungry in the way of a wolf thirsting for fresh blood. Alex could think of no reply. To a man like this, it would matter nothing what he said anyway.

King Hakan knelt and presented the unsheathed dagger to Alex on open palms. "Your Highness, in honor of your birthday, I present you with this dagger as a gift. Take it. It is yours."

His dagger. Alex's stomach clenched. From the tone in King Hakan's voice, he expected Alex's curse to be irresistible. To clutch him in its grasp and force him to prick his finger against his will.

No, he wouldn't be forced into this curse. Not by anyone or anything. The curse wasn't irresistible. It couldn't be. Surely out of anyone in Tallahatchia, he had the intelligence and willpower to fight it off.

He had trained with a dagger for years. Handled them, familiarizing himself with their weight and sharpness, making sure his hands knew them well enough to remain steady when they were in his grasp. There was no reason he should prick himself now after so many years of experience.

Behind the thrones, Alex's mother called, soft and pained. "No, Alex."

Even she thought him so weak-willed that he would fall for the curse.

Heat coursed through his veins, sparking deep inside his soul. He was High Prince Alexander of the Seven Kingdoms of Tallahatchia. Gifted with intelligence superior to all others. He would not be bound to this curse. It had owned him for twenty-one years, but no more.

He had to break it now. His willpower. His cunning. He would take up that dagger, show the curse he would not be forced against his will, and place it back in King Hakan's hands.

His stride was firm as he strolled down the steps to King Hakan. His hands didn't shake as he picked up the dagger he'd been given.

It was a fine dagger. A sharp, crisp edge winked sunlight from the high windows behind the thrones. Leather wrapped the handle below the pommel set with a finely cut ruby. A dagger worthy of a king.

He lightly touched the edge with his thumb as he had practiced so many times growing up and didn't cut himself.

He was master of himself. No curse, no decree, ruled him.

Before him, he could see the light in King Hakan's eyes fading as he realized Alex remained in full possession of himself and faculties.

More footsteps rushed down the hallway and burst

into the throne room. Baron and Baroness Galilahi, Mirabelle's parents, dashed forward, their mouths and eyes wide. "Stop, Your Highness, stop! The king of Tuckawassee, he plots against you. We discovered his treachery only hours ago when we witnessed his army returning without him."

"I thank you for your concern, but I already know." Alex glared down at the king still kneeling before him. "And once today is over, he will be punished for that planned treachery."

He reached to hand the dagger back, and the tiniest pinprick of pain came from his thumb. He stared down. A single drop of blood beaded on his skin.

He couldn't have . . . it shouldn't have . . .

But there it was. The drop of blood. The evidence of a finger nicked on the dagger's edge.

He met King Hakan's eyes, and the king's mouth curved into a triumphant smirk.

Alex's heart beat too fast for him to fall asleep. Surely he wouldn't. This was all a mistake. It couldn't be happening.

But in front of him, the baron and baroness staggered, dropping to their knees, then their sides, as their eyes fluttered closed.

"Alex . . ."

He glanced behind him in time to see his mother sprawl forward still half hidden behind the thrones. Her crown rolled from her head to come to rest a few inches from her fingertips.

King Hakan sagged backwards, his smirk still on his face. "We . . . are . . . free." He breathed as his eyes sank closed.

A weight settled onto Alex's eyes, his shoulders. He was sinking. Down to his knees. Onto the floor. The dagger clattering to the stones between him and King Hakan. A yawn stretched his mouth.

As his eyes closed, only one thought remained.

He had no one to blame but himself.

CHAPTER 31

ROSANNA

The eastern horizon barely lightened with gray as they loaded the canoes. Rosanna left most of her pack with her and Daemyn's canoe on the bank. All she carried was her canteen in case she or Daemyn got thirsty with their planned hiking and climbing. The Kanawhee River didn't have water fit for drinking. She had a small amount of dried meat in a pocket. That was all she'd take with her into Castle Eyota.

Rosanna hugged Isi. "Stay safe."

"We will. We'll follow you into Castle Eyota when we can." Isi stepped back. Her hair was done in a pristine braid, each curl and frizz controlled. She kept her back straight, regal, as she perched in the center of one of the canoes.

Isi, Captain Degotaga, Chogan, Ilma, and Otho planned to cross the Kanawhee in the canoes. If anyone saw them, they would think Isi was the princess and would help or hinder them, leaving Daemyn and Rosanna free to sneak into the castle.

299

Captain Degotaga and Otho slid into the stern and bow of Isi's canoe while Chogan and Ilma took a second canoe.

It was time. After weeks of traveling, it had come to this. She gave them a nod.

The goodbyes, farewells, and best wishes were a blur. Then the canoes were pulling away into the dark mist of dawn along Clearwater Creek headed for the Kanawhee.

Zeke faced Daemyn, his eyes bright, his grip tight on his strung bow. "I'm coming with you. Don't try to stop me."

"Glad to have you with me today." Daemyn clapped him on the shoulder, spun, and led off into the forest down the slope as the top edge of the sun peeked pink and shy over the horizon.

Rosanna trudged behind them, aching as if she carried the full weight of a canoe on her shoulders.

They picked their way down the slope slowly, arriving at a clump of boulders upstream of Castle Eyota.

Through the mist rising from the river, shapes moved in and out of the trees. Shadows of armies shifting into position for a battle about to begin.

Downriver, a fleet of canoes was barely visible, filled with Guyangahela's warriors.

War whoops and shouts shattered the stillness. The clang of metal against metal. The hum of arrows releasing.

Daemyn pointed to a log caught in the boulders at the edge of the river. "We'll use that to help us float across. It should shield us from prying eyes, at least as long as no one looks too closely."

"They won't." Zeke's voice was tight, and he wasn't looking downstream or across the river.

Rosanna followed his gaze. Two canoes appeared out

of the gray morning. Isi sat prim and tall in the center of one, playing her part as decoy and bodyguard.

Rosanna's heart pounded in her throat. If Isi died . . .

She must not think about it. Isi was providing their distraction, and they must not waste time by lingering.

Daemyn waded into the river, keeping one of the boulders between him and the far side. He and Zeke worked the log free until it floated once again. The river tugged at it, eager to drag it to a new destination.

The shouting and screaming and ringing steel increased from the far bank.

Rosanna squeezed her fingers into fists. Her father was out there somewhere. Her mother and Berend too. All of them fighting to buy her time to accomplish one simple task. Wake High Prince Alexander.

Daemyn glanced over his shoulder. "Are you ready?"

It was a question she should be asking him. But she nodded, her toes cold in the gentle swell of the river's shallows.

Daemyn shoved the log farther out into the water, hunched low so the log kept him from sight. Rosanna grabbed a stub of a branch and followed with Zeke behind her. They went deeper. The water soaked into her buckskin leggings, then her shirt up to her neck. Her feet left the ground, and she paddled, fighting the current.

"Just hold on. Let me steer. The current will do most of the work for us."

Rosanna stopped thrashing with her free arm. He was right. Trying to paddle with her hand risked causing splashes that would be seen if anyone looked this way.

But she wasn't going to let him and Zeke do all the work. She kicked, making sure to kick well below the surface of the water so that nothing would be seen from across the river.

In a way, this was like paddling their canoe, yet in the water. Him paddling and steering. Her adding her strength by swimming too. This version was just a mite more wet and had Zeke's help shoving the log in the direction they needed to go.

About halfway across, Daemyn peeked around the end of the log. "No one seems to be looking this way."

She sank lower into the water and kept kicking. The sooner they got to the other side, the better.

Finally, the log bumped against the rocks on the far shore. Daemyn glanced over the log, then slipped from the water, keeping low to the ground.

Rosanna crept after him. They crossed a short stretch of pebbles before reaching the rocks. It wasn't a true, sheer cliff, but a series of jagged boulders and rocks rising as if in giant steps up to the wall of thorns of Castle Eyota rising above.

The stepped nature of the rocks made them easy to climb. She hoisted herself up one by one, Daemyn ahead, Zeke below. The castle grew closer.

Something clattered off the stone below her feet. She jumped and glanced down as something else scraped near her foot. An arrow.

Daemyn swept her around to his other side, putting himself between her and the arrows. "We've been spotted."

They scrambled up the rocks, Zeke right behind them. More arrows flew, missing by inches as Daemyn swung her out of the way and yanked her up just in time.

He flinched. She pulled him up another rock and pressed the two of them behind an outcropping. "You all right?"

Turning his arm, he revealed a red line welling across his upper arm. "Just nicked me."

Zeke slammed his back against the rock next to them, an arrow ricocheting off the boulder where he'd been a moment ago. "I really hope that's the Tuckawassee aiming for us. I'd hate to think cousin Zeph forgot to warn the Kanawhee guard we'd be coming this way."

"We're almost there." Daemyn gripped a ledge, his muscles tense.

Rosanna glanced upward. They had another ten feet to go, then a few feet before the thorn hedge barred their way.

She had to go upward and forward. Daemyn had worked for a hundred years for this moment. Her father and his men sacrificed their life blood in the battle below. She couldn't falter now.

Daemyn met her gaze. She nodded. She was as ready as she'd ever be.

She had time for a deep breath before Daemyn spun around the outcropping. She lunged upward as quickly as she could. Somewhere around her, arrows skittered, but she didn't look. She didn't turn her gaze from the thorn hedge above. That was her goal. Her only goal. If she was shot, if she bled, it was no more than everyone else had already sacrificed.

Her grasping hand closed over grass instead of stone. She rolled onto the small strip of grass between the rock slope and the hedge encircling the castle wall.

She scrambled on her hands and knees to Daemyn's side, sheltered by the wall of vines and thorns.

A cry tore her gaze back to the cliff's edge. Zeke was halfway up, an arrow protruding from his back.

Daemyn leapt to his feet, and Rosanna was only a step behind him. They each grabbed one of Zeke's arms and yanked him upward, dragging him to safety. They didn't stop until they'd worked their way along the hedge where the curve of the castle and hedge gave them a small respite from the arrows.

"That didn't go exactly as I planned." Zeke gasped as she and Daemyn laid him down on his stomach.

Daemyn pulled out his dagger and cut the opening in Zeke's shirt wider. Blood welled up around the arrow.

Rosanna forced herself to take a deep breath. The blood, the arrow, it was all too similar to watching Daemyn take arrow after arrow beside that small creek in Tuckawassee.

"The arrow must have been nearly spent. It isn't too deep." Daemyn snapped the arrow's shaft close to Zeke's back.

"Still feels plenty deep to me." Zeke groaned as Daemyn helped him to his feet. "I'm won't be much help, I'm afraid."

"Let's get you inside." Daemyn pulled one of Zeke's arms over his shoulders. "There's a back gate to the castle here, behind the hedge."

An arrow thunked into the thorns a few yards away. The archers were circling, trying to get her, Daemyn, and Zeke in sight.

Rosanna tore her gaze away from Zeke, taking in the immense height of the hedge of black, dead vines next to them. A few leaves remained dried and shriveled among the stems as wide as her waist. Thorns as long as her arm lanced across any open spaces, crisscrossing each other in a deadly, impenetrable wall.

All along the hedge, even on the dead limbs and despite it being too early in the season, blood red roses the size of Rosanna's head bloomed with such brilliance, such abandon, as if the plant itself threw its last gasp of breath into this final glorious display.

It ached and thrilled in Rosanna's heart. If she could hear the rose thorn's song, it would've been rejoicing in its death, glorying that its one mission was finally completed. She rested a hand on one of the dying strands as if her touch could comfort the plant.

The hedge moved beneath her fingers, shuddering as it drew back. A space opened in front of her all the way to the back gate in the castle wall, the thorns retreating and shriveling. The blooms burst open still farther, choking the air with a scent so sweet it tasted bitter. The death fragrance of the flowers.

This hedge wouldn't regrow. It had guarded this wall until this day, and now its mission was done. She understood that much, even if she didn't know how such a hedge had grown in the first place.

After taking Zeke's other arm over her shoulder, she stepped into the opening. Would Daemyn, like this thorn hedge, wither and die once his mission was complete? She shivered but kept walking, supporting some of Zeke's weight.

The hedge grew right up against the castle wall, no space between. At the gate, she lifted the latch and pushed. The door creaked open.

With a deep breath, she strode into the sleeping castle.

She wasn't sure what she'd expected to find when she'd left on this quest. Something that looked abandoned, perhaps. Overgrown. Crumbling. What a person would expect for a castle that had sat nearly empty and untended for one hundred years.

But time had frozen here. The grass beneath her feet was cropped short as if by some gardener. The garden remained pristine, not overgrown like it should have. The flowers bloomed as they should for this time of year, but were they the same blooms that had been open the day High Prince Alexander pricked his finger a century ago?

It looked so normal, like the gardener would come bustling around the corner of the arched trestle or a groom lead a horse out of the stable near the wall. The kitchen should be ringing with noise while guards, courtiers, and servants bustled across the main courtyard in front of the keep. All the normal sounds, sights, and smells she had seen every day at her parents' castle.

Yet this was empty. No sound except an eerie breeze singing through empty corridors of the keep. She rubbed at the goose bumps on her arm underneath her buckskin shirt.

As Zeke slumped heavier against her shoulder, Daemyn steered them past the garden toward the small kitchen door to the keep. "The servants' quarters are through here. We'll find medical supplies in the kitchen."

She nearly asked how he knew, but of course he knew this castle. He'd lived here, a hundred years ago.

Daemyn took Zeke's weight while Rosanna opened the door and held it for them. As she closed it after them, Zeke stretched out on his stomach on the table, resting his head on his arms. Blood covered the back of his shirt. But at least he was still alert, his eyes open, the muscle at the corner of his jaw tight.

Rosanna snatched a towel off the wooden countertop and pressed it to Zeke's back. Even here, it looked as if servants should be bustling around, stoking a fire, preparing a buffalo roast.

Daemyn set a basket filled with bandages and other

supplies on the table next to Zeke. "Everything looks as if it hasn't aged a day. It'll just take—"

Zeke grabbed Daemyn's wrist. "No, don't bother taking the time. Pack the wound and leave me here. I can watch for anyone following."

Rosanna stuffed some of the bandages around the arrow wound. When Zeke eased to a sitting position with Daemyn's help, she quickly wrapped a few bandages around Zeke's torso to keep everything in place. "That will have to suffice."

"Go." Zeke met Daemyn's gaze. Something passed between them. A goodbye. The understanding of longtime friends.

"Thank you for watching my back one last time." Daemyn spun and headed for the far door.

With one last glance at Zeke, Rosanna hurried to catch up as Daemyn pushed the door open. Rosanna's heart pounded into her throat. What would they find inside?

Daemyn led the way through winding hallways until they stepped into the entry hall by the main doors to the keep.

The front entry hall was shadowed, its only light coming from a high window. The floors, rugs, and furniture remained free of dust, as if a servant had polished them only a few hours ago.

Even with their soft moccasins muffling their footsteps, a faint scuffing resonating down the hall as they tiptoed forward.

At the end of a short hall, a set of double doors hung ajar, though not enough that Rosanna could see far inside.

"The great hall." Daemyn rested a hand on one of the doors but didn't push it open. "This is where High Prince Alexander fell asleep."

Who had told him? Or had he ventured here after the high prince slept? Now wasn't the time to ask.

Rosanna rested her hand on the other door and met his gaze. Was he eager for this moment? Or dreading it? Was that sorrow she saw in his eyes? Hard to tell, for it seemed his eyes had never contained anything but sorrow for as long as she had known him.

He tipped his head in a nod, and together, they pushed the doors open.

The great hall spread before her. High windows streamed early morning sunlight onto the floor. Three banners hung along each of the sides, the standards for six of the kingdoms. The red banner for the seventh kingdom, Kanawhee, hung from above the three thrones on the dais at the far end.

At the base of the dais lay two bodies.

Rosanna swallowed and crept forward, her pulse tripping as if she approached a wild animal. As she neared, a third body became visible half hidden behind the thrones, a woman with long, blond hair spread around her face, a crown near her fingertips. The high prince's mother High Queen Verena.

Rosanna halted a few feet from the two bodies on the ground. Both wore crowns and clothing made of cloth far finer than she'd seen in her life. The man closest to her was middle aged and darker skinned, his shirt fringed with strands of gold as if such riches were nothing to him.

The man closer to the dais was younger with brown hair and bronze-colored skin, but also dressed in fine cloth. A dagger rested on the floor between them, proof of the curse that had claimed High Prince Alexander.

A scepter, a wooden staff embossed with gold and jewels, lay on the dais at the top of the stairs, as if a kingship had been cast aside the day this tragedy frozen before her had occurred.

The moment remained so still, so caught in time, that she couldn't make herself move.

Daemyn stood over the older man, peering down at him. "The king of Tuckawassee back then."

"Considering his descendants have been fighting the other kingdoms ever since, he must have had something to do with the high prince falling into his curse." Rosanna picked up the dagger lying between the high prince and the old king of Tuckawassee and set it to one side. When she woke High Prince Alexander, this king would wake too, and odds were, he wouldn't be on their side.

She grimaced. Two Tuckawassee kings? The one fighting her father outside was problem enough.

Daemyn gripped his hardwood staff, as if prepared to fight the king of Tuckawassee if he caused trouble when he woke. "It's time, princess."

Time for her to fulfill the destiny she'd been given before she was born. She knelt at High Prince Alexander's side, her hands trembling.

The stories whispered about the castle said High Prince Alexander would wake with true love's kiss. But kneeling there, soaking in the stillness of the nearly empty castle, kissing him didn't feel right. She didn't know him. He didn't know her, lying there asleep and vulnerable as he was. That couldn't be the means to wake him.

Over a hundred years ago, the Highest King promised a princess would come to break the curse. But what real power did she have over such a thing like a curse? All she had was the gift to hear.

She hadn't been able do to any of this by herself. Not travel across Tallahatchia. Not get into this castle. She had grown up a princess with no knowledge of weapons or living off the land. Only her skill with a paddle had aided her, small as that skill was.

Perhaps that was the reason she was a princess. A girl of the mountains would've been able to live off the land, travel by herself, fight her way here with the strength of her hands.

But Rosanna hadn't gotten here solely on her own strength. Nor would she wake High Prince Alexander by herself either. This wasn't about strength of body or will. It was about kneeling here, knowing her own helplessness.

A draft curled around her face and touched her cheek. A silent echo of the day she'd been given to hear the trees singing the way the ancient kings had before they had unleashed the curse. She closed her eyes, breathing in deeply.

She was but the lowly means the Highest King had chosen to wake the high prince. He hadn't had to choose her. He could've chosen any number of princesses or girls across Tallahatchia. But he had seen fit to choose her and make her his means to carry out a promise to wake.

And he had even given her the instructions on how to do it that day by the small creek in Tuckawassee as she knelt beside Daemyn's dead body.

Opening her eyes, she pulled her canteen free, uncapped it, and held it above High Prince Alexander. Her arm didn't shake, as much as something deep within her hurt.

She met Daemyn's eyes. Almost she didn't want to wake the high prince. What would happen to Daemyn the moment High Prince Alexander opened his eyes?

Daemyn held her gaze, and his mouth tipped into his soft smile. "It's all right. It's time."

The look on his face, the tone in his voice . . . it hurt so deeply she didn't have the words to describe it. But there was hope in it too and somehow, that hope hurt even worse.

How she wanted to delay this moment. To freeze time as surely as it had been frozen in Castle Eyota for the past hundred years.

Hear, obey, and trust the Highest King with the outcome. That's how Daemyn had survived the past hundred years. If the worst happened, that was how he'd die a few moments from now too.

It's how she would have to live.

With a deep breath, Rosanna tipped the canteen.

CHAPTER 32

ALEXANDER

Alex stood before a turquoise waterfall surrounded by clouds of mist. Instead of the pool, the waterfall disappeared into the crystal floor.

He was dreaming. Yet not the hazy dreams he'd had for the past years—how long, he didn't know. He'd seen things in those dreams, things he thought might be real, but he had still been deeply slumbering, the memories whispers only.

But this dream was one step from wakefulness. He knew he was dreaming, yet he was here too, wherever this was.

He stared at his thumb, the single drop of blood still visible there in this dream place.

What an arrogant fool he'd been. In the end, it hadn't been the Tuckawassee king or anyone else that had forced him into this curse. It had been his own arrogance in taking that dagger, thinking he knew better.

Apparently, intelligence didn't necessarily give wisdom.

"What have I done?" He collapsed to his knees at the base of the waterfall, the roar and mist strangely dry on his face when he longed for its cool touch.

He was a fool. That one moment, staring at the blood on his finger, had torn deep into him, shining a light into places he'd deceived himself into thinking weren't there. Arrogant. Self-important. Oblivious to those around him. Downright horrible to those who served under him. A generally miserable and worthless excuse for a man.

He'd hung his entire existence on his title and intelligence, both nothing but gifts given to him at birth. And he'd acted like he'd somehow earned those gifts. By what, his own ability to be condescending?

"Do you have an answer for me?"

Alex hunched lower at the sound of the Prince's voice, a heat burning in his cheeks, down his neck. He'd marched into the very throne room of the Highest King with nothing but anger and demands. What a self-deceived fool he'd been.

The breeze stirred, cooling his face with the waterfall's mist, an echo of the WaterVeil from beyond, and he heard again the whisper of that question. *Which is the curse, and which is the gift?*

Alex couldn't raise his head, the truth too great a weight pressing him down. "My pride. That's the true curse. It turned the gift of intelligence into a curse and made the curse of sleep a blessing."

He had no one to blame for this curse but himself. Not the Fallen Fae. Not the Highest King. The blame rested solely on him.

What sort of king would he have been without being forced to face what he was? A cruel, arrogant king. Perhaps the Tuckawassee feared truly when they fought so hard to rid themselves of him and the high kings. His reign would not have been good.

Worse, the true curse was still there, deep in his chest, a dark twisting thing in the light of this place.

How had he missed seeing that darkness when he'd walked in the brilliance of the throne room? He must have looked like a dark stain smeared across that crystal floor, even as he was now in this dream place.

He wasn't worthy of waking. He should be left in this cursed sleep for all time, yet even that was a punishment too small. Shaking, he couldn't raise his head from where he pressed against the stone-hard floor. "Leave me here. Please. I don't deserve to wake."

The faintest breath of breeze curled along the back of his neck, carrying with it the scent of streams and forests beyond the WaterVeil. With it came the echoes of that far-off song, the one he hadn't fully understood back then. *Worthy. Hope. Cursebreaker.*

The words weren't meant for him but for the one standing before him. With the mist-laden breeze washing over him, Alex managed to raise his head and look to the Prince, only to find the Prince already kneeling in front of him, a gentle smile on his face.

But when the Prince spoke, his voice held the power it had in the throne room beyond, with all the compassion of water from a mountain creek against a dying man's lips. "You didn't deserve to enter the Highest King's courts, yet you were given entrance in my name. You will wake by the same. Now rise and give place to your pride no more. I have much work yet for you to do."

The Prince took his hand and pulled him to his feet.

With the strength of the Prince's grip and the cool breeze gusting around him, Alex found he could stand, his senses less caught in the dream with each breath.

Alex stared at the waterfall, something in him almost . . . was it reluctance? Was that the tightness in his chest? Even in the curse, he had been given the gift of peaceful sleep unlike any he'd ever known before. Or would know for the remainder of his life. "I will never enjoy such rest again, will I?"

"Not until the final rest, no."

What sort of work did Alex's future hold that he needed so many years of this kind of rest to bear him up through it? He didn't dare ask.

The Prince gripped Alex's arm and pulled him through the waterfall.

Water dripped down his face as Alex opened his eyes. Was it the remnants of that waterfall still pouring over him?

No. A girl stared down at him, a canteen raised over his head. One last drop teetered on its rim. Her black hair had natural highlights of a lighter, almost brown color woven through it. Even though she'd poured a canteen of water over his head, the buckskin shirt and trousers she wore dripped far more water than he did. She was a wild-looking girl, dirty and wet, with her hair frizzing from its braid as it dried.

She was the princess come to wake him, though she didn't look at all like he'd pictured she would. As surely as he had been promised, he had wakened.

"I'm Princess Rosanna." She cocked her head, as if wondering if he was fully awake.

He could introduce himself, but since she was here, she already knew who he was. No, the more important question crowded out anything else. "How long?"

She blinked, but she had her own gift of intelligence, or perhaps the gift to interpret nonsensical questions from formerly sleeping princes. "One hundred years. To the day."

One hundred years. Alex drew in a sharp breath and sat up. Not just a few years or a few decades. An entire century, gone.

Though, it could've been worse. He could've slept for a thousand years.

How much had Tallahatchia changed in that time? What damage had the Tuckawassee done? Obviously, they hadn't been able to kill him in his sleep as planned. But surely, they had caused plenty of other trouble.

The Tuckawassee . . .

"No!" The shout came from beside him, first piercing, then guttural.

Alex turned in time to see King Hakan—or perhaps, former king now—lunge to his feet, dodging around a man dressed in buckskins carrying a hardwood staff, his clothes also dripping wet.

Alex blinked. Jadon? His former manservant's stance was taller and more confident, his hair longer, and his face looked like it should have been lined even though it hadn't aged a day past the last night Alex had seen him. He was Jadon, yet somehow, not Jadon. He was whatever a man became when forced to live a hundred years dedicated to one mission.

Jadon whipped his staff up, taking King Hakan in the stomach. King Hakan collapsed to the floor with a groan, arms wrapped around his middle. Jadon stood over King Hakan, making sure he didn't try anything else.

"Alex!" His mother dashed down the stairs, crashing to her knees and hugging him.

He wrapped an arm around her shoulders. "It's over, Mother. It's finally over."

Those words sank deep into him. After twenty-one years of living for nothing but ending the curse, he was free. And he was changed.

"Princess . . ." Jadon's voice had a strained edge to it. He took a step forward, his staff gripped in shaking hands. The signet ring on Jadon's finger flashed once, going from clear back to the sapphire blue Alex remembered.

"Daemyn!" Princess Rosanna sprang to her feet, steadying Jadon.

King Hakan rolled to his feet, the dagger he'd given to Alex a hundred years ago now gripped in his hand. "I didn't sleep all this time to have victory denied me now."

Alex patted his clothes. He hadn't gained any weapons while he'd slept. All he had was speech. He held out his hands, palms up. "You don't have to do this. It's been a hundred years. Tallahatchia has probably changed more than either of us know. We don't know what we'll find when we leave the castle."

"Tallahatchia doesn't need the return of a high king." King Hakan lunged forward, stabbing with the dagger.

Alex jumped backwards. The dagger skimmed along his ribs, slicing through his shirt and the top layer of skin. His mother dashed for the dais. Hopefully she'd hide behind the thrones again. Behind King Hakan, Jadon appeared to be struggling to stand, the princess supporting him.

"I realize I've been an arrogant prince, and my father wasn't free of mistakes either. But I've learned. I'll change. I'll listen to the grievances you and the other kings have." Alex took another step backwards. Maybe he could lead the enraged king away from his mother, Jadon, and Princess Rosanna. If he was killed, he should at least be able to spare them.

"Easy promises to make with your life in my hands." King Hakan clutched the dagger tighter.

"Over here!" Princess Rosanna's voice cut sharp and hard.

Alex leaned to one side to see her around King Hakan. She stood tall, a dagger—the dagger Alex had given Jadon long ago—gripped in her hand. Jadon stood swaying beside her, gripping his quarterstaff. Was that a streak of gray in Jadon's hair? And had those lines across his face been there a few moments ago?

"I am Princess Rosanna of Neskahana." She planted her feet like she was one of the trees of the forest, her roots immovable. "If you fight the high prince, you fight me."

King Hakan snorted. "Fine." He whirled and stabbed.

Jadon raised his staff, blocking the blow. The force sent Jadon to his knees, his arms shaking. Princess Rosanna stabbed at King Hakan, but he grabbed her arm, tossed her aside, and kicked Jadon in the ribs, sending him to the floor.

As King Hakan faced Alex once again, dagger still clutched in his fist. Alex backed up a step. This was it. Alex didn't have a weapon to defend himself. King Hakan would finish what he'd started a hundred years ago.

Alex tripped on the bottom step of the dais. He fell, landing hard on his back on the stairs. King Hakan stood over him and raised the dagger.

Movement caught Alex's gaze. Mother appeared behind King Hakan, the jewel-encrusted scepter gripped in her hands.

She swung the scepter, tendons standing out on her neck, her eyes blazing. The scepter's end struck King Hakan's temple with a vicious thunk. He collapsed to the ground, his head thumping against the stone floor. Blood spread in a pool from his skull.

Mother gripped the scepter in two hands, shaking. Her mouth twisted. "You took my husband from me. You will not take my son."

Alex approached her carefully, easing the scepter from her grip and hugging her. He couldn't find words, and all that finally came out was a whispered, "I love you, Mama." He couldn't remember the last time he'd said that to her.

He pulled away from his mother, knelt, and pressed his fingers to King Hakan's neck to check for a pulse. He couldn't find one. "Princess Rosanna, would . . ."

When Alex glanced up, he trailed off. Princess Rosanna stumbled as Jadon sagged against her, his hair entirely gray.

Alex jumped to his feet and helped her ease Jadon to the floor. "What's happening? What's wrong?"

Jadon tried to sit upright, but it was as if all the strength was draining from his body, though Alex couldn't see any blood. "I was only promised enough years to lead Princess Rosanna here."

Alex sat back on his heels. Jadon was dying. Not from a wound, but from age as it claimed its long-denied victim. Even as Alex watched, streaks of Jadon's hair turned white, his hands shriveling, the skin becoming papery and cracked, blue veins showing through.

"Daemyn." Princess Rosanna cradled Jadon, her voice cracking, but her face remained free of tears, as if this was something she'd mourned already and would wait to mourn again later.

Jadon rested his head on the princess's shoulder, mumbling something too low for Alex to hear.

This wasn't right. Jadon had given up everything for Alex. Somehow Alex knew that, even without hearing what Jadon had done for the past one hundred years. Maybe it was in those flashes of dreams he'd had while he slept, pieces of the outside world given him. Maybe it was remembering the Prince telling Jadon the cost would be high. But Alex knew without a doubt that Jadon had suffered.

Princess Rosanna cradled Jadon, waiting tears and something deeper in her eyes. An ache, like the pain Alex had seen in his mother's eyes as she'd watched them bury Alex's father. He'd never seen that look in Mirabelle's eyes, nor would she have seen it in him. If they had, perhaps he would've sacrificed more for her and her for him. She'd been right not to stay. Two selfish people as they had been, they would have destroyed each other.

But this was something so much deeper. Love, like that told in the old stories of worthy kings and valiant princesses.

This wasn't Alex's story. He wasn't the hero as he'd so vainly thought himself to be. He didn't break the curse, win the heart of the princess, gain the victory.

He was the one in distress. The person that helplessly, foolishly needed saving.

Jadon was the hero here, and he should receive the happy ending with his princess.

But Jadon was weakening. His hair was pure white, his eyes fluttering closed, his body seeming smaller in Princess Rosanna's arms. Shrunken. Dying.

"Ask."

The Prince knelt beside Alex. No one else seemed to be looking in their direction, as if they didn't see the Prince there, his white clothes stark against the stone floor. Or, perhaps, they weren't given to see at that moment.

The Prince met Alex's gaze. "Ask."

Alex trembled as he had in the place before the waterfall in his dream. *Ask*. It was a command, a command he didn't dare obey. Somehow, he knew, though he crouched on the stone floor in Castle Eyota, whatever he said now would be heard in that crystal throne room beyond. How could he ask anything there after the way he'd approached last time? He wasn't worthy of being heard, then or now.

"When you came in your arrogance, you were heard because I am worthy." The Prince's gaze didn't waver. "When you come in your humility, am I any less worthy?"

No, of course not. The Prince was the only one worthy of standing before that throne and being heard there. If Alex was heard as he had then, it was only because he had come under the Prince's name with the Prince himself standing between them and the throne.

Jadon lay small and still in Princess Rosanna's arms. The princess bent over him, her shoulders shaking. Alex's mother, though she didn't know Princess Rosanna, gripped her shoulders as if to steady her with shared grief.

"To come is a privilege given to few, but to those it is given, it will never be taken away." The Prince's eyes held a depth of compassion that pierced Alex. "Now, come. Ask."

That command stirred deep in his heart, like the draft stirring the tapestries hanging along the walls. Alex drew in a deep breath. What if this, too, was a *no*?

He had to ask—trust—regardless of the answer. "If it's possible, could the years Jadon sacrificed for me be returned to him?"

CHAPTER 33

ROSANNA

Rosanna cradled Daemyn as age claimed him. His face was etched with lines, his hair white. But his eyes were still deep brown as he blinked up at her.

He reached up with one, weathered hand but stopped short of touching her cheek. "Almost I would stay for you."

Almost. But not enough to keep him from wanting the death that was taking him. She gripped his hand. "I know. It's all right."

It wasn't all right. Not even close. But she had promised she would let him go. It was the last gift she could give him.

His eyes flickered closed. The strength in his hand slipped away, leaving it limp in her grasp.

A hand rested on Daemyn's shoulder. Rosanna looked up. The Prince knelt before her.

He was there to take Daemyn home. She loosened her grip on Daemyn's limp body. It was time to let him go, once and for all. If only her heart didn't hold him so tightly.

She couldn't stop her tears any longer as she met the Prince's gaze. She was losing Daemyn forever, yet she couldn't—wouldn't—ask for him to be spared for her a second time. "Please. Take him. He's ready to go."

"You would go on alone?"

She squeezed her eyes shut. "Yes. If that is what you ask of me."

"I ask of you service, but the work I give you is a gift you will never have to bear alone."

"I know." When Rosanna blinked through the blur of her tears, the Prince was gone.

In her arms, Daemyn moved. His hair was gaining color, far more quickly than it had turned gray. His face smoothed, the healthy bronze color of his skin flooding back in like a flash flood tearing down a mountain gully.

He was alive. She couldn't force herself to move. This wasn't an outcome she'd prepared for, as much as it eased the pain in her chest. How would he react to living longer still?

His eyes opened, and he jerked out of her arms, sitting upright.

"Daemyn?" She reached to touch his shoulder, but he waved her away, his head hanging.

His shoulders rose and fell, as if in a deep breath. Shaking off death as he had done so many times before, willing himself to once again pick up the pieces and carry on.

Her heart ached, as if she was losing him all over.

Daemyn rolled to his feet, his posture stiff. "We still have a war to stop."

"I don't suppose just showing my face outside to prove

I'm awake will end it." High Prince Alexander glanced between Daemyn and Rosanna, his eyebrows knit, his jaw a mite slack. It must have been confusing to wake into a time he knew nothing about.

"It might. All seven kingdoms have gathered their armies outside this castle. Hopefully at least some of them will rally to you when they see you've awakened." Daemyn bowed his head, a loyal servant before the high prince he had served for over a century.

Rosanna climbed to her feet and brushed off her leggings. Her task was over. She'd wakened the high prince. She should be relieved, shouldn't she? Then why did something in her ache as if torn open?

"Wait." High Queen Verena held up her hand and dashed back behind the thrones, her silk skirt swishing in a way Rosanna hadn't known fabric could move. What must have it been like back then, when trade prospered and the kingdoms were united?

A lock rattled, and a door grated. A moment later, High Queen Verena returned, holding a large gold crown in her hands. A sapphire winked in the center, matching the stone that had changed to blue in the signet ring on Daemyn's hand. The high queen halted before High Prince Alexander and held out the crown. "You'll need this."

High Prince Alexander stared at the crown, as if it was a bear trap waiting to snap at him. He bowed, and High Queen Verena slid the crown onto his head.

Daemyn stepped forward, the signet ring on his palm. "A hundred years ago, I promised I'd return this to you."

High Prince Alexander slid the ring onto his finger and stood straighter, more the regal high prince Rosanna had expected when she'd set out to wake him.

She had awakened the rightful high king, and it was time he returned.

High Prince Alexander patted the high queen's shoulder. "Please stay here until we make sure it is safe."

High Queen Verena glanced toward King Hakan's still body. Rosanna swallowed. How would the Tuckawassee react to losing a king they had revered as a hero?

"He won't cause you any more pain." High Prince Alexander squeezed the high queen's shoulder, spun on his heels, and strode toward the double doors. Daemyn fell into step after him, his staff at the ready.

After swiping Daemyn's dagger from the floor, Rosanna trailed them. Now that she'd done her part, was she to be overlooked? What was she supposed to do after all this?

As they stepped into the entry hall, footsteps pounded in the passageway to the kitchens. Daemyn pushed past High Prince Alexander, raising his staff and protecting both the high prince and Rosanna.

Isi dashed down the hallway, Zeke leaning against her shoulder. She pointed back the way she'd come. "Major Beshko fought her way past the Kanawhee line with a few of her men. Pa is delaying them as much as he can."

Rosanna brushed past the high prince, swerved around Daemyn's lowering staff, and took one of Zeke's arms across her shoulders. "I've got him. You need your hands free."

Isi released Zeke and spun on her heel, drawing her long knife.

Rosanna helped Zeke sit on the floor against the wall next to a decorative plinth holding a display of what looked like blown glass fake fruit, a decoration that must have been made in Neskahana long ago. "How are you holding up?"

"Fine enough." Zeke's skin was pale around his tight mouth. "How's my uncle?"

"Alive, and I think he's going to stay that way." If he didn't get himself killed trying to stop Major Beshko and this war. Rosanna glanced over her shoulder as the clang of metal on metal echoed down the hallway, growing closer.

At the bend in the hallway, Chogan and Ilma retreated backwards, followed by Captain Degotaga and Otho holding off a press of six Tuckawassee led by Major Beshko.

Major Beshko stabbed forward with her long knife, forcing Captain Degotaga yet another step back. As they poured into the entry hall, the Tuckawassee spread out.

Daemyn dashed to help Rosanna's guard, knocking a long knife from a Tuckawassee's hand. Major Beshko turned to Daemyn and stumbled back, her eyes widening.

High Prince Alexander patted his waist again, as if looking for a weapon. Rosanna held out the dagger. "Here. Take this."

He stared at the dagger for a moment, opening his mouth as if to say something. The clash of knives drew his gaze, and he snatched the dagger and whirled to join the fight.

Rosanna cast about for a way to help. Isi blocked a strike, ducking and swiping with her knife. Captain Degotaga lunged next to her, and against the two of them, the Tuckawassee warrior stumbled back. Rosanna's three guards fought the other Tuckawassee while the high prince hurried to help them.

Daemyn held off Major Beshko with his whirling staff. Major Beshko ducked under his swing, getting past his guard and swiping at his stomach. Only his quick jump backwards saved him from evisceration.

Zeke tried to push himself from the wall, gripping his bow as if he still thought he had the strength to draw it.

Rosanna shoved him back down. "Don't you dare get up. They've got this handled." Or so she hoped.

Major Beshko had Daemyn backed against the wall. As she lunged again, Daemyn couldn't get his staff up to block, not with the small space. Major Beshko aimed her knife at his heart.

Rosanna hadn't had him restored to her to lose him to Major Beshko's knife. She grabbed one of the fake, glass fruit from the decorative bowl next to her. An apple, it turned out. The smooth, red glass fit in her palm. Cocking back her arm, she threw it as hard as she could.

The apple struck the back of Major Beshko's head and shattered, coating her black, puffy braid with shards of red. Major Beshko staggered, lowering the knife and pressing her free hand to the back of her head.

Before Major Beshko could recover, Daemyn sidestepped to gain room and jabbed the end of his quarterstaff into her stomach.

Major Beshko crumpled to the ground. Daemyn sliced one of the leather strings that formed the fringe of his buckskin shirt with a knife and used it to tie Major Beshko's hands behind her back.

Rosanna let out a breath and glanced around. Her guards had the rest of the Tuckawassee subdued. Isi bound the last one hand and foot while Captain Degotaga bowed to High Prince Alexander, saying something too softly for Rosanna to hear.

Daemyn strode across the room and knelt next to Zeke. "Are you all right?"

"Uncle Daemyn. Glad to see you're still alive and causing trouble." Zeke spoke between gritted teeth, his breaths coming harder. He held out his bow. "Here. You'll need this more than me."

Daemyn took the bow and Zeke's quiver. "Stay put this time."

Zeke rested his head against the wall, sweat beading along his hairline. "Not going anywhere."

As Daemyn returned to High Prince Alexander's side, Rosanna glanced between him and Zeke. Should she stay here and help Zeke or follow the others?

Zeke raised a limp hand. "Go on. They'll need you more than I will."

"Are you sure?" Rosanna didn't like the look of the red smear of blood Zeke left on the wall.

"Unless you know how to dig out an arrow and stitch a wound, there isn't much you can do." Zeke had his fists pressed against his sides.

He was right. The quicker they ended the war—or at least stopped this battle—the quicker someone with medical training could tend Zeke.

High Queen Verena appeared next to Rosanna. "I'll stay with him." She settled onto the floor, her skirts pooling around her. She set to work attempting to tear the fine fabric of her skirt, all for a stranger.

At least someone was there to look after Zeke. Rosanna spun and raced after the others.

Isi waited at the far end of the entry hall near the double doors to the courtyard. They shared a nod before Isi pushed the doors open, and they hurried to catch up with the others as High Prince Alexander led the way up the stairs to the wall top over the main gate.

When Rosanna reached the parapet, she caught her breath at the landscape laid out around them.

The thorn hedge remained around the castle walls,

though it had shriveled and blackened even more in the past few minutes. The rose blooms now drooped, petals falling to the ground. In the mountains beyond, white, red, and pink patches marked the blooming rhododendrons and mountain laurel. The sun, now fully risen, splashed warm rays across the mountains and down into the sparkling rivers.

Beyond the rose hedge, the ground sloped steeply down to a narrow valley at the base of the surrounding mountains. Knots of men surged and fought across the valley and up the slope to the castle. Scattered on the grass lay bodies in pools of blood.

Rosanna searched the chaos below, trying to make sense of what she was seeing.

Men and women with feathers tied in their long, black hair had been backed all the way to the thorn hedge by a band of Tuckawassee warriors. To the left, soldiers from Monongadotte, dressed in cloaks made of various animal pelts, struggled against waves of Pohatomie with their blond hair streaming behind them as they charged. On the far right, the ranks of Guyangahelan warriors remained in silent, motionless rows, mere observers of the battle.

There, halfway down the slope, Neskahana's army fought in a defensive formation shared with Buckhannock's army. The young man Rosanna had seen the night before, Buckhannock's prince, called out orders to the formation, gesturing an order to charge forward into the ranks of both the Pohatomie and Tuckawassee.

Berend stood next to the prince of Buckhannock, giving a similar motioned command to Neskahana's warriors.

Where was her father? Surely, he couldn't be among those the bodies, lying wounded or dead.

Isi gripped Rosanna's arm and pointed. "There."

Rosanna's father fought hard at the edge of a small group of his personal guards, cut off from the rest of Neskahana's warriors. He swung his long knife in one hand, a war ax in the other.

His strike was blocked by a Tuckawassee warrior dressed in gold-fringed buckskin and wearing a crown. The current king of Tuckawassee, backed by ranks upon ranks of his men.

One of her father's guards fell. Pitifully few remained guarding her father as the Tuckawassee surrounded him.

Neskahana and Buckhannock were charging forward, but they wouldn't reach her father in time.

Father leapt backward to avoid a strike and stumbled on one of the bodies on the ground behind him. The Tuckawassee king raised his war ax as her father struggled to regain his balance.

"No!" Rosanna glanced about. She didn't have anything she could throw, not to mention the distance was too great.

Daemyn drew an arrow from Zeke's quiver, nocked it, and raised the bow. In all the time Rosanna had known him, she'd never seen him use a weapon besides his staff, not even the dagger he'd worn on his belt.

But hadn't Father told stories about how Arlen Rand had taught him how to use a long knife? And what about the stories that said Jubal Rand was a great archer?

Those were all Daemyn too. He'd had a hundred years to practice any weapon he wished.

Daemyn drew back the bow, his eyes narrowed, and he released.

The king of Tuckawassee staggered and fell, Daemyn's arrow in his chest. A second Tuckawassee fell before he could finish swinging his hand ax at her father's head.

Then the warriors from Neskahana and Buckhannock were there, pushing the Tuckawassee back and enfolding her father into their ranks.

The morning sunlight glinted on High Prince Alexander's crown. In the ranks of the Guyangahelans, a man pointed toward where the high prince stood. Orders were given, and the Guyangahelans marched forward, spears thrust ahead of them.

With the armies of Neskahana, Buckhannock, Kanawhee, Monongadotte, and Guyangahela facing them, the warriors of Tuckawassee and Pohatomie regrouped into a small knot of men and women.

Within the ranks, a few men and women worked their way forward, talking urgently to their commanders. Counseling for more war or for peace?

Rosanna peered closer. Did she recognize a few of those down below? She glanced at Daemyn. Had she seen them last night among Daemyn's relatives?

He rested the end of the bow on the stone parapet as down below, weapons were laid down. "The battle's over. At least for today."

Rosanna sagged against the battlements. Tomorrow might bring more war. The Tuckawassee surely wouldn't take the death of two of their kings lightly.

But, for now, she could take a deep breath and hope that for today, Tallahatchia would have peace.

CHAPTER 34

ROSANNA

With Captain Degotaga, Otho, Chogan, and Ilma at her back, Rosanna pushed into the crowd of Neskahana's warriors, smiling as they stopped to bow and congratulate her on waking the high prince. Isi had remained behind in Castle Eyota to help tend to Zeke.

"Ro-Row!"

She barely had time to whirl around before Berend plowed into her. She hugged him, trying to ignore the patches of blood on his clothes. Based on how tightly he hugged and how fast he'd moved, the blood wasn't his. "Are you all right?"

"Fine. Fine. You did it. You really did it." Berend pulled away enough for her to see the scraggly scruff on his chin and cheeks. There hadn't been time to tease him about it then while running from Major Beshko, but now . . .

"Of course, I did." She swatted his arm with a backhand. "What's with the attempt at a beard?"

He rubbed his chin as if stroking a bushy beard. "You

like it? Some of warriors from Monongadotte made a pact not to shave their beards until the high king was restored, something about a pledge their grandfather made sixty years ago that resulted in this impressive beard down to his knees. It sounded like a grand idea. But then you had to go and wake him before anyone of us from Neskahana could get a good start at it."

Rosanna cocked her head. "Sorry. I think I did you a favor. Your beard doesn't seem to have gotten the message to start growing yet." Beards weren't something many men in Neskahana could grow, much less wanted to.

Berend rolled his eyes with a sigh. "It's humiliating, especially when I spend my nights literally covered in fur."

"It must be un*bear*able." Rosanna found herself grinning. When had she last grinned like this?

Berend grinned and threw his arm around her shoulders. "Exactly. I can *bear*ly contain my disappointment. Now let's find Father and Mother and assure them their favorite daughter is alive and well."

Rosanna rolled her eyes and fell into step with Berend as they threaded their way deeper into the camp.

Men and women set up tents, tended the wounded, and recovered the dead. By nightfall, not a single body would remain abandoned on the field of battle.

"Rosanna." Father stood from where he knelt next to a wounded warrior and dashed to her. He hugged her as tightly as one of Berend's bear hugs. "I'm so proud of you."

Mother joined them a heartbeat later, wrapping Rosanna with warmth.

When Father pulled back, he held out a piece of paper. "Willem asked me to give this to you."

The note contained only a single line. *I'm honored to have you for a sister. Willem.*

Rosanna swallowed back a lump in her throat. She didn't have to ask to know Willem had written only the one note, to be given to her whether she succeeded or failed.

This was home. Not Castle Deeling or the rapids along the Onohio. Home was her parents' embrace, Berend's puns, and Willem's serious expression.

But something deep inside her still ached as if someone was still missing. Part of her heart now belonged elsewhere, a home not found even with her family.

Night had long fallen over Castle Eyota. The king of Pohatomie remained under guard while the other kings, including Rosanna's father, packed inside Castle Eyota's hall to recognize High Prince Alexander as the high king, set a date for the official coronation, and write up an official treaty to deal with Tuckawassee and Pohatomie.

But Rosanna's role in this was over. All she had left to do was figure out what would happen now that her quest was done, the high prince awakened.

She found Daemyn by himself on the wall top over the back gate, gazing down at the Kanawhee River flowing black and shimmering into the deep darkness of the mountains. The stars overhead winked and burned in the depths of the sky. In the far-off distance, a pack of wolves howled to the wind.

He remained still as she approached, leaning against the battlements, his head bowed. She rested her elbows on the stones next to him, gazing out into the night. "What do you plan to do now that this is all over?"

Daemyn sighed and lifted his head to stare up at the

stars. "I don't know. I never planned for this, living after High Prince Alexander woke."

"Why not?" She inched closer. If only they had an understanding between them, something that would give her permission to wrap her arm around his and lean her head against his shoulder. It had felt so right to hold him as he'd been dying, but the wall was back between them now that he lived. She wasn't sure what she had to say or do to make him lower it again.

"My task was all there was. Now . . ." Daemyn's shoulders slumped, his voice strained. "I don't know what to do with another lifetime."

She ached for him, for the years that weighed on him so much that he didn't rejoice at being spared death yet again. She had to swallow before she could force out the words on her heart. "You don't have to live this lifetime alone."

His shoulders slumped farther, as if her words only added to the weight pressing him down. "No, Princess. Don't hang your hopes on me. Go home to Neskahana. Find someone there."

She crossed her arms, heat flaring through her chest. "Why do you always do this? Push me away every time I try to get close. I thought you might care. Look at me and tell me I'm wrong."

"Princess, I . . ."

"Don't." She couldn't stand to hear him say her title one more time, as if it was a shield he held between them. "My name is Rosanna. Say it."

He shook his head. "I can't."

"Why not? Make me understand." She gripped his arm. If there was one thing this quest had taught her, it was to fight for the things that mattered. She had crossed mountains at this man's side, paddled to the headwaters of rivers with him, and watched him die twice.

Perhaps they weren't quite up to speaking wedding vows and pledging their lives to each other, but she reckoned it was about time they scouted things out to see if they could make it there eventually.

"I just . . ." He pulled his arm from her grasp and turned away, but not before she caught a glimpse of his expression. Wide-eyed, brow furrowed.

This wasn't anger. It was confusion.

It was easy to forget, standing where she was, how hard this was for him. She only saw Daemyn, the quiet young man who had led her through the mountains. She hadn't been there during all the other names he'd worn while waiting for the high prince to be awakened. How could she begin to guess what it was like to have over a hundred years of memories yet still be twenty-one years old?

For that's what he was, especially now. He'd been different when he'd woken after dying of old age. Younger, if that was possible. When she'd met him, she'd guessed him twenty-five because the weight of the years he'd lived clouding the depths of his eyes. That was gone now, and she couldn't mistake him for any age other than twenty-one.

If she'd thought herself falling for him before, now something between them fit better than it had. Perhaps now he would be able to smile again. Laugh. Live.

If space and time was what he needed to sort through everything, that's what she'd give him.

For now.

CHAPTER 35

ALEXANDER

Alex nearly ran into Princess Rosanna as she hurried down the stairs from the battlements, swiping at her eyes, though she wasn't sniffing or making any noise indicating she was sobbing. Just shedding silent tears as if even that was a release she barely allowed herself.

He caught her as she stumbled on the last step trying to avoid him. "Princess Rosanna. I don't believe I thanked you properly for waking me up."

She wiped at her face one last time, drew in a breath, and faced him as composed as if she'd come in response to his official summons.

Yet something in her remained the wild-haired girl who woke him. The same one who had casually destroyed a priceless antique glass apple without a second thought. "You're welcome, though I was just doing what I was called to do."

He glanced between her and Jadon's stiff, dark form silhouetted against the stars and lowered his voice. "I left a girl back a hundred years ago, but I think, if I'd truly loved her, I would've tried harder. Don't give up yet."

The set of her shoulders straightened. "I don't intend to." With one last nod, she swept past him, her stride firm.

Alex marched up the stairs. As he approached, Jadon straightened, his posture stiffening in a semblance of how he'd stood as Alex's manservant. But he wore the posture awkwardly, like a shirt that no longer fit him. "Was there something you required, Your Highness?"

What did he require? Alex leaned against the battlements, staring into the darkness dotted with campfires.

In the daylight, he had searched the mountains around the castle, looking for familiar stones and trees. But saplings had grown into towering trees. Old trees had grown still older or come crashing down. Even the river had deepened and changed its course.

And the town of Eyota had been reduced to crumbling homes and rotting stumps of docks, its few remaining citizens trying to eke out an existence in the shadow of the slumbering castle and ever-present threat of war.

He required something familiar. Someone who remembered the way things had been a century ago.

"You don't have to be my manservant any longer. Not after what you've done." Alex rubbed at the signet ring on his finger. "I can make you my seneschal. My chief advisor. Or, if you prefer, I will grant you land and a barony in whichever of the Seven Kingdoms you desire."

Instead of smiling, Jadon stiffened still further. "I will serve wherever you wish me to."

Alex curled his fingers. Why did even his attempt at a reward sound like he was demanding more work and obedience? "No, no. That's not what I meant. I'm trying to reward you. Choose whatever you wish, and if it's in my power, I will grant it."

Jadon was a statue staring into the distance. "I wish for no reward. I merely did my duty."

"You did far more than that." Alex shook his head. "I could use an advisor. My mother, me, and you are the only ones left who remember the Tallahatchia that once was."

"If that is what you wish." Jadon's back was so stiff it looked about to snap.

"Don't. Don't go back to being the silent, dutiful servant. I don't want a servant. I want . . . I want a friend." Alex faced Jadon, palms up. "I need someone unafraid to honestly tell me the truth without any pandering. I didn't have that a hundred years ago, and I was a miserably selfish, arrogant prince. I don't want to return to what I was before the curse, and I'm begging you that, if you can stand my presence after the horrible person I used to be, you'll be that person."

Finally, Jadon turned, his back a fraction less stiff. "You were a mite arrogant back then."

Alex rested his elbows on the battlements, a smile twitching his mouth. "Come now. Don't hold back."

Jadon huffed out a breath, and his posture relaxed still more. "I'm not sure you're ready to hear all of it yet."

"Perhaps not." Alex chuckled, but he wasn't sure how much mirth was behind it. He had a long way to go before he could laugh at the man he had been, and in too many ways, still was.

He shook his head. Enough about himself. "Do you know what happened to Mirabelle?"

Had she been happy? For some reason, Alex needed the answer to be yes. He didn't want to think that by falling into his curse, he'd cursed her to a life of misery as well.

"She had her own curse to fight, but she came out of it with a man she loved deeply." Jadon waved down at the black shape of the dying roses ringing the castle. "She grew those, about a year after you fell asleep, when it became clear we couldn't hold off the Tuckawassee forever."

There was something about those roses, a farewell that spanned the decades. Alex could be at peace with that, knowing she'd had what she never could have found with him. "And her parents? Did I just dream they fell asleep when I did?"

"They woke early. From what I was told, they were never meant to stay caught in your curse forever."

Something in Jadon's voice said there was more to this story, but now wasn't the time to ask. It was enough to know Mirabelle hadn't lost her parents, nor had she been unhappy. It was all he could've wished for her. Hopefully she'd known that, even as she'd grown the hedge of roses to keep him safe for a hundred years.

Alex let the silence lengthen for a beat. "They call you Daemyn."

Jadon's shoulders slumped, as if the name reminded him of a great weight he still carried. "One of many names I've had. It was easier to kill off a previous name than try to explain why I wasn't aging."

"I suppose I should call you Daemyn, then." Yet Alex still struggled to give Jadon another name than the one he'd spent eleven years calling him.

"Doesn't matter to me." Jadon swept pebbles from the wall top with his fingers. "I'm Jadon. And Daemyn. Arlen, Jubal, and all the other names I've worn in the past hundred years."

Jadon had paid a far higher price than Alex had, as if he too had suffered a curse. Something that could have been avoided had Alex not let his own arrogance lead him to pick up that dagger. "Did you have time with your family?"

"Some. I had to keep moving, checking if the sapphire cleared and eventually organizing those loyal to you. But my family stuck by me, best they could." Jadon stared off to the north as if he could see that little cabin in Buckhannock. Was it still standing after all this time?

With the hitch to Jadon's voice, Alex could hear what he wasn't saying. Jadon was there when his parents died, his siblings died, his nieces and nephews died. And still Jadon was here on this side of the WaterVeil. "Did Luke ever forgive me?"

"Not fully, I don't think. Not when he realized, even more than I did back then, how much it was going to cost me." Jadon shook his head.

Luke would've taken his spear to Alex if he'd guessed how much Alex would hurt Jadon in what was then the future.

Alex swallowed and stared off into the night, seeing again that crystal throne room. "Why did you do it? Volunteer to find the cursebreaker?"

It was a question he hadn't thought to ask back then. He'd simply expected it, as if it was Jadon's duty to share his curse.

But Jadon hadn't had to volunteer any more than he'd had to remain Alex's manservant. He could've walked away and left Alex to his own arrogant misery. Probably should have.

Jadon blew out a long breath, staring as if he too saw that throne room once again. "For the same reason I never quit and returned home. I grew up in a large family. I always had friends in my brothers and sisters. You had no one but me."

In other words, no one but Jadon would put up with him. Alex hung his head. He'd been such a terrible person no one was willing to befriend him besides one loyal manservant he'd been too arrogant to realize could've been a friend and the brother he'd never had if he'd but reached out in friendship.

Instead he'd given orders and work and haughtiness.

He would have to be better this time. Because even now, there was still no one but Jadon willing to be his friend.

Alex clenched and unclenched his fingers. Could he learn how to be a friend? Perhaps he could help Jadon this one time after everything Jadon had done for him. "So Princess Rosanna? The two of you seem . . . close."

"Yes." Jadon's shoulders sagged, as if all the stones of Castle Eyota rested on his shoulders.

If Alex couldn't reward Jadon, he could at least remove whatever hindrance remained for Jadon's happiness. Jadon deserved that much after all he'd given, and how little regard Alex had had for him years ago. "I told you, I can make you a baron if you wish it. Your status shouldn't be an issue with her father, and if it is, I'll make sure it isn't."

"That isn't the problem. At least, not all of it." Jadon shook his head, his sigh hissing through his teeth. When he raised his head, it was with the resignation of someone who'd made a tough decision. "Nine times I stood at the threshold of Beyond, and nine times the Prince of All told me I have more work yet to do. Eight of those times, I knew I wouldn't be allowed to cross the WaterVeil even before he spoke. But this last time . . . if he had but held out his hand, bid me enter, I would've leapt through. With nary a glance behind."

The one time Alex had stood on the threshold, he'd felt

the longing, yes, but not enough to make him take a step forward.

"But how can I tell her that? How can I explain that what I wanted more than her was to enter there?" Jadon's voice rang with brokenness, as if he was a shattered blade unable to fight any longer. "I was tired. I was older than a man had a right to be. And yet now . . ."

Alex slumped against the battlements. Had he made the wrong request? Again? He'd asked that Jadon be given more life, yet more life was the last thing Jadon had wanted.

But this time his request had been genuine. There hadn't been arrogance in it. It couldn't have been a mistake, could it?

It had been granted. The Prince said he had more work for Jadon to do, and surely that work remained whether Alex had asked for more life for Jadon or not.

Alex's whim, but the Lord of the Fae's plan. Surely it had to be.

His mind whirled, and something in Jadon's words stuck. "You *were* tired? And now?"

Jadon heaved a sigh and raised his head. "For a hundred years, I didn't age. Not in body and not in mind or heart. But I still felt those years until my only desire was to complete my task and step into Beyond. But this last time when I died of old age, it was as if all the oldness, all the weight of those years, died too. Standing at the WaterVeil, the Prince didn't just tell me I had more work to do as he had before, but also that my life was restored to me."

Alex pressed his palm against the cool stone battlements. No, Jadon's continued life wasn't a curse but a gift. Not merely more years, but a restoration to the young man

Jadon had been and was again so that he could live the life denied him by Alex's curse.

"When I woke, all the dreams and desires I thought I'd set aside a hundred years ago returned, and I feel—I am—more the twenty-one-year-old Jadon Rand than I've been in a hundred years. As if those years didn't happen. I know they did. I remember them. But the weight, the age, all of that is gone. And now I don't know." Jadon's jaw clenched as if he'd remembered whom he was talking to.

"You don't know what to do." Alex closed his eyes as the coolness of the night washed over him. Now they'd gotten to the heart of the matter. This wasn't about being old. This was about being young and uncertain.

They were both twenty-one-years old with their whole lives and huge decisions stretching before them. Having a hundred years of memories—or dreams in Alex's case—stored in their heads didn't make life-altering decisions any easier.

"You must really be in a sorry state if you're coming to me for advice." Alex leaned his back against the battlements. This was a new experience, allowing himself to joke about his failures.

Jadon huffed something that might have been a laugh. "Apparently."

Alex forced himself to smile. "I don't know why you're hesitating. A hundred years ago, you would've liked nothing better than to settle down with a wife and children."

Jadon's back stiffened. "I always wondered if you overheard that conversation."

"Sadly, yes, and I was arrogant enough to believe it was my right to eavesdrop on you and Luke. I'm sorry for that."

Might as well start apologizing now. He would have to get good at it.

Jadon crossed his arms and faced Alex, frowning.

"All right, I'm mostly sorry. But thanks to that conversation, I know how torn you were." Alex crossed his arms. "It took you a hundred years, but I believe you've found a princess raised in a castle whose heart beats with the rhythm of the mountains."

Jadon glanced over to the fires dotting the slope around Castle Eyota, but his posture remained tense.

"As I've learned too well lately, I'm not the wisest man. I've experienced the folly of believing I knew better than the Highest King. I don't know why you were given more time, but it's a gift, not a curse." The words sank into Alex, as true for him as they were for Jadon. He was a man out of his own time now, and there had to be a reason for that. He had work to do here, a hundred years removed from the time he would've lived. "I've done more than my fair share of complaining. You had to listen to most of it."

A breath huffed out of Jadon. Another almost laugh.

"I might know a lot less than I thought I did, but I know that the things we were told there in the throne room are as true today as they were then." Alex straightened. "Now I think I've reached the end of attempting to be friends for tonight, so I'm going—oddly enough—to sleep."

He headed for the stairs. He should talk to his mother one last time before he found his rest to make sure she was still all right. Perhaps before things grew too overwhelming tomorrow morning, he and Mother could slip out to the mountain and visit Father's grave. A grave that now was over a hundred years old, even if Father's loss was only a month past to them.

"Your Highness?"

On the first step, Alex turned and exaggerated a sigh loud enough so Jadon could hear it. "What did I tell you? We're friends. You don't have to use my title."

"Did I use your title, Your Highness?" Jadon was reclining against the battlements. Something in his stance reminded Alex of Luke. "You'll need someone to travel between the kingdoms and deep into the mountains to keep you informed on the needs of the people, both the kings and the mountain folk."

"If you're offering, you have the job. And whatever long, highfaluting title I give it." Alex rested his back against the wall next to the stairs.

He wasn't used to this sort of banter. The kind between friends. Or brothers. It was something he could get used to. Did he dare press this whole friendship thing farther? "And while you're at it, you don't have any pretty great-great-grandnieces you'd care to send my way?"

Jadon's pause lasted too long, like he wasn't sure how honest he should be in this tenuous friendship they had going. "Do you think I'd foist you on any of my great-great-grandnieces? I'm rather partial to my relatives, thank you very much."

Alex grinned for the first time in far too long. "See? That's exactly the sort of honest friendship I'm looking for. Just tell it to me like it is. How about any enemies? Any of their daughters you'd stick with me?"

"The late king of Tuckawassee had twelve daughters. Several of them are around our age." Jadon's shrug was so large Alex could see it even from where he stood on the stairs. "Though I don't believe I'd inflict even them with you."

Alex laughed, but he couldn't help his mind from

racing. Such a match would probably be the right thing to do, politically. Unite Tallahatchia by marrying a princess of Tuckawassee.

But even after all this, he couldn't help but want more than a political match. He wanted what his father had had with his mother. What Jadon could have with Princess Rosanna, if he ever got his mind settled enough to ask her.

Perhaps Alex wasn't meant for that life. Maybe he would serve alone, the last of the high kings of Tallahatchia.

Even then, he wouldn't grumble. He was done complaining and thinking he deserved more than what he was given. It was time he gave joy a try.

"Very true. Even the Tuckawassee don't deserve that punishment." With one last nod, Alex strolled down the stairs. His part as the sidekick of this story was done.

ROSANNA

"You had better really like him to get me up at this hour in the morning." Isi tromped next to Rosanna through the forest outside of Castle Eyota. Somewhere beyond them, Chogan and Ilma scouted the area, making sure none of the Tuckawassee soldiers still wandered the mountains. Not that Rosanna would see her guards unless they spotted trouble. They were to remain inconspicuous.

"I told you. You didn't have to come." Rosanna gripped her small knife. "But I'm glad you did."

"Of course, I did. Someone has to make sure your braid looks halfway decent." Isi ran her fingers through her hair as if trying to put it right after being dragged out of bed far too early. "A girl has to look her best when she's going into battle."

This would be a battle, just not one fought with axes and knives.

The birch trees in this part of the forest had been scoured for their bark many times over the years by the villagers living downstream from the castle, and it took some doing before they found a tree with enough bark to make it worth harvesting. Not that Rosanna needed much. Just enough to get her point across.

She carefully sliced through a section of white, unbroken bark about the size of her hand and peeled it from the tree with Isi's help. Rosanna held the knife out to Isi and grinned. "Do you want to do the next one?"

Isi's cheeks pinked beneath her freckles, and she glanced down. "I'm not sure we're there yet."

"But you'd like to be?" Rosanna waved the knife in front of Isi.

Isi glanced up and took the knife. Together, she and Rosanna harvested a second piece. Once they were finished, they headed for a boulder within sight of the river. There, Zeke leaned against the stone with a blanket pillowed behind his back.

"Did the two of you get what you needed?" Zeke started to push to his feet.

Isi hurried to his side and shoved him back down. "Yes. Sit. I still doubt you should be out here."

Zeke sank against his blanket, his face tight as if that much movement hurt. "Someone has to keep an eye on Uncle Daemyn. He moseyed on down to the riverbank a few minutes ago. If you wanted to talk, now would be a good time, before he sets too long and gets his mind made up."

Rosanna gripped her piece of birch bark and glanced in the direction Zeke pointed. "Would you mind staying here, Isi? I won't be going far."

Isi glanced from Zeke to Rosanna. "Won't be a problem. Holler if you need me."

Rosanna followed the trail Zeke pointed out to the

river. After a few minutes, she found Daemyn leaning against a wide willow tree only a few feet from the Kanawhee's bank.

She sank onto the ground next to him, the willow broad enough that she could rest her back against it as well, though a root dug into her tailbone. She let the silence lengthen for several minutes, listening to the hum of the encampments far up the slope behind them, the gurgle of the river at their feet, and the twittering birds in the branches above.

She set the piece of birch bark next to her and glanced up at him. "Did you get any sleep last night?"

"Not much. Turns out I had a lot to think about." Dark circles shadowed his face under his eyes while a layer of stubble covered his chin. But his mouth tipped into a smile. "I'm sorry I was such a grumpy old man last night."

There was a new teasing in his voice. Being an old man was something to joke about, not his current reality.

"Yesterday didn't exactly go as you'd planned." Rosanna clasped her hands around a knee to stop herself from reaching for his hand. She had to give him time.

"That's just it. It didn't go how I planned." Daemyn huffed out a breath and leaned his head against the willow tree. "After all my grand speeches about trusting the Highest King, it turns out I only trusted him as long as the outcome was what I wanted. It was prideful, thinking I knew better than the Lord of All when I should enter Beyond, as if I'd somehow earned the right to enter there by all the years I'd lived."

Rosanna remained silent. Daemyn need to talk this out, and she had been given the gift to listen.

"I acted like he was a hard taskmaster, and I was the suffering servant earning favor by my work. But the truth is the work is a gift of favor already granted in the Prince's name. It's a joy, not a burden." Daemyn rubbed at his palm, as if feeling the years of work etched in each of his callouses. "Even after a hundred and twenty-one years, I still have only a small beginning of trust and obedience. Perhaps that's why I have been given this restored life. I have much yet to learn."

Rosanna studied her fingers. Hadn't she also wallowed in a form of pride? How many times had she thought herself useless? She'd bemoaned the perceived lack of a gift instead of seeking what the Highest King had called her to do with the many gifts he'd already given her.

No more. From now on, she'd seek the work she was called to do, knowing she'd never have to do it alone. The Prince would be with her. He had and would continue to give her the gifts she'd need to accomplish any task he placed on her.

Though, it would be nice if she wasn't alone in her service because Daemyn was with her too. In his chest beat a faithful servant's heart, one she could cherish all the days they were given.

"Here I'm being given everything I thought I'd lost a hundred years ago, and all I've done is grumble." He shook his head, avoiding her gaze. "I don't know how to reclaim a life I thought I'd set aside."

Rosanna gave in to the impulse and took one of his hands. He tensed but didn't pull his hand away. She traced her fingers over his palm where his callouses hardened the pads of his fingers and the edge of his thumb.

When she threaded her fingers through his, their callouses fit together, and she repeated her words from the night before. "You don't have to live it alone."

After a moment, Daemyn folded his fingers around hers, the tension leaving his shoulders. "Are you sure?"

"Yes." She rested her free hand on top of their clasped ones.

"It doesn't bother you that I've lived a hundred and twenty-one years?"

The answer was there, in his words. He didn't say he was a hundred and twenty-years old. No, he was twenty-one. He'd just been twenty-one for a hundred years.

"Considering you had your twenty-first birthday yesterday and I had mine several months ago, some might argue I'm older than you."

Daemyn raised his eyebrows. "Sort of."

"I've seen the way you interact with my father. You don't act like someone who believes you're older and wiser, but you give him the deference owed someone older than you." She searched his expression, trying to read his thoughts in the depths of his dark brown eyes. "That must have been frustrating, knowing deep down that you should be aging but weren't."

"It's hard to explain. Being stuck the way I was. Even my siblings struggled to still see me as their brother when I was the age of their children, then their grandchildren." Daemyn tore his gaze from hers. "What will your parents think?"

"It will be odd. Especially at first." She stared at the ripples in the river before them. "Do you still see my father as your friend?"

"I remember being his friend." Daemyn shook his head. "But now he's old enough to be my father, and I can't see him as anything but a father figure and king."

She'd suspected as much. He talked about her father as

a friend he'd once had, as if the friendship had been broken as her father aged and Daemyn didn't.

"It'll take time for everyone to adjust." She held up the piece of birch bark. "But that's what this is for."

"Birch bark?" Daemyn took the bark from her, studying it as if trying to find a message.

"I've heard that in the old days, a couple who wanted to get married would build a canoe together." She leaned against his shoulder. "Building the canoe would test their patience, commitment, and ability to work together. In our case, it will probably take us a year with everything else that's going on, and that will give everyone a chance to get used to the idea."

She wouldn't mention the other half of the tradition, the part about what happened if things didn't work out. According to the legends Willem told, if the couple decided not to marry, the canoe was sold, and the profit given equally to each. Or if dissent tore them apart before the canoe was even finished, it was burned, and they received nothing.

For the first time, something almost like a grin crossed his face. He handed the bark back to her. "I'm not ancient. That custom was well before my time."

"Still, it might be a good tradition to try out." She drew in a deep breath and met his gaze. "Will you build a canoe with me?"

He reached out with his free hand and touched her cheek as tentatively as if he expected her to bite. "I'm afraid I'll only get grouchier as I age for real this time."

She shrugged and leaned into his hand. "That's to be expected, I guess."

The smile left him. "I'm not indestructible now. The next time I die, I'll probably stay dead."

Her throat closed with the memory of him in her arms, eyes empty, blood pooling around them. If she married him, would that be their end? Would she have to watch him die an early death a third time?

He still had enemies. Major Beshko survived to return laden with the dead back to Tuckawassee, and it was anyone's guess how the new, young queen of Tuckawassee would react when she received the bodies of her father and great-great-grandfather, leaving her and her eleven younger sisters orphaned.

Rosanna could either love him and risk the loss or not love him at all.

Daemyn leaned back, as if her silence had gone too long and given an answer she hadn't meant to give.

She squeezed his hand she still held in hers. "I understand. But I also know nothing and no one can cut our lives shorter than they are supposed to be."

He huffed out a long breath. "Very true."

Someday she'd ask about each of his scars and all his deaths. But not at that moment.

Daemyn tilted his head toward her. "Do you remember that first day on the river when I said you weren't what I'd expected?"

"Of course. I remember being offended you came to such a wrong conclusion about me."

"I let you think that, but that wasn't what I meant. It had nothing to do with you or that I expected all princesses to be condescending and arrogant. Somewhere along the way, even I was influenced by the rumors that the promised princess would be High Prince Alexander's true love. I expected her to be a fit for him, or at least, for the prince he used to be. I never expected . . . this." Daemyn picked up her free hand and ran his thumb over the callouses on her palm, much the way she had.

This wasn't the outcome she'd expected either when he'd told her she was High Prince Alexander's cursebreaker. But she fit him, and he fit her.

Those old legends, they romanticized the high prince and his cursebreaker, yet missed the fact that the princess fell in love with her guide along the way.

She met his gaze. "Me either. But I rather like it."

"Rosanna . . ." He closed the distance between them, their foreheads nearly touching as he stroked a strand of her hair out of her face.

She closed her eyes at the sound of her name, the first time he'd said it without her title. When she could bring herself to look up again, he was only inches from her, so close she could've shifted only a fraction to kiss him.

She didn't. That seemed the sort of distance he needed to cross on his own without help from her. She had to be patient for him to get his mind settled enough to make that commitment.

"You ain't scared, are you?" She grinned as she tried out the mountain accent she'd been practicing. Based on Daemyn's smile, it probably sounded atrocious.

"A little," he whispered. Then he kissed her, slow and sweet, like a man waking from a long nightmare-filled sleep at her kiss.

When he pulled back, he leaned his forehead against hers. "Yes, I'll build a canoe with you. And if you'll still have me when we finish, I'll paddle it with you all the days you and I are given together. And we'll do a lot of paddling. I have a rather large family scattered through all seven kingdoms that we'll need to visit."

Daemyn's unique relationship with his family would

take some getting used to, not to mention being Zeke's great-great-great aunt, which Zeke probably wouldn't let her forget.

She grinned and gripped his hands, her heart thrumming with the call of the mountains and the song of the trees. "It'll be an adventure. Wherever the river takes us."

But dreams have a price, and gifts can be curses in disguise. What will it cost to stop this curse from tearing Tallahatchia apart yet again?

Fairy tales meet the Appalachian Mountains in this adventurous fantasy retelling of the classic Cinderella story.

Buy Now!

THE BLADES OF ACKTAR

Dare

Deny

Defy

Destroy: A novella

Deliver

Decree

BEYOND THE TALES

Dagger's Sleep

Midnight's Curse

Poison's Dance

Goose Princess

Acknowledgments

Thank you, readers, for picking up this book and making it all the way to the acknowledgements at the end. I'm thankful both for the new readers picking up one of my books for the first time and for the readers who loved *The Blades of Acktar* and were willing to take the plunge with me on this new series, especially since it has been over a year since *Deliver* released.

Thank you so much to my family for your encouragement while I was struggling through writing this book. My mom for being the best local salesperson ever. My dad for helping with the final polish. My brothers and my sisters-in-law for being awesome.

To my friends Bri, Paula, and Jill. I know I can always count on you guys.

To my Realmie Roomies: this book would not have been written without a late-night idea discussion two years ago. If not for your enthusiastic response to what was then a jumbled idea, I would have given up on this book so many, many times.

Once again, thank you, Sierra, for your critique of *Dagger's Sleep*. You're the most amazing critique partner ever!

Sarah Addison-Fox: Thanks for all the encouragement

and author chats over the past few months. If only New Zealand wasn't so far away!

To Kara and Mindy: thanks so much for reading and proofreading this book. Those pesky typos would get the best of me otherwise. Thank you, Bethany, for an additional proofread before the release of *Goose Princess*.

Thanks to Kathrese for a stellar edit and seeing what this book could become within the mess of a draft I sent you.

Thank you to the students and teachers at the Protestant Reformed School and Heritage Christian High School of Dyer, IN for being so enthusiastic about *The Blades of Acktar*! I really enjoyed visiting your school. Also, thanks to the students and teachers at Covenant Christian High School for welcoming me to speak to several classes.

But most of all, the glory and praise belong to the Most High God. His glory is the only reason to do anything worth doing.